Cover design by Allan Gibbons
Jacket photograph 'The Big Wave'
Vinz Klefer © 2016

ISBN 978-1724641472

For Kathy Kessler, the girl out of time

Low ebb, high tide
The lowest ebb and highest tide
I guess we took us for a ride...

 -Michael Stipe

We didn't have flotation devices.
We didn't have leashes.
We didn't have helicopters waiting to scoop you out.

If you fucked up, you were on your own.

 -Greg Noll

But if we had not loved each other,
none of us could have survived.

 -James Baldwin

Who the hell do you want me to be?

 -Miki Dora

CONTENTS

1 PROLOGUE: BILL AND FRED'S EXCELLENT ADVENTURE

7 WIPEOUT

9 WE'LL MEET BEYOND THE SHORE

11 THOUGH MUCH IS TAKEN, MUCH ABIDES

14 NOCTURNAL INTERMISSION

15 DRAWS REIN AND SINGS TO THE SWING OF THE TIDE

23 THE CLOCK STRIKES TWELVE

30 THE SUN BOYS

35 IF I FOUND A LUCKY PENNY I'D TOSS IT ACROSS THE BAY

42 BRING IN DA DOG AND PUT OUT DA CAT

47 NOCTURNAL INTERMISSION II

50 HUNGERS BREAD AND CIRCUSES CAN NEVER APPEASE

63 TELL ME NOT TO BE LONELY

77 ONE MORE LEADING NOWHERE JUST FOR SHOW

90 NOCTURNAL INTERMISSION III

93 FROM WHAT I'VE TASTED OF DESIRE

117 NOCTURNAL INTERMISSION IV

121 PANTIES IN THE ICEBOX

136 BUT YOU CAN LEAVE 'EM TO THE BIRDS AND BEES

158 YOU'RE NEVER ALONE, YOU'RE NEVER DISCONNECTED

170 DIE IM DUNKELN SIEHT MAN NICHT

196 NOCTURNAL INTERMISSION V

200 SILVER THREADS AND GOLDEN NEEDLES

213 GLORIOUS FOOD

234 NOCTURNAL INTERMISSION VI

238 THE MIDDLE GROUND BETWEEN LIGHT AND DARKNESS

265 IF I COULD FLY LIKE BIRDS ON HIGH

287 AFTERWORD

PART I:

EPIPELAGIC, 1962

THE SUNLIGHT ZONE

Plink.

On the nod in the bathtub, my cast in a plastic bag so it won't get wet. Trying to remember. I was thinking about water once, about the desert. Pip was reading Vonnegut. We argued. Khrushchev and Castro were about to blow up the entire world, yet our small lives went on, our petty concerns persisted. No matter ever disappears entirely. No matter.

I stick my toe in the faucet to stop the drip. *Après moi, la déluge.* One of the Louies. The Sun King? No, Fifteen. Knock yourselves out, peasants; the chaos will make you long for my brutal order after I'm gone. He wasn't wrong. A fine little girl, she waits for me. Revolution, Marie at the guillotine, Marat in the bath. Oh, baby, take me where you gotta go. I pull my toe out again.

Plink.

Plink.

The point of a city, it always seemed to me, is that it's not the wild. You are sheltered from the elements, or lack thereof. Municipal powers that be will provide. But water is like hope; a little can be worse than none at all. And for a long time, a little was all we had. Just enough to sustain a few thousand; no orchards or gardens, let alone pools. We were fated to be a one-horse burg, it seemed, never as big as San Francisco's boom. A pity, what with our fab weather and beaches. But more kept coming— from back east, for their health; from up north, sick of seeking gold. By 1904 there were over a hundred thousand of us, dusty and thirsty, and the rain was unpredictable.

So we called Bill.

William Mulholland and Mayor Frederick Eaton went back, from their days digging ditches for the Water Department. Bill supervised it now; he knew his water management, and was a man who got things done. Started scouting locations—there were a few potential sources in the area, he claimed, but nothing near big enough for what they had in mind. This was untrue, but Fred didn't argue.

Eureka, Bill told him a few months later. I've found it. The Owens River.

Are you nuts? said Fred. It's 250 miles away, and the farmers—

Bill just waved him off: minutiae.

Fred started wheeling and dealing, buying land in the Owens Valley—we'll only take a little water, he vowed, you'll hardly notice it's gone—working connections from Joe Lippincott at the Bureau of Reclamation, paid as consultant so they wouldn't block the project, right up to Teddy Roosevelt, convincing him this water would be better used quenching Angeleno thirst than watering crops for hayseeds out in the middle of nowhere. H.G. Otis, 70-year old editor of the 'LA Times' and slightly to the right of Attila the Hun, whipped us all up into such a lather that the bond passed easily, and construction on the aqueduct began.

Skullduggery ran rampant from the start, but anyone asking questions was dismissed as a malcontent, a progress-hating Red. Bill worked his men to the bone out in the searing sun, fed them garbage, paid less than half what they could earn up north. They started striking, and he brought in scabs as the 'Times' shrieked of the bone-lazy bums—it was *your* money they were wasting. Your water. By then no one thought of it as belonging to the farmers of Inyo at all. It was ours, just wasn't here yet. But tempers grew short. It had been three years. What was the goddamned holdup?

Socialist Job Harriman cast his hat in the ring for mayor in 1910, calling the whole operation a boondoggle. There were enough broke people watching the city rifle their pockets as the rich got richer, and still, still no water, that it looked like he was going to win. Can you imagine that, a pro-prole LA mayor? Our whole lives could have been different.

That fall the 'Times' building blew up, burning to the ground. Twenty died, many more were injured. The cops rounded up the MacNamaras, two brothers who had been organizing the workers. Harriman rushed to their defense, but they confessed to planting the bomb, and our great utopian dream was lost in a flood of anti-labor hysteria. We shut up after that. The project was finished without further mishap, and LA was never a union town again.

I take a deep breath and go under. *Tiefer.*

Thousands have been flooding in all morning for the event; there are speeches, fireworks, bands playing Sousa. Children chase each other, hollering and excited, but they all fall silent as a man approaches the red, white and blue bunting-draped stage.

This is it. They prepare their bottles to catch what they can of history.

There is no trace of greed or cruelty in Bill's face; he does not look like a man entrapped by hubris. A breeze ruffles the shaggy grey hair, the walrus mustache, as he gives the signal to open the sluices. The water spills out, the trickle becomes a torrent. A cool mist rises into the faces of the grateful Angelenos crowded around. His eyes burn with triumph. The LA Aqueduct was a project on a par with the Panama Canal, and he'd done it in six years—and under budget, too. It is not every day that you get to be a god. He raises his arms to the cloudless sky.

'There it is,' he cries to his disciples. 'Take it!'

And they did.

They took it all, and wanted more, so Bill gave them more, diverting the entire Owens River as the lake sank and sank and then vanished; as the farmers of Inyo watched their parched herds wander off, their crops wither. They begged us for mercy, for reason, and we ignored them, drunk in our paradise of orange trees and lush lawns, a swimming pool for every starlet. We struck oil and were rich overnight; lured rag-trade nickelodeon Jews sick of waiting for the sun while hassled by Edison's goons out to build Hollywoodland, its sign 45 feet tall and luminous, and, oh, there was water, so much water, everywhere. If California was America squared, then Los Angeles was America infinity: our burro paths become dirt roads become highways paved with gold.

And still they came: by train, bus, jalopy, ship, by shank's mare all the way from Texas. Demanding a dream, denying the paradox of a desert in bloom. Bound to go where there ain't no snow, the wind don't blow, the sun shone every day. Where they hung the jerk who invented work. Big Rock Candy Mountain, Incorporated.

In 1920 we shot past Frisco to become the largest city in California, annexing the San Fernando Valley in a shameless *Anschluss* planned by Fred years before, building subdivisions in a frenzy, paradises of palms and papier-mâché, laying down five miles of new road daily in a fantastic madness of movies, oil derricks, fast cars, and wild coke-fueled parties that never ended. Klieg lights strafed the night skies, and every store opening was hopped up by acrobats, elephants and circus freaks. The farmers of Inyo watched the orgy from afar, their fury growing as their lives were baked into hard dry ground.

And that's when the bombings began.

Spring of 1927, there was a deafening explosion as the aqueduct burst open and a flood soaked the desert sand. An angry Mulholland patched up the damage, offering a huge reward for any info leading to the culprits. The farmers stayed *schtum*. There was another bomb. Another. Bill pulled together a posse of starving WWI vets to defend his work. Let's go, growled the Inyo boys. We've got dynamite for days, plenty of guns, and nothing to lose. There will be blood.

Bill could have sat down with them, still. He could have said, look, we screwed up, we're sorry, here's a fair price for destroying your lives. They might have accepted that, even then. But he didn't. The bombings continued, ten of them throughout that summer. Bill gritted his teeth, building a series of dams and reservoirs to safeguard our precious resource, patching up his beautiful baby, stewing at the loss.

Who knows how long this violent détente might have continued, had the Inyo County Bank not failed? Turns out the owners had not only been sponsoring the bombings, but doing a fair amount of speculation on the side—and now it was gone. All of it. Everyone's life savings had evaporated like desert dew.

The Wattersons were sent up for a dime at San Quentin—not for the crime of fucking these farmers forced to beat their plowshares into swords, but for funding them in the first place. There were no other arrests—local cops refused to cooperate—but now the farmers truly had nothing. They gave up the fight. Mulholland expressed hope that 'the city and the valley can join hands in peace,' moot sanctimony by then. There was no valley left, only deserted ranches and desiccated orange groves. We had sucked it dry.

The biggest dam was located in San Francisquito Canyon, 50 miles east of LA. Bad idea, the engineers warned. The sandstone and schist aren't stable; it's unsafe. By then a crabby 70, Bill was in no mood. Just do it. No, go higher. But we'll have to expand the base. You dare question me? Bill roared. I am William Fucking Mulholland, and I know what I'm doing. The St. Francis reservoir contained 12.4 billion gallons of water, enough to sustain the city of LA for quite a while, so the engineers complied with the specs, but they weren't real happy about it.

Cracks appeared almost instantly. Perfectly normal, said Bill. Concrete shrinks. Patch 'em with oakum. *Oakum?* the engineers mouthed. Is he mad? But they did as he asked, using rope to fill in the cracks. Water began to seep under the dam: muddy water, indicating an eroding foundation. They begged him to deal with it, so he grumpily agreed to an inspection on March 12, 1928. Fine, he proclaimed, nothing to worry about. If it would set their minds at ease, they could lower the water levels in the reservoir a little. Just a little. Pussies.

The hydroelectric stations provided LA with 90% of its juice; the dam held, and despite all their dark jokes, the residents of the canyon didn't leave. It would be fine, Bill had said so. But late that night, as one of the anxious engineers watched from his porch, the lights of LA flickered and went out.

Oh, goddammit, he thought. This can't be good.

And then the dam burst.

A wave ten stories high rushed down the canyon, carrying everything in its path: trees, phone poles, cars, houses full of sleeping people. Some escaped to the hills to radio ahead: get out. The path of destruction to the Santa Clara Valley was long enough that most Ventura residents were able to flee. A few managed to cling to trees in their pajamas. The rest were battered to death, buried in mud, or swept out to sea.

It was a disaster second only to the San Francisco Earthquake. As many as a thousand people were killed; most were undocumented immigrants who were never found. Bodies were washing up on the beach for days as we wandered the streets, desolate, desperate to help. There was nothing to do; those left alive were unscathed. Aimee Semple McPherson beat the Red Cross to the scene as usual, handing out blankets, soup, and words of comfort we weren't able to comprehend. How could this have happened? We had been living the dream, blessed and invincible. Where was our god on that day?

Our god was in his office, weeping over his folly. He tried to tender his resignation to the Water Board, but they wouldn't accept it, unwilling to lose face. They would compensate the victims, they announced, no questions asked, but didn't want the hassle of lawsuits. Act of god, was all. Business would proceed apace. Four million dollars were allotted, and the Foursquare Church and the movie industry matched the funds.

The people were paid off and went away, and in time we forgot about it, simply turned on our faucets and didn't consider the source—or the distinct possibility that St. Francis, patron saint of animals, the natural environment, and the grace of the Holy Land, didn't really like us that much. *Praised be thou, Lord, for sister water, who is noble, humble, and chaste.* Workers were sent in to eradicate all trace of the dam: nothing happened here, folks. Nothing at all. Our inexorable eye turned towards the Colorado River.

This is where I live. This is my home.

The brand-new City Hall opened two weeks later. We were 2.2 million strong now, the swiftest and most massive conurbanation in the history of mankind. San Francisco was left in the dust.

We wrestled the florid mouthful of *El Pueblo de Nuestra Señora la Reina de los Angeles del Rio Porciúncula* down to Los Angeles, then to the streamlined LA. With half the population of California and only 0.06% of its natural water, there would be no small portions for us.

We'd host the Olympics in 1932—mysteriously, ours had been the only name on the Committee's list—so we began importing palm trees from Mojave and Mexico to cement our status as illusory oasis, miles and miles and miles of them. Palms don't magically appear in the desert; they need water, too. Quite a lot of it, in fact.

Après moi, la déluge.

And we were just getting started.

It happens a lot, more than anyone knows. If it doesn't, you've stopped trying. You never see it coming, either, mind elsewhere on the water, far from the landbound masses, straddling your board, legs dangling in the ocean, shouting back and forth. Allow the worry in, like the thought of sharks, and you wouldn't be out there in the first place.

You can spend a lifetime in all that edgy serenity, especially with mushy surf, just kidding around, waiting for that ninth wave—but then you sense it: there she is, the one. Your brain shuts down, and something else takes over. Everyone's paddling hard, popping up to rip the curl in to shore, and you're steady, owning her, crosswalking up to the nose like a god—but it's easy to forget how precarious it all is: one goof and you're gone. Leap away before the wave swallows you so you don't get dinged, bashed by forty pounds of glassed balsa falling out of the sky to kill its master, a circus tiger in a sudden rage.

And then you're under.

But still it doesn't hit you. Not for awhile.

Time really does slow down underwater, even if you aren't drowning. That gasping instant as you fall, loosening your limbs as everything else closes up tight, then the whirlpool of arms and legs all around as your mind tries to sense which way is up. There.

No, there.

No, over there. Shit!

You're a rag on spin cycle, bubbles rising, kelp whipped back and forth, sand scraping your skin, saltwater pummeling and pushing into every helpless crevice and pore. That rush and roar of the waves, the blood in your ears, joining rhythm. And then comes the moment of calm. There. That clear greenhouse light filtering down from the surface—that's where you need to be.

But not just yet.

Sometimes you're entangled in kelp or wedged in a rock, and tons of water are holding you down, far below the surface. There are times you don't even want to come up again. The worst is the loneliness. Everyone else is off in another dimension, and maybe they'll think to look for you after it's too late, maybe not. You don't know. But where you are right now—you've never been this alone.

The last of your air escapes in bubbles, silky rats deserting a ship, your lungs in desperation are trying to con you into breathing underwater, no problemo, kiddo, *in utero,* like riding a bike, and after a time your brain is edged with black, let go, you don't have to stay here, it'll be so easy, like falling asleep—then some rarely used part of you roars back, no, man, don't sleep! FIGHT!

You tear loose, savage, superhuman, and are free, clawing for surface, breaking through into the world. Your body opens up to suck in air and it's the best thing you've ever felt, better by far than food or fucking. Your noodle arms are swimming for shore on their own, you reel in to fall face down on the warm sand, rolling around in its gorgeous grit, your mother and best girl, good old terra firma, forever and ever, amen.

Once you've stopped choking up Neptune's cocktails, your heart slows, vision becomes more than a series of dazzling snapshots. No one came for you; you saved yourself, again and again, losing count of stitches, of fractures, hold-under blackouts, miraculous close calls. Time returns to its old complacent pace as you breathe deep, sit up. Brush off the sand, then look around for your board.

And then you go back in. I mean, it's not like you have a choice, right?

Gazing out to sea after sunrise, nothing on my mind, just rocking on my heels, resting my eyes. Breakers rolling in from New Zealand, the peaceable warp and woof of currents, that shush of curl and slough, choppy foam sidling up to my toes to burst in sly tickling bubbles. The crabs are checking each other out, slapping claws, dodging the gulls gliding down on the warm breeze. Ricky's out there dancing solo, while the rest of us hold back to give him his space. You know what Daddy's like before his coffee.

This is home, 300 degrees of sky and sea, nothing to obscure it but the pier and an occasional far-off tanker, sand strewn with flag napkins and yesterday's fireworks. We tend to our manic asylum, making sure fires don't spread to the dunes, staying on the bottles and cans. Leave your board here overnight, and no one will lay a finger on it; the throngs all give us a wide berth. Ricky's got his shack of scavenged telephone poles, and we can crash in our cars if we're too wasted to drive.

A Jerry Lee tune's going strong in my head, that roiling rhythmic piano that creeps into your hips, burning you up; my fingers are playing with themselves, drumming on my thigh—and then, out of nowhere, there she is. Beside me, her presence so sudden I almost start. None of your Zeus-juice Venus rising from the water crap, either; this girl is entirely self-made out of sand and sunlight. Blink. Still there.

To say she's the most beautiful thing I've ever seen would be silly, for she's the most beautiful thing *anyone* has ever seen. I try not to swallow my tongue. She says nothing, just stands there looking out to sea with me, although by now of course I'm not pretending to look at anything but her. After a minute or so, I clear my throat.

'Help you?' Anything, just don't leave yet.

'Where do you go?' she asks. 'When it's all over?'

'It's never over. And I'm not a bum, you know. I have a home.'

'Ah,' she says, gesturing with the code we all know. America's golden children, with nothing to complain of, ever. 'Yes, I have one of those.'

'Is it a good home?'

'It's a place.' Draws a line in the sand with her toe, shaking hair off her face. Blue French bikini; her navel would bring tears to a man's eyes. 'Books, a bed, food on the table. Parents and such.'

'Come here to surf?' Girls do. They're rarely serious, mostly just here to check us out, and this girl won't ever have to be serious about anything. But she could be—she has that look.

'Be nice to learn, I guess. More to life than lying around reading *Bonjour Tristesse*, right?' Eyes Ricky, tucking his hips in for an elegant swerve. 'It just looks so...risky. Wonderful.'

It is, full of wonder. Like seeing God. Like being God, over and over.

'You're taking chances, sure. But it feels so...it's worth it, I swear. If you want, I can show you how. You know. If you like.'

She hesitates, struggling with something. 'Not yet, I think. Not just yet.'

Her eyes meet mine then, like water-worn stones at the bottom of a clear stream, golden-green and honest. She grins up at me. There is an infinitesimal gap between her front teeth, and every part of me longs to reach in, grab hold and never let go. At least get a number, a name—oh, hurry up, you damned fool.

But then she is gone. Just walks off and disappears, as I struggle to find the words to make her stay. And after a moment, Jerry Lee is back, pounding in my belly.

Breathless-hahhh.

That day. As if she'd reached into me and flicked off the bad. I caught every wave, never wiped, just feeling the rhythm of it, relaxing into the warm wet pleasure. Slept through the late afternoon, waking only to the evening sound of crackling sparks and clink of beer bottles, odor of charred dogs teasing my belly.

Easy laughter, U-Boy handwalking around the fire, Mysto hollering about Jayne Mansfield, Pip standing shyly at the edge: a younger me, all ribs and freckles. Emerge from dreams to join them, fingering sand out of my hair, grown long over my eyes, pale with sun. Fluke hurls himself in for a tackle, knocking me off my feet, and I rouse myself to wrestle him. Time to bring on the night with my brothers.

We're a motley crew, like one of those units in the war movies, or girls at a whorehouse. Ricky's the dark grifter, our elder statesman, knighted by Kahanamoku. Mysto's the philosopher, Fluke the tough wiseguy, U the rambunctious jester, Pip our mascot waif. I'm the sensitive one all the girls go for, before realizing what a zero they set their sights on. I'm a decent guy, and clean up well; you can bring me home to mother. But there's no traction there, no staying power. I get in too deep, too soon, then run away to sea.

Slip into the house many hours later, a bungalow off the shitty part of Mulholland, all trailer parks and liquor stores. The oldest trick of our long-avenued town of climbers is that deception of a nice address, the blurry border of Hollywood High. The turquoise paint is peeling, lawn overgrown with dry crabgrass. Light's still on in the kitchen.

'Mama?'

Silence. The air in the living room is hot and close, smelling faintly of moldy oranges. She's asleep at the kitchen table, an empty glass on its side; the old silver shakers gather dust on cupboard shelves now. Check for warm breath. This again. Used to scare the hell out of me as a kid. She comes to as I pick her up.

'Tomas?' Nestling into my chest, eyes at half-mast.

'Ja, Mama, ist bin. Wie geht's?'

'I can walk, liebling. Let me walk.'

'I don't mind.' But she wriggles down, to steady herself on the floor. It hurts, how small the whole of her is. So easy to wipe out: in an instant, gone. 'Where's Ray?'

'In bed, like you should be. There is lamb in the oven, we left you cake. Maybe come home early tomorrow?' In her voice: we miss you. Please.

'I should find my own place, Mama. I'm almost twenty.'

'No.' Stops climbing the stairs, doesn't slur. 'You don't have to leave us, Tomas. I don't know where you get these ideas.'

'Some of the guys are talking about a house in Venice. I could get more hours at the store to swing it, maybe sell some boards.'

'And who would feed you, in Venice? The bohos and junkies?'

'Why, you old hepcat!' I crack up, despite myself. Not drunk, I think, just exhausted. 'Where do you pick up this stuff?'

She strokes my face, somber. 'Your mother is not such an innocent.'

'All right, Philippa Fallon. Go to bed. I'll get my dinner.' Bend down so she can kiss me on the forehead, a calming benediction. She's right. What would I do without her?

'Sweet dreams, my liebling. Gute Nacht.'

The mamaloshen is different for us all, and as inescapable. This is how love sounds to me: the educated Viennese drawl of dropped L's and R's, the near-French German softened by enjambment. The insula cleaves to it like a scent, imprinting. This sound means love, will always mean love. The tongue of those who care about you, even as they're punching you in the face, shoving you into ovens. But you can't be trying to kill me, you think. You love me, you mean love.

The brain is some tricky shit.

Sock Ray before sliding into bed, growling, 'Where the hell were you?'

He rolls over, swipes at me. 'Where were *you?*'

'You have to keep an eye on her, man. She needs us.'

He moans, rolls back again. 'That's not my job.'

Whose job is it, then? To take care of her, of all of us? We're falling apart here. Something bad is imminent, but I'm too tired to think what. Sink into sleep watching shreds of newspaper burlesque their way down to the murky ocean floor, tiny indecipherable words and parts of faces curling and glowing in the watery sunlight, falling and falling, softly, slowly, to disappear into the darkness.

NOCTURNAL INTERMISSION

The dream is always the same. She and I are six years old, and she looks so cute, like Judy Garland in striped pajamas, but something's not right. I take her hand and tell her it'll be okay, really, we'll get all the kids in town on our side, put on a show, and then everyone will understand. She thinks about that and smiles: *Mein Onkel hat eine Scheune.*

And there it is: a red barn, brand-spanking new, as if built just for us. Bet there's cows inside, sheep, and that sweet hay smell. I can't wait. Heave the door open, but before I can follow her inside, it wrests itself out of my grasp, slams shut behind her. And then the buzzing starts. Here comes the twister. That's when my brain kicks in—I've done this before, a hundred times. I keep forgetting.

Get her out, get her out, is all I know, and I'm hollering, pulling on the door with all my might, the bees are coming closer and closer and I'm hammering till my hands are bloody and the bees are swarming out of the sky in a dark cloud, millions of them in a cyclone right down the chimney and I'm helpless to stop it, just screaming and screaming, pleading till I run out of air, *Geh raus! Bitte! Raus! Bitte, bitte!*

I always wake up with half the pillow stuffed in my mouth. Even as a kid I knew not to wake anyone, to shut up about this stuff. We don't talk about it, not even here. I don't know why, exactly.

Because bad things will happen if we do.

Don't give them any ideas.

We don't talk about it, at all.

Work unloading produce at Tony's early the following Wednesday, then get in a few primo sets before collapsing into sleep. The blessing of summer: class-free on the beach till fall, nothing but endless fun. Roll over and stretch under the rays, sun stroking my mind into visions of the Pipe. Ricky's filled us all with this need to make the pilgrimage out to Oahu, face the holy grail of swells, triple-overheads even on a mild day, shaking the earth like a quake as they crash down. You haven't surfed until you've met them, he says. The perfect wave—it's out there.

Dream of riding so high I'm flying, touching the crest to drop in, that 20-foot plummet, cutting back to rip through the barrel, miraculously shooting through it all, the green roof over my head sheltering me from the world. Crazy. I need to do this before I die. Even before I wake, am already totting up the cost of a ticket. I'll eat pineapples, sugar-cane, coconuts right off the tree. Sleep on the beach. Hawaii. Just saying it fills your soul to the brim: that lonely, sensual yearning. *Ha-why-eee.*

Haole, they called the sailors washed up on their shores. The breathless ones, their pale faces like the fishbelly skin of the dead. The way these vampires spoke: all those brutal consonants. C'mon, you guys, relax a little, enjoy. The *haole* did not relax. It ended badly for the Hawaiians. Always ends badly for someone, huh? Life and its zero-sum games.

Malibu is a tapped-out imitation of this plundered paradise, jostling crowds of clueless kooks copping our waves; Huntington, Redondo and Windansea nearly as bad by now. Santa Cruz is breaker city, but will freeze your nuts off in August, and those waves will smash you against the rocks as soon as look at you. No rocks in Waikiki, no why's in Waimea—just wave after giant, body-warm wave. Probably kill me, but I can't imagine a happier way to die.

A shadow falls across my face, and I struggle into consciousness.

Oh.

It's her again—on a horse this time, a huge black creature who might eat me if he felt the need. Smiling down at me, in jeans and a ponytail. Barefoot, bracketed by sun. Even her goddamned feet are lovely.

15

'You came back,' I murmur. 'Mmm. I hoped you would.'

She says nothing, merely beckons.

'Are you real? Is this a dream?'

'The bitchenest,' she says. 'We're going away now. Hop on, Hopalong.'

I sit up, shaking away the webs of sleep.

'I can't,' I confess. 'I don't know how.'

'That's okay, I do. Get a move on, before I change my mind.'

Rise up, unsure, but it's not like she needs to ask twice. The guys have come in, keeping their distance down by the waterline, just watching, poking each other a little. Fluke does a happy little jig for me; he saw her that morning, but I saw her first, and haven't shut up about her for days. I have never been on a horse before. I like them enormously; just seems rude to jump one someone's back and ride them around without so much as a by-your-leave.

'Hold him still now,' I say nervously, trying to keep my feet out of the way of those giant hooves. 'Don't wanna wind up on my ass.'

Put my foot in the stirrup, push up hard with my arms and swing my leg over, just like jumping a wall—a warm muscular wall, between my legs now, and before I can even gasp with the sudden apprehension of all this horsepower, she clicks her tongue and we're off, trotting down the beach as the guys break into cheers. Raise an arm in farewell, bouncing around like a ragdoll, bones coming apart, saddle digging into me. Jesus. Wherever we're going, I'm never going to make it.

'Hold on,' she says, and I reflexively dig my heels into the horse's sides, then grab her by the waist as we lurch into a gallop. The wind against me, all that thunderous speed and energy thrusting in and bursting out, has me petrified, clutching, sure at any moment I'm going to fall to my death. I can feel her laughing against my chest.

'You're kidnapping me,' I protest. No idea what's going on; I just woke up, and the world is all abrupt chaos flashing by, beachgoers a blur of faces. 'And I don't even know your name!'

16

Shakes her head against my lips — the scent of her hair like honeysuckle or the jasmine you'd smell on a warm summer evening on a leisurely stroll through a nice neighborhood. I used to live around smells like that. Holding my breath under the pool's wavering surface for as long as I could, only to breach and let it flood my brain: this is your home. You get to be here.

Looking down makes me dizzy, so I shut my eyes and hang on, nothing but the thud of hooves, the splash of surf and squelch of wet sand, then we slow, climbing into the canyon. Further and further into the trees, only the insect buzz and swish of eucalyptus leaves against our heads as we bend for the branches, until we come out into a clearing.

'Here,' she says, and I think, *here what?* Hardly daring to wonder.

'Georgia,' she says, and then I do say it. 'What?'

'That's my name. Mom's a 'Gone with the Wind' freak. Long story.'

'No, it's great. I mean, you could've wound up a Rhett, or an Ashley. My brother's named after Raymond Chandler.' Not sure why that's relevant. Consider getting off the horse, tearing up mouthfuls of grass, shake my head, trying to clear it. Girls are Maries and Michelles, the occasional Helen. Who's named Georgia? No one I know, no one. Why does it still feel like I'm asleep?

'I've been thinking about you.' No lilt in her voice; she's not flirting.

'I've been thinking about *you*. You have no idea.' How clever of her to have hustled us past the awkward chitchat. 'I give up. How do I get off?'

'Same way you got on. Lean on Buckley, down you go.' She gracefully demonstrates.

I slide down, landborne again, surprised to find my leg shaking a bit. She lays a hand on my thigh, and it calms instantly beneath her touch.

'That's normal, for the first time. All that adrenaline.'

'Wasn't what I expected.'

She nods solemnly. 'I know.'

'You think you'll be flying—but you could die. I never dug that, with cowboys. Like riding a motorcycle over a bumpy road, and I was—'

'In his head?'

I nod. Like the most savage, exhilarating sex ever. I just got fucked hard, and liked it. By a horse. My ass hurts.

'Why Buckley?'

'Watch.' She pats him on the neck, then says, 'Buckley, pinko!' His head swivels around to roll a jaundiced pale-blue eye at me, and then he sneers, baring long yellow teeth.

'Oh, that's a crack,' I chuckle. 'Looks just like him.'

'Doesn't he just? My old red-baiter, aren't you, Buck?' They nuzzle each other, and she turns to me. 'Hungry?'

'Always.'

'Then we'll eat first.'

First? I want to believe she—but no, she's a nice girl. Not pretend nice, either. Actual nice. And smart, and rich, and way out of my league, and only—I can't tell. One of those faces that could be fourteen or forty. Oh, hell, I don't care. Whatever she wants, I'm in. A blanket comes out of the saddlebag, a long loaf of bread and some cheese, and a bottle of wine—the good stuff, not Gallo. I pull out my knife for the corkscrew's virgin struggle, another thing I've never done before.

'So, um...how old are you, exactly?'

She's taking off the saddle, watching me. 'Writing a book?'

'Come on.'

'I'll be sixteen come Sunday.'

'No, come on. Really? No. You're not fifteen. Are you?'

'Does it matter?' Her eyes flash, daring me. *I'd make it worth your while.*

18

'You're awfully cute, but I'm not up for prison.' Set the bottle down for a second, unable to joke. 'I mean, aside from the shanking and whatever they do to cradle-robbers in there.'

She hands me a smile, then reaches into her back pocket for her license. Seventeen. In six months. Close enough. Shit. No. What am I thinking?

'Don't worry, I won't let you them bust you. You couldn't live without all this, could you?'

'It'd break me,' I admit. 'I can't even go a week in winter. I get dumb. Cantankerous.'

She nods sympathetically, and whips the blanket into the air as I catch the other side; together we spread it on the dying grass.

'It's not even you I'm worried about. It's...'

'My parents? Nah, they trust me. And they're not real big on authority.'

I sit down, slip my shades off. We blink at each other for a moment, faces naked like babies, drinking each other in.

'Well, this is a helluva start,' I say, extending my hand. 'I'm Tom.'

'Huh. I thought you were Rodney. 'Hey, Da Rod, hanging ten!"

'Oh, that. Just a dumb nickname.' The heat in my neck.

'Dig the rides, do you?' Her glance is mischievous; I'm going to have my hands full with this one, I know. Feels good, though—all that soft, busy weight, anchoring me.

Pick up the bottle and turn the corkscrew once more, wriggle it a little, wrestling, and the cork bursts out of the bottle, splashing wine. She meets my eyes with a level gaze, raises my hand to her lips and touches it delicately with her tongue—and then my hands are in that bounty of golden hair and we're kissing like we've been doing this our whole lives. Maybe we have: suddenly everyone I've ever kissed is a cloud of dust, disappearing as I gun it down this road.

She's a great kisser, too, tastes like herself, not gum or cigarettes. Warm and honest. No makeup. I never understood people who wear makeup to the beach; they spend the whole time making sure their mascara isn't running, and miss all the fun. My hand wanders up her back, under her chambray shirt, thumbing aside her bra.

She pulls back. 'Thirsty?'

'Yeah,' I breathe. Her eyes make my mouth go dry.

Hands over the bottle. I drink deep, head back, liquid cascading down my throat. I've always been a beer man—wine tastes like sour grapes to me—but I get the allure now. The warm current in my belly runs down my legs, up to my heart, and still, still, that thirst.

Her eyes are on me, finger caressing my neck; she drinks, too, and then we're kissing again, hands frantic for each other. Not many clothes to lose, so before we know it we're nearly naked, nothing to hide us from the relentless gaze of the sky. Now I'm the one to pull back.

'Wait. Hold up a second—we need to stop.' I'm not good with words. Especially not these ones.

'No! Why?' She gazes up at me, puzzled.

'Because we shouldn't, you're not...' I can't think of a polite term.

'Easy?' She laughs a little. 'No, I just want you.'

'That's not what I meant,' I say. 'We should stop, cause—'

'Because you think you're smarter than me.'

'No,' I say with some conviction. 'No, I wasn't that bright to begin with, and I'm definitely out of my depth here. But we can't just lunge at this. It takes time, if we want it to be good. And I do. I like you.'

'But it can be good now. I like you, too. I want this. I've been thinking about it all week. And I don't *have* time.'

'Sure you do,' I say. 'What are you, dying or something?' Girls do that, too. You'd be surprised.

'We're all dying,' she says, and sits up. 'And who decided we needed to wait? Why do I need to save myself like I'm some fucking Fabergé egg? If you'll pardon my French.'

20

'It's German,' I say. 'Look, do you trust me?'

She doesn't answer.

'Do you?'

'Why else would I be here?'

'Then listen to me. No, *listen*. You're cool. You really are. Whatever you do, you're always going to be Fabergé. No one can take that away.'

'Then why not? Don't you want to?'

I fracture at that; I've got a woody you could park six boards on and still have room for Miss Pasadena. Turn my head away from her nipples, the swell of her breasts. Nothing ever looked as tempting, not in this world.

'What?'

'I just want to take you out, if you'll let me. It'll be better that way.'

'Will it?'

'Oh, man...the best. I swear.' And it will. I can feel the certainty with every molecule: no crapping out this time. 'Now, clothes on before you break me, Quentin quail. Please.'

She throws her shirt at me, but we put our clothes back on, eat, make out some more, finish the wine. Go for a long tipsy walk through the eucalyptus trees, the sere yellow grass brushing against our knees as we talk and talk until sundown, working our way back to the start.

She's going to be a vet, she tells me—it takes as long as med school, but animals are worth saving. Not like people. I tell her about my classes at City, my hopes for Oahu; even about Mama and Ray. Ask her if she'd like to go get a soda. She smiles, yes. Chintzy, but I'm better than bent till Thursday, so big spending will have to wait.

The scrap of paper with her number on it burns warm against my thigh, the number I should've had from the start. Can't believe we wasted seven whole days bothering with anything else in the world.

I've never met anyone like her.

Absolutely who she is, brave about saying things no other girl would dare to. Hell, that no one would. I can talk to her, and I know she'll be straight with me. She's not the sort to hold back. I can trust her.

As if she'd been inside me all these years as I chased other girls in vain, and out of nowhere, here she is, beauty made moot by her brain, navel a third eye in that tan belly, begging to be caressed. This is like a dream I could fall through any second to wake, cast away on my island once more. And you wanna know something weird? For the rest of my life, the smell of eucalyptus will make me incredibly happy—even happier, somehow, than I was that delirious golden afternoon. When I can't sleep, sometimes I go into the bathroom and just sit there for a while, sniffing the Vicks.

Yeah, yeah, I know. Fuck you.

I used to go to the movies alone a lot. Sometimes I'd let Ray tag along, but it felt better on my own. I was one of those stringy kids with bad haircuts who sits in the back of the class daydreaming and doodling instead of dwelling on Venezuelan exports (oil, umbrage) and the Red invasion (imminent). The house on Mulholland was our new home, a crash pad in every sense.

Dad was a prick, who had made life unbearable for us all before we fled and were replaced with his secretary. Ray and I spent that whole year in shock, floating around Mama like Sputniks, hoping she wouldn't die and leave us with...we weren't sure what, and didn't want to disrupt the delicate balance of our existence by asking. Junior High was bullshit, as far as I could tell. I knew no one, nor particularly cared to for a long while, and the feeling appeared to be mutual. Life was a thing to cruise through back then, in an invisible, miserable daze.

One Sunday afternoon in March, I scrounged a couple quarters and went to a matinee. I'd overheard some kids talking about this new movie that sounded slightly more fun than reading on the porch while our screaming neighbors grilled dogs and spilled Scotch on each other. The theater was crowded when I made my way in: teens spilling out into the lobby, jabbering, pushing each other, jostling for seats. Then the lights go down, and there's an expectant hush.

Leo comes on and roars, and a snare starts up, a staccato beat. Words roll on the screen: 'We, in the United States, are fortunate to have a school system that is a tribute to our communities and to our faith in American youth. Today we are concerned with juvenile delinquency— its causes—and its effects. We are especially concerned when this delinquency boils over into our schools. We believe that public awareness is a first step toward a remedy for any problem.'

We're staring at each other, stunned. This wasn't what we'd been promised—just another shoddy trick, to lure us in and yell some more. We're well aware we're a problem; we have been told so all our lives.

Then a new beat explodes: 'One-two-three o'clock, four o'clock rock!' I hear a girl scream, a fearless battle cry, there's a mad scramble and half the audience is jumping out of their seats to rock it in the aisles. This doesn't seem safe. What if there's a fire? I glance around to see the manager standing by the door, helplessly wringing his hands, while half the ushers have joined in the fray.

Oh. We *are* the fire.

Before I can break this down, a girl with dark hair and eyes grabs me by the hand, pulling me out of my seat, grinning, then I'm dancing too, can't help myself. No idea what I'm doing, but mirror her, swinging my arms and jitterbugging along, and kids are caroming off each other in a big sweaty melee, total madhouse. *Till broad daylight.* Feels like I just woke up—for the first time in a year, everything's coming through crisp and clear, and so wonderfully, unbelievably loud.

The movie starts, so we all plop down in our seats, tripping over each other, panting and dropping our popcorn, and this flick is nuts, we go ape for the story: Artie West is this badass JD, a whaddayagot Brando who'd kill you in your sleep, and it isn't the teacher, but Sidney Poitier who's the hero. I never knew black guys, let alone teens, were allowed to be heroes, strong and good like that under the delinquent mask. And so smart, too, smarter than any of the teachers. 'Blackboard Jungle.' First time I saw Monroe. Was that it? No, no, that was 'Asphalt Jungle.' So many jungles came to find us in those days.

I think that's how it all happened, really. We'd been so quiet for so long, sitting on our hands and minding our manners and doing well in school or else, because there had been a Depression and a War and by golly what did we know about Uphill Both Ways in the Snow. Be seen and not heard, you unfortunate little accidents of nature, and you know what, unseen is fine too.

Our paved-over civilization is starting to bust open, cracks spreading everywhere, wild tendrils bursting through to drag us in, our folks drinking hard and smoking like chimneys, popping Lord knows what, laying into us kids and each other, getting divorced only to remarry and make more families to fuck up, and we're sick to death of watching TV where there's nothing to explain any of this. Jack Paar and Steve Allen can't break down this diseased despair in every one of our good, good homes, our hopelessly inadequate good homes.

We don't even know what the term's supposed to mean—you walk past the gilt address, the picket fence and perfectly pruned roses, open the front door and, man, there is nothing good or happy or even civilized in there, at all. Home is insane and school is a scam; marriage and work and the army are all suicide traps peddled by our resentful elders, and our government is the most shameless peddler of all. The leader of the Free World looks a baby's penis, and does nothing all day but play golf and sell us out to the warmongers.

That's how the jungle got in: we broke under the strain of shutting up. It's harder to pretend as a kid, because you're not numb yet, can't bite your lip forever about the emperor's ass hanging out in the middle of the street. And when we get together (we get to, whatever anyone says, it's in the damned Constitution), we get brave about it. Brave, and *loud*. You will hear us, if it's the last thing we do.

That was the year that really got it going: 1955, Elvis and Chuck and Jerry Lee and Little Richard were surfing the airwaves, as the race music denied us for so long was turned into rock by the original Moondog, this mad Jewish alchemist Alan Freed—from Cleveland, of all places—synthesized and shipped direct to our hungry ears. You'd walk into any Woolworth's in America and bring the jungle right into your living room, and Mom and Pop would just have to deal with it.

Our bodies were rocking, hearts racing with soda and hormones, and these guys sang to us with the straight dope, songs that told us it was fine that all we wanted to do was fuck and fight and soup up our cars to drive even faster. To crash and burn still hopeful and pretty, an entire generation of James Byron Deans. Even a quiet kid like me...I'm not sure what I would've done without those songs. Probably wound up in a loony bin by the time I was fifteen.

Usually people are hushed coming out of a movie, still in that dream state, mulling it over, but not us, not that day. It's like we all know each other all of a sudden, we're looking into strangers' eyes and yelling our heads off. *Did you see? Did you? And when he?*

The girl brushes by in the crowd, tips me a wink. I nod and mumble, 'Thanks for the dance.'

Don't know how she heard, but she did. Turns back, checking me out. 'You're a pretty ace dancer.'

'Oh, no, gosh, I—' Did I just say 'gosh'? Well, that's that, nerd, blown it. Where's a goddamned earthquake when you need one?

'No kidding, you are.' She has that great *pachuca* accent, like her mouth is full of plums. Her hair is wild, too, all ratted up high and raven black. 'Come on, let's get outta here before we get trampled.'

She pulls me through the revolving door and we lean against the wall, letting the crowd flow around us, and she talks. Her name is Tina, she's thirteen, and boy, can she talk. I love it; in a minute I know everyone in her family, her girlfriends and favorite singers—she *adores* the Orioles, Johnny Ace and Rosemary Clooney, but feels Sinatra's overrated, which I can't argue. I believe her words were 'dumb jumped-up wop.'

'Rosemary Clooney's a wop,' I venture. This is untrue, I discover later; Rosemary's a mick who sings like a wop. But she's very convincing.

'Yeah, but she's cool, not dumb! Hey, how old are you, anyway?'

'Fourteen.' I'm just tall enough for this not to be an obvious lie.

'Oh.' Her nose wrinkles. 'Too bad, I don't date older men.' My face must have fallen, as she hoots with laughter. 'Just playing! I know you're— what, twelve?'

I nod, blushing, not meeting her eyes.

'And I bet you're a...Pisces? No, Aquarius!'

'I don't know.'

Her eyes, lined with black like a feline Cleopatra, go wide.

'You don't know your own sign, dumbass? When's your birthday?'

Open my mouth to tell her I'll be thirteen in a month, when someone shoves me from behind, hard. Stumble into her chest and she teeters in her pretty pencil skirt, nearly falls.

It's not that Raoul is large, exactly—he's not that tall, and there isn't much of him beyond the greasy DA and leather jacket. But he projects largeness in a way I never will, even if I get to be as big as Grandpa Joe. It's beyond the shadow of a doubt that I'm about to get my ass kicked here, so what the hell, I shove him back, and then we're circling each other like dogs, for all the world like this is a real fight.

Never been in one before, just kids messing around on the playground. Everything else fades away and all I can see are the slits of Raoul's eyes, his grim angry mouth. Throw a punch at it, nail his nose instead, and he slams me in the chin with an uppercut so hard I think he's broken my jaw. Uh-oh, comments my brain, ever late to the game. What the hell were you thinking? He's gonna *kill* you.

Then a hand reaches out of the crowd, eases round Raoul's chest in a half-Nelson, a switch in the other. Not threatening, exactly, just sort of indicating the possibilities. This guy actually is large; he looks at least sixteen, and like he shaves twice a day. I've never been so happy to see anyone in all my life.

'*Este pequeño no vale la pena,*' he says, then gently adds, '*Cabron.*'

My savior drags me off in one direction, as Raoul drags the girl off in another, but she grabs my hand before we part.

'Tina Vasquez,' she yells. 'Sorry about my brother. But it was very nice to meet you!'

'Tom,' I manage. *Call me*, she says, and is gone.

My head's in a whirl, but when the guy lets go my arm, I say thanks.

'What'd you tell him?' Finger my jaw. It hurts to talk.

He laughs shortly, tucks the knife away. 'How good his mother's pussy tastes, now that he quit fucking her.'

I gasp a little. 'For real?'

'Sure, beaners love it when you talk shit about their moms. Calms 'em right down.'

'Okay, yeah,' I groan, 'That was—'

'Your first fight? Never woulda guessed, *stugatz*. You're bleeding, by the way.' Hands me a hanky. 'I'm Eddie Fallucci, but you can call me Fluke.'

I press the linen to my lips; it comes away stained bright red against the white. My blood. I had almost forgotten it was in there.

'Hey, you like to surf?'

'Like to what?' I say absently.

And that's how it all began. He takes me to the pier, where we hang over the rails watching the guys down on the water. Something loosens in my chest, watching them glide over the waves like Jesus, bodies swift and sure, at ease in a way I've needed to be for a very long time.

'What's it mean?' I ask. 'Your name, I mean. Fallucci?'

He gets this look, like he's been waiting for someone to ask that. 'Well, you know what a phallus is, right?'

'Sure,' I say. 'Like an argument that doesn't hold water.'

'Naw, man, dick. It means dick. And *lucci* means light. So like the sun shines out of my dick.'

Wow, I think. Italians truly are magical people, with their art and songs and delicious food, with their names that call a spade a spade and still make it sound like the most exquisite thing on earth.

Fluke's trying not to crack up. 'You're beautiful, kid, no joke.'

'Oh, hardy-har-har. What's it *really* mean?'

'Light-maker. My family made candles, back in the old country.'

'That's cool. Though the dick thing would've been cooler.'

'Abso-fucking-lutely. How about yours?'

I shrug. We don't get into the family history that much. 'I think it was Bäcker once. They changed it to Beck.'

28

He grins. 'A baker and a candlestick maker, nice. Tell you what. Come on down tomorrow. I'll show you how to surf, maybe even introduce you to that guy.' He nods over the railing at the dark elegant fellow in the ragged cutoffs, the center of everyone's furtive attention.

'Who's he?'

He laughs a bit, barely able to believe my ignorance. 'Dig it, dog, that's Ricky Morrow. He's the *butcher*.'

When I get home, I open up the phone book, find four pages of people named Vasquez, and am somehow still brave enough to start calling the next afternoon. I get to thirty-six before I find her. Her sister shouts her to the phone, and we date for three thrilling, terrifying months before she dumps me and I cry all night, all the light gone out of my world. Tina Vasquez, the first girl who ever let me in.

And I don't go to the movies alone anymore.

THE SUN BOYS

There was this great 'Twilight Zone' episode once: the earth has been knocked out of orbit and is now speeding towards the sun. The heat is beyond belief and everyone's gone north for relief, water is scarce and these two women are the last ones left in their building, just sweating their asses off, waiting to die—when the younger one wakes up, and it was all a fever dream. Whew, right?

But then the doctor nudges the older one out of the room, and tells her not to spill the beans: that the earth really *has* been knocked for a loop, but now we're all going to freeze to death instead.

I'm not a big TV guy, but Ray had talked me—and somehow Mama, who is even less of a fan—into trying the Zone 'just once!' and we were instant junkies. I'd come home early on Friday nights so the three of us could curl up on the couch and watch it on the black-and-white. That show never failed to rattle us, though in a good way; it was like this thing we shared that got us all excited and talkative, which was neat, because we each had our own orbits, rarely intersecting, and that can get a little lonely.

So we're sitting there quietly freaking out, because this felt like a thing that could really happen—that's how Serling always got you, with that deadpan honest face (the crooked incisor, for some reason, always made me trust him completely), plying us with all these scenarios that weren't too far out of reach. But then Ray points out that it's pretty improbable—anything strong enough to knock us that far would just demolish the whole planet instantly.

Whew, right?

We wander through life vaguely aware of the sun's power, taking for granted that it won't vanish, nor come too close and burn us all up. That tiny window of tolerance, our delusional notion of extremities to be braved upon our perfectly placed planet, all alone in the middle of this vast dark nowhere. What were the odds, of any of this?

30

I was talking to these two Swedish stews once about the winters there, and apparently they go for weeks without seeing the sun at all, like in Alaska. I'd go off the deep end, I think. It's not that I'd be afraid of the dark, or die of sadness or rickets or something, but because I'd need the dawn, you know? To know it was coming. Doesn't show for a while, you start to lose hope.

I was not really an outdoor type before I got into surfing. Liked to swim and hike, but mostly preferred to hole up, read, draw, dream, gazing out the window while listening to old jazz records. So I was a pale little goose, and new to the things the sun does when you're out in it all day. Your eyes, when you take off your shades: dilation, contraction, *snap.* Your appetites swell in strange ways, but you're more laid back about it, too. There's a kind of self-sufficiency to it, like you're photosynthesizing whatever you need from water, air and sunlight.

Hungry? Food materializes. Lonely? Plenty of people to talk to. Bored? Surf, swim, fish, horse around, have another beer. Stretch out on the sand, lick the salt off your lips and feel that warmth creep up between your legs, lock eyes with any of the girls hanging around on the fringes, and there's the grass in the dunes or the backseat of someone's car, all hot skin and mindless joy—and then you go back and surf some more, maybe party a little that night or see a show at the Civic. Go home and sleep like a log. There is no feeling of remorse or lack; this is just what humans are supposed to do with their lives.

Sex was part of the appeal, of course. Surfing is hard; it sculpted our bodies into their ideal forms, nearly nude Leonardo dreams of graceful latissimi and trapezii tapering to hungry waists, clear skin, bleached hair, easy eyes. The sunny languor made us forget that lust was bad. We all wanted to fuck, all the time, so everything we said and did became infused with a lucent sensuality that never felt awkward or unwanted. Everything. Eating a hot dog, rubbing oil into skin, the music and wild laughter all around. The rushing hush of the waves. I'd always felt so small, so trapped, like I couldn't do anything right, but I blossomed here, expanding like a flower.

We'd head home or back to school, see the sad constriction in the faces there, and think, oh, you fools, don't you know how easy it could be—come, join us. Look beyond, beyond. Let my people go.

31

I became a different guy there; it wasn't an affectation. The sun burned away the angst of the night. Far as I knew, I was the only Jewish surfer on the beach besides Kathy Kohner, neither of us big religious types, but after she left for college, it was just me. There was Doc Paskowitz, of course, but he was much older and traveling the world, this mythical uncle who rarely visited.

The Saturday after my thirteenth birthday, when every nice Jewish boy in the world dons a prayer shawl and shows off their Torah skills, I shot my first curl. All the guys nodded wordless acknowledgement, Fluke clapped me on the shoulder, and Mysto handed me a beer. I chugged it: *bad-Jew, bad-Jew.* Apparently not-Jew was not an option.

Our people don't surf, you see. We study hard, get good grades, and grow up to be doctors and lawyers and faithful, law-abiding husbands. *Lantzmen* are responsible, clean-cut and four-square; we buy insurance like it's going out of style. We are not reckless fellows who goof around on the beach all day in pursuit of pointless pleasure. Well, I am. But you can't disengage from this stuff that's seeped into your genes till you'll never wrest it out. Which side are you on, boy? I honestly didn't know.

Jews came of age in Egypt, I think. Buckled down, realizing it wasn't enough just to be miserable slaves; that they had to have a code to keep themselves incorruptible, apart and safe. They wouldn't worship Ra's gang of cats and jackals, but the one God who'd protect them—until he wouldn't, which was always their fault somehow. Flip a coin, if you ask me. Ten plagues and Pharoah's army getting drowned in the sea aside, my people didn't seem to be having such a swell time of it. May as well move back to Memphis and worship the sun.

Sam Phillips subscribed to that, with an unerring ear for the guys who'd get us: Elvis, Jerry Lee, Johnny, Carl, Roy, chosen to unleash their song on the world. Our parents were right to fear these beams of light that shot from Sun Studio to knock us out, transform us into lunatics with their Bacchanalian exhortations. That energy that slid into our hearts and hips, made us run wild, dance our asses off, and flee the city with its stultifying homes, churches and classrooms. Make a beeline for the ravenous sea, to baptize ourselves in its brine and found a cult with its own rituals and language. Look beyond, beyond.

We were proud to be Americans, for the first time not playing second fiddle to the old country. *Ich bin nicht ein Berliner,* motherfuckers. We dropped castoff food and clothing on them out of the sky, then forgot all about their bullshit. We knew what they had done. We were the cool ones now--and surfers were the ones your mother warned you about. We weren't, mostly, but the moldies assumed we were, which just made us seem cooler. Best of both worlds.

Hawaiians had brought the sport over to the mainland, spreading the aloha, paid in pain, but it didn't catch on with many but a few obsessive diehards till after the war, when it became an act of defiance. We were a generation in transition, just a bunch of bums not that interested in being lost to the machine.

And Ricky Morrow was our Helios, son and heir to the men who'd haul hundred-pound planks out into the water and surf straight on, never swerving. The guys he started with were all gone by then, out west to Hawaii to ride the serious waves, up north to work the fishing boats. Making movies, starting magazines, spreading the gospel of our dream. Grown up? Maybe. I don't know that you ever grow out of surfing, any more than you do out of Judaism. But Ricky was the last one standing: the Moses of Malibu, enforcing his law with a mighty hand--he was fluid and flexible on the waves, but nowhere else--and we gravitated to him cause he was a bona-fide outlaw, funny and cool, and the most righteous surfer any of us had ever seen.

Fluke was the first. Just marched into the sea one day and claimed a wave. Mysto was a nerd who came to the beach for his bad skin, then found more interesting things to do than quote Kierkegaard and fall apart around girls, all klutzy chivalry. One day he hauled this kid out of the water where he was playing shark and copping feels, beat his ass and christened him U-Boy. When U jumped up, unrepentant, and took off with his board, Mysto slid his eyes over to Ricky, who nodded, *let him go, see how he does.* He did good, and kept at it. I was a sarcastic shellshock case, but within weeks had mellowed out to where I wasn't getting dunked on a daily basis. Pip came from nowhere, had no one, and never spoke—but he never left, either. This was our life now.

Others came and went, but we were the core, craving Ricky's respect as much as the anarchic discipline he imposed. Not yes men, exactly; we just never said no. Of all of us, Fluke was the only one who didn't take any shit. 'Chill pill, Magill,' he'd growl when Ricky would go off on him. 'Peaceable kingdom. I'm just here to fucking surf.'

You were free on the beach as nowhere else, but within these strictly circumscribed limits. Ricky's vibe may have seemed all sophisticated diffidence, but defy him or drop in on his wave, and he'd make you pay in a hundred ways. Might even ban you from the beach altogether, a fate reserved for the weak, the chicken, the rat-fink kooks who would never get this game.

Chaos and confusion might reign elsewhere, but this world was simple clarity itself, even as we grumbled under the fascism that made it possible. And those of us lucky enough to remain in Ricky's barely-tolerated second circle were the ones who'd learned the lesson Icarus should've gotten from the get-go: you can fly, all right, but not too high. Don't fuck with the sun god.

Georgia and I meet for a soda that night at the Crescent. I offered to pick her up, but she just raised her eyebrows at Mayhem, a '49 blue VW Beetle I'd knocked the rear window out of for my board. All bald tires and scabs of rust, and I love her. Not a beauty, but you could depend on her in a pinch. Sort of.

'What,' I said, mock-offended. 'Volkswagen has the best safety record in the world.'

'That hunk of junk? I could crush it like a beer can with a stern look.'

'Well, yeah. But nobody ever got knocked up in one.'

She punches my arm, giggling. That night, she's already there when I push open the smudged glass door: leaning back in the booth, seeming to study the menu, secretly spying on the other diners. I slide in.

'Thought you didn't like people, KGB.'

'I don't. Not all of them, anyway.' She lays a hand on mine and smiles as my entire body turns to hot fudge, spilling over the vinyl seat. 'Did you know the jukebox has a dozen songs about the Twist?'

'They do seem to be grinding that one into the ground.'

'I mean, 'Twistin' Postman?' *Ubi sunt,* Marvelettes? It's like last call on a sinking ship—let's take our biggest hit and slap a hot dance on it. Those idiot kids'll buy anything.'

'What's that mean, *ubi sunt*? I love Latin phrases. *Dulce et decorum est. In vino veritas. Vincit labor.*'

She tosses her hair back, considering me. "Beats working,' right?'

'Work's for suckers. Trick is to seem like you need nothing, then people fall all over themselves to give you everything.' Ricky taught me that. Not sure I'm entirely on board, but it does sound cool.

'*Ubi sunt qui antes nos fuerunt.* It's from poetry, 'where are those who've gone before us."

'So like 'Ozymandias.' Tragic transience and mortality.'

'Someone was listening in English.'

I shrug. 'You might be rushing the write-off. The Marvelettes, I mean. 'Beechwood' is doing okay. They'll be back.'

She shakes her head sadly. 'Kiss of death, the hit-dance combo.'

'But they're not even twenty. They can't have peaked already!'

'People peak too soon all the time.' Slides the sugar over, and I take it, at a loss. All I can come up with is Bobby Fischer, probably just wishful thinking cause the vulpine little prick makes me feel so inadequate.

'Humans are odd, don't you think?' she murmurs. 'The way they cling to things. Why not just write a new song?'

'Oh, so you're a shrink. A social anthropologist. Examining us all under your microscope, ether and pin at the ready.'

'Sorry, don't mean to get analytical. I'm just, y'know, kind of a Martian. A little green stranger trying to figure you all out.'

'Most of us feel that way. Lotta this gets better after high school; bet it did even for Camus. Probably got his ass kicked all the time, babbling to the jocks about existential alienation, and look at him now.'

She frowns. 'He's dead now.'

'Yeah, but at least we take him seriously.'

'Hmm,' and she traces a tiny tight pattern on the table. 'Seems like a pretty steep price to pay.'

'So tell me about animals. You're right, most people are vake. Useless.'

'Animals don't lie, and they love you forever. But you like Fluke, and your mom. What about your brother?'

'Ray? Oh, he's a good guy, crazy smart...but he's got his own life. We're like kitchen chairs, I guess—we'd notice if one of us disappeared, but not a lot of deep convos. You?'

36

Her face shutters. 'No sibs. Dad's cool. Not around much. He loves me, though; he'd do anything I asked. So I don't.'

She wouldn't, no. 'And mom?'

'Ah...she's the strongest, smartest woman I know.' Stops there. I wait. Mama drama over boys and hem lengths? 'But she's sort of...well, she had it pretty tough growing up. German, so not exactly Thrillsville.'

Oh. Not just hard work and snow. 'Tough' means something else now.

'You mean she was in the...'

'Never mentions it.' Her eyes drift out the window to watch traffic. 'A few times, when she was plastered. But it's always there, you know? The elephant in the room. I think...'

'What?'

Presses her lips together, before it rushes out. 'It won't go away, ever. She came here and no one could handle it, just pretended like it never happened. And she's never going to get better. Not ever. No one can tell; she dresses up for parties, travels a lot, wins at Mah-Jongg, that sort of thing. She has her little...habits, hobbies, whatever, but it's like she's not here. It's not real. She never got to scream her guts out about what they did to her, cause we were all too afraid we'd drown in it. So now she never gets to be normal again, just this terrible...survival robot.' Her hand goes to her mouth. 'Sorry, I'm sorry, this is dumb. Don't know why you'd care. I'll stop now. Moving on.'

I'm silent for a moment, chewing on this. Then, 'No one knows this but Fluke—but my mom, too. Sort of, not like yours. She got lucky, they got out in time, her and her dad. Left Vienna in '37, right under the gun. She talks when she's been drinking, too. It's like she can't shut up.'

'I *know!*' Her eyes are aflame. 'You want to walk out—and then you hate yourself for being a jerk. But I'd almost rather not know.'

'Exactly. And *everyone* felt that way, even as it was happening.'

'No one would listen. No one. No one would even let them in, just told them to shut up and go home. Hey, you know us Jews, always making some big fuss over nothing.'

'Yup.' I toy with the fork tines, pressing them into my thumb. 'Her dad got visas somehow, but her mother dug her feet in, wouldn't come, said it would blow over. Finally agreed, but only after he got settled, found a job and a place to live. My mom was sixteen, but she knew the score, so she got on the boat—and they never saw her again. The letters stopped in 1940. Grandpa was desperate, tore up the embassies with calls and telegrams. Every dime went to bribe officials all over the world—who took all his money and didn't do jack. If it weren't for my mom, he'd have gone back, and...'

Our heads are drawn together, voices hushed: our shameful Zionist conspiracy at this table of formica and chrome, 'Twist and Shout' on the jukebox, neon and raucous laughter and milling feet all around. I was never bar-mitzvah'ed, have never been in a synagogue; by now probably couldn't find Israel on a map if you had a gun to my head. This has never bothered me before.

'And...nothing?' she asks, after I've been silent for a while.

'Nothing, but he wouldn't give up. Till he saw their names on a list.'

'Their?' Her eyes are shining with pain or curiosity. Maybe both.

'There was a sister, too. Rachel. She'd be...she'd be about thirty by now. Their whole family, all their friends, just—poof. Smoke.'

'Jesus, Tommy.' She takes my hand. 'Your crazy Aunt Rachel.'

'Yeah, I had these dreams about her for years.'

'But maybe the lists were wrong. I mean, they might be in Israel, for all we know. They took in so many...'

Shake my head, teeth clenched till my jaw aches. 'Nah, the Nazis were pretty thorough. Wasn't like they had to hush it up.'

'No one cared. It's hard to wrap your head around, but they didn't.'

No point being bitter, right? It's over, and we're told *never again*.

'Did he ever...y'know, did he ever move on? Your grandpa?' The delicate trace of hope in her voice.

38

'You could call it that.' I knock over the salt, set it right, toss a pinch over my shoulder. 'He taught college, and wrote. Serious rabble-rouser, and oh, man, such a cool guy. HUAC was after him for years because he was supposed to be this big Commie, and he really wasn't. I mean, yeah, he was—but he loved America, was super gung-ho about it. They got him fired in the end. And then...'

'What?'

'Oh, hell, you don't want to hear this.' She waits, biting her thumbnail. 'Okay. He, um, he hung himself. We were busy that week, so didn't get out to his place for a few days, and that's when we found him. No note.' I pause, clear my throat, check the ceiling fan. It's still going, round and round in lazy circles. 'She'd held it together, but after that...' No. I won't tell her how she fell apart, how everyone ditched her but me and Ray. Leave her that much.

'Oh, Tommy. Do you want to stop talking about this now?'

I'm afraid I'll explode if I stop. Drive her away, if I don't. Those troubled green eyes, raking mine; I can't believe she hasn't walked out on me already. Why the hell would we bring this up, either of us?

'Do you?'

'I guess. This is supposed to be our happy first date, right? The big romantic one we tell our grandchildren about.'

Relax a bit. Perv that I am, in that moment I want nothing more than to fill that beautiful belly with babies. 'Yeah. I shouldn't have—I'm sorry. We can drop it now.'

'Never would've pegged you, though. You don't look Jewish at all.'

'Neither do you.' We gaze at each other, wondering at the compliment: the absence of schnozz, of pale skin and dark sad eyes. Two nice blonde *Kali Kinder,* who might pass if you didn't scratch too hard, hanging out in a diner, all quick repartee and easy affection. Unburdened by the old neuroses, the weakness and fear; puzzling over the twists of fate that brought us to this place. Must be half a million here by now, changing our names, cutting off our noses to spite our faces, so we can't even recognize each other. Go to Israel or New York if you want to be a Jew.

Here is where you come to masquerade. Hiding in plain sight, as far from our old lives as we could get without leaving the planet. Dying to put it all behind us forever.

'You know the worst part?' she muses. 'People freak out, or tell you they get it, cause their hamster died. I just stopped telling people, in the end. I don't know what my face is supposed to do.'

I nod, unsure what my own face is supposed to do right now.

She squeezes my hand, and then the waitress appears, the relief of real life in a pink nylon uniform, sneakers and a starched cap. Shifts gum to one cheek: 'Getchu?'

Georgia's eyes meet mine, and we smile wryly. What do you order? What divine nectar could possibly bring all this under control?

'Cherry Coke,' Georgia says, and I nod, same. She's back in seconds, and we suck at our straws.

'So,' I say.

'So.' The word slips out, falls to the table. She clears her throat. 'So this guy dies and goes to Heaven. Tells God a joke about Auschwitz. God doesn't laugh. Ah, well, says the guy. Guess you had to be there.'

'Good one,' I say, and it is. The only good one I've ever heard, and I've heard a few. Her eyes are on mine, probing, fingers thrust in a wound. I have the strangest sensation of us falling out of the sky, into the sea, deeper, deeper, no need for anything but each other, entwined in this moment, extended into eternity.

She grins, and it passes. 'So...how 'bout them Dodgers?'

I shrug. 'Eh. They should go back to Brooklyn, da bums.'

'Oh, come on, sourpuss, they're doing great. Koufax is on fire!'

'Didn't know you cared.'

She perks up. 'My dad's a fan; he helped fund the new stadium. And the enthusiasm's contagious. But at the same time, baseball's...I dunno, it's

just such a funny exercise in time. Always feels like it should go way
faster than it does. Why does it have to take so-ooo-ooo long?'

'You want everything to go fast, don't you?'

Under the table, her foot has slipped out of its sandal and is touching
my calf. I harden instantly, some nerve writhing like a snake at the base
of my spine.

'Not all of it, no,' she says. 'But the shitty stuff, sure. We learn nothing,
so why not cut to the good parts and linger there? Because evil really is
just that, isn't it? Boring.'

'Come surf with me then. You forget it all when you're out on the water.
All of it, I swear. Nothing out there but right here. *Undas rego.*'

She smiles; the hook has landed. Her foot creeps up my thigh, and my
breath catches in my chest. I think, no, I know she would have liked
him. She and Grandpa would've gotten such a kick out of each other.
And it *is* shitty that they'll never meet, shitty and pointless and above
all boring. I'd give anything to change that.

Her toes are toying with my fly, prehensile, and her eyes are looking
into mine as if all this were the most natural thing in the world, as if it
happened every day. My mouth is sweet with need and fake cherry
flavor, my right hand's holding my left to the table, heart pounding in a
slow, hard way that can't be invisible in my eyes.

And that's when I realize I'm screwed: I'm never going to be able to
look at another girl as long as I fucking live.

41

Late afternoon, I'm in the little stretch of parking lot off the beach, head deep in Mayhem's bowels, tinkering. It's not looking good. Fluke comes up from behind and slaps my ass.

'What's the word, bird?'

Bonk my head on the hood. 'Fucking gasket blew. I think she's seized.'

'Oh, you always think the worst, asshole.' Peers under the bumper, sees the spreading pool of oil. 'Okay, yeah. You may be screwed.'

He and Mysto make a quick parts run, then shunt me aside. Fluke's dad works for Lockheed, and taught him everything he knows; pretty sure he could repair a B-52 blindfolded in midair. Total wizard. Whatever he can't fix, he fabricates—one way or another. Finally steps back, wiping black grease on his trunks, eying his handiwork.

'Start 'er up.'

I start her up, and there is grinding noise and a cloud of smoke, and I shut her down. All the guys have gathered by now, and there is a groan of disappointment.

'You know what this means,' Fluke says. There is a gleam in his eye.

'No,' I say.

'Paaaunnch.' He drawls it out like caramel, relishing.

'No.'

'Oh, yeah. Paunch, paaunnch,' and then the others join in, chanting it. Ricky's chuckling, in his element. Fagin sonofabitch loves this shit even more than surfing.

Not sure why we call it that, maybe a cross between poach and punch, a rebellious blow to the soft underbelly of America. But I never could rest easy with it. It's not a political act, for Christ's sake, just stealing—and while LA's wealthy probably don't lose any sleep over the credit cards and jewelry Ricky palms at parties, he boosts from everybody on the

beach, too. Rich or poor, he doesn't care. Even from us. He's not Robin Hood, and the rich don't drive Volkswagens anyway. But I can no more
lay my hands on $200 for a new engine than fly to the moon, so hold my hands up in surrender.

'All right, you goddamned hyenas. Just this once. But two conditions: we hit a new car, something nice. Maybe Brentwood.'

Fluke is grinning, jiving, getting psyched. We've never pulled anything this big before, not even close. 'And the other?'

'We put my old engine in the car.'

Everyone stares at me, befuddled. 'What the hell for?' says U-Boy.

'So they won't know they've been robbed. Let them think, I dunno, that it just broke down. And then...maybe they can fix it?'

'That's the lamest shit I ever heard, dumbass,' says U-Boy, and cuffs me upside the head. 'A, you think the mechanic won't notice a ten-year old engine in a new car? B, it'll add an hour, minimum, and we'll get busted for sure. C, you're a fucking douchebag.'

Hadn't considered that. 'Okay. But still, someone who can afford this.'

'My little chickadee.' Fluke ruffles my hair affectionately. 'Toughen up, man. This world is going to eat you like a hungry cat one day.'

Ricky wants to leave right away, but the others talk him down to the more reasonable time of midnight, so we sprawl out on the sand and build a fire. Someone makes a beer run, and a few girls show up with weed. By witching hour we're all wasted. Mysto says we should wait till tomorrow, but Fluke is adamant, so we bid the girls a fond adieu and pile into his campervan.

I'm down on the floor, dreaming in a heap of towels, U-Boy singing 'Yakety-Yak' out the window, carefree and off-key, all the time in the world for a ride with our hoodlum friends. I suppose we should be concerned that Fluke's put away a joint, six beers and half a fifth of tequila, but he could probably drive blind. Ricky's resting his feet on my belly, and for once, I don't mind.

'You're sinking of her, aren't you, dahlink?' He pulls this asinine Zsa Zsa accent when he's drunk or stoned, like a Transylvanian fairy. Usually bugs the shit out of me.

'Mmm,' I reply, on cloud nine. Tomorrow night I get to see her again—she's picking me up for a movie, her treat. I was taken aback, but she said we should Dutch the dates, and I could tell this meant a lot to her, so me and my empty wallet swallowed our pride and allowed it.

'Don't get in too deep, dearie. Miles out of your league, you know.'

'I know,' I say, although I don't. True love doesn't care about money or good looks, and this baby was written in the stars.

'She'll tire of slumming, and—' he drops the accent. 'No kidding, Rods. You want to watch yourself. I know the type: trouble in a kitten suit.'

'Fuck off, Ricky,' I say uneasily. 'You don't know shit.'

'Yeah, shut up, Ricky,' says Mysto. 'She's aces.'

'Wahine,' someone murmurs ecstatically.

'Teeny-weeny wahine queenie.'

'Your weenie is teeny.'

'Your mother's weenie is teeny.'

'Bite it, asshole.'

There is laughter and a minor scuffle up front, as U turns back to whine like Lucille Ball, 'But Riiicky! Why can't I date the gorgeous gal with the big bazongas?' Everyone fractures but me and Ricky; we're glaring at each other. This has been a long time coming.

'Oh, sweet Jesus, those tits,' says Mysto. 'No offense, Tommo, but you don't deserve this kind of luck. I'd walk through hell in a snowstorm to get my hands on—'

'That ass!' and then the van explodes with her various body parts and what they'd like to do to them. Fluke calls back crabbily, 'Leave him be, ya fucking pricksters. Can't a guy be happy for once?'

I say nothing, just remove Ricky's feet and sit up. We stare each other down for a long heavy moment, streetlights washing over us in soft blue light and shadows, before something shifts in his face.

'Your funeral,' he says. 'You always did learn hard.'

'The boy's been Circe'd, Ricky,' Mysto says solemnly. 'Calypsoed. You're never gonna save him now.'

U-Boy's head jerks around. 'There!! Over there! Check it out!'

The van slows, and we case the scene. Bright blue Beetle, '61 if she's a day. Berkeley bumper-sticker, perfect. Parked under a jacaranda on a dark corner, good cover. Fluke backs it in and we all pile out with tools, a flash, a board and a rope. Jack it up, disconnect the hoses and wires, ease it down onto the board, slide and wrestle it into the back. We can't see for shit, and aren't in the best shape to be doing this anyway—Pip trips over the curb and falls flat on his ass, Mysto loses his grip and the engine nearly lands on my foot, there are bruised fingers and a fair number of whispered curses, but within thirty minutes, the job is done, and far more quietly than I would've given us credit for.

Fluke wipes the Beetle clean of prints and we all pile back in—Pip on someone's lap this time to make room—and make our getaway, merry men waiting a full block to cheer. Don't make it much farther before Ricky calls to slow down again; there's a party going on, a big one, cars for half a mile around. Crashing it is out of the question—we're all barefoot, covered with grease—but Ricky has something else in mind. He leaps out as Fluke slows, begins trying the cars on the dark street. Drunks rarely lock doors, and some of the convertibles don't even have their tops up. I love that people are content to rely on the kindness of strangers. Ricky loves it, too, though not for the same reasons. Hits five cars before a German shepherd suddenly lunges out of a dark yard; we all shout in terror and he high-tails it, leaping inside just ahead of the teeth. Fluke floors her, and we're out of there.

Ricky's pocketed the cash, but he lays out the rest of the haul on the engine, pills and pot and doodads, a purple yoyo for Pip. Passes me an album, still in its bag. His apology: Dick Dale, 'Surfer's Choice,' live at the Rendezvous. I'm on there, stomping and hollering my appreciation.

'Oh, man,' I say, genuinely moved. 'You shouldn't have, Ricky.'

'Naw, kid. I know how you dig him.'

He's like that. He'll fuck with you endlessly, in little ways you can't make a scene about but that build up till you're ready to kill him—and then he'll turn around and do something so perversely decent it'll break your heart. I shake my head.

'You take some awful chances,' I mutter. But I keep the record.

The pills turn out to be not Dexies but downers; back at the beach we stumble around for a while, feeling every care slip away, a trail of shed clothing behind us. Georgia wanders through my mind as I breathe in her scent, lips on mine, hair slipping through my fingers. Ricky's wrong. I've seen trouble before, and this isn't what it looks like. By three, we're all passed out on the sand.

The lifeguard hollers us awake the next morning, and Fluke and I put the engine in. Well, he does. I hand him tools, tighten bolts and learn from the master. Starts right up after we top off the oil, gurgling like a cat over a dish of warm milk, and I have a ride once more. The two essentials in every Angeleno's life: transportation and obliteration. All we ever have to do is reach out, and they fall right into our hands, ripe oranges off a tree. Truly, we are in Eden.

The most important movie I've never seen is *Nuit et Brouillard*, directed by Alain Resnais. I was thirteen when it came to town, and told Mama I was going to Fluke's for the night, riding my bike over to Hollywood instead. It was only playing for one night, and the tickets were sold out, but I wanted to...I don't know. I wanted to be there. They hadn't made any movies about the Holocaust yet, and things aren't really real until you make movies about them, are they? Just idle gossip.

Sat on the curb across the street, knees drawn up under my chin, and watched all the unchosen ones who hadn't gotten tickets either milling around outside. Hundreds, some in camp uniforms, like a bizarro high school reunion. Part of me wanted to join them, hear what they were saying, but I held back, having had enough of it: the veiled references, the ominous doom and gloom. The helpless pathos, as if this was all my people were good for.

Thought of the images I'd seen in newsreels, tried to imagine what was going on inside. All I knew about it was that it held up the horrors of our black-and-white past (documented so proudly by Goebbels' crew, serial killers dying to get caught) with the tolerance of our Technicolor present: see, all better now. Hitler's *Nacht und Nebel*, the Night and Fog policy that cloaked the Jews' extermination in utmost secrecy, so as to avoid the brouhaha bound to ensue should the world find out.

They needn't have bothered. The excuse, of course, was that such an atrocity was inconceivable—but in truth, no one cared. I don't know that France would've even made the film in the first place, had they not wanted to whitewash their own Vichy cooperation, needing to pretend the whole country had struggled valiantly against the occupation, that they hadn't surrendered overnight before falling all over themselves to ferret us out for their overlords. The French perceived the camps as tragic, not because the Nazis were killing Jews there, but because they were killing resistance fighters. Real people. France, as America, always had a hard-on for the moving image, never more so than when it made them look good. But it was all smoke and mirrors.

There was so much I didn't know then—basic stuff no one bothered to tell me, truths that might've helped make sense of it all. The smallpox blankets we sold Indians so we could take their land without a fight, as if all our guns and lies were not enough. That the term 'concentration camp' was actually invented by the upstanding Brits, who herded South Africans into them during the Boer War. 130,000 civilians died, black and white alike. Kids, mostly. That a million and a half Armenians were slaughtered by the Turks during WWI, and no one gave a damn except a young lance-corporal named Adolph Hitler, who took careful note of the world's indifference for future reference.

The Germans didn't invent genocide, just as they didn't invent lying to their people. They were just more efficient about it. But America was no slouch when it came to befogging its citizens; I hadn't plumbed the full depths of it yet, but sensed we were all being bamboozled pretty badly. I didn't want to play this game anymore, I thought. Didn't want to be a Jew, led like a lamb to slaughter. An American fatted calf, battening on lies. Wasn't even sure I wanted to be a Communist anymore. All it ever did was get my ass kicked, and for what? Stalin and Mao were even more enthusiastic about killing their own people than anyone else.

No, I would be free of all that. I was a surfer now. I was cool, and I had cool friends, and girls liked me. Fluke had my back, I was getting better, and one day even Ricky might look at me with respect. When the foggy nights rolled in, we'd build fires on the beach, surfing through the mist. We couldn't always see where we were going, but that was the point, wasn't it? We lived forever on this razor edge of death. Serenity resided at First Point, a stoic ferocity that turned down the volume on the rest of the world.

I realized something that night, though I never did wind up seeing the movie—only thirty minutes long, it never could've measured up to the shit my brain concocts to torture me anyway. But I had been wandering lonely in a cloud for an awfully long time. There was a *lot* I was not being told. Not by my teachers or parents or anyone. They'd just laugh and say I was too young—although I spent my share of time skulking around eavesdropping, and couldn't help but notice no one was talking about this in private either, all the vague things I so desperately needed to know about sex, and death, and why humans were so incurably evil.

Grandpa was the only one who'd ever leveled with me, and he once told me there were two types of ammunition: bullets and facts. Now that he was dead, it was up to me to get those on my own. I was still too young to buy a gun, of course, but no one can stop you from going to a library. On the contrary, the fools even encourage it.

Resolved, then: I would be a secret agent, gathering data on the sly, storing away dossiers for hard times to come. Everyone would see me as this laconic blue-eyed surf bum, but inside...I would *know*. I'd be wise to all this shit, and learn to fight, and maybe even get a gun someday, and no one would ever hurt us like that again.

So that is what I did.

HUNGERS BREAD AND CIRCUSES CAN NEVER APPEASE

It is exactly 6:25 when the coffee spills down my slacks; I was checking the clock yet again, and didn't notice what I was doing. Lukewarm, thank God, or I'd be dealing with second-degree burns all over my dick, on top of losing my last pair of clean pants. Curse, kick the cup across the floor. Bounces off the table, spins over the rose-patterned linoleum, imperturbable, unbroken. They don't make them like they used to.

'What now?' Ray says from the living room, feet up and sounding about as concerned as the cup. He's taking a break from recreational rocket physics for a Captain America comic, while I race around like three jets getting ready for my date. When I wail in utter despair, he saunters out to have a look, and determines that I will wear his blue slacks instead, three inches too short. He can let them down, he says. Mama does it all the time; how hard can it be?

Hard, apparently. The minutes tick by while we find the sewing kit, turn on the living room lamp, and start picking at the hems, side by side on the couch.

'You're taking too long,' Ray says. 'Thread the needle.'

'I don't know how to sew,' I protest. 'You do it.'

'Do I look like a Home Ec boy, you galloping moron? I took shop!'

I'll figure it out. Get the thread in with fumbling fingers on the sixth try, and by then Ray is done with one leg and ripping away at the other. 6:40. I eyeball the hem, fold it, stick the needle in, and prick my finger.

'Wrong side,' mutters Ray, pulling the last of the threads out.

'Look, can't we just use masking tape?'

'We can't use tape, it's tacky.'

'Adhesive humor, funny. You're a real comedian. Hurry the fuck up.'

'Wrong side. When do you need this by?'

'Seven. What wrong side?'

'You're sewing the wrong side, genius. Hem goes on the inside.'

'But I can't *see* on the inside,' I panic.

He throws me the look you'd give a sick calf that wandered into your living room. 'Turn the pants inside out, you goof.'

'Oh...right.' My brain unfreezes, and we begin stitching as if we've been doing this all our lives, albeit with big spazzy stitches that yaw all over the cuff. I moan about this, but Ray brushes me off.

'Unless she's got an ankle fetish, she won't notice a thing. Does she?'

'Not to my knowledge.'

He pauses a moment, then asks begrudgingly: 'Is that all we get?'

Prick myself again, drawing blood. 'What more do you need?'

He laughs, almost angrily. 'Jeez, Tommy, you've been walking into walls for two weeks. You're obviously gonzo for this girl. What's the plan, show up in a month to tell us you're getting married, and as far as you know she doesn't have a thing for ankles?'

'I like her,' I say, unable to squelch my foolish grin. 'A lot, so I'm a little antsy. She's...oh, Ray, she's perfect. Her name is Georgia.'

'You big sap,' he says. 'Georgia? What is she this time, colored?'

'No, Jewish.'

'Okay, Jewish girl is progress; Mama'll like that. She is...nice, right?'

'Man, you don't know the half of it.' I stop sewing, my thread run out. 'She's something else. You guys are gonna love her.'

The front door opens and I startle, still in my shorts, but it's just Mama, home from the office. Comes in to kiss us hello, wearily taking off her hat and gloves. Ray finishes his leg, we cut the threads and hold the pants up, as she struggles to subdue her horrified expression.

'Let me fix.' She pulls at them.

'No time,' I plead, pulling back. 'She'll be here in five minutes.'

'At least iron.'

Ray rushes for the iron, drops it on the rug and we lunge for it, cracking heads and yelling, more in vexation than pain. Ray clocks me in the arm, I punch him back, then pick it up, and we go stand by the ironing board rubbing the tender lumps on our scalps as Mama ignores us, quietly toiling away with the steamer—and with a minute to spare, I'm dressed, shod and waiting at the front door like a racehorse as they circle me, brushing lint from my shoulders.

'We are going to meet your *Freundin, ja*?'

'Not today, Mama. It's not serious yet, and I don't want to scare her.'

'What nonsense is this! Who is scary here? Ray? I am not scary.'

Ray chortles as we exchange her patented look of askance. 'Our friends are all terrified of you, Mama. You can be a little intimidating.'

'This is completely untrue! Eddie, now, he likes me very much.'

'You're nice to him, because he's not scared of you. But you'll meet her soon, I promise.'

'*Brauchst du Gelt*?'

'Nah, I'm set.' Can't tell her a girl is paying my way; she'd have a fit. 'Do I look okay?'

They kindly comfort me with how handsome I look in my ragtag pants, tight blazer and grey fedora. Just then there's a honk, so I sprint out the door, tossing thanks over my shoulder, and leap into the dark-green Corvette convertible idling at the curb.

'Cherry car,' I babble. 'Good year, '59. Hi, by the way. Where we going?'

'Cherry hat,' she replies. 'Say, aren't you going to introduce me?'

She points to the lace-curtained window under the banana tree; Ray and Mama are stationed there, staring and shameless. Ray grins wide and gives us a big thumbs-up. Mama waves, and Georgia waves back enthusiastically over my head. Oh, man. I can't get them together, not yet. They'll eat me alive.

'Some other time,' I mutter, slouching down. 'Just drive.'

Throws me a look, but obeys. As we pull up to the light, 'Why not?'

I shake my head. 'Too complicated right now.'

'Seems pretty simple. Pleased to meet you, shake hands.'

'It's not you, honest. Or them. Just...not yet, okay? Don't want to jinx it.'

'Too late, ya big galoot. It's clinched.'

I sigh, a deep shudder. Hadn't realized I was holding my breath. Sink back into the seat, so low my ass is inches from the road, legroom for days. VW's are midget rides; even with the seat all the way back my knees are round my ears. Eye the sleek narrow dash, run a surreptitious hand over it, coveting. Everything about this car is so smooth, so easy. And the speed, forget it. There's a passenger grab bar set into the dash, that's how fast they assume you'll be going. Controls and gauges are all set up for the driver like a damned rocket ship; I don't even know what half those switches are for. Fluke said he tested one once, some work friend of his dad's, and it went zero to sixty in six seconds. I don't think he was pulling my leg, either. Takes me about a minute.

'You like it,' she says, a strange relief in her voice.

'Sure, it's tight as hell. When'd you get it?'

'Dad gave it to me, after I'd driven his car for a year without a ding.'

'Must be nice.' No flies on Dad. Bucket seats, no backseat, low top. Even harder to get knocked up in one of these babies than a Beetle.

She shrugs. 'It is nice. I'm not one of those people who apologizes for having money, Tommy. It makes a lot of things more pleasant. Not everything. But a lot.'

'Don't apologize,' I say, and mean it. 'Money's great stuff. Wish I were a bit better at getting it. Hardly ever feel that way, but a car like this...'

She throws me a sidelong glance. 'If there were something you wanted, you could make money, easy. Just have to find one thing you're good at, that you can do with a clear conscience.'

'I'm good at surfing. That's about it.'

'Then figure out how to make money from that.'

I snort. 'They don't pay people to be bums, Georgia.'

'No, it could be anything. My mom had this thing when I was little—she'd read papers. I mean, obsessive-compulsive, no-tomorrow-style. We had subscriptions to the 'Times,' LA and New York. 'Washington Post,' 'Wall Street Journal,' 'Variety,' everything. Some from Europe and South America she got weekly. Even 'Pravda.' She'd sit there with the dictionary and read them all, cover-to-cover, tens of thousands of words every day. It seemed pointless to us, borderline neurotic. She didn't hoard them or anything; she was very tidy, tied them up and put them out for the Scouts. But it was strange.'

'And?' I ask, unsure how this relates to surfing. 'She went to work for the CIA? Someone paid her to read the papers?'

'No,' she says, and raps a knuckle on the steering wheel. 'When I was six, she borrowed a grand from Dad, and started buying stocks. He just thought it was a lark, you know, real cute. But she swore she'd pay him back by December.'

'And did she?'

'She made ten grand that year, after commission.'

I whistle. 'How?'

'She thought about it, not even very hard. Her brain was so packed with information that it started to form patterns for her. She'd predict trends in real estate, science, fashion, politics, before they'd even gotten going. The year before the Russians got the bomb, she bought a bunch of rock-bottom stock in this little outfit down in Texas that built backyard nuclear shelters—and it exploded. So to speak.'

'Jeez. That's the greatest thing I ever heard. Savvy.'

'It gets better. See, after the Depression people were still gunshy about investing, but then things started to loosen up, money started coming in. Stocks go up, then everyone wants in so they appreciate even more.

Right now it's like someone dumped a bucket of chum in the water. Everything's through the roof.'

'Sounds like you know what you're talking about.'

'I do, actually. Got into it myself for a while.'

'Really? How'd you do?'

'I made enough for *college*,' she bursts out. 'I took my bat-mitzvah money, and made some pretty good guesses—Mom nixed a few, and there was one flop—but I made enough for all eight years, all by myself, housing and tuition and all that. I won't owe anybody *anything*.'

I don't know what to say to this. My mind is a whirl of pride, surprise and overall feeling that I'm in the wrong business. But it takes money to make money, right? 'Yowza. No offense, but you don't really seem the type. This is straight out of left field.'

'People never think of me that way because of...well, this.' She sweeps a hand down her body dismissively. 'Which is just some dumb accident. But the money is mine. I did that.'

'With that crafty Jew brain lurking behind those doe eyes.'

'But you've got one, too. Get off your high horse, ditch your precious surfer vow of poverty, and go for it. Look at Kathy Kohner.'

'Arrgghh. Pull over, I need to commit hara-kiri. *Gidget?*'

She clucks, 'You're missing the point. You could do it *right*. Your way.'

'Oh, come on, I wouldn't know where to start.' Mull it over. 'There is one thing...but I, well, no. Maybe. I'd have to think about it some.'

Restless, my brain humming, I fiddle with the lighter, the immaculate ashtray. Switch on the radio, just for the distraction: 'And this is KRLA with the man, the superman, Da Emperor Hudson, feeling all you hepcats and kitties tonight, and signing off till Monday, moondoggies. Keep 'em crossed, and don't forget to—'

We belt it out: 'Clear the freeways, peasants, da emperor is coming!'

She laughs and shimmies a little in her seat as the next number comes on, *you broke my heart, cause I couldn't dance...*

'You like to dance?' I ask, peering over at her profile, her eyes intent on the road. She's a good driver, not the hot-rodder I expected. Doesn't take chances. The Vette would be wasted on her, if it weren't so pretty. Not nearly as pretty as she is, though: dolled up in a narrow-waisted blue dress with white cuffs, hair rolled in some complex old-timey style not many girls could pull off.

'Kidding me?' She does look at me then, just for an instant. 'Love it!'

'Good,' I say. 'I'm going to take you dancing.'

'Ciro's?'

'Ciro's!' I scoff. 'What am I, dead? No, someplace cool. You'll dig it.'

'Ciro's *is* dead, you dope. Went under five years ago.' Flicks my hat off. 'Ow, you're bleeding!'

'No, I'm not.' I check the rearview; a smudge of blood on my forehead. 'Oh, yeah. Hit my head earlier, it must've...' I fumble in my pockets, and she hands me a hanky, pulls a Southern accent. "Never in all your born days have I known you to carry a handkerchief."

'Fiddle-dee-dee, baby.' Check the mirror, dab at my head. 'Hey, um— mind if I ask a stupid question?'

'Sure.'

'It's really dumb.'

'Try me.'

'Are you...oh, you know what, forget it.'

'Don't make me turn this car around.'

I blurt it out then. 'Are you just...slumming? I mean, with me?' Stare out the window, unable to face the blow head on. Now why did I have to say that out loud? Fucking Ricky. After a minute, I sneak a look at her. She's staring straight ahead, one hand on the shift. Pensive, absent, as if she were quite alone in the car. 'Are you?'

'And if I were?' Looks over at me, kind of pale.

'I guess that'd be all right,' I say humbly. 'I just want to know.'

She says nothing. Pulls into Lucky's, parks with a screech, disappears, door slamming behind her. Not a word. I wait for a few minutes, hating myself, then follow her inside, where I find her in the liquor aisle.

'Screw you.' She folds her arms over her chest. 'Get lost.'

'No.'

'How could you *ask* me that?' She grabs my hat, issues a flurry of quick blows upside my head. 'How could you? I thought you were okay with the money, I thought you—'

'Godammit, Georgia,' I protest, dodging the hat. 'Ow. Quit it. Ow!'

'I thought you were into me. That you were *you.*'

I stop dodging; she stops hitting. 'Who else would I be?'

'This isn't you. It's not.'

I flush, hang my head a little. Fucking *Ricky.*

'Look at me, Tommy. Do I seem the type with some big diabolical plan? I saw you, was all. Didn't even know why I was down at the beach at six o'clock in the morning...and then I saw you, and I knew. I *knew.*'

'I know,' I say. 'I did too. But it seemed impossible. Fairytales aren't— and the horse—'

'Oh, for the love of Pete,' she groans. 'I knew Buckley was a bad idea. I just—I didn't have time to shilly-shally and swan around hoping you'd notice me. I had to sweep you off your feet.'

'But you did. You did, right away. You're smart, and beautiful, and yeah, you're rich. You could have anyone, and for reasons unclear, you went and picked me. Really, I'm fine with whatever you want.'

She leans into me, head against my chest. I put my arms around her. 'I'm sorry I don't have a big pile of dough,' I say. 'That's never going to happen, frankly, and I've never been sorrier.'

'Oh, come off it. Like I care about that crap.'

'Really?'

'No. And I'm not *slumming*, you clod,' she says. 'What an awful word.'

'Agreed. Forget it, let's go see our movie. Will you tell me what it is?'

'Will you buy me some vodka?' She grins up at me.

'I'll buy you an ice cream cone, miscreant. What's your flavor?'

'Black cherry. Yours?'

'Chocolate.'

We get a double scoop, and I feed it to her as she drives, dripping on the dark leather seats, happy again. I don't know what happened there. It was a legitimate question—she could've just said no. Hell, she could have said yes, and I'd have gone with that, too, resigned for the axe to fall one day. There's a dab of ice cream on her nose; at the light, I lean over to lick it off, and then we are kissing, the traffic fading away, the music easing into the rush of blood in my ears.

'I love you.' It just falls out, and so help me, it's the truth. I've said the words before, but never like this. It's the kind of thing you'd say to a girl after you'd gone out a few times, maybe after sex if you really dug her. I'd never wanted to be untruthful, but neither did it seem like this thing you had to hoard till interest rates went down. What it meant was: that felt good, it's cool hanging out with you. This is different—ridiculously, unbelievably right. A warm yellow light is filling my brain, like coming up for air. This girl is killing me.

'I love *you*, asshole,' she says. 'Is it too soon to say that? Oh, I don't care. I do, I really do. All in.'

Someone honks, and she drives on. I crunch the last of the cone, then just sit there beaming at my lap. After a while she says, 'What's on your mind? Do I want to know?'

'I don't know,' I say. 'Nothing dirty, just...'

'What?'

'There's this picture Fluke has in their parlor, alongside DiMaggio and the Pope. Kind of a shrine. Jesus going up to heaven after they crucified him. I don't know who did it, no one famous, but he's good. There's all these cherubs and stuff, but that's not...all you see are the eyes.'

She nods. 'They follow you?'

'No, it's the expression, sort of...ecstatic. Calm. You know how right after someone wakes up, their eyes are soft, like an animal's?'

'There's no fear there. They're not all tangled up in our mess.'

'Exactly. That's how I feel right now. Untangled.'

She looks at me fondly. 'This is such a sloppy old chestnut...but it's like I've known you forever. It's not fair that it's taken this long to find each other. But there's still that fear, you know?'

I don't. I don't know, I tell myself. I'm not scared anymore.

'I read this story once, two kids were walking over a frozen stream, and one of them fell through and was caught in the current. The other boy could see him through the ice, and it was horrible. Because he couldn't save him, you know? He couldn't break through, and he was just a few inches away, looking right at him. I'd close my eyes at night and—' She shudders. 'It's so hard to find the people you're meant to. And so easy to lose them again.'

'I've never even been on the ice,' I tell her. 'No worries.'

She shakes her head and doesn't seem to want to say any more, so we just listen to the radio. After a while, she asks, 'Never?'

'Never even seen the snow. I don't like cold places. Never left California, except for Baja a few times. Why bother?'

'You're nuts,' she laughs. 'Hawaii? New York? Rome? There's this spot in the Rockies, you'll think you're in heaven, no joke. And Barbados! Oh, Tommy, the water's so clear there you can see the fish way down at the bottom—and those waves!'

'But everything I need is right here.' I put a hand on her knee, so happy I can barely breathe. She rolls her eyes, smiling at me.

59

'There's something I want to show you before the movie—it's right up ahead.' She hangs a left onto a dirt road that winds up to a crest in the hills, then pulls over. 'Check it out.'

I look. The entire city is spread out, dark purple-brown, silhouetted serene against the sky, quilted with lights moving slowly through it: all of us made one by this mass, from Watts to Santa Monica to Pasadena. The sun is almost gone now, only a faint golden murmur painting the underbellies of the clouds that slouch across the arc of horizon over the sea, rose-pink and pale lavender, a last bastion against the encroaching violet haze and oil spill of nightfall. A sliver of moon hangs in the sky, and from it, suspended like a hypnotist's pendulum, the North Star.

'That's something else,' I say. 'Though I'm more of a sunrise kinda guy.'

'Not me. There's this anticipation to sunsets, like a message from God: get ready, baby, here comes the night. The big adventure.'

I don't know what to say, stymied, unable to manage anything clever, but every cell is amped, tingling with possibility. She stretches, cracks her neck. 'You know it's the pollution that makes it that pretty?'

'Really? How so?'

'A refraction off the particles; my Chem teacher told me.' She sighs. 'You know...this goddamned town. It's all paying off in breathtaking sunsets, isn't it? We'll keep building highways and pumping out crap, and the sweet young things from Ames, Iowa will keep turning up to get turned out, until the whole place goes belly-up in a big bang of filth and beauty. I can hardly wait.'

'Yeah, but it's not like we were ever going to end well, right? And think what a glorious sunset it'll make. Bikini times a hundred.'

We watch it go down, alone in our minds with this *Götterdämmerung*, until night has drawn over the sky and a few more stars are visible.

'We should go,' she says at last. 'We'll miss our movie.'

I chuckle when I see the sign over the Easter Island head: Mission Tiki Drive-In. All palm trees and aloha shirts, jokey tropical names at the snack bar. Our cheap island getaway. Then I see the marquee: 'Lolita.'

60

Groan. 'You're really gonna rub it in, aren't you?'

She chuckles, pleased with the payoff. 'Plan to. Seen it yet?'

'Not yet. Helluva book, though. Who directed?'

'Same guy who made 'Spartacus.' Dad brought him home once. He got drunk and I think tried to hit on my mom, and we never had him back.'

'Sounds like a keeper,' I say. "Spartacus' was sweet, though—the flick that broke the blacklist. But what'd you think of him?'

She shrugs. 'He seemed cool. All directors are weirdos, but he was like this smart, friendly Jewish troll. Shtann-lee. From the Bronx, yet.'

'The Bronx' is said in such a way that lets me know people shouldn't be from there, though I'm not sure if this applies to directors or Jews.

The movie, while not quite as twisted as the book, is still pretty insane. They skipped her dying in childbirth at 17. Maybe it was too much, though I don't know how it could've been more so. And I wouldn't have gone with Mason for Humbert; I had him pegged more as an attractive Alfred Hitchcock, if that makes any sense, and Lyon's a little long in the tooth to achieve the full creepiness of a twelve-year old seductress, but after half an hour I'm shifting in my seat, shamefully aroused. Georgia glances over.

'This is turning you on, isn't it?'

'Yeah, kinda,' I confess. 'Sorry.'

'Don't be,' she says. 'All part of the plan.'

Throws a switch; the roof closes over us as she climbs on top of me, straddling my legs, and we're kissing as the world disappears, drive-in and all. The seat goes back, I harden against her warmth, her breasts soft against my chest, nails delicate on the back of my neck, and when I move my hands up her skirt to find nothing underneath, I am this close to abandoning my notion that she deserves privacy and a bed and many, many pleasurably uninterrupted hours.

It'll be good, my brain gasps, don't blow it. Just hang in there a little longer, keep her here.

I didn't think it was possible to get any harder, but when she starts whispering those things in my ear, I find I was wrong. Dolores Haze murmurs from the speaker, *I learned some games at camp*, and then we are speaking to one another in an ancient tongue no one ever needed to teach us at all. Our teeth find flesh, her fingers are rough in my hair and she is grinding into me, the bone beneath her tenderness hard against my cock, until all the times tables in the world can't hold me back. And that's how I spoiled my second pair of pants that day.

There is this commonly held belief that a big dick is a gift from God. It's not. I'd just like to clear that up. Queers have been hitting on me in the john since I was a kid and didn't even know what they were up to, just there to pee and scram, but regular guys are even worse. They'll check you out on the sly, and half the time make some idiot comment or try to pick a fight, like I'm threatening them with this thing I never asked for in the first place.

Grandpa Joe used to go in with me after the first time I came running out all upset; he was a solid guy with meaty fists and a scary scowl like Mama's, and you'd best believe no one screwed with me when he was around. But after he died, I was on my own, and gym class, when they made us all shower together, was not a big barrel of monkeys. I weighed maybe eighty pounds soaking wet back then; there was a lot of teasing and towel snaps, and I could feel a fight brewing for which I was no more prepared than a butterfly is for a windshield on the highway.

When I started hanging out with Fluke, he taught me a few moves. He didn't want me to be caught in another Raoul situation, so we practiced under the pier for a few days, sparring until he's sort of satisfied, but not really. One day he pulls back, sucks his tooth and considers me.

'Thing is,' he says, 'You're missing a certain essential, how the French say, Jenny Say Kwah.'

'What's that?'

'Like the spirit of kicking ass.'

'Oh, yeah, like the French would know a lot about that.'

'Fine, then, go get your punk ass creamed.'

'No, man, don't bug. Sorry. All ears, great master.'

'Yeah you are, Jughead,' he says, mollified. 'You're a skinny young thing, one day you'll grow into yourself. But for now, what you want to work on is your mad-dog.'

'My what?'

'See, best way to win a fight is to avoid it. Don't yell. Don't even beat him, less you have to. Just make him think that though you may seem like a puny nerd, you're stone cold, so batshit you'll fuck him six ways from Sunday, tear him apart in ways he can't even imagine.'

'So, like a crazy look.' I attempt this, and Fluke winces.

'Naw, man, no. Like this.' He doesn't change at all, really. Hardly at all. But suddenly he looks like he's going to reach down my throat and pull out my spinal column.

'Whoa! How'd you do that?'

He smiles, his old affable self again. 'Ahh, I could feed you a line about Sicilians, but...well, all right. Swear you'll never tell, though.'

I cross my heart, as a wave licks my foot. Tide's coming in.

'Ever watch 'Rawhide?"

'Sure.'

'So you know how no one ever fucks with Rowdy Yates?'

'Well, sometimes they do.'

'Yeah, but they live to regret it—anyone looking into his eyes can tell the motherfucker's insane. The guy who plays him is a total health nut. Runs on the beach a lot, early, when there's no one around. We talked a couple times—he's actually a pretty nice fella—and one day I got him to show me how he does it.'

'How? Like this?' I growl a little, narrow my eyes as I raise my fists.

'No, dukes down. You're ice. Focus on the eyes. You're about to feed this guy his own dick, with relish.' He makes the face again and I take a step back, then try it myself. Fluke groans, then feints with his right, coming up on my left as I try to block it and catching me hard in the shoulder. I wince, trying not to cry out.

He throws up his hands. 'Jesus, kid, you're killing me here. Defense, defense—didn't your dad teach you *nothing*?'

I freeze. I haven't thought about him in weeks, but now it all comes rushing back, a dam busting open, vision swimming with a hot plastic shimmer. What he did to her, how much I'd like to—

'That's it!' Fluke hollers in triumph. 'Damn! Just like that!'

'Don't talk about him,' I say. My voice is liquid nitrogen, face inches from his. 'Don't ever mention him again. I don't talk about him.'

He's nodding, nodding, and looks a little rattled though he outweighs me by a good fifty pounds. His dad loves him so much they're ready to kill each other half the time, and Mr. Fallucci would walk in front of a semi before he pulled that shit, but I know Fluke understands.

'I don't talk about him.' I can't feel my lips.

'I know, Tommy. I know, man, I get it. Never again.'

I get it, too. For the rest of my life, whenever I need to scare the shit out of someone, I flash on my father's face. It is the only time I think about him at all.

I won't lie: my love for Fluke is just plain weird. I follow him around, a dumb puppy copping his moves. Talk like him, dress like him, mimic his loose-limbed rolling saunter. Come over to his house, befriend his parents and five sisters, help him put his baby brother to bed. Sit at their kitchen table and surreptitiously observe how he eats spaghetti. Memorize 'Che la Luna' to sing very earnestly for Mrs. Fallucci, a big Louis Prima fan, as the whole family rolls around on the floor in tears of joy, till Fluke takes me aside to explain what I'm singing.

One morning we're waxing our boards—mine a dinged loaner from Mysto—when he suddenly sniffs the air. Turns his head, to give my awkward DA a strange look.

'Tommy, did you, ahh...did you put butter in your hair?'

I blush like a madman. Fluke howls with laughter, then explains the superior qualities of Brylcreem (for the heavy duty jobs, but a bitch to wash out, you gotta use Coke or dish soap) and Vitalis (for hot dates, so the chick's hands don't get too slippery). I hit a drugstore on the way home, and for four bits am hip once more. God Bless America.

A few months later, we both toss the greasy kid stuff and go full surfer. I throw my soul into sanding down every part of me that is not as cool as he so effortlessly is, getting back on the board again and again and again and again until I don't shame him, until I'm damn near as good as him. Until that fateful day I ride his ass off, and have to choke back the roar of triumph rising in my chest. Play it cool back up on the sand, but I can feel his eyes on me; when I finally dare look up, he's grinning like a guy who just won a bet. You neither brag nor rag on anyone here, not about this. It may be the best part of surfing for me.

Fluke is the one person on the planet I feel totally comfortable with, though, and I know he's fine with what you might call my megaphallic situation, so when he lays that idiot nickname on me I just let it ride. After a few months I even come to enjoy it, which is pretty much what he told me to do from the get-go.

'Be happy with yourself, Rod. Anyone who isn't can go straight to hell. And consider this free advertising; you'll thank me when the chicks are lined up around the block.'

Word does get around. Los Angeles is a smaller town than everybody thinks; a few days after Tina and I broke up, Carole Kushmaro sidled up to me by the bleachers. She was fifteen, but had been left back twice, not cause she was dumb, but cause she really, really did not like people telling her what to do. She had this thick red hair she never cut, just wore in two long braids. People gave her grief for being old-timey like that, but she didn't care. She never did.

'You wanna go out tonight?'

'What?' I said, caught off-guard, watching some guys tackle each other on the field. Football always seemed so aimlessly painful to me, like the ball was beside the point and all they really wanted to do was kill each other. I liked swimming, but hadn't worked up the courage to try out for the team yet. Carole repeated her question.

'Sure, I guess. I'm strapped.' I wasn't sure how she knew me.

She nodded, 'That's jake. We can go to the park.'

And that was that. I got all dressed up and she took me to the park, where she pulled me into the bushes before we'd exchanged more than a few minutes' conversation, and fucked me. Not much better at kissing than she was at talking, but let me take her hair down, and it smelled like apples and felt like we were hiding from the world in it, and she had some nice moves, although she made me pull out, still a difficult thing to gauge back then.

'That was sweet,' she said, pulling her skirt down and combing leaves from her miraculous hair. 'Tina wasn't lying, you're good.'

No idea how Carole and Tina even knew each other, and I'm pretty sure I was very not-good at this, all elbows and nervous contrition, but she was into it, and after awhile we didn't bother with the chitchat. Saw each other a few more times, and then there was Katie Kingston and Shelly Dubois, and Gladys Pfeiffer for a month, and then came Angie and Beryl and Corinne and Edith and Mary-Jane and there were girls on the beach and women at parties and by the time I was fifteen I stopped trying to remember names. I keep my mouth shut, and this discretion makes me a popular guy; they pass me around like a pint of ice cream at a party. Nice girls all, but kicking over the traces, you know? I was just happy they seemed to like me for a while.

Don't get me wrong, the sex was fantastic, I was very grateful and did improve over time—do anything for long enough and you will, though Mama had thrown up her hands with me and the piano lessons. But it wasn't like it'd been with Tina. Maybe I was too heartbroken or dumb or whatever to feel whatever it was I was supposed to be feeling, and I'd wait around for it to show up, but it never did.

I could always pinpoint that moment they started to slip from my grasp, too. Their eyes would go flat, and my heart would sink, knowing all the vague excuses to come, our charade of unity growing thinner and thinner until I was sick with it, knowing there was no coming back, not even to this thing that hadn't really been there in the first place. Kept hoping some bona fide nice girl might slip up and get to liking me, but the nice ones were no slouches; they avoided me like the plague. After a while I learned to simply have some fun and walk away.

With a few, I couldn't get it in there, and wasn't about to hurt a girl. They were happy enough just to touch it, though, like some kind of good luck totem. Little did they know. But broken or not, no one turns down a handie. My hormones were so crazed back then I'd have stuck my dick in a car muffler, and bought it dinner first, too.

Fluke would see me sidling back to the pit with that dumb grin on my face, and one day took me aside and asked if anyone had told me about the birds and the bees. I said sure, although no one had.

'Look, don't knock 'em up, is all I'm saying. Bad enough when you have to get hitched, and God only knows what they'd do with your juvie ass. You're pulling out like I said, right?'

I was. Most of the time.

He then proceeds to give me this convoluted and somewhat erroneous explanation of the rhythm method, and looks at me significantly. We're both a little red, and I say, 'I can't ask them *that*. We're not on those kinda terms, and it'd kill the mood.' He groans, and I add, 'And why am I taking advice about this from a Catholic with six siblings?' He cuffs me upside the head. That night we pull Operation French Letter, breaking into a pharmacy to steal two gross of rubbers to stow with Ricky, who then of course attempts to sell them back to us.

I point out that they're ours, and he says, possession's nine-tenths, price just went up to a quarter; I holler, they're the people's prophylactics, goddammit, and there is a general uprising as we liberate the rubbers again, smuggling them home to stash. We didn't always remember to use them—there were a few pregnancy scares, and U-Boy caught the clap three times from the same biker chick—but overall, we were very lucky. Very lucky indeed.

Da Rod's reputation blossomed, and frankly, that was fine by me. Guys seemed to respect the Casanova shtick, although I was caught in a few snafus where I'd screwed their girls by mistake, or someone they felt should be their girl, or had just broken up with; it wasn't my job to keep track of all this crap. By then I'd gone through a growth spurt and carried a reputation as a serious maniac, so the few that did come after me didn't do too much harm.

Overall it felt good to walk the halls and have everyone fall away like I was Charlton Heston parting the Red Sea. Takes something out of you, though, especially when you're trying to keep your grades up and all the teachers want to flunk you for being this notorious JD surfer, and you're not even sure how that happened.

Mama kept getting called in, and couldn't understand it. At home I was this perfect angel, even though I was home less and less, always over at the Falluccis' or out on the water. Always for some nothing shit, too—either someone had picked a fight, hardly my fault, or else I'd corrected one of the teachers in class yet again. Never failed to go to bat for me, but I could see it pained her. She had to take time off from work—a friend had gotten her a gig with an insurance investigator, and she was indispensible enough that he allowed it, but still docked her pay. She loved me, though, and wanted to see me have a good life. College and all that. I don't know what she was thinking.

I'd been suspended this time, having piped up in Civics to point out that I didn't think the Russian people were having such a great time, all things considered. Khrushchev was no picnic, and they were hungry and scared, yet still kicking our asses in sports, science, and technology, and maybe we could cut them some fucking slack. I didn't say 'fucking' or 'asses,' but they were definitely implied, so I was sent to the principal for manifesting subversive tendencies, where it was determined that I was corrupting the youth. They didn't make me drink the hemlock, but I was exiled for three days, with option to renew until I realized the error of my ways. This involved an essay.

'You must stop with the smart talk,' Mama tells me in the car, for the 87th time that year.

'Yeah, wouldn't want smart in school,' I mutter, staring out the window, hands clenched between my thighs.

'Tomas. You are an intelligent boy, you know this. I know this. Even Ray knows this.'

'I'm not writing the essay,' I growl.

'Tomas, *es ist nicht wichtig. Gibt ihnen etwas Unsinn.*'

'Not giving them sh...anything. And it *is* important. I won't apologize. Russians are human beings too. They're being used, just like us.' I don't mention Grandpa, but we can feel his ghost in the back seat.

She groans, but I know she's in my court. I spend the next three days fixing up the house, mowing the lawn, and at the library writing essays: one about American suburbia and Potemkin villages, another on the flourishing kibbutz movement, and a real crowner about Guevara and Castro and how bad things are under Batista. Briefly consider *Animal Farm*, but it's not what I'm looking for, so I go with *Grapes of Wrath* instead. I type up each brilliantly articulated expression of political criticism—and Mama nixes them all.

Friday rolls around. The school calls to see if I am ready to apologize. I am not. They call Mama at work, she comes home that night in tears, and Ray takes me out to the yard where I let him beat the crap out of me, thinking it will make him feel better. It does not. Mama falls off the wagon that weekend, and by Sunday Ray is no longer speaking to me.

They probably think I'm being a stubborn idiot, a rebel without a cause who can't keep his mouth shut to save his life—and you know what, they're right. It's not like one guy is going to change jack shit about this system. McCarthy may be dead of decency deficiency, but HUAC is still king. Congress isn't our judicial body, and it's a free country; you can believe whatever you want—at least that's what they tell us. The whole surreal melodrama was staged by fiat fascists as we wrung our hands, oh, it's not *constitutional,* oh, they can't *do* that. They could, and they did, and they do. You can do anything you want if you have the balls, while the rest of us shlubs have to sign a loyalty oath and suck Hoover's dick even to get a job as a gas station attendant.

Lie on my bed that afternoon staring at the ceiling, watching a spider build a web in the corner. Before it's done, a fly bumbles in, is quickly incapacitated and wrapped up for dinner—but as the spider gets back to work, it manages to wriggle free of its sticky bonds and fly dizzily away. It's fucking hopeless. Communism's gone bad, too many broken eggs—but it's not like capitalism is working, either, and socialism is just a slippery slope cop-out. There's gotta be some simple, obvious solution

Sonntagsleere: the inescapable emptiness of Sunday, no busy weekday repetition to shelter you from the glare of your pointless asshole life. A faucet is dripping in the bathroom sink, echoing down the silent empty hallway as I doze off.

In the dream, I am three, up on Grandpa Joe's shoulders, hands twined securely around his forehead, chin resting in the nest of his thick grey hair. He is striding through a forest like a giant; we are on our way to an important meeting where there will be people who know me well, who will pick me up, hold me on their knees and tell me what a good boy I am. We'll eat good food and sing proud songs and listen to people speak about the wonderful future that awaits us. But we're not there yet. For now, we're just walking through the calm quiet forest, the smell of pine all around, the occasional sunbeam breaking through, and he is singing in a deep bass voice that fills it all like a bell: *Alte Not gilt es zu zwingen, Dass die Sonne Schön wie nie...*

Wake up sobbing. Let the old woes be forgotten, that the sun may shine again. Easier said than done. I cry for an hour, which hasn't happened for years. I'd grieve terribly, then be wholly happy again. I was a merry little fucker, once upon a time, could roll with the punches.

Eventually I dry my eyes, get up, and go to the closet. There's a stash I keep in there under a pile of outgrown clothes: an ancient Red Sox cap, Ray's Cub Scout uniform, two pairs of cords, my stamp album—and under it, a little squashed, the box.

I pull it out and look through it—old photos and drawings, notes from Mama, birthday and report cards, tattered copies of 'The Worker'— until I find the America First pamphlet Grandpa showed me one night. We sat at his desk and went over everything that was wrong with this bullshit, till I was able to argue any fascist dullard into the ground.

Gibt ihnen etwas Unsinn, give them some nonsense. I copy it all down, word for word, two pages of the stuff. It is the most un-American thing I've ever done, and I know it wouldn't make him proud. We are nothing if not original here, in this brave new world. He always liked that about us. He wouldn't have liked any of this, though. Not them doing it, not my craven surrender. He'd have torn them limb from limb; it was only himself he was no good at defending. But this is how I choose to protect myself. I'm a turncoat now, a scab—and a chickenshit cheat to boot, even if I'm faking it. These uncrossable lines meant something to him: a Rubicon that did nothing in the end but kill him dead.

His last act as a human being was to break Mama's heart, and that's not something I can do. I will live for her, if not for myself, even if that life winds up crushing me. There are no other choices, no happy ending. And there should be, you know? There really should. This is America. The happy ending is the whole fucking point.

They accept my essay, take me back, and everyone is relieved but me. I don't shower or change that whole week, and at night fall into bed in my clothes, sleeping so badly I'm too groggy to brush my teeth come morning. I can't play at being clean anymore.

Thursday night Connie Brutelli picks me up in her old man's Chevy and teaches me to eat pussy. It doesn't turn me off at all. I love being buried here between her warm solid thighs, my lips on hers, fingers sinking into the flesh of her beautiful ass, tongue making her moan and clutch at my hair. Her cunt tastes more real than my entire life, like fish and flowers, and after she comes I fuck her so hard she screams in pain, and it turns out I like that, too.

'You look tired,' Fluke says the next night. We're unloading cases for the luau. I barely hear him. Everything's been underwater for days.

'Ungh,' I say, and pull a church key to crack a beer. Fluke places the last case on the sand. Night is coming down, the fire's going hard, there's food and booze, and a cute little ultramarine record player with a stack of 45's Ricky boosted out of some bopper's room at a party in the Hills last weekend. Mysto passes me the bottle he's nipping at. I've never had vodka before, but take a taste. A deeper one. Deeper.

Can feel it run down my body like gasoline, an inspiring Molotov, and Mysto guffaws, slaps me on the back.

I grin and take another long belt before Fluke wrestles the bottle away, tries it and grimaces. The music is playing, hooked up to a car battery, and U-Boy is flipping through the records, tossing them aside, finally opting for the new Crickets. This song has been on the radio hitting us like a freight train for two weeks now, *sehyew gonna leave, hyew know it's a lie cuz*—Mysto grabs my hand and we are dancing, two guys in jeans and T's bopping around, kicking up sand, helium bubbles of that Lubbock accent rising into the cool night air. The happy is creeping in through the back door, and I'm trying just for once not to break it down and ruin everything.

I love Buddy Holly, no lie. Here's this buck-toothed guy with goofy eyes and horn-rimmed glasses, hiccupping and yodeling while managing to be even cooler than Elvis, outrageous in his claim that you can be a dork and a rocker both. He's not trying to look cool, see—he just lets his passion shine through, so that he actually *is* cool.

Every skinny geek in the country is rooting for him, cause you know that hillbilly's scoring mad pussy, and we're stoked to be along for the ride. Almost Christmas, another winter festival in our parched snowless paradise, and we've got our ocean and our Buddy and each other, and maybe life isn't the pits after all. Monday morning I'll have to face the zombies again, but for tonight—damn, man, I am *alive*.

Cars start pulling in: the HB and Venice crews, a few of those insane Windansea pranksters, two of Fluke's cousins down from Santa Cruz. Strangers show up on Harleys, a Fairlane spills a gaggle of girls onto the sand all laughs and clattery chat, and we're rocking around the bonfire, bodies intertwining, singing to the heavens, happy as clams.

I'm draining the last of the vodka, drinking anything I'm handed, senses flickering as I shotgun beer after beer. Things go a little muffled, and I'm struggling through the waist-high waves, screaming my guts out, knocked over to choke on the dark saltwater flooding my mouth. Fluke is hugging me from behind as I punch him away, telling me something I can't grasp as he drags me out of the water and carries me into Ricky's shack, where I pass out.

And then Denise shows up.

Denise is, well. Denise. A peach of a girl, a woman, really. She's twenty, with curly black hair and brown eyes, red pillowy lips she has this way of licking that gets you instantly hard, tits so nice you just want to rest yourself there and moan. Surfs a little; she's not bad, but mostly she just comes down to fuck with Fluke's head. Been around the block, but he doesn't care, he's nuts about her, would marry her tomorrow if she'd have him. She's the only one I've ever seen get him tongue-tied, falling all over himself to get close to her—and for some insane chick reason, she won't even give him the time of day. It's cruel.

When I come to, she's on her knees by the bed, fiddling with my fly. It's pitch dark in here, and for a moment I have no idea where I am.

'Shtah,' I tell her, and push her hand away.

'You're all wet,' she says. Not sure what she wants me to do about that.

'M'fine. Go away.'

'It's okay. Ricky just wants me to take your clothes off, cause you're soaking the mattress.'

'Oh.' I sit up for her, raise my arms, and she pulls off my shirt, tousles my damp hair. There is a fragrance of cinnamon and sweat to her skin, her hair's brushing against my face, and those lips are so close to mine, too close. Hold up, something's rotten here. I don't want her to take my pants off, but her touch is cunning and sure; before I know it, they're around my ankles. Fuck, fuck. Try to pull them up, but she pushes me back, runs her hands down my chest, and no part of me is working anymore. Almost no part.

'You're a good boy, Tommy.' She traces a finger over my lips.

'Don't,' I manage. *Oh, God, please, please do.* 'Sorry, you're really pretty, but please don't.'

'Sshh, honey. It's going to be all right.'

Her mouth is on mine then, running down my chest, tongue flicking against the head of my cock, and all words desert me as those lips take me in. A better man would've stopped her, but I am in no way a better man, and I am this close when Fluke appears in the doorway, checking up on me. The flashlight blinds my eyes, Vi haff vez of making you talk, as I come, hard. And then he's gone.

Everything after that is a fearful shamed blur of racing down the beach after him, stumbling and pleading for him to listen, I didn't mean it, spineless fuckhead that I am, please wait, Fluke, *please*. I do remember the moment he stopped and turned back: the moon had just come out from behind a cloud, and was shining bone white and cold-clear on everything: the monotone of the pier, the waves slurring in to shore, the grass bent over by the wind in the dunes.

'I'm sorry.' I'm sobbing, half-naked, shivering like a mongrel caught in a rainstorm. 'I am so fucking sorry, Eddie, please.'

He smiles, but there's something cruel about it. 'Don't mean nothing, Roddy. Just a chick. They can't come between us, right?'

'I didn't mean to, Eddie, I fucked up. I love you, man. I'm sorry.'

And then I puke on his feet.

One of the few people who ever really got me in this life was a girl named Sharon Cox; we dated for a while when we were freshmen. She was a nice girl, shy and pretty with a thing for squirrels, but she was kind of a mess, couldn't walk down the hall without getting hassled, and not just over the name. Her tits had started in fourth grade; by thirteen she was a double D, not the sort of thing you could hide with hunched shoulders and bulky sweaters.

Guys would corner her by the lockers or in the girls' room, and a few teachers did too, and no one but me ever did shit about it. All the girls gave her the cold shoulder and called her a slut, which was such bull, because she wasn't, not at all. The whole time we were together, all she let me do was hold her hand or kiss her cheek; try for anything more and she'd go rigid. It was hard, when you'd meant no harm.

I got bored and wandered off after a while—but I still think about her, cause she dug what it meant to be this Midas freak. There are things you get in this life and think, 'Oh, man, this is so great, wait till I show everyone, what a *gift*.' And it turns out they aren't gifts at all. They just wind up hurting you and those you love, till you can hardly fucking live with yourself.

I pulled it together after that night. Kept my mouth shut at school, did my homework without cracking wise, got a job at Tony's to help out Mama. Remembered where my loyalties lay. I didn't touch another girl for a long time, and Fluke and I stayed friends, but things were never quite the same. Our friendship, so easy and true, was tarnished now by this idiotic two-minute blow-job. That ease had been a real gift, broken before I had the chance to appreciate it.

A year after the party, Buddy Holly's plane went down in a storm over Clear Lake, Iowa. There were no survivors.

After my date with Georgia, I barely sleep. We've just met, but she's the one; there is no doubt about this in my mind. In three months I'll be leaving my teens behind, and it's time to get my act together. Not going to ask her to marry me tomorrow, but when we're ready, I want to be— I dunno. Somebody, not a bum. Have something to offer...no, you know what, fuck the world. Myself. Me and her.

Her dad's one of the top agents in town, probably worth about a zillion and change, more than I can make in ten lifetimes no matter what I do. I mean, the girl's so far out of my pay grade it hardly bears thinking on, and my thirty a week won't be enough to support us, not even in a style that would be a major comedown from what she's accustomed to. She wouldn't care, she claims, but she probably would, if we come right down to it—and I most definitely would. Stone truth: there is nothing romantic about poverty. A kiss don't pay for your humble flat, nor help you at the Automat.

It ought to, though. A place where you could get sandwiches and cake out of a wall in exchange for kisses? Now there's a business idea. Shit, I'd eat there every day. Who'd you kiss, though? I'm a decent kisser, but surfing is the only thing I'll ever be great at. And I don't know how to sell that—or if it's even right to.

I toss and turn, and at four finally get up, switch on the desk lamp and quietly start taking down notes. Things must have been fermenting in there, cause by the time the clock begins to jangle and Ray stirs under the sheets, I've got twelve pages of sketches and ideas and, so help me, cost analyses and profit projections. Turn off the alarm and go back to bed, smiling to myself. The business classes I've been bumbling through are finally paying off; God bless Governor Brown and free Santa Monica College tuition.

This is going to be a tightrope walk, though, and not just with Ricky and the guys, because it feels like a sellout, no matter how I cut it. Surf shops are springing up like mushrooms all over town, but our crew has always been above that gig, mocking the money-hungry rat race.

The thing about the beach, maybe the most important thing, is that it's a place without class, where money means nothing, nothing is for sale. The great equalizer, where we're all stripped down as far as legal, often beyond. Can't tell who's a big shot here, and it doesn't matter anyway—Morlocks are indistinguishable from Eloi here, all milling around in our sunny kingdom. Who cares who's who, right? There's enough to eat, plenty of beer, and no call to fight each other. But that urge dies hard, and you can't hole up in this bubble forever.

We crawled out of the sea 250 million years ago, didn't have Corvettes or Brooks Brothers suits or Tiffany bracelets back then, just tooth and claw and each other. Eventually we evolved into whatever we are now—yet there's still that urge at our core, that primal need to feed and breed. We kid ourselves about our moral superiority, but we've all got parents supporting our deadbeat selves, or a half-assed job, and Ricky's got his little outlaw pursuits. America is rolling in dough, and we can scavenge quite comfortably off the fringes without the sacrifice of an empty belly or a dead heart.

But I'm sick of scrambling for crumbs.

People have always loved the ocean, can't stay away. However far we've come as a species, we still long to return home, physically needing that with every part of our being. We're amphibians, after all, neither fish nor flesh, and have to keep wandering back and forth, crawling up onto the sand, only to flee back to the sea. It's that ambivalence that feels like home, because I love the land—but I long for the ocean. Salt, water and air, just like us, hardly any difference. There are days when there is no difference. Something like that is too precious to pollute, though we happily do so anyway. Surfers didn't need to read Rachel Carson to be aware we were spending our lives immersed in a swamp of sewage, oil and toxic waste. I suppose it'd be worse if we were new to this scene, but when you're born in Mordor, you get used to it.

Money does tend to ruin things, sometimes as much as its lack. You lose sight of what matters, the joy going jaded until there's nothing left. I can give that pleasure back to people—for a price. Pretty sweet little irony, I know. But anything that packs the line-up even further is a concession to the carpetbaggers, a betrayal of the tribe.

You can spot a true surfer straight off—there's an ease there, a leathery looseness; the eyes start to get that faded faraway look. Waves wash away the need for niceties and status symbols, and the sun burns you till they stay gone--but you can hang out at this party too long, taking that rejection of society too far.

Just don't want to wind up like Ricky. Thirty-four seems ancient to me, embarrassingly so. Older than Jesus was when he died, with a lot less to show for it. Sure, he's a god, and he loves that, you can see it in his eyes. People all over the world know how good he is, one of surf's few real naturals. He's had articles written about him, and even stunt-doubled on movies, although he pretends to hate all that.

And yeah, I admire how he's made this philosophy out of the whole fuck-you-and-the-money-you-rode-in-on, standing by it with every fiber of his being, though he's aware that it's a pointless approach that screws people over. You can see that in his eyes, too. There's no peace there; maybe that's why he's such a crab all the time. He's selfish and stingy and ruthlessly antisocial, and thinks he owns the beach and all the best waves, and I suppose he's earned that. But it doesn't make him very pleasant to be around.

There are other kinds of surfers, though, who love the beach without living there full-time. I've met a few. Not the wishful fishbelly hodads— I mean the guys who started before the whole scene went to hell, the lifeguards turned into jackboot-jerks and the siren song of *Gidget* brought the hordes out of Hawthorne and Pasadena. Who take this seriously, as more than a hobby or even a second job. It's a love affair for them, a spiritual quest, and you can tell it gives more meaning to their life than anything else. That they might die without getting out there on a regular basis.

Thing is, it *is* a job, one that never ends. The hours revolve around the tides and winds, in a natural rhythm like farmers and fishermen have, hard to reconcile with any other kind of life. You're either in or out, and so have to make your own time—but so few of us can. You get a job, go to college, start a career and get married and then she's pregnant and there are bedtimes, barbecues and twelve hours a week on the Ventura, and then you wake up at forty having wasted your life, so you buy a Jag and fuck your teenaged secretary, unaware what a joke you've become. You can skip all that if you're rich enough. But I'm not.

I don't know. I'm muddling this, but here's the deal: I'll have to do something different here, something new, and grasp and connive and juggle to make it work. I can whore out the one thing I've ever loved, to get the love I long for—but I can't slide into that surfless desperation, ensnared and held under. Not for Mama; not even for Georgia.

Cause I'm going to marry that girl. I am. And she's never going to want for a goddamned thing, never mend our clothes till there's nothing left, never stay up late at the kitchen table, trying to decide between milk and electricity.

Never.

So it's gotta be this.

There's this old guy, shows up at the beach sometimes. Not like Ricky old, I mean *old* old. Methuselah old. He's in great shape for a geezer, though—not an ounce of fat on him, and surfs like nobody's business. Been coming down forever. He'll catch a few waves, then be gone for a week; come back when a front moves in and the sets are high and he's out there owning it—then vanish for months. Real mysterioso loner. Some people just are, and you leave them be, so we've never talked. But one day, a few weeks before my eighteenth birthday, he says hi.

'Hey,' I say, and leave it at that. The sun's just come up, and we're alone on the beach, towels on our shoulders. I'm scarfing down one of the peanut-butter sandwiches I brought for breakfast.

'Surf's good.'

'Yup.'

'Nice board. Where'd you get it?'

I swallow and sneak a look. He's dripping, and his face is...it's hard to describe. Long intelligent forehead, thinning hair, huge schnozz, like someone bigger is trying to push its way out of him. Not a lovely face, sure, but one you couldn't help but respect.

'Me and a friend made it.'

'That so?'

Holds his hand out, and I pass him the board. It's a nice one, 9'6", not some cheap foam pop-out. Fluke and I drilled out the balsa to make the core low-density; the stringer and rocker are high-quality redwood. I still have a scar on my hand from planing the rails while sweating my ass off. Twin-fin, for better control. Sunset-orange with a pale-orange stripe down the center, and Fluke's sister Sophia painted a gull on the tip in dark purple. Five coats of glass give it that smooth deep Barris car glow, and I watch him give it the once-over out of the corner of my eye, trying not to let on how proud it makes me.

'How much would you want for a board like this?'

That's not what I expected, and my face falls. You don't just muscle up to a man and ask to buy his wife. 'It's not for sale.'

'Not this board.' He looks disappointed in me, too. 'A board *like* this.'

Oh. Shit, I dunno. Damned thing took forever. 'I guess...fifty bucks?'

He throws his head back and laughs, a rowdy, rusty sound like an old door. Doesn't seem like a guy who gets a lot of yuks. Hell, I knew that was too much, just threw it out there.

'Tell you what. You make me a board like this, navy blue with a white stripe, single-fin, I'll give you 150 dollars.'

It's my turn to laugh. Pretty sure he's not queer, and I'm not Velzy here, I'm nobody. 'Yeah, sure you will.'

'Don't sell yourself short, boy. This is solid work. Can you have it ready by next Tuesday?'

I'm staring; he's fucking serious. He'll give me a C and a half for a board. 'I think...well, no, wouldn't want to rush it. We might, but the glass won't cure right. Still be tacky.'

'Well, as any of my wives would be the first to tell you, I'm a tacky man. Now—I don't know your name?'

'Tom.' This has gotta be some kind of prank. Any minute now, Fluke and Mysto are going to stagger out pissing themselves.

'I'm John. I have somewhere to be, but call me when it's ready. And take your time; some things deserve that.' He passes over a business card, shoulders his board and disappears. I tuck it into my shoe without looking, cram the last of the sandwich in my mouth, then head up to the pier to call Fluke.

It's only later that I pull the card out. The name sounds familiar, maybe one of the silent stars? No. Damn...it's on the tip of my brain's tongue.

'Hey, Ray, who's John Paul Getty?'

Ray snorts, head hanging off the bed as he reads. He says it makes you smarter. 'My Algebra teacher, numbnuts.'

'No, come on, help me out here. I need to know.'

He lowers the book, throws me a glance of pity and wonder. 'You really don't know, do you, Astro? What is this, for a crossword?'

He's an oil baron, turns out. The oil baron. Owns drilling rights to half the planet, and 'Forbes' just named our first customer the richest man in America. Wildcatted out in Oklahoma, then retired to marry three seventeen-year olds in a row, juggle an endless supply of women, mess around with surfing and cars—only to get back into the oil game two years later. I guess the ocean isn't the only thing that's irresistible. Invested wisely during the Depression, and is now worth a number followed by more zeros than I've ever seen outside of a chess club.

Holy fuck, Scrooge McDuck. You'd think he'd have a fancy beach all to himself, but this is California, we don't do that. Owns a mansion off the Pac, luxury pads all over the world, a castle outside of Rome, hotels in New York and Acapulco. Born in Minnesota, a citizen of the world, but keeps coming back to Malibu. This is home.

Not a fan of the autocrats, I want an excuse to drop this. Some closeted skeleton that'll fall out, give me a reason to blow him off. Fucks around a lot, but you know, glass houses. Cheap as hell; installed a pay phone so friends would stop running up his bill. This only makes me like him more. Five wives, six kids, none of whom he's particularly fond. Just

opened a section of his house to the public as a gallery, with all these
Roman statues. And he surfs.

I turn off the microfiche and leave the library, dizzied by the sudden sunlight. Huh. Well, I'll be a monkey's uncle.

But after the thrill of nervous elation that he wasn't fucking with me, that he'll give me five paychecks for a few hours of work I love, he goes back to being John. A solitary old man who hangs out at the beach and rides the waves like a killer. And that's who we make the board for.

Two weeks later, Fluke and I are lying on the sand.

'I don't feel so good,' I complain.

He lifts the empty bottle of Chivas and hurls it out to sea. We'd brought the board down to the Getty building this afternoon. Ricky said we should go in trunks and huaraches, but we had sport coats on, slacks, hair slicked down, very official. No ties; there are limits. Fluke got cold feet in the car, so I rode the elevator alone up to his office on the top floor. John nodded approvingly at the board, not saying much. Paid me in cash, we shook hands, and that was that.

We were going to save the money, honest to God, seventy-five apiece, maybe split a six-pack. But then John threw in a couple of Cubans and another ten for delivery, so we went a bit crazy. Oysters were involved, and caviar, which tasted exactly like you'd expect raw fish eggs to taste, bursting between my teeth with swift tiny pops even worse than the flavor. A rare Porterhouse bigger than my head, and a lot of high-shelf liquor. I'm down to fifty bucks, nothing to show for it but the sneaking sensation of having been conned somehow. I've never smoked a cigar in my life. I think I'm going to be sick.

'Shouldn't litter,' Fluke murmurs to himself. His eyes are glassy, but he gets to his feet, wobbles over and fishes the bottle out of the tide. Plops down again, cross-legged. A huge moon is hanging in the sky. 'Did you ever find a message in a bottle? Like, washed up?'

'Couple times,' I mutter, swallowing hard. 'Water'd gotten in, though. Not much left.'

'Huh,' he says, and we listen to the waves for a while.

'Why, did you?'

'Once,' he says, burping softly. 'I was eight. Floated right up to my feet, y'know? It was cool, like it traveled all that way just to get to me.'

'So what'd it say?' I sit up too.

'Not much. Some girl up in Santa Barbara. Gave a number.'

'And?'

'And nothing. I called, we talked. Said she'd thrown twenty bottles out six months before, as an experiment. I was the only one to call.'

'And?'

'And nothing, really. That was it. Kind of a letdown.'

I'm wondering what his point is.

'Thing is, Tommy, it was important somehow. I just didn't...I let it go.'

'Ever call her again?'

He shakes his head. 'I don't think that was it, know what I mean? She was twice my age, we didn't have that much in common. But something was meant to happen; I was supposed to do...something. Just couldn't figure out what. And that's always bothered me.'

Light dawns. 'You think this was a message? Him buying the board?'

'Yeah. Don't laugh, but I do. I mean, the guy's a notorious tightwad. There's no way he'd have paid that much for any old piece of shit. So we must be onto something, you know?'

So we started shaping for kicks; we'd sell a board from time to time, but never really made that much, so it petered out. We had more important things going on. A year later, I come home, and there's a package on the kitchen table. Open it up and it's a box of chocolates, a couple sticks of wax, and a note from John. Happy birthday, it says. He loves the board, has taken it all over, and it's holding up great, barely a ding.

Can't help but think of this thing I made with my own hands, travelling the world like a righteous ambassador. It feels absurdly cool. How'd he know it was my birthday? Or where I live? Has he been digging up dirt on me, too? I don't know whether to feel more flattered or spooked.

Write a thank-you note right away, so I don't forget, and after dinner split the candy with Ray and Mama. Fall asleep that night considering messages in bottles, and what Grandpa Joe would've made of all this. I know he would've roared at me to go for it, that every comrade must be productive, make art and bread. But then I think about John, all alone in his Malibu mansion with his marble statues and stacks of money, and I can't commit to that life any more than I can to Ricky's.

And that's where things stand when I knock on the Falluccis' door that evening. I'm pushing twenty, serious about a girl, and ready to drop this whole bird-on-a-wire act.

Fluke opens up. 'Hey,' I say. 'Wanna go get a beer?'

He comes out, shrugging on a shirt, as his ma yells to shut the door and not get me in any trouble. We walk through the sunset streets, twilight settling around our ears. After a block I say, 'Boards.'

'Indeed. What about 'em?'

'Time to quit fucking around. We can do this.'

He stops to light a Camel, exhales long. 'Whatcha thinking?'

'Three-tier workshop. Pop-outs for the grems, tart 'em up with bright colors and cute slogans. Medium grade for everybody else, and every so often a really nice custom design.'

'Our pieces of resistance.'

'Exactly. But that's not all.'

'Okay, shoot.'

85

'We make a proper store out front of the workshop. A nice one, where they can buy gear. Not just the things they need, Eddie—the things they want. The things we tell them they want.'

Nods, that paunch light in his eyes. 'T-shirts. Records. Hawaiian crap—'

'No, that's just it. None of it'll be crap. Well-made, quality stuff, with prices to match. Like one of those exclusive clubs, only for those in the know—or who think they are. You have to deserve to own our shit.'

'So you're selling a style. A life they can cop.'

'Yeah. Even if the tourist kid from Podunk can't use a board, he can still get a shirt. It adds up.'

'*Our* life.'

'Don't start with me, Fallootch. We didn't invent this shit, and it hasn't been ours for a long time anyway. Other people get to have a crack at it too, even half-assed phonies.'

'And we'll do nothing but pimp it out.'

'No. That's the genius part. We open when we feel like it. We want to surf all day, that's what we do. Want to come in, we're in.'

He laughs, almost with relief, because I've blown it right there, and there isn't going to be massive fallout with Ricky. 'Don't be an idiot. No one's gonna go for that.'

'No one over thirty, but that's not our market. Supply and demand. The harder it is to get something, the more you're willing to pay.'

'Still...seems like a risk.' He takes another drag, as we wait for the light before crossing into Venice. 'What about the competition? Velzy and Sweet? Oh, and Noll? We cut into his business, he'll have us killed.'

'They do great work,' I shrug. 'Taught us a lot. But Kennedy's right—new day, move forward, all that. You wanna make bank, you market a fantasy, a Camelot wet dream for losers to jerk off to. Noll sells junk. Sweet and Hobie are selling real boards to real surfers. Quigg and Velzy are goddamned geniuses, but they're old-school, small-time. Purists.'

'Isn't that a good thing?'

'Can't eat purity.'

'Dave Sweet sold six hundred boards last year. He's eating fine.'

'Yeah, and he's been in business for ten years. I bet you next year we sell a thousand.'

'You're off your rocker, you daffy fuck.'

'Yeah, but you know I'm right. Catch it, Fluke. This shit isn't going away tomorrow, but it's not going to be this big forever. We wait too long, it'll mush out.'

'Ahh, man. This all sounds great, but—well, shit, what are we gonna do for money? Don't think a bank's gonna take Mayhem as collateral.'

'I've got a few ideas. Let's figure out how much we'll need first.'

We walk into Olivia's, where I spread my notes out on the table, and we scribble down more. After two cheap steaks, a side of slaw, some sweet potato pie and half a dozen beers, Fluke is so stoked, that back at the house he rousts his dad out of bed. Mr. Fallucci hears us out—and not only doesn't knock our heads together like Stooges, he agrees to help us write up a plan and even cosign on a loan application. We're making so much noise down in the living room at this point the rest of the family joins us in their pajamas, Mrs. Fallucci pours Chianti, and *salud,* we're in business.

'We gotta look professional,' Fluke points out. 'Or they'll laugh us right out of the bank. You're gonna have to get a haircut, Thomasina.'

'You're gonna have to get 'em all cut, Sasquatch.'

'Ah, man, not my crowning glory,' he moans in desperation that is not quite mock. Fluke really does have boss hair. What kind of L7 hell am I getting us into?

'Relax,' says his dad. 'Way you eat, it'll grow back in three days.'

'I'll do you both,' declares Elena. She's just out of beauty school, works over at Bonwit's. Mostly sweeping up, but you gotta start somewhere.

87

'Settle down, you vultures,' Fluke growls. 'Plenty of time to shear off our pride and joy. And don't make this one look too pretty. He does enough damage as it is.'

We never talked about it. Not after that night, not a word. He wouldn't say her name, and I didn't dare, and Denise stopped coming around, so eventually it sank and was silted over with five years of our lives. Something like that doesn't just vanish on its own, though. I'm going to work my ass off and square this, if it's the last thing I do.

Cause I'm not just some surfer bum freak of nature, you know. I have other qualities. I see patterns others don't. I learn hard, but then I never forget. And when I latch onto an idea, I'm like one of those hunting dogs that clenches down on its prey and never lets go. I know I've got it in me to make something happen here, something big for us both; it's bursting out of me, clear, pure and sharp. This certainty, this ability— they, too, are gifts. And not the shitty kind this time.

It's well after midnight when he walks me out to Mayhem. The sky is clouding over with bellies of grey and blue, the moon has disappeared and the streetlights are all haloed with rainbows. You can smell the coming rain in the air, like wet concrete.

'Piscadoo,' says Fluke, wrinkling his nose. 'Non surfiamo domani.'

We probably could surf in a hard rain and not, you know, die. There are places with worse water pollution. But around here every time it rains, it rains, not pennies from heaven, but a landfill's worth of garbage, the torrents sweeping up every butt and used rubber in the city, every dog turd and tin can, broken bottle and bloody hypo; motor oil and paint and DDT and God knows what, dumping it all in the LA River, where it sweeps down the cement runoff to land smack-dab off Santa Monica, our little portion of paradise.

Used to be even worse, between untreated sewage and oil spills, and it was only the prospect of losing all those sweet tourist dollars that made them cap that, but it's still pretty bad. Staph is the surfer's malady; people lose limbs. So, you know, you can surf in the rain if you want.

I just wouldn't recommend it. The first drops fall and we turn our eyes to the sky. Since when does it rain in July?

'Is this really happening?' I ask him.

'God, I hope so. I've never seen you like this. Motherfucking shark.'

'Zero to sixty in six seconds.' Put an arm around his shoulders. He's not as big as he used to be.

He yawns. 'Man, we are gonna be *minting* money.'

'Not at first—and maybe not at all. It's a gambit, okay?' He yawns again, and I relent. 'Ahh, go get your beauty sleep, Samson. Tell your ma sorry we woke everyone up.'

'Wilco, Tommy. G'night.'

I start her up, turn the wipers on and wave through the window. It's really coming down now, but Fluke doesn't seem to care. He takes one last drag, then flicks the butt into the gutter, where it is washed quickly down the street, into the sewer, and out of sight. Turns and walks back into the house. I wait till he's inside before I drive away.

Fluke and I are on the Titanic, and the last lifeboat has just sailed. I'm racing from one deck chair to another, trying to figure out how to lash them together, while he's kicked back in one, blowing smoke rings and drinking beer. The musicians have hauled the piano and strings out onto the deck; we even got a few minutes of 'Maple Leaf Rag' before the bandmaster made them settle down and go back to hymns. Everyone seems to be having fun in some vague way I fail to grasp.

'Jesus, Tommy,' says Fluke. 'Quit running around in circles already, and take a load off.'

The deck is tilting hard, and the piano is starting to roll bowside, so I go over and lean against it.

'We're not even *here*,' I tell him, sliding into a squat and bracing myself. 'We aren't even *born* yet. I'm not supposed to die. This is unreasonable.'

'Well, you know how it is. There was a lot of hubris involved. Bound to happen sooner or later.'

I push my fists hard against my eyelids, trying to think. Spangles of orange and yellow are exploding against the red, with an aftermath of undulating checkerboards. I can almost hear the radio operator's last desperate signals over the screams and music: seek you, Dee. Come on, girl. *Dahdit dahdit dahdahditdah dahditdit.* Title of my doo-wop song: Come Quick, Danger.

'They're not gonna make it in time,' I say, and it's true. This is it.

He exhales some smoke. 'Probably not.'

'How are you so fucking *calm*?'

Downs the last of the beer, belches into his fist. 'I'm not, Tommy. But I'm not gonna spend the last hour of my life going nuts, either. And look on the bright side: bar's wide open.'

I groan, and he hands over a bottle of Hennessy. 'There you go, bud. Your own personal St. Bernard.'

Glance over the side. The lifeboats are hovering a few hundred yards from the ship, lanterns twinkling in the dark, safely out of reach of our suck. 'At least some of the women and children got away.'

'Lotta rich guys, too. But hell, maybe they're worth more than we are.'

'Communist revolution coming in five years,' I note, and take a long hard swig of the brandy. It tastes like doctors and important occasions. 'Pure coincidence, I'm sure.'

'Check it out, though—see that couple over there? The old ones?'

Follow his finger, sight a well-dressed pair heading into the cabins. He's holding the door open for her, and the look on his face, that resigned tenderness: he's sorry to be here, but there's no place he'd rather be. That's what love looks like. You don't see it that often.

'Yeah?'

'Isidor Straus. The son of a bitch owns Macy's. Coulda got out easy, but he wouldn't leave while there were still women on board. And she was damned if she'd go without him.'

'Shit,' I say, can manage nothing more, but Fluke knows what I mean. The deck lists under us, hard, and the piano pushes into my spine. I'm not sure how much longer I can hold it. There is a groaning, cracking shudder; one way or another, we're going down in minutes. So much for unsinkable. People are clinging to railings, but I'm beyond panic, just trying to figure out if I want a quick drown or a slow freeze.

Nod apology to the pianist, then rise clumsily and stand aside. We all watch the piano careen down, smashing into a wall before falling to its demise with a spectacular splash. I have heard the mermaids singing, each to each. I do not think that they will sing for me.

'Listen,' I tell Fluke. 'Put in a good word for me up there, okay?'

'Man, I told you to get right with God. You always leave this shit for the last minute.'

I say nothing. You don't see these things coming.

'Ahh, you'll be right by my side, ya dumb fuck. Think I'm just gonna ditch you?' He stands, takes the brandy, and we pass it back and forth as the band goes into another number, 'Proprio Dei.' I was hoping for more of a Deus Ex Machina situation.

'Darkness be over me, my rest a stone,' Fluke sings in his sweet tenor. 'Yet in my dreams I'd be, nearer my God to thee.' He sounds like a brave angel, with those strings soaring behind him. I am not a brave angel. I'm about to piss myself.

'Remember that first time at Redondo?' he asks, and I nod. Double-plus overheads, I couldn't stop shaking and cracking wise. I took the plunge though, knowing there was no way he'd let anything bad happen to me. 'Remember San Francisco?' Oh, I remember. Witch's tit, and this is gonna be a lot colder. 'Say it.'

Try not to whimper. 'It's a good day to die.'

'It's a good day to die.'

I shiver, glance up at the sky. The moon is a sliver of waning crescent, as if turned away, unable to watch, but the stars don't appear to mind. I hear a baby wailing in protest.

'Fluke?'

'Yeah?'

'I'm ready to wake up now.'

'Soon's we hit the water.' There is another cracking sound. 'Okay, okay, this is it. Go. *Go!*'

You have to wake before you hit bottom, I think as we leap.

We do not.

We're out there forever, freezing our asses off as the band plays on, clinging to the deck chairs, saying less and less—and then we're dead. There are no angels, no harps, no white light. Only darkness, and I'm alone in it, and Fluke is gone. And my eyes are open.

I don't mention this dream to Fluke for years.

One of the worst-kept secrets about LA is that there's nothing old here. I dunno, it's like some kind of unwritten law: a building has to burn or be demolished by earthquake or wrecking ball before fifty, otherwise it gets declared a landmark and there are Development Problems, bitter conflicts between City Hall and The Ladies with Too Much Time on Their Hands. You want old? Go to a museum. We leave enough behind so as not to feel entirely unmoored—Spanish missions, the synagogue on Wilshire, the Bradbury Building and California Club, a few Victorian mansions. There's some pretty boss new Googie stuff like the Union 76 in the Hills—but overall we're just a bunch of faceless buildings, neither old nor new, but out of time altogether.

Kind of funny, when you think about it. Go anywhere in the world and they'll have all these ancient temples and elaborate churches full of art, castles thousands of years old, colonial mansions Washington took a shit in once—but come out to LA, and we'll proudly show you a beige fire station from 1912. We don't much like time here, nor people liking things, so periodically we stomp them all down, then sit back and wait for them to sprout up again, maybe just for a change of scene.

Take the Rendezvous Ballroom. It was built back in 1928 right smack on Balboa Beach, to hell with rising tides and shaky foundations. Docked like a ship when we were drowning in money, no idea what to do with it, throwing it around on all these in-your-face fantasy buildings like Grauman's Chinese Theater, grandiose diners shaped like cows and owls and derbies. But they finished Hoover Dam in 1930, and the loony visionaries all took off to go build Bugsy's Wonderland, while we still needed places to live and learn, eat and drink, dance and gas up.

So they brought in some cut-rate Levitt disciple who said, 'Don't bother with skyscrapers or civil engineering, this ain't San Francisco, we got land for days, just slap up ten thousand gussied bungalows, clapboard-stucco structures with terracotta roofs like Mexican churches converted into train stations and whorehouses, connect them all with a hundred highways, that'll do ya.' Went back to running the Pasadena Mail-Order School of Architecture and Design, the developers made a zillion bucks apiece, and that's been our look ever since.

So most buildings here aren't that old, but look like they might be. Like aging stars, there's a mystique there, a quality that transcends Chronos, as if you're briefly glimpsing something solid through a shimmering veil. The Rendezvous felt holy in just that way. Even gazing at it from the beach, you felt like it had been there forever, poised on the planet's final frontier. That someday it would simply...float away.

A block long, and you couldn't tell if it was a church, a whorehouse, or a train station, because it was all of those. Took off with the jivecats and flappers, a new band every night: Goodman, Dorsey, Calloway, Krupa, dances till dawn and beyond, vodie-odie-odie-oh. Fire took it in '35, but we rebuilt, a phoenix rising from the ashes to suck in the tide of sailors and soldiers and sweet young things come to kick it at the Bal. Top spring break destination for the West, all through the Depression and the war, for we are California, fools—what do we know of such things? Only sun and sea and happy, happy, happy.

The great wave of money had ebbed out by the late 40's, however, and didn't come back for a while; it left the Rendezvous in its wake, a whale beached up on the shore, forgotten and forlorn. Stan Kenton bought it in '57 as a home for his various jazz bands, each louder and larger than the last—I saw him play there once with an ensemble of a hundred guys, no joke—but jazz was comatose by then, and the band often outnumbered the audience. At one point Newport Beach shut it down for 'immoral dancing and racy rock music,' and then it was dark for a while; shuttered for good, it seemed.

So the heyday was over by '59, when we went to see Dick Dale and the Del-Tones. Dick practically had to break into the place to play, and his dad had to sign an agreement that it wouldn't be a rock show. Their idea of enforcing this was to make us wear ties, passed out at the door as we walked in, all bare feet and ragged trunks. We were game, for it is always a joy to watch two-bit fascists make fools of themselves.

He played a few namby-pamby tunes to palm off the squares—but then he got down to the business of making our ears bleed. That show was just me, Fluke and fifteen other people. The next had fifty, though, and by '61 you'd get 4000 surfers in there, all hollering and stomping and bouncing off the walls. And Dick, oh, man, he was a force of nature. We loved that cat, and that joint, and over time they became inseparable.

94

Did try to keep a lid, but word gets around. It's hard to stay mum when someone blows your mind like that—and our minds were more than ready to be blown by then. It had been a rough patch.

The rock rebellion had been going strong for only three years when the backlash began: Little Richard, the frenetic queen who'd started it all, saw Sputnik 1 over Sydney one night and took it for a fireball sign from God, so he tossed ten thousand bucks of jewelry in the bay along with his boogie-woogie anthems to wild sex, to go preach for Jesus. Elvis was drafted, shaved down, and sent to Germany; Jerry Lee Lewis married his thirteen-year old cousin and overnight became an unperson, his name erased from airwaves and shows. Buddy, Richie and the Big Bopper went down over Iowa: stomp, stomp, stomp.

Ask not for whom the bell tolls, baby.

One singer after another was lost to drugs, disease, disaster, to racism or general folly. W.C. Handy, Big Bill Broonzy, and Billie Holiday all bit it within a year; Chuck Berry was sentenced to two years in prison on Christmas Eve, 1959, for taking a teen across state lines, and then Eddie Cochran was killed by a London cabbie and we all thought, well, this is the end, there's no one left. Because that November, they had come for Alan—and boy, they really stomped the shit out of that man.

Hard to explain how much that one hurt. It was like if the Romans had captured Jesus and, instead of crucifying him, just cut out his tongue. Alan Freed was our spiritual leader, the DJ who'd released rock-and-roll on us all, pulling together sounds from all over the country—rhythm-and-blues singers from Detroit and the Delta, doo-wop groups from Brooklyn, country singers from Texas and the deep South, gospel from all over—stirred them into a pot, and said to America, take, eat, it is our body. And we did. And it was *good*.

Sure, there was a lot of cash floating around changing hands, but who gave a shit? We knew the government's concern had nothing to do with artistic integrity, that it was really about us looking across race lines and realizing we had nothing to fear from each other, and could all just hang out and dance and have a good time. That was the last thing they wanted, because frightened people are a lot easier to control.

So when Freed, chain-smoking Jewish hepcat and 'known associate of Negros,' stood his ground and refused on principle to sign a statement declaring that he had never accepted payola like everybody else in the goddamned business, the House Investigation Committee hauled him up on bribery charges and fined him. He was canned from WABC on my 17th birthday, sent off into the wilderness to bounce from one small-time station to another and die six years later, allegedly from cirrhosis, but probably more of a broken heart.

It was Grandpa Joe all over again. He was just...fun, you know? He was fun. A nice guy with big ideas who'd never done us any earthly harm. It didn't need to happen. But it did, and then there were none, and we were looking at the prospect of spending the rest of our natural lives with Pat Boone and Doris Day and Dick Fucking Clark.

And that's when we bolted: East went folk, but West went surf. Hard.

Betrayed, bleeding, stampeding with rage, we sure as shit didn't want to talk about it. True surf music has no lyrics, no tricky pretty words to disguise or apologize, nothing but guitars and bass and drums, maybe a little organ or sax thrown in, wet reverb for days like surfing stoned—and those amps! Dale had them stacked up to the ceiling from the start, set as high as it'd go before exploding in a shower of sparks, till our bones were vibrating with the rhythm, organs pulsating, aching for more. Drawing our line in the sand: stomp, stomp, stomp. No more compromises. The cocksuckers would hear us, if it killed us all.

So that was where I was taking Georgia that night: to this whorehouse-church-train station that would tell her more about me than anything I could possibly say. Not Ciro's, no.

Drive over to her house Saturday afternoon, worried that she won't like Dick, or my friends, then realize that she doesn't like me all that much either. That her folks will take one look and give me the bum's rush. Keep checking the rearview to make sure I'm not being tailed through this quiet velvety neighborhood, in which Mayhem is as inconspicuous as a tarantula on a piece of angel food.

I get lost twice, I'm that distracted. I've only ever been here with Ricky and the guys, never driving. Honest, motoring the Hills is no more fun than cruising Watts for me; I don't really care how the other halves live, so checking out their coops is not high on my list. When I pull up to the gate, there she is waiting. My heart clenches, cause she looks even more nervous than I am.

'Don't,' she waves me back. 'Park out on the street, okay?'

Okay, I think as I back out. Okay. Probably, all things considered, not a bad idea. But I must have a look on my face when I walk up the drive, as a crease has appeared between her brows and she's holding her lip in her teeth. And then it clears up.

'Oh, no,' she says. 'It's not like that. A Benz would've been just as bad.'

'Huh?' I have no idea what's going on.

'That's just how she is, Tommy. She won't have it in the house.'

'Have...what? I don't get it.'

She throws me a look, like I of all people should understand, and then it hits me. The People's Car, invented by our good friends the Nazis.

Allies bombed the Wolfsburg factory in '44, then rebuilt it after the war and brought it home so our people could dig on the whole Strength-Through-Joy groove, too, and I have never bothered to consider this because I am a class-A asshole, a bad Jew who should've known better, but was too busy scarfing down BLT's and being this big prolier-than-thou Commie amnesiac to consider boycotting the guys that killed my mom's entire family. I can't go in there now. God knows what other landmines are waiting for me. I'll slip up somehow, probably panic and start singing *Deutschland Über Alles* just to get it over with.

Georgia chuckles. 'You should see your face. It's not a big deal, honest, she just...doesn't want it around. But you, she's going to love.'

I take a deep breath, struggling with the temptation to sling her over my shoulder and run off into the night; to explain that I'm Austrian, not German, and that I obviously had nothing to do with any of this. It's usually the moms I do so well with, too.

'Do I look okay?' She takes my hand. 'Wasn't sure what to wear.'

Her hair is in loose braids, bangs brushing against her eyes. Jeans, blue sneakers, a red-and-white checked halter-top that stops and starts in all the right places. You can see her bellybutton over the Levi's button, and I don't know why you'd want to look at anything else, ever again.

'Well, Dick's probably gonna be pissed at you for stealing the show, but yeah, you look fine.'

She kisses me then, and I'm no longer nervous. God, she's so *warm*. Her back beneath my hands, her lips on mine—how is she so warm? I don't know why this surprises me, any more than I know why she asks if she looks okay, so seriously, as if she couldn't don a barrel and combat boots and still leave a trail of butterflies and broken hearts behind her.

Leads me up the hewn granite stairs, through the large wooden door guarded by two lions and a gargoyle, into a foyer the size of our entire house. Smells different from other houses. Better. Not like cooking or mildew or cleaning products. More of an absence of all those things, a security in them being taken care of by ghosts. We walk into the living room, where a woman in a long green dress is standing by a fireplace, waiting. We stand there for a moment in silence, sizing each other up.

I don't know how to say this without sounding like a complete jerk, so I'm just going to say it: this woman is exquisite. Like, very possibly the most beautiful person I've ever laid eyes on in my life, onscreen or off. An older Georgia, with dark red hair and emerald eyes—and there's this expression on her face, like you're a book she's reading only because there's nothing else in the house. I don't know what I was expecting, exactly—some starveling in striped pajamas?—but no way was it this. Glance over at Georgia, waiting in vain for an introduction. Not sure what I see on her face.

The woman tilts her head. 'Life,' she says.

'I'm sorry?'

"Life,' September '61. In the background, a surfboard on your head.'

I look at Georgia. *It's her little game,* say her eyes. *Just go with it.*

98

'Yeah,' I say shortly. 'I asked him not to shoot me. Didn't take.'

'And your name?'

'Oh.' I fumble my hand out; she shakes it. 'Tom. Tomas Beck.'

'Beth Lustgarten. Would you like something to drink, Tom?'

'I'm fine, thanks.'

'Cigarette?' She gestures at a case on the coffee table. Is this a test?

'I don't smoke, sorry.'

She seems to soften. 'But tell me about yourself. You like to surf?' She has no accent; doesn't sound like she's from Germany, or California, or from anywhere, really. Elocution lessons will wipe all that out. But you can hear it in the last word, if you're listening close: *sssehrff*. Like the waves themselves.

'Very much.'

'Why?'

Georgia groans. 'Don't grill him, Mom.'

'No, it's cool,' I assure her. 'Nobody else gets it either. Surfing is...well, it's fun, for a start. You're out in the ocean all day, which is always nice. And I started during a time when things were a little, uh, difficult, and I think it kept me out of trouble.'

'You do not seem like a boy who would be in very much trouble.'

'Ah, well, you know how it is.' I shrug. 'Sometimes it finds you.'

'And where are you taking my daughter tonight?'

'To see a musician I like.'

'And no trouble will find you there?'

I smile to myself. 'No, ma'am. It's not that kind of place.'

'Very well, Tom. It was a pleasure meeting you; you may go up and see my husband now.'

99

Surreptitiously check the clock as Georgia takes me upstairs, footsteps soundless on the thick carpet; an hour till showtime. Hope the old man isn't a big talker. She pauses outside his office, poised to knock, then beckons impishly. His voice foghorns through the door, surprisingly calm, considering the words.

'Now listen to me, you overpaid halfwit twit, tell that *ferkakteh* fuck he has two hours or we walk. I'm not screwing around with you scumbags this time. My goddamned cat shits better films than he—what? Oh, yeah? Well, in that case, I love you too. Lunch, sure.'

Georgia knocks once and opens the door, and a balding brown-haired man removes his glasses, pushes his chair back from a massive mess of a desk and blinks happily around.

'Where's my baby? It's all a blur! Help! Where'd she go?'

'Right here, nerd,' Georgia kisses the top of his head and gestures at me. 'This is Tom.'

Leaps to his feet and runs around the desk to surprise me with a hug, then holds me at arm's length, examining me and beaming. He's not that much shorter than me, though he moves like a small man. Quick, like he's trying to catch up.

'You're Tom! Good grief, Georgia fed me such stories, I was expecting a hardened criminal. The relief, don't ask! I had my shotgun all ready!'

Georgia swats at him. 'Don't pay him the slightest bit of mind, Tommy. He does this to everyone.'

'He's much cuter than you let on,' he stage-whispers behind his hand.

He's pretty cute himself. I've never lived anywhere but here, so I have nothing to compare it to, but can't help but wonder if this is something real people do: play the role of themselves. Everyone's an actor, every location one you've seen a hundred times in dark theaters. The shtick we peddle, every seamstress and starlet and soda jerk watching you vaguely with glazed eyes, waiting for you to shut up so they can shine, privately thanking the Academy, everyone but me with their lines down pat. I wasn't even given the script.

been taught to crave. There are moments in my life I wouldn't mind a little truth, a sliver of authenticity, but I play along.

'I'm not that cute, sir,' I tell him. 'I just try to stand in flattering light.'

'Oof, this one! So where are you two crazy kids headed tonight?'

'The Rendezvous Ballroom, sir, it's a music club on—' He and Georgia burst out laughing.

'You don't have to explain, Tommy. He practically invented the place.'

'The Voo was a blast, I tell you. Supermurgatroid.' He lights a cigarette, exhales long. 'Shame it went downhill.'

'It's back, though,' I say. 'Different sounds, but you should see this guy, he's like Krupa. Nothing else around.'

'Daddy was a serious jazzbo in his day,' Georgia chimes in. 'He wrote *poetry* and everything.'

'Not poems, darling, *songs*. Such terrible, awful songs.'

'And he played saxophone!'

'I did,' he acknowledges. 'Which was even worse.'

'Oh, Daddy, don't! Your sax is fantastic! Tommy, you should hear him someday, he's just being modest.'

'Don't torture the boy, *bubbaleh*. Why don't you go get your purse?'

'Okay. Play nice, you two.' And she's gone.

The office, study, whatever, all brown leather and flocked maroon wall-paper, is like some kind of warm-wombed brothel. I'm surprised there's no player piano in the corner. Everywhere are headshots, scripts, books, and not the kind you buy by the yard: exploding from the shelves, in piles on tables and floor, upside-down on the long red velvet divan. Can't help but trust a guy who lets the books run roughshod. A few paintings on the wall, one of which—oh, no. There's no way.

Blue girl in a nightgown, contemplating a bowl of soup, looking sadder than you'd think a human being could possibly look about soup.

'Sir, is that a Picasso?'

He chuckles. 'Enough with the 'sir.' Just Ira. Mr. Lustgarten, Esquire, if you're feeling formal.'

'Is it?'

'Yeah. Why, you a fan?'

'No. Not really. I mean,' I pull at my ear, struggling to articulate my deal with Picasso. 'He was pretty great when he started out. Blue period, the harlequins, 'Avignon.' But after that...'

'After that what?'

'He cashed in. Which is fine, really—who doesn't want to make money? But he never did the good stuff anymore, unless he's hiding it in some Swiss vault or something. It's all just so much mass-produced Cubist nonsense, with no...'

'Soul?'

'I guess. You look at them and feel nothing. Wallpaper.'

He nods. 'Well, you're in luck, Tom, cause that's one of the good ones. Got it in Paris, during the war. Gave the lady my watch, boots and all. Told the sarge I got rolled, because we weren't supposed to be doing that, buying their art. Cultural exploitation or some such. But they were starving, and there was no way I was leaving without it. One of the most beautiful things I'd ever seen, and I had to spend a year with it all but shoved up my ass.'

'Wow. Must be worth...I don't even know how much, by now.'

His eyes darken. 'Me neither. I wouldn't sell it for anything. Didn't even have it appraised; could well be a fake. I don't care.'

'Oh, it's no fake.'

He looks amused. 'How do you know?'

'I don't. But look.' The two of us are beneath it now, close enough to smell the paint, peer into the girl's troubled eyes. 'That's his signature, it's gotta be. I've faked my mom's enough times to know how hard it is to get that right. And it's just—that's him. When he meant it.'

'His friend had just committed suicide.'

'That girl?' She does look close. Must've been some pretty awful soup.

'No, a buddy of his. Went into a funk for three years, but painted his ass off the whole time. Best work of his life.'

'And 'Guernica.' 'The ugly may be beautiful; the pretty, never.' So what, he could only paint right when he was depressed?'

'You can't choose what makes you passionate, son. Happiness isn't the same. Listen, if—'

Georgia bursts back in. 'Come on, come on, we're gonna be late!'

He grins at her. 'Be good, my darling. Home by one, okay? Don't make me call out the National Guard again, they're sick of me.' He turns to me. 'Tom, take care. Pleasure.'

We shake hands, and his mouth is still smiling, but his eyes say clearly, *if you hurt her, even a hair—you're a dead man. I know a guy, but I won't bother waking him up.* I nod, jaw aching with all the things that can't be said. That I'll stand in front of a train before I let anything hurt her. That I'm going to get my ass in gear, and when I'm worth something, I'm going to ask her to marry me, dedicate my life to keeping her safe. I swear it. He nods, too, as Georgia pulls me away.

'Jeez, you two, get a room. Next time, why don't you just take my dad to the Rendezvous, and leave me at home with my knitting?'

We beat it then, hustle down to the car and heave a sigh of relief. We're almost a mile away before either of us says anything at all, and then we both start talking at once.

'You first,' I say.

'No, you. So what'd you think?'

'Oh, man. They're something else. Intense.'

'But did you like them?' She fingers one braid and glances at me, an earnest farmer's daughter.

'Yeah, I did. Didn't see that coming, either. I thought—I dunno. That they'd take one look at me and burn me to the ground.'

'Nah, Dad likes you already, I can tell. He either hates you on sight, or he'll go to the wall for you no matter how many times you screw up. You never get to change his mind.'

'And your mom...how'd she do that? That 'Life' thing? My name wasn't in the article, and no one else noticed the shot. I mean, the guys, yeah. But no one else ever caught it. Your mom's never even met me.'

'She never forgets a face.' She gazes out the window. 'Sure I look okay?'

'I wouldn't lie to you, Georgia. You look stellar. Just right.'

'And we'll have a good time?'

'The best. And my friends...well, don't let this go to your head, but they dig you. I mean—' I pause, not sure how to say this the right way. 'They see all girls as chicks, you know? Betties. But they see how happy I am now, and they love you for it. They're like your dad: once they're in your corner, forget it.' All but Ricky, of course. But he never likes anyone.

'What about everybody else? It's a lot of people to meet all at once.'

'Oh, you know, surfers. Bound to be some rowdies, but we're pretty laid back. It takes a lot to shake us up. You'll do fine.'

She fiddles in her purse, pulls out a silver cigarette case identical to her mother's. I didn't know she smoked. Cracks the window, extracts a joint and puts it to her lips. I put my hand on the lighter to stop her.

'Georgia, whoa, there's a cop two lanes over. Not the time.'

'Oh, they don't care.'

'They do, actually. And guess who winds up in cuffs—the bum in the clunker with three priors, or the under-aged rich girl?'

She puts it away in silence. Then, 'Sorry. I wasn't thinking.'

'That's fine. It's cool. Later, okay?'

After a minute, she whispers, 'It helps. I'm not good with crowds.'

I check her out. 'You wanna go catch a movie instead?'

'No, really. I want to have a fun time. I'll be all right.'

'I won't leave your side. You'll be fine, I promise.'

She puts her head on my shoulder, sighs, and I can feel it go out of her. All of it. I get the feeling it's been a while.

Parking is a bitch, so the party's already in full swing by the time we make our way inside, Chuck Berry wailing, everybody rocking it on the floor. Clasp fingers so as not to lose each other as we move through the sweaty, writhing bodies. Catch sight of the Laguna guys across the far wall, they toss shakas over the crowd, and I raise my hand back, thumb and pinky extended in salute. People are hanging off the mezzanine like gorillas, the dancers are throwing each other around, and everyone's on fire. It's going to be a hell of a night.

We stake out a spot by the stage and dance together for the first time to 'No Particular Place to Go.' She's a sweet dancer, loosening up after a minute to swing it with me, twining her hips, eyes smiling into mine. Someone staggers into us from behind.

'Roddy! Rodrigo Aragone! Long time, dog!' It's Chi, breath strong in my face, eyes unfocused, with two of his friends from Muscle Beach. Big guys, come down to pump, but they get a little surf in. 'How ya been, what's the kate? And who's *this* little darling?'

'Can't complain,' I shout back. 'Georgia, meet my boys Chi and Huey.' Can't remember the third guy's name. Louie? Dewey? She waves a little, still dancing, and they bow exaggeratedly before lumbering off as the lights dim for a slow number.

She relaxes into my chest as we sway; it's starting to get hot in here. Really hot. AC must have broken down, and good luck getting anybody out here on a Saturday night. We'll be stuck with fans, and with this many people jumping around punishing the parquet, things get steamy fast. The mirrored balls overhead scatter snowflakes of blue light over our faces; everyone looks half-wasted, soda dispensers spiked again. Thousands of bodies all pressed in together gets me nervous; I never realized that. I'd just get drunk. Well, drunker. Georgia fishes for a hanky, dabs at her cheeks and neck, wipes my brow.

'Sorry,' I say. 'Didn't realize it was Tropics Night.'

Her hand on my hip, pulling me into her. I can feel her fingers on me through the denim. She's so tiny, not even up to my collarbone. Comes across as bigger, somehow.

'It's making me sleepy,' she murmurs, and I lay my cheek against her hair. She'll wake up soon enough.

Just then there's a drumroll, and the lights flash. All right, here we go. The MC comes out, mopping his head, grinning until we calm down.

'We have a very special treat for you all tonight, before we bring on The Ventures, and the one and only Mr. Dick Dale—' Massive cheer from the audience. He waits for the cries and stomps to subside. 'They just signed with Capitol, ladies and gentlemen, but you know them best from their hit 'Surfin'.' Please join me in welcoming for the first time to our own Rendezvous Ballroom...the Beach Boys!'

There are silences less dead in cemeteries. The few desultory claps are quickly subdued as the curtain goes up on a barbershop quintet in tight white ducks and striped shirts—but they are professionals, by gum, and launch right into their hit, as if to get our attention.

Oh, they've got it. A hand falls on my shoulder; Fluke, shaking his head. Georgia is looking up at me, confused—I put an arm around her and smile without conviction. The crowd's too tight to escape, and they're beginning to shove us up against the stage. A dull moaning roar starts up at the back, rolling in, punctuated by shouts here and there:

'You suck!'

'Get those goddamned pussies off the stage!'

106

The booing grows as the boys head into the bridge, sweating bullets. I take a quick look around, then pull Fluke and Georgia down as a bottle arcs over us, smashing against the amp. I'm about to drag us out of there, crowd be damned, when a few more missiles fly by, connecting with the drum kit. Dennis throws down his sticks and rushes the edge of the stage, another bottle catches him in the chest, knocking him back into Carl, and then, oh, shit, it's on.

Here's the sad thing about Dennis: I like him. Unlike the rest of those blando twerps, he's a stand-up guy. Two years younger than me, with old-gold hair and long burns, he's seen his share of shit, and is a decent surfer with no more love for his dad than I have for mine. We've dated a few of the same girls, hung out at parties. I can't just ditch him.

'Go with Fluke,' I tell Georgia. 'Get out! Now!'

Fluke picks her up without ado, thrusts his way through the throng like a linebacker—and Dennis leaps off the stage, four guys jump him, and I dive in, trying to break it up, tearing them off, getting elbowed in the stomach and punched in the face for my trouble, so amped I'm barely feeling it. But it's the screaming I hate most. We get it, you're angry. You don't have to yell.

Chi and Huey move in to fend off the crowd as I get a still-struggling, cursing Dennis back onstage, where the rest of the band are standing like limp astonished puppets. Brian drops the mike, and a shrill shriek of feedback tears through the audience as the bouncers hustle them out the back. We all take a deep breath, sigh it out, the threat fended off. I shake myself, annoyed, and go in search of my friends.

Cast an eye over the parking lot: woodies and camper vans, as far as the eye can see. Convertibles, a VW or two. Motorcycles, an incongruous purple Caddie. They're standing by it, sharing a smoke, and Georgia's laughing her ass off. Fluke's good that way.

'Cue me in?' I take the butt, draw deep. He winks at me, and I raise my eyebrows, cough, and hand it back.

Georgia says, 'He was just explaining what happened back there.'

'Oh, this I gotta hear.'

Fluke nudges her. 'Go ahead.'

Folds her arms over her chest and does a gruff impression of me: 'Instro forever. Fuck folk. Pop is prefab crap. Top Ten is them, Dick Dale is us. The Ventures and Shanties are cool, and Jerry Lewis is still the Killer— though technically rockabilly, not surf.'

'Hardy-har-har. Chantays,' I correct her, smiling. 'And Jerry *Lee* Lewis, bite your tongue. Hank Ballard, and the Coasters. Though also not surf.'

'Not technically, no,' says Fluke wryly. 'And yet boss. Beggars belief.'

'Elvis?'

Fluke groans. After 'Blue Hawaii,' that shmuck was dead to us.

'Jan and Dean? Just trying to confirm what my choices are here.'

We simultaneously say, 'Sure,' and 'Oh, hell no,' then sock each other a few times. It's a sore spot: hodads with the same faux-surf deal as the Beach Boys, but the songs are more automotive, boss enough to pass with some of my less discriminating brethren.

'Still seems like an overreaction. You were about ready to lynch those poor kids, and they meant well. And they were trying so hard!'

I sigh. 'Look, the Beach Boys...they're not even hodes. They're nothing. Softy folk nerds who never got their feet wet, and never get it right. We're not going to let them scam on our thing—not here, anyway. We get to have one place they don't invade.'

'Uh-huh. Like my mom and the Volkswagen.'

'That's not a fair parallel,' I protest, though it actually kind of is.

'She's got a point, Tom; we might have been a little hard on the Beav,' Fluke reflects. 'Brian's got a sweet voice, and Dennis, well. Token, can't drum for shit, but deep down you know he's okay.'

'Whoa!' I sock him. 'Et tu, Brute? No Beach Boys.'

'All right, kookaburra, cool your jets. No Beach Boys. I'm gonna see if we can't get the AC up and running, or we'll be dying in there tonight.'

'See you around?' We slap palms.

'You know it. Georgia, you're all right. Keep this guy on a leash for me.'

They trade a grin, and I sigh, relieved. He digs her, and the Fallucci seal of approval isn't easy to come by. Stretch, crack my back and wince as something catches in my ribs. Georgia moves me under the streetlight, fingering the swelling around my eye.

'Do they have a First-Aid kit here? There's a cut on your cheek.'

'It's fine. I'm about ready for that joint, though. Shall we?'

She takes my arm, and we descend the narrow cement stairs to the deserted beach; everyone who didn't race in for the fight is now jostling for The Ventures. The breeze blows through our damp clothes as she lights it up, carrying the smell of burning herbs over our shoulders and out to sea. Shards of moonlight skate over the waves as we walk along, scuffing through the sand like kids, passing it back and forth.

'So much for this not being that kind of place,' I say. 'It isn't, I swear.'

She exhales a laugh. 'No, you know what? That was oddly entertaining. I mean, part of me was convinced I'd never see you again, but it was pretty decent of you to stick up for him—and it made me think. This is such a weird cult for you guys. Why don't you open up a little?'

I scoff. 'Yeah, 'open' sounds real great, until you remember Sutter's Mill and the Gidget Paradox. Share your nice unspoiled thing and whoops, here comes everyone to spoil it.'

'But you're all so dead serious about it.'

'Serious, I dunno…maybe. Music should be fun, right? And surfing. We didn't used to be like this, just need a little…elbow room.' I can feel the dope start to take hold; speech is always the first to go. 'But what would you do? I mean…if you never saw me again?'

'I'd swear to mourn forever, then run away with Fluke.'

'Good choice.' My tongue is definitely dragging now, a soft bright fog spreading through my brain. Senses dulled yet acute, tuning it all out for a few seconds, then letting it rush dizzily back in: her presence, our legs moving slowly down the strand, the damp sea air in my nostrils. The wail and thump of the music behind us. We're missing it. And yet we're missing nothing.

'I'm kidding.' She drapes her arm around my waist. 'I'd be inconsolable.'

'I won't, then. Go away, I mean.'

'I won't, either.' Her voice is so round, all around me, echoes joining together in a cloud. Take a last hard drag, nearly burning my lips, and toss the roach. She trails down to the water, crouches and picks up a lost crab, gently brushes some sand off its shell. 'What do you think this place looked like a hundred years ago?'

'I don't know,' I say, because I don't. We rarely discuss our history, in school or out. Everything before the invention of the motion picture is a blur of Chumash Indians and Spanish missionaries, gold and grapes and oranges, dinosaurs trapped in tar pits for eternity. But the ocean is the same. The ocean will always be the same. *Humawilo*, the Chumash name for Malibu: the surf sounds loudly. *Sssehrff*.

'Hey, Tommy?'

'Huh?' I'm waving my hand, watching the trails of imagery it leaves.

'Don't disappear on me, okay? I'm serious.'

'Why would I? You're cool. We'll disappear together, maybe run away to Mexico. It'll be a blast.'

She laughs a little. 'But where would we live?'

'We could hang out in Mazatlán, or some other little beach town. Live on fish and tortillas. I know Spanish.'

'Oh, do you now?' Her lips on my neck. 'Tell me things in Spanish.'

'Mas cerveza, por favor. Vamonos a la playa. Te quiero, querida.'

'Andale pues.' Her hands on my ass, thrills running down my legs.

'See? We'll be fine.' My thoughts are no longer pretending to cohere, with each passing second, it becomes more of a struggle to remember what we're talking about. This isn't just pot we've smoked, not even very strong pot; I'm starting to sense that.

With one mind we come down to the sand. I can feel her lips on mine with every nerve, singing their ecstatic way up to my brain; my whole body needs to feel this way, right now. Push her gently back, run my fingers through her hair, kiss her harder as she rolls me over, biting my neck, fumbling with the buttons on my shirt, running her fingers over my nipples as I groan, *too much, oh no, no, don't stop.* Grab her arms, roll her back under me and then it all hits in a rush of fiery synaptic crackles, blowing fuses. My brain is beginning to melt like butter. Jesus. What's *in* this stuff?

Musta said it aloud. She says, 'Don't know. It's...I'm really stoned.'

'I'm toast. Wholly toast. The host with the toast. Hey, you know what'd taste great right now?' My tongue begins exploring her navel, licking her belly. Tastes like butter, like buttered toast. Butter. Sounds like the silliest word in the world. Butt-tar. Better. Bed her. Is this a real word? I'm undoing her top, giggling into her breasts, helpless with it, and she lifts my face to hers so we're gazing into each other when it happens, and I swear I'm not making this up.

We swap bodies—I'm in her head, seeing through her eyes. The ocean over my shoulder, the dust of freckles on my nose, the blood on my cheekbone and curl of blond hair over my eyes: wide and washed clear of everything impure and imperiled, pupils so huge they're edging out the blue. Feel her knowing me, loving me anyway. Something cracks in my chest, like an egg fracturing open to reveal a damp dark chick: hopelessly striving, hideous and blind.

Then I'm back, urgently unzipping her jeans, sliding my hands down into her warmth. She groans, shifts under me and my shirt is tented over my head and there is nothing here but this fragrance made flesh, just me and her sweet soft heat, the depths of it, and I am hard, *hard,* and more than anything in the world I want to plunge into her, held back only by the memory of encounters past.

Sex on the beach sounds so great, doesn't it? So exotic. Feel free to jerk off with a handful of sandpaper, if you ever want to approximate the experience. She's swelling against my mouth, hands on my neck, breath halting and rough, then fast, gasping my name and *there* and *oh* and *there* and then that sweet rain is coming down to greet me, oh Christ, nothing in this world ever tasted this good, and our mouths meet again to share it, speaking in tongues, shaking a little, what the fuck, what the holy fuck is *in* this stuff?

Everything is haloed in miasmas of purple and blue: our bodies, the palm trees, the ballroom. Vibrations of sound are visible over the roof, the whole joint rocking and quaking, about to explode and blow us all to Kingdom Come. Stomp-*stomp*. Stomp-*stomp*.

'We should get back,' I whisper into her belly. 'Before Dick comes on. You really want to see this.'

'Don't leave, Tommy. Please.'

'I'll never leave, I promise. You're right here.' Shake my head to clear it. 'I am, I mean. Right here.'

Her eyes close, then open slowly as if she's waking up. We rise like an old couple, put each other's clothes to rights, laughing and brushing sand off our asses. I hug her close and we just stay like that for a while, hearts knocking against our ribcages like two kids socking each other on the playground. I can feel my brain begin to crackle and smoke in my skull, but as long as I am here and she is here, I am safe.

'Are you on fire?' She won't let me go. Not even to put myself out.

'I must be,' I say. 'Must be. Are you?'

And then we're down again.

I never did find out what we'd smoked that night, though I did a fair amount of digging in later years. The CIA was experimenting with a lot of stuff at the time—a *lot* of stuff—and it might have been ketamine or PCP or STP, or any of the strange chemicals they'd inject into prisoners or crazies or broke students or Vietcong POW's. So much shit was floating around in those days in the grey zone under the law's radar, and she'd bought it off some guy who'd bought it off some other guy on

Sunset whom no one ever saw again, so we never managed to duplicate the experience. But that night still comes back to me, in dreams so clear and rattling I wake up and have no idea where or who or why the fuck I am, or if I'm even still alive.

By the time we get back, the drug is beginning to lull, ebbing away to leave us lucid, before rushing back in to knock us off our feet. The stage is empty and the crowd half-mad with anticipation, clapping in perfect rhythm in the darkness, stomp*stomp* clapclap stompSTOMP clap.

Seeps into your body when it's all around you like this, wrenching your heart into the groupbeat; in the dark, we could be anywhere from Siberia to South America, at any time in the history of man. Beethoven would roll over, sure, but you know he'd dig it, rocking out with the earnest children of the peasants that washed over these shores; the gates of Sicily, Scotland, Scandinavia, opening up to spill them out in a flood of kilts and kerchiefs, bearing hope in packs on their backs along with akkordolia and bodhrans and ciaramedda, traditions of centuries that began to alter soon as they got here, but always this at their core: Stompstomp *clap*clap. Stompstomp *clap*. The curtain rises, and we cry out, fall silent: the darkness is total, but they've got a blacklight spot, performers and instruments glowing like skeletons.

And then it begins.

Richard Anthony Monsour does not play like anyone else on the planet; he's Boston-Lebanese, for starters, and grew up on all sorts of weird Middle Eastern sounds that filter into his music. Righteous goofyfoot surfer, a southpaw who never bothered to restring his guitar, just plays it *upside down*, because that's how his brain works, like you could drop him into a funhouse where everyone else was walking into the mirrors, and he'd stroll on through, easy as pie. On top of which he plays faster than any other human being alive, and better, of course, goes without saying. The staccato-fingered things he does with that guitar—mere mortals can only shake their heads in awe. It's like watching Ricky surf. We'll never be that good, but damn if it isn't a pleasure just to marvel. And then there's the volume—because Dick doesn't just play loud. He sets amps on *fire*.

113

He's backed by two additional guitars and a bass, a drummer and a sax, and is ripping the hell out of a new song, some kind of Greek-sounding tune, but sped up, loud and rough, thrusting into your ears. It sounds like...well, you know how a good rock song will make you want to fuck, and a great song will make you want to fuck *it*? This song is fucking *you*. Sax twines around the archaic melody, the primal drive of guitars pushes through, and from time to time Dick barks into the mike as if it's bursting through him, too, tearing his chest wide open. No one's even dancing; we're all just standing, riveted, mesmerized, unwilling to miss a single moment of this.

Georgia is in front of me, my arms crossed under hers, around her belly, and I can feel the waves of tension rip through her, fade and rip again, and she's getting it, she gets it, and everything's starting to blur and change again—as the song draws to a close, the lights come up and Dick appears to be turning into a kind of purple octopus backed by a crew of grinning dolphins, and who knows how or when this is all going to end, or if we're going to wind up in a padded cell somewhere, but by now I don't even care.

We dance for hours, jumping, twisting and shaking, bopping around like tribesmen, sweating like mad—Fluke jury-rigged the AC, but it can't keep up with this many of us—and God, we're thirsty, so incurably thirsty. Go up to the bar for one Coke after another until my money runs out, then switch to water, but still can't slake this. We don't care. The drug is washing out of our systems now, leaving a cool cerulean calm in its wake. I ask the time and am told it's nearly one; Georgia goes out to the payphone to call home and let them know she'll be late, as I head into the men's for a much-needed leak.

Dennis comes in while I'm at the urinal; he's changed back into his old shirt, jeans and motorcycle boots. We nod to each other, unzip, piss for a while in companionable silence. Splash some cold water on my face at the sink, eyes back to their old washed-out blue around normal pupils. Shiner's coming in.

'Thanks,' he says, almost grudgingly. Checks his hair.

'No problem.' I'm looking for a single clean spot on the roller towel.

He's about to leave when he stops, hand on the door. 'Can you just why not, Tom? Can you tell me that? Why the fuck not?'

Give up, wipe my hands on my pants, soaked anyway. 'You know why.'

'We're *good*. You know we are.'

I grimace. 'You're really not, Dennis. You're good *enough*, okay? The world loves good enough, so go out there and knock 'em dead. Make a million, get a Jag, fuck juicy young pussy for days. But don't bring that shit in here. You of all people should know that.'

He looks about ready to sock me. But then his face softens.

'You really think we're going to be big?'

'I think you're going to be very fucking big.'

He cocks his head a little, thinking about that.

'Well, guess you can't have it all. See you round, Tommy.'

We slap-shake our farewell, and I never see him again in my lifetime. Not in the flesh, anyway.

People are starting to stream out of there as I wander around looking for Georgia. Not by the phone, not in the ladies'. Finally spot her over by the coat check, call her name. She turns and smiles at me through the crowd, and there is such clarity there, such sweetness and trust, that I can almost believe I'm not going to fuck this up.

'I'm ready,' she says, and something stirs in her voice.

'To go home? Your chariot awaits, milady.'

'No, I'm ready to surf. Can you teach me, Tommy?'

I nod. 'I can do that, definitely. Tomorrow.'

We drive home, and I park outside the gate and walk her up to the door, and her dad doesn't kill me, and her mom doesn't freak out and accuse me of colluding with the Nazis. It wasn't a perfect date, exactly.

115

But that's why it was beautiful. I want to go on dates like this with her forever, for the rest of our natural lives. This shit is not only possible, it's actually happening—and you know what? It doesn't hurt this time. Not a bit.

You'll be watching a movie sometimes, when the flow of the dream is interrupted by a flicker. It rights itself, then stutters again, and breaks loose from the sprockets. Before you know it, a brown spot appears, the projector overheats, the celluloid begins to burn, and that's that for that particular story. If you're lucky, you'll get your money back—but you can't help but wonder: *what happened, in the end?*

Four years later, just after its thirty-eighth birthday, the Rendezvous Ballroom burned to the ground. Not much registered for me by then—I was *non compos mentis* for what I'm told was one of the most exciting times in our history—but I do remember that day. Fluke and I drove out the next morning, parked on the street and crossed the tape along with a few dozen others, circling the smoking ashes that were still too hot to touch. Must've been one hell of a blaze. There was nothing left to take home, even as a charred, disfigured souvenir. Not a goddamned thing. Some of us were crying; no one said much, and then we all got back in our cars and drove away.

The lot was vacant for a while, and then they turned it into condos. You can't cling to anything in this life, I've found, or its loss will tear you apart. Not much you can do; everything changes, no matter where you are—but here, the wipeout is always as total as it is inevitable. That's LA for you, though. Nothing old can stay.

Two Jewish movies came out in late 1947: 'Crossfire,' a noir about an anti-Semitic murder with three guys named Robert, and 'Gentleman's Agreement,' about the more genteel type of hatred. It had been a trend to mention intermarriage or country clubs occasionally, but Hitler had made us bold, and these two openly addressed the Jewish Problem in America for the first time. I was only five, but it was a pretty big deal—especially as, two weeks later, the UN finally passed a resolution in favor of a Jewish state.

It had been a tense gathering by the radio: Grandpa's Party cronies, two of Mama's college girlfriends, Dad nursing a whiskey in the corner, sulking over this invasion of his living room. All clamor silenced as the vote began, and Jake Hartmann took up his pen to keep score.

After a minute, I felt this boredom creep up my back, a helpless anger at how it was being drawn out. They were really gonna milk it, y'know? Make us beg. No one in the room said a word, not even a whisper, as if any expression of joy or outrage would affect the vote either way, so it wasn't until we got to the P's that anyone dared to breathe. Pakistan—Against. Panama—For.

Paraguay?

The Republic of Paraguay votes...for Partition.

It was like a bomb went off. Pretty sure every Jew in LA, New York, London, Paris, Jerusalem—hell, at that moment every Jew on the planet was screaming his fool head off. You could hear us on Mars. After two thousand years, we had our home back. I mean, I had always assumed home was here. But everyone loves a party, right?

Not Ray. When all that shouting burst out, he began to cry, and he wasn't the only one. It was almost his bedtime anyway, and Mama was weeping in the arms of her friend as they ran through the rest of the countries, so I took his hand. One more triumphant roar from the Reds followed us up the stairs as the USSR sided with the Jews. We'd brushed our teeth already, so I tucked him in.

'Can I have a drink of water?'

'No. Dad's deal was dry bed, or you go back to the crib.' I nudged him over, showed him a map.

'That's why everyone's so excited,' I explained. ''Cause we get to live there now.'

He squinted at it doubtfully. 'I can't see it.'

I got the magnifying glass out of my top drawer. 'Right there.'

'It's too little. We won't all fit.'

'Well, it's bigger in real life.'

'Why can't we live there?' He points to the sweep of Saudi Arabia.

''Cause that's where the Arabs live. And there, and there, and over there. Just this part is ours.'

'But the Arabs don't like us.'

I stared up at the ceiling and tried not to think about the rivers of blood they had promised. 'They'll get used to us.'

'We'll be lonely.'

For the first time in my life I actually thought the words 'little pitchers have big ears.' I'd said the very same thing to Grandpa, and he'd scoffed, 'There are worse things than lonely.'

'You don't have to live there. But now you can if you want to. Just go to sleep, okay?'

'Okay.' And instantly he was out. I held him like a teddy bear until I dozed off, too, and then it was morning and school, graham crackers and milk, Cowboys and Indians. Life was back to normal.

It wasn't, though. Four months later, 'Gentleman's Agreement' won the Oscar. At that point, I put my foot down: Grandpa had to take me. Confused by the story of Gregory Peck masquerading as a Jew to write an exposé of anti-Semitism, I kept quietly asking who was really truly a Jew, not just pretending to be one—or not be one.

All the cryptic name changes and jiggery-fakery were perplexing, and finally I got told to shut up by the rudenik behind us. Grandpa stood up, all 6'5" of him, and stared the guy down, but I sank into silence. Just wanted to get things straight, you know? I wasn't sure why Jews needed the cavalry to ride to their defense—why couldn't they call out the jerks themselves? Peck seemed like a decent guy, but it burned. I was all for self-reliance, even then; if you couldn't stick up for yourself, I reckoned, you weren't worth much. Grandpa's doing, I expect.

It was my first encounter with a hatred more insidious than genocide, and to our own passivity in the face of it. I'd never thought about this before: society's need to keep us at arm's length, judge our noses, ban us from their precious reindeer games. Even in the land of the free, you couldn't get a decent job if you were Jewish, couldn't marry people's sisters or join country clubs or play golf, although I wasn't sure why anyone would want to do any of those things.

Impatient with adult dawdling, I'd learned to read at three; I liked to swim, eat, and read books, and didn't foresee my horizons expanding much beyond that. If they did, well, I'd go to a place where the rules were different. I'd liked the movie, though. At least it was honest.

America seemed to like it too. It got Best Picture in March 1948, and two months later Israel declared independence. I wasn't sure why it had taken so long—independence was a thing you inscribed on parchment, then tossed the Brits out and *voila*—but apparently Jews were supposed to keep quiet and politely wait our turn.

And the Arabs had not gotten used to us, after all. For reasons unclear, seven countries were now trying to slaughter us and take over our little splinter of land. The war went on for nine months; casualties on both sides were enormous. By the time the dust had settled, I was in second grade, and thought, well, that's that, then. They get the picture now—we're a force to be reckoned with. They'll leave us be, go back to doing whatever it is Arabs do.

They didn't, of course. But we changed, all of us. We now had our own country, and a pretty *starker* army, and if you tried to kill us, there'd be consequences this time. We held our heads up high, no matter where we lived, and if people still wouldn't let us play golf, we could always move to Israel and play there, make the desert bloom and dance the hora while fending off the hordes.

So this meant a lot—but Israel was very far away, a dim idea in most Americans' minds, and didn't carry much weight on the playgrounds of Los Angeles. We'd been an exciting trend for a brief glorious moment, but trends fade fast, especially if you're a kid. You got your Oscar, for crying out loud, you got your stupid country, and it's not like we killed *all* of you. Shut up already.

And there were no more Jewish movies until I was a senior in high school, unless you count 'Ten Commandments' and fifteen versions of Anne Frank, which I most emphatically do not.

No one ever leaves this place. Not really. We're like one big body here, and your pancreas can only travel so far before it needs to come home again and make, I dunno, bile or something. You need bile, if you're going to digest stuff. We're the gossip capital of the world, sure, with a million coy tattle rags, but they're hardly necessary, cause we all know when one of us is hurt. Like waking up in the middle of the night when you've bashed your elbow or are sleeping wrong on your neck. You don't need to think, you just know: pain. It spreads through the city, arcing over synapses until all news is yesterday's.

When my eyes open that Sunday, I know: someone's dead. Check on Ray, curled around his pillow, hair tousled, face so kid-smooth in sleep that I can't help but plant a kiss on him. On Mama, gently removing the paperback from her chest, *Stranger in a Strange Land*.

Then I call Georgia. It's early, but I know she's awake: today's the day I get to teach her how to surf. I've never done this before—maybe given a few tips to the grems—but I remember Fluke teaching me, and in my mind have been adding a move here and there ever since, maybe for a kid of my own someday. I know she's going to be an apt pupil, and the waves will rise to meet her—but the phone just keeps on ringing and ringing. Is there any sound lonelier? Now the worry's starting to gnaw at my stomach.

Dress in silence, the sun coming through the curtains, a few sparrows twittering outside the window. It's probably nothing. Maybe she's still asleep; it was a crazy night. Maybe she's on her way down to meet me. Slap together a meatloaf sandwich, humming 'St. James Infirmary,' then ease my board into Mayhem and head down to the beach. We all have our churches.

I tell you, I've had some weird rides in my life, but nothing to beat that one. Barely any motorists—and this is LA, there are *always* cars. People are moving sluggishly along the sidewalk, heads down as if mugged, coming to in the middle of the street, looking around—and no one is so much as honking. Even the mutts seem forlorn. One of the checkers is on the sidewalk out front of Tony's, broom in his hand, a lady sobbing on his shoulder. His face is blank, hand patting her on the back like an automaton. The light changes before I can roll down the window to ask what in Mary Mother of God.

No one's out. The guys are all standing around in an aimless huddle. Plant my board. 'All right, already, *what*?' I probably sound a little testy; by now I'm thinking missiles on Manhattan. Mysto says nothing, just hands me the 'Times.'

The picture's from a year ago, when she got her square by Grauman's. She and Jane Russell are down on their knees on the sidewalk, and she's looking up at the camera with that wide-open grin she always had, the one that made it hard to do anything but adore her: *Ain't life grand? Can you believe all this for little old me?* My eyes skitter over the article, snagging on words like *Nembutal, depression, coroner.* Cause of death: *Failed to find happiness as Hollywood's brightest star.*

If you can imagine.

My eyes wander up to the sky, as if hoping to find some explanation for why someone like this was simply...removed from the world. Snatched away as if we'd misbehaved, warranted a walk to the woodshed instead of an ice cream cone. But there's nothing up there, not even a shred of cloud. A sky so bright blue, so implacable, it hurts to contemplate for long. Almost every day is like this. I've lived here my whole life, and occasionally you want something different, you know? Weather should be moody, at least change once in a while. This shit ain't normal.

'Say something,' Fluke mutters. My throat's closed up. I got nothing. You can see it coming a mile away, and still not be ready.

'Well, shit,' Mysto says, and U grumbles, 'Waste of a fine piece of ass.'

Ricky grabs his board and takes a step towards the water.

I say, 'Got a dime?'

Ricky does not have a dime. Ricky wouldn't give you a dime to call the fire department if you were in flames, though he might consider pissing on you. But Fluke tosses me one, and I head up to the payphone on the pier. Dial her number once more, just to feel like I'm doing something. She picks up on the third ring.

122

'Hello?' Muffled and distant, as if talking through a pillow.

'It's me. Are you okay?'

'I keep...pulling it together, doing stuff. And then I'm crying again.'

'I'm on my way.' Don't wait for her to argue.

On the drive over, I keep waiting to feel anything but numb. Shift into third, think of her hand, skin soft but cold now, slipping out of the blanket to hang off the stretcher, then be thrust into an ambulance. Taken off to the morgue, never to be seen again. Never again to touch a warm living body, write a letter, play piano, never let water run through her fingers in the bath, frisking the bubbles.

But why did it matter? Wasn't like I was some big gaga fan, gone on her every movie, up-to-date on her latest dress or love affair. But still. She was so nice, you know? She had been around for practically my whole life, and she was just so fucking *nice*. So harmless and friendly. You could imagine sitting quietly with her, holding that hand, never asking for more. And no one should have to die in fucking Pasadena.

I met her once. I've never told another soul about that. It was at a counter-demonstration in front of the Russian embassy, I guess Miller must've dragged her down there. I was fourteen, on my own, playing hooky and missing Grandpa Joe so much I wanted to die, and I tripped over the curb, falling hard to my knees and dropping the sign. Someone reached out through the crowd, helped me up and dusted me off, all hangdog and mortified, and then I looked into her face.

She wasn't wearing make-up, and had a scarf over her hair; I guess she didn't want to be recognized, and she could just vanish like that. And she was so much smaller in real life, like you wouldn't believe, this tiny little elf. She winked at me, put a finger to her lips—and then she was gone. Maybe it was just a dream. I never mentioned it because—well, just because. Georgia opens the door with a wan smile, still clutching a Kleenex, and it punches at my heart.

You wouldn't notice it right away. Different noses, and Georgia's hair is long and straight, streaked honey from the sun, but once you'd caught a glimpse of that expression, it can't be unseen: *Please don't leave, don't fuck me over, please.* Like a kitten in the gutter, barely hanging on.

Moves into my arms as I whisper, 'As long as I walk this earth, you'll never be alone like that. Not on a Saturday night. I swear to you.'

'This wasn't supposed to happen.'

'No, it wasn't.'

'She was supposed to grow *old*. Have kids and grandkids. Take them to the circus, and cuss out the columnists, raise hell drinking and dancing, doing sixty up Sunset in a convertible full of screaming fairies, and everybody'd shake their heads because what a shameless old lady, and why wasn't she home with her knitting and she'd just laugh, cause they were morons, and she was Marilyn Goddamned Monroe.' She stops to catch her breath.

'I know,' I say. 'I know, I know.'

'They killed her, Tommy! Miller and DiMaggio and the Kennedys and all those fucks, they pretended to love her and left after they'd sucked her dry, and she just had no one, ever, no one. And she tried so hard! Nobody gets that!' She pulls back, weeping. 'Everybody thought she was this dumb little Twinkie, that this all came so easy for her...and she was so fucking lonely, and she was trying *so fucking hard!*'

'I know,' I say desperately, although I didn't, really. 'I know.'

I've got nothing here, and it's scary, how hard she's taking this. Like some tectonic shift has laid bare an ancient aquifer of rage and sorrow; I have no idea what its source is, nor how to drain it. My chest is wet with tears, and I'm nudging her into the house, muttering words that mean nothing. Nothing, really. Random sounds you make to comfort the grieving, like a mother gorilla.

'Where is everyone?' The place is breathless, curtains drawn and silent.

'Carm has the day off,' she says, and swipes at her hair, blows her nose. 'I think she's at church. Mom's out to lunch, and Dad's in New York. He took the red-eye last night, called at six.' She sniffs. 'I'm just so tired, Tommy. He said he didn't want me to get the news from anyone else. Must've blanked on the time difference. He was really upset.'

Probably left right after I'd met him. Took a car to the airport, sat on a plane, waiting to rise into the sky. Strange, how we can all disappear so easily. 'Doesn't he ever sleep?'

'We're not big sleepers. Sometimes we have little insomnia parties in the kitchen, but mostly...' her voice catches, and she starts to sob again.

I pick her up—she's even lighter than Mama—and take her upstairs to her room, a melee of books and records and clothes, and in the middle of it all, an incongruously tidy bed. The snoozing cat raises his head to glare: *bastard, what have you done?* Nudge him over to lay her down, which does not improve my standing. She turns away to hide her face with one hand, weeping, curled into a ball. Impossibly alone with this, as if I'll never understand.

Not knowing what else to do, I fetch some water and sit on the edge of the bed, hand on her ankle, trying to feel anything but this blankness, this strange humming in my ears. After a while, her weeping slows and she turns over to regard me. Wiping her eyes, smiling apologetically, because she didn't even know her, really. None of us did.

I don't know how to console girls. Always start out well enough with *there, there,* and *it'll be okay,* but then realize that it won't, and start talking about that till we're both miserable. Only two things I know work every time, and I don't think surfing is what's on the menu today. She sits up and we look at each other, knowing what we're about to do, unable to stop it. Reaches out to touch my face, I thumb a tear from her cheek, and she smiles, starts to unbutton her pajama top. I swallow, heart pounding, take my shirt off to keep her company, she's pulling off my trunks, and then—well, there we were.

I let it all happen, good sense washed away by emotion. I'd wanted this so badly for weeks, until the thought of being inside her had begun to consume every cell in my body, warring with the need for it to work out this time. Can't always be the one steering the boat, though—there are times you just have to rest and drift where the current takes you.

What is it the dicks are always looking for in the pulps? Motive and opportunity. And here we were at last with both, in this nice big bed in this nice big empty house, no witness but the cat.

I thought it would be beautiful, you know? Romantic. Didn't have any elaborate seduction planned out, no hotel rooms in Paris or rose petals or honeyed words—but I had it in my head that it'd be this big holy thing somehow. Never really is, though, is it? No matter where you are, or with whom. It's not meant to be. Just two animals going at each other down in the dirt. Making you face things you're too proud to with your clothes on. I love this girl so much my bones ache, I want her to be happy, she's giving me this sweet tender gift—and I'm, God, I'm feeling *nothing*, like washing the dishes or taking out the garbage.

It's always gone bad for me after that. People stop being people once they've fucked, treat each other in cruel senseless ways till they have to split up or die. You keep at it, because it feels good; the sadness only comes later. And you can rob Peter to pay Paul till doomsday, but let me tell you, that vig adds up.

I learned that when I became a monk at fifteen, and it all came crashing down. School-work-home-bed, days a blur. Only time I woke up was on speed or out on the water, and that's when I started surfing every day, in any weather. But I longed for that warmth, that plunge into another, and after high school I slipped back into my old ways, desperate for that post-screw serenity, with no more success than before. The Pussy giveth, and the Pussy taketh away.

This is my first time with someone I truly loved since Tina, though, and losing her might actually kill me. Not like suicide. More an uprooting, my soul yanked out. I don't know if there'd be enough left to carry on. It's not healthy to need another person like this, especially not one that, let's face it, I barely know.

Because the other thing I'd had in my head was that she was a virgin. There was no basis for this idea in anything she'd said or done—but my heart needed her to be a pristine princess waiting for me in her lonely tower, so it took my dumb ass a few moments to realize the truth. And then I lose it, go limp. I'm not sure what to do; this has never happened to me before.

'What's wrong?' She struggles to her elbows as I pull out.

'Nothing. It's, ah, nothing. Thought I was hurting you.'

'You weren't, of course you weren't.' I say nothing. 'Tommy, look at me. What's going on?'

'I don't know,' I whisper. 'I'm sorry. I need to—I'll be right back.'

Get to my feet, edge through the chaos towards the bathroom, and with every step the voices are screaming, *get back there and get it up, or she's through with you* but also *go back now, and you're through.* I'm fucked either way—but I can feel the grief rising, pummeling at my throat, and I can't cry in front of her like a crazy person. Close the door behind me, turn on the shower. Feel the water drumming cold and hard against my head as I clamp a hand over my mouth, the tears burning out of me, washed away and still coming. We didn't even have a chance to start, and already I've killed it.

Death is always so simple in books and movies, isn't it? The gunshot, the sword thrust, the fall off a cliff. The doctor lifting a limp pulseless wrist, glancing at the clock on the wall. Right this moment, is when it happened. The neatly transcribed time, the close of the chapter that began with a red-faced squall long ago. Tidy like that. But you can take that tidiness away from people, just as you can take yourself away without a word of explanation.

They say he was angry, Joe. Furious, that night he came down to the set and found her shimmying over the subway grate, a goddess in ecstasy over the blasts of hot air that caressed her thighs, lifting her skirts, a spectacle for a thousand rock-hard New Yorkers with slack jaws and aching hearts, knowing they'd never peel off that pure white dress, lay bare what lay beneath, spread her out under their hungry bodies.

He didn't think, it's just a story, that's my wife up there, she's all mine, I'm the only guy who gets to know her like that. He didn't think, I'm the Yankee Clipper, King of America, I've got a notion of what it means to be adored like this, how vain the headlines and golden accolades, the warm fickle waves of love that lap around you and are gone.

No. He thought, that fucking *whore.*

Any doctor could've taken one look at the proud Italian blood rising to his cheeks, that clenched jaw and eyes of jealous shame, and clicked a stopwatch: kaput. Time of death. They'd continue to love each other for all eternity, but that's the moment they could no longer live with one another. She came into the shoot the next day covered in bruises, and a month later they were divorced.

That moment of insanity came back on him in spades. You can hate him for beating on her like that; I do. Even that goofy Rod Serling face of his couldn't save him from that. But I also know that after that surge of rage had ebbed away, he was just really goddamned *sad*.

You can't deflect these moments simply by recognizing what they are. You can't. But it helps a little, to know precisely when they've come. At three AM, the housekeeper got suspicious and called the shrink, and together they broke down the door, too late. So who the fuck knows when it came for her? It hurts, to be left without even that little crumb of awareness of what the world was up to in that moment. How you were otherwise engaged, while you were meant to be there. It hurts. Believe me.

I'd had a new drawing to show Grandpa that day; it was pretty good. Robin Hood and Friar Tuck are going at each other with longstaffs, and Tuck's just lambasted him right off the bridge. Robin hasn't hit the water yet, but the splash is imminent, and the motion and perspective are pretty well-done for a twelve-year old, and there are all sorts of little details that make a good drawing great—cattails and ripples; a fish leaping out of the water; one of the Merry Men peeping out from behind a tree, amusement battling horror on his face. I've been toiling away at it for a week, hiding it in my notebook and sneaking in work as the teachers go on about congruent angles and Magna Cartas, and I jump out of the car, race up the walk and, wait, wait, something's off. Because the door is open.

Not all the way—just a little ajar. But I know instantly something is wrong, because he always closes his door, and locks it, too, and my first thought is *burglars*, so I'm tense, ready for them to jump me as I move through the kitchen, skin crawling on the back of my neck.

The smell hits me like a rat has crawled up somewhere and died – and I'm in the bedroom, and at first my brain can't swallow what I'm seeing and I'm trying to lift up his dead weight with all my might, screaming for Mama to come cut him down, please please please keep him here, we have to hurry, *please*!

There was no point in hurrying, really. The Boy Scouts had taught me mouth-to-mouth till I could do it in my sleep, but the only way I could've saved him by then was with a time machine.

He never said goodbye. And he never told us why.

Not why, exactly, I mean, duh, that wasn't too hard to figure out. But he never told us *how*. How he could just leave us like that. *Er war unsere Sonne,* so brilliant, so full of fierce fiery life, and the three of us revolved around him like...no, not even planets. Moons, reflecting his light. Nothing without it.

That whole year, it was so dark. Even in this town where the sun never, ever stops shining, I'd wake up each morning and there'd be a moment of birdsong and delight before the fog would roll in: still gone. Maybe reality was more fluid for me then, but for that entire year I thought I was going to wake up one morning and it would all have been one of those really long bad dreams. It wasn't until I'd voiced this hope aloud, talking to Fluke a few weeks after we'd met, that I realized the truth.

Grandpa wasn't coming back. Ever.

There is a knock at the door, and I turn off the water and wipe my face. Want to tell her to come in; it is, after all, her bathroom, and I'm being a putz however you cut it, but I can't trust my voice just yet. The door opens anyway, and the curtain is pulled back.

'Hi,' she says, still naked.

'Hi,' I say, beyond embarrassment. 'I'm okay now, sorry.'

She steps into the tub, takes me in her arms. 'Wanna tell me what just happened there?'

Shake my head against her hair, comforting myself with its smell.

'Uh-uh, big boy. Don't cop out into some dumb manly silence. Spill, because right now I feel like I have the scariest pussy in the world.'

Laugh. 'Your pussy's a work of art, hon. Just didn't see this coming, was all. Bad timing, and now I've gone and screwed it all up.'

'My fault, too, Tommy. You don't get to be responsible for everything.'

'Well, I'll grant you have been hounding me a little, but I wasn't exactly unwilling prey to your femme fatale ways, was I?'

'You wanted to be the one to bust my cherry, huh?' That gorgeous sailor's mouth, saying these things. I can't look away. I've never felt as much anything as I do around her.

'Guilty,' I say, running my hand down her back to trace the heart of her ass, so pale against her tan. 'But it's not what you think.'

'You don't know what I think.'

'What you might suspect, then. I've never been with a virgin. I hear it's painful and bloody, which isn't my gig, and it's not a contest anyway. But I know how guys can be. Even the best of us are kind of shitty, especially to girls. I wanted to get in front of that.'

She sets her jaw. 'You think I can't defend myself?'

'I think you shouldn't have to, Georgia. If I'm good for nothing else, at least I can beat the shit out of anyone who hurts you. Or not let that happen in the first place.'

She nuzzles into me, chuckling. 'You're a piece of work, Tom Beck. I'm nuts about you, and there is a distinct possibility I'll lose my mind and marry you some day. But for now...'

'What?' I can barely hear myself. My heart is singing. Loud.

'I'm going to fuck you till you can't stand up. Get naked for me.'

I grin, looking down at my body, rising again to meet her.

'I mean *really* naked, Tommy. Because this time, it's gonna be good.'

Then we are under the covers, staring into each other's eyes.

She whispers, 'Right here.'

'Right here,' I tell her.

And then we stop talking.

'Put your clothes on, barbarian.'

'You put your clothes on. No, just kidding, don't. Who's Etta James?' We're putting her room back in order. Well, she is. I'm mostly going through her records.

'From Chess...? Ugh, you're so hopeless, dope. Here, listen.' Takes the record, places it carefully on the hi-fi, and holds out her arms.

'I can't dance in the raw,' I protest. 'When's your mom coming home?'

'Not for hours. Come on, dance with me.'

She sings into my heart, an ache in her voice, about a dream that she could speak to.

'It's not always this bad,' she murmurs as we sway. 'My room, I mean.'

'I don't mind,' I say. 'Ray's the messy one with us, though. I have to put everything in its place, or it takes too long to find, you know?'

'Must be nice, having a brother. I always wanted one. More than one. A whole houseful.'

'Oh, you'd regret it. Boys are terrible. We yell a lot, and fight and break things. And we smell weird.'

'I don't care. I like the way you smell; I want more just like you.'

I stop dancing. 'Shit. Shit, oh, double shit. I didn't use anything.'

'It's okay. I'm on the pill.'

'Pill? What pill?'

'Birth control? Enovid?'

'Oh. But isn't that only for married ladies?'

'I have a pretty simpatico doctor. 'Menstrual problems,' don'tcha know. Which covers every woman in America.'

'So it works? Like, you can't get pregnant?' This is how cheap I come: I'm hard again already.

'Foolproof. And hey, only took forever.'

I'm quiet, thinking, holding her close. It's almost better than the sex, this closeness. Almost.

'What is it?'

'Nothing,' I say, coming to. 'Just...wow. This changes everything.'

'Tell me about it.'

'We can feel this way all the time. Without running around in circles every other month cause someone's missed a period.'

She nods. 'I don't think they have any idea what they've done here.'

'Probably had some inkling. They'll catch flack—but hey, they can take comfort rolling around on their beds of money, right?'

'Nothing to stop us, and we won't have to get married anymore. This is gonna be so much fun, like stepping out into space.'

'Well, there's still the clap.'

'Ah, yes, the Russian Tragedy. The Burning Bush. Did you ever...?'

Hold up three fingers. 'Never, Scout's honor. Got crabs once, though.'

'Oh, God,' she laughs. 'Giant crabs crawling all over you.'

'No, they're more like—'

'I know.' Her fingers crabwalk over my thighs, and I groan.

'Let's fuck right now.'

'Let's never do anything else again.'

We dive under the covers, and she's giggling until I'm infected with it. Huge crabs, prowling around our bed, tickling us with their antennae, examining our goings-on with strange stalk eyes. Ten-legged beings, trying to figure out what the hell we're up to. Join the club, my crazy crustaceous friends. Join the fucking club.

We take the board out to the pool, and there in its waveless safety I give her lesson one. New suit today, a gold number that blends into her tan so evenly she'd seem naked but for the green paisley pattern over her nipples and crotch that make it hard to look anywhere else. We each have our quivers—guys their boards; girls, their bikinis. No way can she wear this to the beach, though—there'd be riots.

Dives in. I follow her through the water, bubbles trailing in her wake, clinging to her skin like minute pearls. Her hair streaming through my fingers, the shift and glance of bodies, vague shadows on the bottom. We come up for air, and she slides a hand into my trunks.

'Take them off,' she whispers, and I laugh.

'Christ, you're insatiable.'

'I just want to see what you look like, under the sun.'

'Yeah, skinny-dipping is a strictly nocturnal affair. Learned that one the hard way.' She raises an eyebrow, so I explain. 'Fluke dared me to go out to Pirate's Cove this one time, and I said that I would if he would— but he had to get naked, too, cause you know otherwise that bastard would find some loophole. And we did! We actually did it! Still can't believe we went through with it, and him blushing like a schoolgirl the whole time. Seriously, I thought he was going to die.'

Her shoulders are shaking with mirth. 'Poor old Fluke, I can see it now. But how was it? How long were you there?'

'A while. First five minutes were the longest of my life, but honestly, after that it sorta clicks off, and you don't get why this was ever a big deal. Fluke spent most of the time hiding in the water, but I got into a conversation with this nice lady—'

She snorts. 'Oh, I'll bet you did.'

'No, it wasn't like that, we were talking about Castro. Anyway, she must have been eighty or something, but cool. It was a strange place, you know? Not the types you'd expect, just normal people, hanging out in their bodies. And no one was being creepy, even though we were all naked. But I lost track of time, and then realized that certain parts of me that had never seen the sun before were getting a little pink, so we went home.'

Ducks her head, shoots water between her teeth. 'And?'

'Brick red. Three days of agony. Balls were the worst. My mother kept wondering where all the yogurt had gotten to, and I was like, heh-heh, I dunno, but I'll be in the john for the next hour or so, hum-di-dum. Then it peeled, which was super attractive. Naturally, Fluke's swarthy shy ass escaped unscathed.' I pause. 'Why am I telling you this?'

'To get out of taking your shorts off.' That unfettered merriment in her voice. 'Just do it already!'

'Not today, *mamacita*. Wait till the moon is full.'

Hops on the board then, and man, she is solid from the start. Paddles as I shout instruction, leaps into her goofyfoot stance, loose hips and knees, over and over, perfecting balance, finding her sea legs. Roaring with pleasure when she gets it right, practicing her wipeout till she no longer needs to use her brain for it. Think out there, and you're lost. You stiffen up, punk out. But she won't, I know. One of those lucky few, born without a fear bone.

I tell her the truth: that no matter how good she gets, she's gonna wipe. A lot. Until it seems there's nothing in the world but the hard smack of saltwater up her sinuses, ears blowing out, board bombing down on her head, being held under, nearly drowning, bones breaking, reef rash. Staph and sunburn, surfer's knots and sharks. As if trying to warn her off, though I omit the crucial part: if she gets sucked into this, she won't want to do anything else with her life. Ever.

She absorbs it all and nods; she knows how hard this is going to be, and how hard it's going to rock. I feel alive, a clean breeze blowing through every part of me, because this person—she isn't just my girl, you know?

She returns the favor by teaching me to make a cake. We keep throwing stuff in—chocolate, cherries, pecans—until she cuts me off at beer.

'855, 856,' I count, arms aching. You never use a mixer, she tells me. It ruins the taste. 'Can I lick the bowl?'

'Course,' she says, smiling to herself. 'That's the best part.'

'988, 999, 1000. You grease the pans?' She holds them out, and I pour in the batter: half in one, half in the other, just right. 'Can we frost it?'

'Sure. Gotta bake it first, though. Typical rookie mistake.'

So we bake the cake and find something else to keep us occupied for a while, up against the pantry wall. It gets a bit singed around the edges, so we cut those bits off and coat it with a pale yellow buttercream, and I'll be damned if it doesn't come out looking like something straight out of 'Better Homes and Gardens.'

Georgia purrs, 'Happy birthday, Mr. President,' and we laugh instead of crying, cause didn't Norma Jeane just blow all those condescending douches out of the water that night? That woman was in such pain, and she spun it into this shameless sexy humor that made the rest of us want to go on. It's something, that. Most of what you make out of life is nothing, but that wasn't. It was something. A reason to be happy.

Can't believe we get to eat this delicious thing we made all by ourselves. When Mrs. Lustgarten finally gets home around dinnertime, she finds us passed out on the couch in front of the 'Creature Feature': still in our suits, half the cake gone, crumbs everywhere. Years later, she told me we were smiling.

'Maybe we should just call it 'Don't Tell Ricky',' I groan. I'm lying on the bedroom rug, trying to balance an open bottle of Coke on my forehead. It's probably not a good idea.

'He'll come around,' Fluke advises from the desk. He's working on a model, a Lockheed F-104 Starfighter, abandoned when I was fourteen. His hands move over it with care, fingers tweaking a rocket, shifting a wing. 'Don't get your panties in a bunch.'

'There's a name. 'Don't Get Your Panties in a Bunch, Incorporated."

'Beats anything else we've come up with. 'Sticks?' How many nights you lie awake over that one, brain trust?'

'Oh, blow me.' Take the bottle off my head, sip precariously. 'Read what we've got so far.'

'Why am I on fuckin' list detail? I'm doing important shit over here.' He folds the paper into a plane, zips it over and opens a bottle of paint.

I sit up and unfold it. "The Extraordinaires?"

'Yeah, that was more of a band name.'

'You're not in a band.'

He shrugs. 'Guy can dream. Extra something, though. Exes, Axes. Axis? Hey, what's that thing you always say to your mom? You know, when you tell her how bitchen you are.'

'Huh?'

'Y'know. She says, '*Tomas, macht du* garbledy,' and you say, '*Ja, Mama,* I'm bitchen."

I spit Coke on my hand. '*Ein bisschen.* It means a little bit.'

He puts the paintbrush down, picks up the pad. 'Spell it.' I comply, and he says, 'Where does the umlaut go?'

'Can't we put one in there anyway?' I sigh heavily, and he says, 'Ugh, humorless fuckin' Krauts.'

'I'm Austrian, fuckhead.'

'Quiet. I'm concentrating.'

'Even 'umlaut' doesn't have an umlaut. Could we call it 'Umlaut?"

'No 'Umlaut.' Check it out.'

I peer at the bold ink letters on the page: BISSCHEN. 'Reasonably boss,' I admit. 'But I don't think even Ricky's ready for a Nazi surf shop.'

'Too soon? C'mon, there's some good shit coming out of Germany now. Cars, cameras, art. I hear some band's blowing it up out in Hamburg. Might be the wave of the future.'

'Naw, fuck Germany, man. Hitler didn't surf. And quit hanging out in Army bars already; those meatheads will just brainwash you. First time outta Podunk, they think they know the world.'

'What about pirates?'

'They have pirate bars? Sweet. Disneyland for grown-ups. Let's open up a pirate bar.'

'You're too young, June. No, pirate names. Like 'Arrr, Matey."

'Pirates didn't surf. How 'bout just 'Arrr'?'

'Captain Cook surfed. What about 'Yo'? Or 'Ho'?'

'Cook didn't surf, he just wrote about it—and he wasn't a pirate. How about 'Sex Marks the Spot'?'

'Irrelevant, your honor, it's not a topless bar. 'Fallucci and Beck's'?'

'Blah firm. Haberdashery. 'Swell Effects'?'

'Novelty shop,' he nixes. 'How about just 'X'?'

I'd taken a breath to rejoin with some flippantry, but stop right there, cause that's it, gotta be. Toss out a few more, but damned if 'X' isn't the one. Sure, there were moments we came to regret it later, usually after turning away the tenth unshaven perv that day in search of stag flicks and jerk mags, not to mention the occasional perplexed Nation of Islam disciple—but overall, it suited our ambivalence about the whole affair. We'd excommunicated ourselves both from society and the temple of unsullied surf, so were as ex as you could get—but if you followed the treasure map, you'd find us.

Fluke finishes painting the plane, leaves it to dry on the desk. Now all we need to do is get a business license, lease a site, fix it up, get stock, install the tools and shelves, make a few dozen boards, learn to use the register, put the sign up and the word out. Oh, and get a loan to pay for it all. Lead pipe cinch, right?

But first, of course, we have to get our hair cut. And tell Ricky.

We hit the streets. Malibu's commercially zoned, but fancy and far from our financial fingers, so our best bet is probably Venice. We scanned the real estate section this morning—check us out, reading Real Estate instead of 'Alley Oop'—and five spots might work. We wander around scoping them out, then narrow it down to three and call the realtor. We're meeting a *realtor*. This is officially insane.

'Don't be alarmed,' Fluke is saying over the phone. 'We may not look like much—' I frantically wave my hands as he ignores me—'but we're a legitimate concern, I assure you. Ten o'clock, then.' Hangs up. '*What?*'

'Don't blow it! Don't apologize! He won't take us seriously now.'

'He's a chick. And I think she was feeling me. She had a nice voice.'

I raise my eyebrows and look down at my burgeoning agenda, every scribbled item of which seems like it needs to be done first, if we're to manage all the others. This is starting to feel like one of those Chinese puzzles, made for finer minds than mine. We take it to the beach, to confer secretively between sets, our last outing with hair intact, just till we get the bureaucratic bullshit out of the way. Fluke's dad was right— it'll all grow back.

138

Piles of people, far as the eye can see. August, and half the city's at the beach. Half the planet, it seems, all come out to suck up our golden Cali dream and crowd the waves, making surfing an agonizing nightmare. Most know to clear out when we're coming through, but it's not enough anymore. Ricky's face is getting grimmer by the day; last week he skegged some kook's back for dropping in on him, and things got ugly. No charges, but there's always a next time.

'What are you two dudes up to?' he asks. We're huddled over the pad, scheming. This is going to take at least a month, don't know why I thought it would be overnight.

'Writing a love song, *dude*,' Fluke shoots back. 'We just need a rhyme for June.'

'Goon. Baboon. Buffoon.'

'Moon,' U-Boy sings out, and suits the action to the word, setting off shrieks of horror amongst the towel girls.

'Dune,' Mysto calls from the firepit. 'Swoon. Maroon.'

Pip mumbles something, and we all say, 'What?' because Pip never says anything. He shakes back his hair, smiling beatifically. 'Soon.'

'Nice one, Pipster,' I tell him. 'I think you nailed it.'

Ricky tries to get a gander at the pad, but I hide it behind my back. 'Wait till it's done, okay? Soon.'

And then it's time for the cruelest cuts. Elena seats us in the kitchen, throws towels around our shoulders, then spritzes us down. Snip, snip, testing the scissors. Something rumbles in my gut, a strange painful heat working its way down into my groin. Sofia runs a comb through my hair, clucking over the tangles.

'Am I hurting you?'

'No, no,' I reassure her. 'You're fine.'

'Don't give me a crewcut,' Fluke wriggles. 'Swear on our mother.'

'Ahh, shaddup, you,' says Elena. 'I'm a professional.'

'Professional pain in my ass, is what you are. And don't make me look too square, okay? Just normal.'

The girls collapse on each other's shoulders. 'Normal's not an option,' giggles Elena. 'No one's that good. But you'll look nice, don't worry. This is the Exi: business but hip.'

Fluke and I grin at each other. The Exi. It's a sign, right?

'Credible,' adds Sophia. 'Sophisticated.'

'Like someone you'd just hand over five grand to?' I say anxiously.

'Gonna be more than that,' Fluke says. 'Rent alone is half a buck a foot.'

'Well, that's not that much.'

'Times a thousand? We've got to clear a grand a month just to keep the lights on and the sharks at bay. More, if we want to get paid.'

I swallow. Spending my life dicking around at Tony's is starting to look better and better. We're not building a treehouse, I know, but I did think it'd be cheaper. All fire and brimstone, and now I'm not so sure. What if surfing really is just a passing trend? But that's what they said about the talkies. Nothing ventured, right?

'Be cool,' he adds. 'Don't pussy out, or blow it all on wine and women, and we'll be jake.'

Elena is trimming his hair now; Sophia and I turn to watch, his eyes squeezed shut as bits of him fall to the floor.

'Don't touch the burns,' I remind her.

'Yeah, and don't cut my ear off.'

'And make sure to—'

Sophia shushes us, 'Don't talk while she's working.'

Elena's good at this, her hands as quick as Fluke's, maneuvering the hair about, into clips, between her fingers, stepping back for a moment to squint at his head like a true artiste. At last she razors his neck down, combs and pats the hair into place.

'You wanna blowdry, *fratell*?'

'Nah, just gimme the mirror.' Looks at himself for a moment, as we all hold our breath. 'Not bad, sis. Nowhere near as faggy as I expected.'

She slaps his arm, plants a kiss on his damp head. Then I'm up.

It's a strange experience, getting your hair cut. Like you went through all this trouble, drank your milk and ate your Wheaties and brushed and washed it, only to turn around and mow it down like a lawn. But it feels good, the kind of touch you don't get from anyone else, like that of a really caring doctor. Mama used to take us to this barber from the old country, and he felt like that. We went on our own for a time, and then I saved the money by hacking away at it myself, with varying results. So it's been a while.

I trust Elena—Fluke looks sharp, in a cleaned-up way: like himself, but also like the sort of person you could take to court as a character witness. I've known her since she was eleven, though, so it's funny to think she could have this skill, be all grown-up like this.

'Tilt your head back,' she says. 'No, like this.' Her fingers gently push my chin up, and the scissors ease their way over my brows, across my bangs, tufts of hair falling on my eyelids and cheeks. Fluke brushes them off. Trust. That's another thing. You're putting yourself in the hands of another person who could kill you in an instant, just plunge the scissors into your neck or something. Don't all those mobsters get killed at the barber's, just when they've relaxed into a nice hot towel? Or shot while eating at their favorite restaurant? Or—why the hell am I thinking this? No one's going to kill me. I don't know. These thoughts pop up sometimes.

'Oh, man,' Fluke says, and there's a smile in his voice.

'Dreamboat, Tommy,' Sophia agrees, and Elena is pulling the towel off, whisking my neck.

'No shave?' I say, eyes still closed. They laugh.

'No call, Peachfuzz,' Fluke says, and I open my eyes. 'Take a look.'

I check the mirror. 'Aww, man. I look like Dennis the Menace.'

Sophia pats her own impeccably bouffed black hair, dismayed. 'Oh, no you don't, Tommy, you look handsome! Elena, fix his cowlick.'

'No, I look okay. Just not used to it. Sorry, Lena.'

'It's all right, Tom. Personally, I think you look good. Trustworthy.'

'True fact,' says Fluke. 'I'd buy a used car from this man. Not Mayhem, but maybe a Ford.'

'Booo,' I tell him. 'FoMoNoGo.'

'Aahh, bite me, Bolshie.'

'Well,' I stand up, brush off. 'That's that, then. Let's go get ourselves a slice of that good old American pie.'

'Picture first,' says Sophia. She's got the Polaroid ready, so we crowd in together, me still twitching off the itch of clippings. *Flash*. We crane over each other's shoulders as Sophia waves the picture back and forth, blowing on it softly.

I can't get over the developing process, watching the grey emulsion give birth to these ghosts, outlines filling in with color and detail, then after a minute, our selves—there we are, tiny and glowing. We do look cute, I admit, bangs rounded and brushed long over to the side, sides fading to a short back. But like two guys who could run a business? I dunno.

'Wanna eat?' Fluke asks, opening the fridge. 'We got ziti and peppers.'

'Nah,' I say. 'My stomach kinda hurts, just want to hit some waves.'

'Well, let's go then. How's Georgia doing?'

'Sweet. Pulled her first cutback yesterday, can you believe? Right out of the blue, zoom! I mean, she wiped, but still. She's better than I've seen anyone start out, really.'

'Better than Brackie?'

Lady Bracknell isn't her real name, of course. It's Estelle Harriman, a dignified matron type, likes dogs and golf, without being too butch about it. Rich leather queen; husband owns a chain of stores, both her sons surf, she took to it and is way better than they are now. Super pretty for her age, she rips the Pipe and is buddies with Rabbit Kekai, so we're all in awe. Doesn't socialize with us much, but we like to watch her work; even Ricky gives her dues. Plays the noble, aloof queen to his moody king, and they book-end the beach, rarely saying a word to each other—but she invites him to all her parties, and he shows up and robs her blind, and it's cool, she just thinks it's funny. Relationships with Ricky are rarely pure, and never simple.

'I think she could get there, you know? My little Amazon.'

'She's a keeper, all right. You really lucked out there, you fuck.'

'Yeah, well, you gotta get up earlier, Birdman. Shall we?'

The guys, naturally, are in shock. Fluke blows them off with the claim that we're starting a band, and Ricky looks at our hair for a while, running his thumb back and forth over the stubble on his upper lip, saying nothing. We catch some great sets—the Santa Ana's are in early, devil winds blowing up the waves, air and sea near indistinguishable in their warmth. Everyone's allergies are acting up, but my stomach calms down to the point where I'm able to scarf down two bowls of chili and a slice of pie at the diner. Stare down at the empty dishes for a while, lost in all this. My stomach is bursting, but at least my head is clear.

Wide awake in bed that night, Ray snoring softly. Realtor tomorrow, then we meet with Mr. Fallucci that evening to draw up a business plan for the bank. I'll drop by Dave Sweet's for some industrial espionage, ask him about suppliers. Be straight with him, though; he won't be happy with the competition, but he's always been decent to us. I should probably get a suit.

A suit! I'm about to ask the bank for five grand, and I don't have the money for a damned suit. Good grief. I sit up, stomach aching again. Chili was not the wisest choice.

143

thought. I turn over half my check every payday like clockwork, but am starting to realize it doesn't go that far. It's all been on her, the rent and food, clothes and all the rest, for seven years after Grandpa's insurance ran out. Dad's never given her one thin dime.

'Tomas,' she says. 'It's half midnight. Wherefore are you up?'

Her accent thickens like that, when she's tired. Or angry, or when she's excited and happy, which is not often enough. I want it to be more, you know? I want to take care of her, give her some time to put her feet up. She gets to have a life, too.

'I have a stomachache,' I tell her. 'Wherefore are *you* up?'

Gestures at the bills. 'I like to do it late at night. It feels clean, *ja*? Then I sleep like a baby. Shall I make you some chamomile tea?'

'Like Peter Rabbit? I can do it.' I put the water on, take a deep breath. Now or never. 'Mama, I want to tell you something.'

'What is it?' She looks alarmed; these words have rarely given her cause for much else.

'No, no, it's a good thing. Big. But good, I hope.'

'You're getting married! To this girl I have never met! Oh, Tomas, no— tell me she's not—'

'No! Nothing like that, don't flip! I'm going into business. With Eddie.'

'Oh, ho, is that all? *Das ist schön.* Will you sell lemonade on the beach?'

Ouch. 'No, this is serious. We're opening a store together.'

She takes her glasses off to stare at me like I've fallen from the moon. 'But what—where?'

'Venice. We'll make and sell surfboards, and all sorts of other stuff.'

'But who will buy such things?'

'Plenty of people, Mama. Really a lot right now. It's gotten huge.'

144

'A store, though? From where will you get the money?'

'A business loan.'

'From the bank?'

'Sure, from the bank. What do you think, from the mob?'

'But Tomas, it's...I don't know. It's a big risk, *ja*?'

The kettle shrieks behind me, and I pour the water into two cups of tea, bring them over.

'It is a big risk, Mama. That's why my stomach hurts.'

Her face softens, and she puts a hand on mine. 'Not to worry, Tomas. It will be a success.'

'Then why am I scared?' I have to tell someone; I don't know how I got myself into this.

'It is a big step, but it will go well.'

'How do you know?'

She shrugs. 'Remember when you wanted to go on the hike with the Boy Scouts in Yosemite, and I said no?'

'And I sulked all weekend, and they all came home with salmonella and poison ivy, and Chuck Krinshansky fell off a cliff and broke his arm? Yeah, pretty hard to forget that one.'

'And the first time you brought Eddie home for dinner?'

'You said he would be a good friend to me.'

'And was he?'

I nod. Smile a little, nod again. 'So you're a witch, then.'

'Eh,' she shrugs. 'Maybe. But a good witch.'

'Best in the West. Okay, I feel a little better.' And I do. My stomach has begun to unclench.

'Drink your tea now, liebling, and go to bed. We both have long days tomorrow. And Tomas?'

'Yeah?' I blow lightly on the tea and sip it; it spreads through me, warm and soothing, tasting of sleep.

'Bring her to dinner on Friday. I want to meet this Georgia of yours.'

'Okay, Mama. I'll ask her.' And...there goes my stomach. Damned chili.

Fluke checks his watch for the third time, worried. 'I know we said we'd meet her here. Think she got the right address?'

'It's her...you know, thing. Property. She probably does.' I yawn, rub the sleep from my eyes, and palm my aching abdomen. We're on Horizon, by the beach. Foot traffic looks good. Loads of kids milling around, tan and lovely, trying to look as cool as their parents' fat wallets will permit. Fish in a barrel, baby.

'You were right. She probably thought I was some punk, pulling a—'

'Excuse me, are ye noat Mr. Fallucci? The fella I spoke to on the phone yesterday?' Our realtor: not merely a chick, but a serious fox. I nudge Fluke, and he says, 'Yes, that's me.'

'Sheila Mackenzie.' An accent as brilliant as her curly red hair. Irish?

'Mrs. Mackenzie, how are you this morning?' Fluke recovers quickly. 'This is my partner, Tom Beck.'

'Just the Miss will dae nicely, thanks.' *Dae.* Scots, wa-hey—and single. She fumbles a key ring out of her purse, and Fluke gives her a hand with the rusty riot gate, each pulling a screeching accordion shutter to one side. Security's nice, though a little WD-40 wouldn't hurt.

'Now, this particular property is going for a song.' She holds the door for us and goes into her spiel, flicking on the light. 'Bit of a fixer-upper, but bones are sound as a pound. Drywall, a few coats of paint, and she's golden. Are ye good with your hands then?'

The desire to crack wise forms over Fluke's head like a cloud; I step in. 'We do okay.'

'And what is it ye're planning to sell, if I may ask?'

'Surfboards.'

'Oh aye! You're surfers then?'

'Oh, aye,' says Fluke. 'Aye. We be.'

'Are ye making fun of my accent, lad?' She looks amused.

'He can't help it,' I hurry to explain. 'It's magical flowers, every time you open your mouth. You must sell a lot of houses. Been here long?'

'Oh aye, but some things die hard, ye ken? Tell me about surfing, then.'

Fluke and I glance at each other. He knows I'll just rattle on about Tom Blake till she's comatose, so he gives her a rundown of surf culture and our plans for the place, while I wander around. She wasn't kidding, it's a real mess. Empty boxes and bottles, a few broken chairs amidst a snarl of yellow crime tape. Half the wall's torn out in the back. But the floors are solid hardwood, and if the price is low enough, a few days' elbow grease could save us a ton.

Pipes are intact, thank God. Toilets work, faucets are chugging rusty, but all the lights go on. Check the cupboards: no sign of rats or roaches. There's a cash register up at the counter, big black sucker that looks to be from the thirties. I play around until I've figured it out, and Fluke comes over, picks a penny off the floor, hands it to me with a wink.

'Man, I like this place already,' I whisper. 'Feels like us. Even smells like it should. Salt and sawdust.'

'Price is right,' he whispers back.

'We should look at the other sites, though.'

Sheila coughs. 'I'm afraid there's a reason it's priced this low.'

We look over at her, half-holding our breath.

'It's a bit macabre, and I probably shouldnae tell ye.' We wait.

'We're not legally obligated fir a lease, and my boss'll have my head, but ye're nice lads, and I couldnae bear it.'

'What is it?' Fluke folds his arms over his chest. I knew there was going to be something.

'Last tenants were running a restaurant. Two brothers. Got into a wee bit of a scrap over a girl, wound up shooting each other. Tragic, it was. Most hear that and want naught to dae with the place.'

I exhale a laugh. You never know with Venice; thought she was going to say it was condemned, or built on an oil or sewage pipe about to blow. Haunted is fine.

'No worries,' Fluke says. 'Tom's a good fellow, he'd never shoot me.'

'I might,' I qualify. 'With sufficient provocation. This one threatened to vote for Nixon, and the rat bastard had me going for weeks. Weeks!'

'No regrets,' he chortles. 'Nada. Thought you were going to lose your damned mind.'

I poke him. 'We do like it. And we'll try not to shoot each other.'

We go look at the other places, just to be sure. One's too far from the beach, and the other's way too big, and the lease is twice as much.

'Methinks Goldilocks here hit it on the first try,' Fluke says to Miss Mackenzie as she closes up behind us. I nod, but something's not right. This was too easy. Some major obstacle is going to hit us hard, when we're already bound and committed.

'It's $37.50 off.'

'What?'

'Per month, per body, oan the lease. And nay, I'm noat making it up.'

Fluke and I stare at each other. Seventy-five bucks. We just hit some kind of morbid realty jackpot.

'We'll take it,' he says, and I nod, affirmative.

We walk her back to her car, where she gives us each a business card and takes Fluke's number down to call him in the unlikely event of an even better deal. He gazes after her as she disappears down Ocean, and I nab him as he's about to wander out into traffic.

'Don't hit on the realtor, Romeo. Least not till we're done here, okay?'

'*Moi*? The very model of a modern major gentleman?'

'Please, Fluke. I know that look.'

'Fine, one week, and I'm asking her out. I mean, Jeez, did you *see* that?'

I'm about to rib him when a flare of pain hits hard. I gasp and clamp my hand to my side. Holy shit, that hurt.

'Whoa,' Fluke says, grabbing my arm. 'You okay?'

'M'fine,' I manage. 'Just my stomach again.'

'Always with the bellyaching.' He puts a hand to my forehead. 'Hold up, you feel pretty hot.'

'Don't hit on me either, okay?'

'I'm not kidding, asshole. We haven't even secured the loan yet—how the hell do you have an ulcer *already*? Wanna sit down?'

'Nah, really, it's fine. Should head home, though. See you tonight?'

'Yeah, after dinner. Pop says it's simple, just draw up the projections and overhead financial stuff, then type it up to show the bank.'

'Okay then, I'll see you around seven.'

'Aces. Go home, take some Alka-Seltzer. And Tommy?'

'What?'

'Stop worrying, ya big galoot. You've had this look on your face for days now like you're about to explode—and this is gonna be a cakewalk. Bank of Italy, my dad knows the loan guy from Knights of Columbus.'

I grin. 'The Guinea Conspiracy comes through for us at last.'

'Exactly. We told him it was for sporting goods, cause surf'll be the kiss of death with these guys. So we're in like Flynn on the money end—and the rest will just be fun. Otherwise we shouldn't be doing it, right?'

'Okay, gotcha. Fun or bust.'

We're getting there, I guess. Sidewinding towards this like two knights in a game of chess. I never was very good at chess, though—too many options. Unlike surfing, it wasn't that much fun for me. And we still haven't told Ricky.

I take a long nap that afternoon and have dinner for the first time in weeks with Ray and Mama, who want to hear about the new business. Don't want to jinx it, but I dole out a little, including the new property and how we'll fix it up. Start getting excited, too, beginning to gush as I see my stoke reflected in their eyes. It's funny, this back-and-forth of energy. Worry conveys itself to others, spiraling into bad things actually happening, but so does the good stuff—and it's always neat to share it with someone you love. Ray has his own news: his solar project won first place in the Science Fair, and he's taking it to State.

'Ray, that's righteous,' I say. 'Gonna save the world, you big nerd.'

'Aww, g'wan,' he says, but I can see how pleased he is. 'We can't all be bums like you.'

We rag each other as Mama makes coffee and brings it to the table.

'Say, you look pretty tonight, Mater,' Ray says. 'Hot date?'

He's kidding, of course. But she says nothing, and Ray and I turn to each other, eyes full of surprise and a little consternation. She hasn't so much as mentioned another guy since Dad.

'All right, you slyboots,' I say. 'Out with it, pronto. Can't believe you've been letting us rattle on.'

'Just a movie, with a man I met.'

'Where'd you meet him?' I say. 'What's his name?'

Ray adds suspiciously, 'What does he do? Is he a good person?'

Are we going to have to kick his ass?

'His name is Charles, a fireman. I met him on an investigation.'

'Charles what?'

She sighs a little, resigned. 'Brown.'

'You're dating Charlie *Brown*?' Ray whoops, unable to believe our good fortune, and we drum on the table and serenade her with the Coasters until she shushes us.

'Behave yourselves. He is not a Peanut, not a clown. He is a very nice, very serious gentleman. You are not to make fun of his name.'

'Sorry, Mama. But are you serious about him?'

'No, I am a wild girl, just out for kicks with Good-Time Charlie.'

We snicker. This is a huge step, and brave. No wonder she looks lighter lately; the things people get up to right under your nose!

'All right.' I drain my coffee. 'I better jet. Have a good time. And Mama?'

'Yes?'

'Watch out for that little red-haired girl, okay? She's a sneaky one.'

Ray snorts, she bats at me, and I'm out the door. Good news all around, buoying us up together. It's about fucking time.

'Think we should we round it up to six?' Fluke asks, hunched over the typewriter. 'Just in case?'

'I don't know,' I say. I'm lying on the couch, trying to swallow the acid rising in my throat. I'm definitely coming down with something. Soon as we're done here I'm going to bed. 'I guess. Five-five already seems like a lot, though. How does this loan stuff work, anyway? I mean, what if we can't pay it back? Do they just take all our boards and T-shirts, or do they break our kneecaps, or what?'

He darts a look at his dad. 'Pop's putting the house up for collateral.'

'What?' I sit straight up. 'Mr. Fallucci, you can't do that.'

'It's all right, Tom. I've known the guy since high school; he's not gonna take my house.'

'No, because no way am I letting you do this. It's too big a risk.'

'Calm down, son. I know what I'm getting into. There's some money socked away, so if you boys have a hard month, I'll chip in till you're on your feet again. And there's going to be a few hard months, believe me; that first year is a bitch. Running a business is not for the birds—you can't nine-to-five it. Gotta work your ass off. But I believe in you two, or I wouldn't be putting myself on the line like this.'

'It's all going to be on us, though, Tom,' says Fluke, leaning back in the chair. 'I know you won't flake on me, but you need to get this straight before we go in there tomorrow—in or out?'

'Uh...wait. Just give me a sec, okay?'

Put my head in my hands, trying to breathe, a clammy sweat against my fingers. That weird heat rises in my gut again, spreads through me, and then I feel it all coming up. Dash for the bathroom, reaching the toilet just in time as it explodes out of me in a sour flood, spasms wringing my body clean of what feels like everything I've ever eaten. The pain is back, a hot knife stabbing and twisting inside, and Jesus, this hurts, it hurts, it's really bad. I can't do this. Moan into the toilet bowl, tiles cool on my knees, the room tilting and closing in. Retch again, come up dry. Few more cramps, but I think that's it. Rise shakily to my feet and totter over to the sink, splash water on my face.

The guy in the mirror isn't a businessman, just a kid. A sick, scared little boy with goofy hair and freckles. Don't know who the fuck I think I'm fooling with this shit. We should've told Ricky, been straight with him from the start. He'd have talked us down, and we'd be fine, back on the beach instead of teetering on this cliff, about to step into oblivion. Even Wile E. Coyote always realizes at some point he's not standing on anything but air; that all his drive and Acme trickery aren't going to save him from falling to his death.

Rub some toothpaste on my gums, eye the brushes lined up, each in their own place in the chrome holder on the wall. Eight people, I'll be putting out on the street. Gargle, rinse, spit into the sink. Eight people who believe in me with all their hearts, willing to bet their house on me not screwing this up. I can't pussy out on them.

Open the door to find Leo: spurs, hat, Lone Ranger mask and all.

'Well, howdy, pardner,' I say weakly. 'What's going on?'

'Ain't your day, varmint,' he informs me, and I'm inclined to agree.

His capgun comes up then, and it all slows down, the frames of a movie crawling to a stop until the deceit of motion is revealed, the cruel trick of flick after flick deluding us into a sense of progress.

Bang! goes the gun. Bang!

The sound echoes off the tiles as the pain erupts, blasting right through me. I cry out and grab at the wall, crumple to the floor, not sure myself if this is a game anymore, but as the light fades I hear Leo screaming, 'Eddie! Help! Pop! Oh, God, get in here, I killed Uncle Tommy!'

The fear in his little voice! I long to tell him I'm fine, honest, it wasn't him, I'm just playing around, but the agony is everywhere and my mouth is mute with it, all sight and sound rushing away in waves of bright burning pain, out and out and out until I'm gone.

It is the smell that awakens me, I think. That sweet burnt-flesh odor of hamburgers grilled just right, slathered with ketchup and mayonnaise, piled high with pickles and onions, crisp lettuce and tomatoes on a toasted-just-so sesame-seed bun that's soaked up all that good meaty grease. The thought of it on my tongue is making me drool. And that's how I come to open my eyes and see Ricky, kicked back in a chair only two feet away, really going to town on the sucker.

Oh.

I'm dead, I guess, and Hell is going to be guiltily watching Ricky eat a burger for all eternity. It's surprisingly cool and dark for Hell, the light from the hall the only illumination.

153

'Gimme some.' The voice is barely a croak. My throat feels bruised.

'Hey!! You're alive! Nurse, get in here—Ray's awake!'

Ray? He whispers, 'You're Ray for awhile. Just be cool.'

The nurse bustles in, shines a light in my eyes and checks my blood pressure. As she puts the cold stethoscope to my heart, I ask for water, and Ricky pours me some.

'Drink it slowly, through the straw,' she orders. 'Hold it in your mouth first to warm it up.'

'Will someone tell me what's going on?' I rasp, then suck like a maniac. Ow, fuck. Slowly. 'Where's Fluke? Where am I? And...what time is it?'

She shoots a glance at her watch. Writes on her clipboard.

'It's 4: 45 AM. Can you tell me your name?'

'I'm Ray Beck.' And I am. I just don't know why. Suck again.

'You're at the Marina Cedars-Sinai; you had appendicitis. There was pain for a few days before you got here, nausea, a fever. Bad, right? You didn't tell anyone, though, and then your appendix burst, so it's going to take a lot longer to heal. But you're conscious, which is an excellent start. Next time you're hurting like that, say so, okay?'

'Damned straight,' growls Ricky. 'Out for days. Thought we'd lost you.'

'Where is everybody?' Looking around, I can see traces now; roses in vases, scent mingling with the burger, vanished down Ricky's gullet. On the bedside table, my worn *Fellowship of the Ring*, an issue of 'Surfer,' half a dozen get-well cards and an optimistic stick of Parowax.

'Sent them all home, man.' He yawns. 'Your mom was worn ragged, and Fluke's been by your bed the whole time saying non-stop rosaries. Rest of the guys got banned last night for playing wheelchair bowling in the hall. Your girl was here, but—'

'Georgia? She came?' Try not to sound too eager. Sip some more.

'Yeah, both days. Daddy put his foot down about staying overnight.'

154

Before she leaves, the nurse switches over my IV feed of antibiotics and injects some stuff into the line. What is it? Ohhh. Something good. Something really, really good. I feel all the tension and pain melt away, all problems disappear. A filial warmth toward Ricky fills my heart. We watch her leave, then I lean in.

'All right, debrief me, Catboy. Why am I Ray?'

He answers low. 'It was Fluke's idea, and pretty genius, though the rest of us did our part. He and your dad ran every light on the way here—'

'*My* dad?' My heart lurches.

'His, I mean. What'd I say, yours? Dads, shit, who can keep track? At any rate, they race you in, and Fallucci Senior's screaming at the docs to get you into OR toot sweet, and poor old Fluke's so rattled that, gosh, he went and put Ray's name on the form. You know Ray, right? The one who's still insured under your mom?'

Oh. Damn, Fluke, that's some grace under pressure.

'Bet my mom had a few nasty words for him on the side. You do know she investigates insurance fraud for a living, right?' My heart sinks a bit. The German is *Krankenversicherungsuntersuchung*. Not really looking forward to that conversation.

'Not after he showed her what the bill'd be. Appendectomy, anesthesia, a course of antibiotics and Demerol, plus a week's stay? Gonna be at least $1200, so she may just let this slide. Not to mention whatever it's costing to feed you through a drip.'

'Well, I can take care of that right now. Gimme one of those burgers.'

'No food for a week, buddy. Liquid diet for another. You start chowing down now, you're going to rip your guts all to hell, buy the farm for real this time. Check it out.' He raises the blanket for me, and we both stare down at my bandaged torso, draining blood and pus into a tube.

'But I'm *hungry*,' I moan.

Look longingly over at the crumpled Bob's Big Boy wrapper. I just want to lick it a little. 'Lucky to be alive' doesn't mean much when you feel like this, so hollow inside it seems like you'll never be fed again. Alone but for the one guy I don't really want to face right now

A week in the hospital. Two without food. Can't believe Mama is letting us get away with this grift. That no one's figured it out. You think you know people, right? She could lose—I don't know what, but there'd be major repercussions for sure. No one can find out, ever. Poor Mama. It's always something with me. I try to look as Ray-like as possible, sinking further down into the pillows as the Demerol takes hold.

'Ricky?' I say drowsily.

'Yeah?'

'Can we call my mom? And Georgia and Fluke?'

'Let them sleep, man. I'll go out and call at six. All of them.'

'Ricky?'

'Yeah?'

'Can you open the curtains? I wanna see the sunrise.'

It's better when you're facing west and can't see the source: like the world decided to lighten up all on its own. He opens the curtains, and we regard from a new angle this scene we've watched together so many times, the black brushed away by tentative tinges of grey, whispers of pink and orange illuminating the streets. It can take an hour for the sun to come up, but for once, we've got nothing but time.

"Nature's first green is gold," I murmur. "Her hardest hue to hold." Can't remember...something-something, fade away. Flower? Leaf?

Ricky casts me a sidelong glance; my fingers suddenly long to touch his crow's feet. "So Eden sank to grief," he says reluctantly.

"So dawn goes down to day.' Never figured you for a Frostie, man.'

'Yeah, well. He's a California boy, and I got the same bullshit education as everybody else, didn't I?'

'You're one of the good guys, Ricky,' I tell him. 'You are, I swear. Not perfect. But good.'

'Ah, you're delirious. Get some sleep, hophead.'

'Ricky?'

'Yeah?'

'We're starting a surf shop. Me and Fluke. Didn't want to tell you.'

He nods. 'I know.'

'How?'

'Fluke told me a week ago. Oughtta beat your cloak-and-dagger ass, you little mongrel.'

I laugh softly into the pillow. Fucking Fluke.

'I thought you'd be mad. You know, that we were spoiling the beach.'

He stares out the window for a while, lost in thought. Everything is fading into visibility now, as the sun muscles its way over our heads. Gotta love those fresh starts, when anything could happen. It's cool we get to have one every twenty-four hours.

'I've been doing this for thirty years,' he says at last. 'Shoulda been here back then, cause it was sweet. Best break in the world, always will be. But the crowds, the cops, the crazy...don't know if I can take anymore. May be time for clean cups. Australia's nice. Biarritz, or Jeffreys. Peru, Brazil, Indonesia...whole world of waves out there, Tommy.'

'I'm Ray,' I remind him, sliding into a warm, weary pool. 'Don't leave just yet though, okay?'

'Not going anywhere, man. I'm right here.'

I say no more, asleep. And that's how we tell Ricky.

157

I am fourteen years old, and there is a swastika on Malibu wall.

No, hold up. Let me go back a little further.

It is an unfortunate truth that most surfers have shitty dads, or none at all. Fluke was the only one I knew of with a proper one, someone you could rely on and love. And Ricky, of all people, got to have two dads.

But it was one of those gifts, you know? Because there was his real dad, Mr. Zoltan Morrow—*Zoltan*? I'd asked Fluke when he'd told me, and yes, Ricky's dad was apparently a Flash Gordon villain, but was actually this nice Hungarian guy, a snazzy dresser and suave with the ladies, the way Ricky could be when he wasn't bent on being, well, a Flash Gordon villain—and then there was his stepdad, who really was a villain. Flash Gordon surfed, by the way. So did Tarzan and Buck Rogers. And so did Edgar Funk, Ricky's stepdad, the original Surf Nazi himself.

I don't mean 'Nazi' in the sense that he was really into surfing and territorial about his waves, though he was. Or that he was a fascist son of a bitch, a bit too quick with his fists—though he was those things, too. No, Edgar Funk was a straight-up, goose-stepping, card-carrying member of the Bund, the American Nazi Party. It's not as uncommon as you'd think, even in our mellow ranks. Usual suspects, though every so often someone will come at you from out of left field. But Funk was also the best goddamned surfer in the state, which at the time meant the country—although I imagine if he'd lived to see Hawaii join up, they would've shown his *haole* ass a thing or two.

And more than anything in the world, Ricky loved to surf, even as a kid. Zoltan had taught him at four when they came over from Hungary, and he'd ride on his own down in San Onofre while his dad hung out with that crowd, dicking around in their aloha shirts with their ukeleles and beach bunnies. In 1940, though, his parents divorced, and Edgar Funk wound up marrying Ricky's beautiful Beverly High debutante of a mom, taking the boy under his crazy violent wing—and the rest, as they say, was history.

He beat Ricky. He beat Ricky's mom. Zoltan would pack Ricky off to military school, but he kept running away or getting kicked out, and finally just wound up coming home again; where that was by then was anyone's guess. The only child of only children, as if the family were trying to drum itself out of existence, he kept getting passed around, the hot potato no one wanted. He'd get into these massive arguments with Funk, or try to stop him from killing his mom during one of *their* big screaming drunken fights, and Funk would put him through walls and windows, like those saloon brawls in the Westerns, except for the part where all the extras get up and walk away.

Ricky'd flee to his grandma's house—the only woman he ever truly loved in his life—and Funk would come tearing over and drag him out by the hair as Grandma screamed at him in Hungarian, cussing out this lunatic invader and flailing at him with her broom. Funk would throw him in the car—then they'd go surfing like nothing had happened.

And the things he did to that kid—don't get me wrong, we all grew up under dads with fists and belts, even Fluke got the occasional beating from his ma—but not like that, and the stuff we heard about was only the tip of the iceberg. There was a rumor going around that he'd made Ricky get circumcised when he was twelve, which, considering Funk's position on Jews, was pretty goddamned weird in and of itself.

Here's the thing about Nazis, though—there's no reasoning with them, as they're completely deranged. I don't say that cause they're trying to kill me, though I'd really prefer they not do that, but cause every one—from Hitler down to the lowliest Murphy Ranch lackey with his shaved head and Iron Cross tattoo—is not dealing from a full deck in any way. Try to coax them out into the light of logic, you'll just wind up getting sucked into their demented swamp yourself.

But Funk could get away with it. The cops all thought he was aces, big law-and-order man, and if his wife and kid kept falling downstairs, well, they should be more careful next time. He was preaching a gospel a lot of Americans wanted to hear, not just the ignorant and down-trodden. Charles Lindbergh, Walt Disney and Henry Ford were national heroes; wealthy, well-educated men—and serious Jew-haters all. Ford passed out thousands of copies of *Elders of Zion* to his workers, and his book *International Jew* was Hitler's bible.

159

Even Roosevelt didn't give a damn about us, he knew all about the gas chambers and refused to bomb the tracks to the camps. Shit, he turned the St. Louis around in '39 to send nearly a thousand Jews back to their deaths in Germany. Little kids were on that boat, even younger than my aunt Rachel. It was a hard thing to discover about the man who'd always been my working-class hero, maybe the only president who ever did something for the little guy. The polio was bad enough—but those cruel feet of clay were far worse.

There had always been a refuge we could flee to when things got dire: Spain, Holland, Poland, Arabia. Not this time. Every country on the planet turned the boat away. All the boats. My people were sentenced to die by the rest of humanity. The Brits wouldn't even let us into Israel. We knew where we stood, after that.

Back in 1933, there'd been a big Nazi rally in downtown LA. Organized by German immigrants, it attracted all kinds of groups—the Klan, the Bund, the Silver Shirts, America First, and the big one, the Friends of New Germany. Leon Lewis, a lawyer, WWI vet and founder of the Anti-Defamation League, was startled enough by the storm of fascist hysteria that he recruited four couples to infiltrate the organizations.

The agents' reports were even more damning: not only were these guys planning to overthrow the US government, but they were going to kill every Jew in the city. Father Coughlin and Gerald L.K. Smith had been spewing venom over our radios for years, so this should've come as no surprise, yet it did. You want to believe California is different. It's not.

Lewis went to LA Police Chief Edgar Davis with solid evidence about the groups' intent to take over the US mints and armories and conduct a mass extermination. Davis cut him off, I kid you not, to defend Hitler. Germans couldn't compete economically with Jews, he claimed—who were all Reds anyway, far as he was concerned. They'd been forced into this. Now get the fuck out of my office. He got the same response from the Sheriff and the FBI.

Lewis filed a suit with the Supreme Court, though it meant exposing his operatives as witnesses—and the judge decided in favor of the Nazis.

In 1934, Lewis and Senator Samuel Dickstein formed a group to ferret out Nazi subversives in the US: the House of UnAmerican Activities. As you may recall, that ended real well for us, too.

J. Edgar Hoover decided that Reds posed a more dire threat to America than Nazis, though Hitler targeted LA from the start, agents bearing millions of dollars and Nazi propaganda streaming into this mecca of cultural influence, aircraft factories and bases. They recruited on the street, infiltrated the movie studios and fired all the Jews, sabotaged the Lockheed lines—and no one tried to stop them. By '39 there were over 800 Nazi groups active in the US, with millions of members. We were sitting ducks.

After being shut down, Lewis went into high-drive. Upped recruitment, and met with Irving Thalberg and Rabbi Magnin to raise funds from LA Jews reluctant to rock the boat. Over the next decade, his crack team foiled plots to drive through Boyle Heights and gun us down, gas our homes, and kill Hollywood figures from Louis B. Mayer and Samuel Goldwyn to Al Jolson and Jew-adjacent Charlie Chaplin. They turned the Nazi groups on each other with well-placed innuendo, so that their plans to defeat the war effort and ensure German victory fell through. It was great. If one man was responsible for not letting these fuckers take over the world, it was Leon Lewis, whom Hitler had dubbed 'the most dangerous man in America.'

The public didn't find out till years later. The authorities knew, and did nothing. We were nice and polite about it, as usual, didn't fire a shot—but we were on our own. We were *always* on our own.

So, yeah, it could happen here.

Still might, if you get the right sellers. Pretty people can always get away with murder, and Funk was indisputably pretty, tall and blonde and *Übermenschy*, the way a surfer is supposed to look. Ricky, on the other hand, was just this short swarthy kid who'd do anything for a pat on the back from the guy, and I mean anything. He emerged from that fire one of the best surfers in the world—and, though it pains me to say, it was because of that, not in spite of it. Brutality and an iron will can bring genius to the fore, if it's in there.

But Christ, did it come at a cost. Funk was gone by the time I met Ricky—fucked his back up in some drunken car crash, no longer able to surf, he disappeared into Mexico and died a year later under suspicious circumstances—but his insanity will haunt his stepson for the rest of his natural life. Ricky always said he was murdered, and who knows, maybe he killed the bastard himself. Fluke and I were the only ones who ever dared suggest this, and if the Fiasco Kid were in a good mood, he'd smile and claim that he could neither confirm nor deny.

But there we are. Mid-summer, 1957. I know all this stuff, and yet. I am fourteen years old, and there is a swastika on Malibu wall. On *our* wall.

I'm not blind, of course. I've seen them before. We really went off on a Nazi kick after WWII—our dads brought home captured helmets and flags, they marched through our newsreels for years, and their broken crosses appear in clumsily-inked incarnations on bathroom walls and notebooks to this day. Cause they were cool, you know? What could be more exciting than a Nazi, let alone hordes of them, untrammeled by the chains of civility and compassion that held us back for centuries?

Those of us that were born later and didn't have to fight them got off on it, too, running around shooting at each other, yelling *Achtung* and *Mach schnell*, and yeah, I was one of them. It was fun, though if Mama or Grandpa Joe had caught me—well, they wouldn't have had to do anything at all, as I would've died right then and there from the shame. But that was part of the thrill, I think—getting away with something this slimy. It palls, however, and I grew out of it quick.

Still, I couldn't help but feel like this wasn't my fight. Technically, I'm not a Jew—I've never been to synagogue nor donned a prayer shawl; never eaten a bagel nor plotted to take over the world's banks. The only Yiddish I know is from 'Mad' magazine. It's just me in here. I'm not a threat to anybody, and anyway, not really a Jew. Not really.

Dr. Stein didn't know that, though. He was the guy who'd removed my appendix at Cedars-Sinai and kept close tabs on me ever after, stopping in each morning for a chat. Young guy, only a few years older than me, with a beard and a yarmulke fastened to his curly brown hair with a bobby pin, but he's pretty hip.

The appendix is a vestigial organ, he informs me. No one knows quite why it's there, but I could survive just fine without it. He seems more concerned when I ask him where I could get Demerol on the street.

'Kidding,' I say. 'Ha-ha. It just feels...calm. Like I can breathe again.'

Eyes me for a moment, a little sadly. 'Don't get caught up in that mess, buddy. Drugs are a sucker's game. If you're experiencing anxiety, you should talk to someone.'

'What, like a shrink?' I bristle, insofar as one can bristle in the throes of a Demerol high. It's like trying to pick a fight while swathed in cotton candy. 'I'm not nuts.'

'Ahh, come off it, that's not what psychologists are for. Jury's still out, of course, but talk therapy doesn't actually help the bona fide insane. A shrink's just someone for regular people to talk to, who doesn't judge you, and can offer constructive solutions.'

I shrug. I have Fluke for that—it's called a friend. This fucking town. Everyone's seeing a shrink here; even the shrinks have shrinks. It solves nothing but your excess cash issues.

'You aren't doing drugs, are you?'

'Little grass now and then.' He scoffs.

'Actual drugs, I mean. Heroin, cocaine. Recent studies have shown that marijuana does not, in fact, lead to Communism.'

'Yeah, in my case it's more the other way around. But no, I'm not.'

'Interesting reading material, for a Commie.' Nudges the bible.

I blush, busted. 'I was bored. Don't get too excited.'

'Too bad you have to stop halfway through. Only the *goyim* get to read the sequel, find out how it ends.'

'No harm in peeking, though, is there?'

He holds his hands up in mock horror. '*Toyve*. Take my advice, don't bother with all that 'turn the other cheek' nonsense. Never worked out for us. But you're healing up fine. Should be going home in a few days;

we'll give you some aspirin for the pain. Stay off the solids, and you'll be back to surfing in no time.'

And then he is gone, back to his rounds, and if I could feel anything, it'd probably be panic. *Aspirin*? Are you fucking kidding me? A voice in my head points out that I may have a problem here; I point out that it should go fuck itself, and return to the Queen for a Day melodrama of the Book of Job. I don't let it slip to Stein that I'm not Mr. SuperJew, though. He's cool, you know? I want him to think well of me.

I stare at the swastika, half-hypnotized. It's pretty well-done —usually you get some sort of garbled mess with the legs pointing the wrong way, as if the artist were rushed or ashamed, but this one is bold and black, its lines clean, pure, almost beautiful. Someone really took their time here, creating a threshing machine that could take down anything in its path. I could just walk away, shrug it off.

I could. But I don't.

Walk into the nearest hardware store, the bell jingling, greeted by that one-of-a-kind odor of lube and lumber, rope and tin. Simple measures for your problems, easily solved. Here's a washer, no more leaky faucet. Box of nails and some two-by-fours, you've got your fence back.

'I have a quarter,' I tell the guy behind the counter, who looks like he expects me to stick up the joint. Not sure why. All I'm wearing is cut-offs, not a lot of room for a piece. 'How much paint will that get me?'

His eyes narrow. 'Depends what you want it for.'

I gnaw at my lip, at a loss for a credible lie, then just tell him the truth. Fuck it. Not like the world could think any less of us.

His face grows hard. He hands down a pint of grey and a cheap brush, waves off my coin. 'On the house,' he tells me. 'I was at Normandy. You go wipe that filth out before it spreads. Goddamned punks.'

I thank him and head back. Look around; the coast is clear, at least of Ricky. Shake the paint a little, pry it open with my housekey, and start eradicating anti-Semitism, one stroke at a time.

Funk aside, I doubt I'd be dealing with this right now, but for one odd twist of fate. The swastika's been around for thousands of years; the word just means 'lucky charm' in Sanskrit, so when Pacific Systems started manufacturing their big guns, the monster redwood boards they were putting out in the 20's, they burned a swastika into every one, because surfers needed all the luck they could get out there. Cute as a four-leaf clover, it was—and they kept at it right up till '37, when it was becoming clear even to the dimmest that these Nazi guys were not interested in good fortune and righteous waves so much as world domination and racial extermination.

But the boards were everywhere by then, and surfers refused to stop using them just because some useless kooks across the pond had stolen our symbol. The more guff we caught, the more determined we were to hang in there—cause fuck you, that's why. Ironically, this symbol that had come to represent relentless fascist oppression to the rest of the world meant rebellion against the very same, for us. Do not ever tell us what to do. If we're holding a gun to our head, it's our gun, and our goddamned head.

It wasn't just us. Bikers, draggers, pachucos, any thuggish punk on the outs with society could throw a swastika up there for a clear message to the squares who'd rejected them: because fuck you, that's why. Like a pentagram. You know it's just empty posturing, and yet you don't mess around with people who don't give a shit to such a degree that they'd get into bed with the devil.

You can only play at being a monster for so long, however, and the rigid surf ethos was close enough to the Nazis' that it wasn't that much of a flip. Closer you get to the border, the worse it gets, too. Orange County, some of those guys, Jesus wept. Surfing all day, then going out at night to beat up Negros and Mexicans, Jews and queers, which is just...that's what I don't get about hatred. It's not even that it's evil and pointless, it's *exhausting*. Who has the energy for that shit? It's nighttime, for Chrissake! Go the fuck to sleep!

We close ranks around our own, so we put up with that, too—and it does spread. It's appealing, this sense of power, especially when you've been denied it all your life. If you're not that smart or talented or good-looking, it's one way to earn respect. But none of those apply to Ricky.

He of all people does not need to stoop to this, not after dealing with Funk all those years. Messed up as he is, he's still one of the sharpest cats I know—handsome, funny as hell, and could have any girl on the beach, were he interested in anything but the next wave.

And he's...well, he's Ricky Morrow, that magnificent bastard, and never got into the really bad shit, it would compromise his cool. So we let it slide, laughing over his antics and rants, taking pictures of him surfing in full Nazi mufti, trenchcoat and all. We smile and smile and smile and smile...and today, I no longer feel like fucking smiling.

I step back.

You can still tell what it is, so I turn it into a figure eight, a nice infinity symbol. A snake, eating itself. Then hear a voice, that laconic drawl that has never once acknowledged my presence, never once addressed me directly in the two years I've been coming here. Not once.

'My, my, what have we here? Your kindergarten let you bring paint to the beach, Gremberg?'

My hand jags a little, just a little. I go on painting.

'Not too fond of the décor, Jeebie? There's the door, right there.'

He gestures out beyond the wall, to the city we all came here to escape. You can't bar anyone from coming to the beach, not legally. It's a public place, belongs to all of us. But you can sure as fuck make it unpleasant enough that they stop coming. Don't believe me, ask the next Negro you see frolicking in the surf. Not too many, are there? Huh. Wonder how that happened in California, the golden antidote to Mississippi. He doesn't get to do this to us. Doesn't get to do this to *any* of us.

Fuck infinity, I'm just sloshing paint on like Jackson Pollock. He pushes me, hard. I drop the brush. Bend to pick it up, knock the sand off, and keep on painting, not a care in the world. Quite alone on this beach, just me and my concrete canvas. The scent of trouble spreads fast, and I can feel the murmur of people gathering round, slavering over what's sure to be a lynch worth the watch.

He slams me up against the wall, and his voice comes hot in my ear. 'Just apologize and walk away, Roddo. We don't have to do this.'

166

Some tiny part of me is dancing a jig because he knows who I am, but I free my arm and lay on another stroke before he shoves my hand up between my shoulder blades. I go limp for a sec, shocked by the pain, frayed nerves turning to fury. You want to play little Nazi games with me, fuckhead? Fine. Let's play.

My head rears back with everything I've got, to catch him square in the nose. Bellowing with rage, he falls, then jumps up to spin me around, fist slamming into my face so hard my head cracks against the wall—then I'm down and he's stomping me, no more Gentleman Jim, yelling like he's lost his mind, kicking the shit out of me like he's remembering how this was done to him. Fluke and Mysto are pulling him off, holding him back, as I roll over and stagger up, vision white with rage. Hawk blood at his feet.

'*Das ist unser Land,*' I scream, holding up a fistful of sand. '*Unser Land! Du nimmst es nicht,* you fucking Nazi clown! *Und du...du bist nicht mein verfickter Vater! Klar?*'

Throw the sand in his eyes and stalk off. Next thing I know I'm home, head down in the sink, having walked five miles barefoot, bare-chested, covered with paint and blood, probably ranting and punching the air like a madman. Find some turpentine and clean myself up with a rag, the fire seeping into me nothing against this feeling of ferocity. I've never felt like this before. Not just after a fight, after anything. There'll be hell to pay, but oh, was it worth it, for the look on his smug superior face. I'm in the shower when I realize I left my stuff back at the beach. Ah, to hell with it. I'm still grinning when Mama comes home.

'I do not know what this means, 'pearl,'' she frets, fingering my cheek. I keep my shirt on; she doesn't need to see the rest of me.

'I told you before, Mama. It's when you go off the nose. Like diving for pearls, get it?'

'I would not think water could hit you so hard.'

'Water can be very tough,' I say. 'You have no idea.'

I help her get dinner, Ray and I do the dishes after, then we all play gin. Phone rings halfway through our second game. It's Fluke.

Excuse myself, edge into the pantry, close the door and huddle down to stare into the eyes of the Quaker Oats guy, wrapping and unwrapping the cord around my wrist.

'Hey,' I mutter. 'Is Ricky pissed?' Like I care.

'Naw, man. He thinks it's a gas.'

'What?! Really? Fuck you.'

'Yeah, he's mad as a hornet.'

'Oh.' My life, collapsing like the house of cards it always was.

'But the whole beach is talking about it, Tommy. I was on the pier, and these two Marines up from Pendleton asked me if it was true the great Ricky Morrow got shut down by a grem. So that's how he's gonna play this, big yuks. You okay?'

'Hmm, I'm fine. So should I just...lay low?'

'No. Come on back tomorrow, like nothing happened. I'll be here.'

'I'd have to anyway, I guess. I left my, uh, everything, back at the—'

'Yeah, yeah, I got it. Keys, wallet, shoes, board. Your shirt. You know, one of these days—'

'I know, man. You're gonna get tired of picking up after me.'

'And?'

'And I'm a fucking retard.'

'And?'

'And thank you, Fluke.'

'Damn right.' He hangs up.

Mama gives me a ride to the beach the next morning. I pick my way down to the pit, heart pounding in my throat so I can barely breathe. The air is still cool and damp with shreds of mist, and the guys look up from waxing their boards, salute me with grins and chin nods. U-Boy throws me a shaka, and then Ricky comes out of his shack, yawning. Sees me and stops.

Everyone stops then, all these hands frozen in time, and I see Fluke's shoulders tense like a cat's. Think, well, enjoy, because this is the last thing you'll ever see. Goodbye, ocean. We had some pretty sweet times together, didn't we?

Ricky comes over, slow: nose taped up, lip scabbed. Draws his hand gently over my jaw as I try not to wince. His eyes look almost...sorry. Wishful thinking, I know.

'We cool?'

I hate how my voice is shaking. That it's even a question.

He nods. 'We cool.'

Everyone exhales, and we all head out to the break. It's far from over between us, of course; this is, after all, Ricky. There are still goads and jibes, tasteless Holocaust jokes and arguments about the Rothschilds around the fire as everyone groans and begs us to shut up already—but he treats me like a person, with as much contempt and ill-tempered abuse as he does the rest of the crew. Like I actually exist, you know?

And no swastikas ever appear on Malibu wall again.

'Can I see it?'

'Get away from me. You're like some weird little kid with this shit.'

'Fuck you. Stitches are cool, that close to your dick. Chicks'll dig it.'

'Would you quit it already? Trying to suck up some beach here, and I'm on borrowed time.'

'I promised your mom I'd have you home by six, and that you wouldn't go in, or run away, or eat, or talk to strangers, and about a million other *verbotens*, but we've got an hour. How you doing?'

'Holding up.' No danger of me doing any of those things. I barely even made it down, leaning on Fluke's shoulder. Eyes half-closed, I let the incoming tide surge against my ankles, heels sinking into the wet sand. 'Feel pretty good, actually. Kinda high.'

Might as well be broke and drooling at a restaurant; I'm dizzy from the foodless, drugged-out week and being back in the world of fresh air and sun, this close to it all. It's a dubious tonic, though, cause I'd kill to be on a board right now, moving through a wave, not just watching, body amped and aching with temptation.

Like ball players, surfers have very specific stances—you could spot us a mile away just by how we ride. Ricky and I are elegant dancers, working subtly from the hip, a delicate shift of foot against rail, our unconscious hand gestures. Pip's flex, a leaner who steers with his whole body, going so far over you can't believe he isn't going to wipe out, but he always comes back. Almost always. Fluke charges, attacking the wave like he's going to tear it apart, back knee bent low, feet planted sturdy on the board, born to own bigger waves than these. Mysto and U like to clown around and take chances. They wipe a lot, but they pull off some pretty dazzling tricks, too. They never give a heads up—they'll kick-flip, pull spinners and handstands, switch boards, turn turtle and come out the back only to catch the next wave. It's all about the stoke. We just have different ways of getting it.

'Stein said the stitches come out in three days. Can you go in after that?'

'Not for another week or so. Infection and all, and then I'll need to get back in shape.' The world tilts a bit as I open my eyes again, recalibrate. 'Listen. I need a favor.'

'Name it.'

'A few Mills, if you can find some. But I'll settle for anything.'

'Shark days back?'

'Not yet. But they're sitting there, waiting. I can't come off the Demerol with that baby aspirin bullshit they gave me.' My voice is gruff, trying to keep the panic out. 'Just three or four.'

Fluke rubs his chin, pondering. 'I've got some Dex in the van.'

I laugh. 'Nah, then I'll just be energetically grumpy.'

'I'll see if I can't score you something, bring it by tomorrow.'

'No rush.'

'Yeah,' he says. 'Rush.'

That's what we call them, so as not to admit the weakness: shark days. There's only one thing scarier than public speaking or losing your mind, and that's sharks. I get it, sure—they're big animals that come out of nowhere to chew you up, which can be disconcerting. You're far more likely to be eaten by a grizzly or a wolf, or hit by a bullet or a car or lightning, but those aren't even on the fear radar for most of us.

They never sleep. They're super fast. They have cruel weird faces and cold black eyes. And they're the world's most perfect predators, able to smell one drop of blood in a million of water, zip on over and tear you apart with insane teeth. You can't hope for mercy; even if they knew the meaning of the word, I sincerely doubt they'd be on board with it. The only way we can spend this much time in the ocean is by locking this into our brains: this is not a thing that exists in the here and now. When it does, we'll deal with it.

Emotions, especially in crowds, aren't super logical things, and no one wants to start a freakout over nothing. Attacks are rare, but I've talked to people who've survived them. Most do, because sharks aren't even interested in eating us, they just enjoy being assholes—and apparently there isn't as much pain involved as you might think.

It's like getting hit by a silent locomotive, a quick tearing pull. You look down and a sizable chunk of you is missing, and ho-hum, you appear to be bleeding to death, no bigs. Adrenalin rush and blood loss conspire to put you into shock—and that's where it's touch-and-go, because your brain is scoffing that nothing dramatic is going on and not to make a fuss, and it's so sudden that you're too out of it to fight or call for help. Once the pain sets in, you start screaming, trying to paddle in pronto before you bleed out. It hurts, but you're actually in less danger at that point: you know you've got a problem.

That's what those days are like. I'm better at seeing them coming now, but they still hit pretty hard—and there's never any specific sadness. Instead, I'm bowled over by a tank of blank despair, quietly bleeding to death. But I don't want to bother anyone with this thing that, let's face it, isn't a problem, or shouldn't be. It's hard to keep a grip on these two lifesavers: this isn't real, and it's going to pass.

It first started after Grandpa died; whole chunks of my day disappeared, sinking under the surface of this paralytic tar pit. I'd spend hours in the boys' room at school, perched on the john, staring at the graffiti'd vitriol on the stall walls. I couldn't move, didn't see what for. And no one noticed I was gone, which made it even worse.

The bell would ring at 3:15 and I'd go home, sit on my bed and stare at those walls, watching myself seep out onto the floor. I'd think *kitten butterfly little girl dancing,* and my brain would respond, *Holocaust suicide lynching H-bomb.* It wasn't a fair fight. Even if you could keep your kitten safe and burrow out from under all this, you'd look each other in the eye afterwards and wonder, what's the point? So we can keep drawing breath on this brutal, soul-crushing planet? Why waste the oxygen?

Never seemed to know what day it was and went a little deaf and blind, unwilling to let anything in. Stopped drawing, writing, even talking, afraid to let anything out, either. Ray, of all people, was good about it— I don't know if he understood what was happening, but he helped hide it from Mama, nudging me when it was time to speak, set the table, go to bed. He'd come and lie down with me on the rug, pillowing his head on my back so I didn't feel so alone. It meant a lot, though I never told him so at the time.

And this went on for months. Once I got into surf and sex I was able to get on top of it, except for those few days a year, usually in the winter, where it shows up out of the blue and suddenly my leg is gone at the knee, femoral artery spewing crimson into the water. Most people have an unreasonable fear of sharks; I don't. Shark days are another matter, and only Fluke and Ray know how bad they can get.

'Hey,' I say suddenly. 'Hey. Did you ever call her?'

'Call who?'

'Don't play coy with me, comrade. You know who. Realty girl.'

He grins a little. 'We're going out tonight.'

'Hotcha! Where you taking her?'

'I was thinking Chinese, then a walk on the pier. Too booge?'

'Nah, just right. Respectful, and who doesn't like Chinese?' I try not to think of egg rolls dipped in sweet-and-sour sauce, and fortune cookies full of love and lucky numbers. I'm having a Vitamix shake for dinner, maybe Jell-o if I'm feeling festive. 'Gonna get her flowers?'

'Nah, I'm tapped. Think I should?'

'We've got roses in the yard. Throw in some ferns, make a bouquet.'

'Look at you, hidden talents. The orange ones?'

'Yeah. Mama took a flower-arranging class once, it's not that hard. And you save a ton, if you're a dating man.' The water is up to my shins now. 'I'm just glad to see you back in the game.'

Denise aside, Fluke has pretty good taste in girls, but he takes the same approach as he does with waves, charging fast, not really looking where he's going. Case in point: the notorious Lurlene of Pensacola, who did seem nice at first. She had done a few cameos and prints, maybe not the brightest bulb, but cute as a button and obviously very gone on Fluke. They had this passionate thing going for months, and were hard at it one morning when this Navy guy walks in, somewhat taken aback to find his wife in bed with another man.

He was pretty decent about it, in the sense that he let Fluke get dressed on the landing after throwing him down the stairs. We snuck back the next day and waited till the guy left, to retrieve his Zippo and St. Jude's medallion, Fluke grumbling all the while about the indignity of getting his ass kicked by Popeye, and how chicks in general were a treacherous and unreliable species. Lurlene was all full of wide-eyed apologies, and probably would've talked him into a parting quickie had I not been there staring her down. But Fluke was discombobulated enough by the whole affair to lay off for a while, and he's really the kind of guy who needs to be around women to feel alive.

'What do orange roses mean, anyway?' he asks. 'Don't wanna send the wrong message.'

'Red means love; white means purity, or death or something. Yellow is Texas. Orange ones...I dunno, friendship?'

'Well, scrap that then.'

'Don't be a douche. Be her friend first, before you go all crazy with the Roman hands.'

'Hardly running off a stellar record yourself, Miss Lonelyhearts.'

'Nah, trust me, play hard-to-get for once. She's got a brain and a job and no guy, so don't fuck this up. Even if she's not Italian.'

'Ah, don't matter,' he says cheerfully. 'Ma'll hate her no matter what; no one's ever going to be good enough for her *bambino*. And Pop likes the smart ones, so he won't care.'

'Well, obviously. He married your ma, didn't he?'

'Knocked her up,' Fluke whispers. 'Don't ever tell her I told you.'

'Shut the fuck up. Your ma?'

'It's hardly rocket science,' he shrugs. 'Their anniversary's in March, Angela's birthday's in October.'

'You're blowing my mind right now.' I feel dizzy again.

'You shoulda met my nonna. Buried two husbands in Naples, then came over here and took a lover she never bothered to marry. Let's just say quiet time with her gentleman caller wasn't quite as quiet as it could've been. Apples and trees, and I say that with full respect to my ma. This may come as a shock, Tom, but we didn't exactly invent sex.'

'Yeah, but…well, how come they keep making us feel like we did?'

'Cause then we feel guilty, and take out the garbage. How long you waiting with Georgia?'

I say nothing, suddenly fascinated with something far, far out to sea. He nudges me, and I duck my head, smile into my chest.

'Why, you crafty little fucker! When? Wait, no, don't tell me—that day Monroe died. You had that shit-eating grin all over you the next day. Oh, man, I *knew* something was up! And here I thought you were just excited about the shop. I'm hurt, to be honest.'

'I was gonna tell you eventually, I just didn't—'

'Yeah, yeah, big gentleman with your chivalry. Using that poor dead girl as an aphrodisiac. You oughtta be ashamed.'

'Don't,' I say, and stop smiling. 'Don't. It wasn't like that.'

'Ah, don't sweat it, Tommy. She would've dug it. Fitting tribute and all. So do I get to hear all the sweaty pulsating details?'

'No, you don't, perv.' I swat his hand away. 'And let it go already with the fucking scar. One more week, you can look at it to your heart's content for the rest of your life.'

'All right, crankypants. Time for your nap. Ready?'

'No.'

'Come on, man. We'll come back tomorrow if you're up for it.'

Back at his camper, I lean against the door, heart pounding, dark fog rolling into my vision. He gently guides me into the passenger seat.

'Damn you and your sweet talk, I shoulda just taken you straight home. You're skin and bones.'

'No, c'mon, don't say that. You know I needed this.'

'All right, but take it easy, okay? We've got all the time in the world.'

'It's not that I'm ailing, really, it's...' I say, and stop.

'What?'

'Haven't slept for days now, even with the Demerol. I stopped wasting time on pedestrian shit like eating and walking around, so I had all this energy. Just caught up with me for a sec, is all.'

He turns onto the Pac, glances at me. 'What'd you do instead?'

I yawn. 'Can't say. You'll laugh your ass off.'

He shifts into fourth and puts on a burst of speed. He knows I'll crack.

'All right...I read the Bible. It was right there in the drawer. Everybody was asleep and the only other option was a pamphlet about leukemia. And don't give me a hard time—but it's not bad. Battles and heroes and hot girls, poetry and crazy sci-fi shit. It's a real page-turner.'

He grins to himself.

'What?'

'Just lost a bet with my ma, is all. She always said you'd find God.'

'Yeah, don't go all hosanna on me, hombre. It's a good book, all right, but that's all it is—a book.'

'And I'll lay even money this is about Georgia, too. Capitalism, and now that good old-time religion. What's next, Scientology? How's your mom feel about her, anyway?'

'Hard to say. Says she's 'very nice,' but you know Mama. She's got some kind of hair up about her, and won't tell me what it is, or even look me in the eye. It's weird as hell.'

'Well, she never liked any of your girls. Neither did I, but moms are just like that. Doesn't want to see your dumb ass get hurt again.'

'This is different, though. I fucking...I love her, man. It's the real deal. Mama won't say what's bugging her, and it's not like she ever kept her opinions under wraps before.'

Fluke pulls up at a red, punches the car lighter. We're silent as it pops and he fires up a Camel. 'I would say forget it, but she's got that mojo, you know? She's been right about a lot of stuff.'

Flash on two kids standing on ice, moments before it begins to crack. My heart is skipping beats. I don't want to talk about this anymore.

Fluke walks me in, and we throw some flowers together before I send him off to court his Scottish fox. The sea air must've done me good, as I undress, fall into bed and sleep like a dead man. No, not dead. Like a man coming back to life, having survived the sharks and rid himself of outdated vestigial appendages. Ready for it all to begin.

I should nearly die more often. People go all kind on you, revealing truths kept close to their chest, suddenly grasping the brevity of life. Like jump-starting a car, that instant connection. Can't imagine how boring we'd become if we never got to die, you know? Vampires always seem witty and philosophical, but that's only cause they're not actually immortal—every sunrise could spell their doom.

Wake to a warm weight on my chest, that newly familiar scent drifting into my nostrils.

'Hey,' I say, open my eyes. She rolls her chin around to my sternum, blinking at me with a gaze that seems greener today.

'Hey, babe. Just listening to your heart. Sorry. Was that snoopy?'

'More Lucy, I think.' I clear my throat. 'The doctor is in.'

'Poor old Lucy. She got a bum rap.' She drapes a lock of her hair across my lip like a mustache.

'She's a terrible shrink, always telling people what blockheads they are.'

'They should stop being blockheads, then. Hey, how come your mom doesn't like me?'

Oh, boy. I'd hoped she wouldn't notice. 'She's kind of a Lucy herself—not really in the business of liking people. But she's a softie underneath. You'll grow on her.' Shift under her warm weight, run my hands down her shoulders, and she gives me a peck on the nose.

'It's so good to have you back, Tommy. I didn't want to make a big deal, but that was scary. All Fluke said was hospital, so I thought broken leg or something—and when I walked in there I think my heart stopped, cause you looked...embalmed. All those tubes and machines, your face was that awful waxy color, like you weren't there at all. I could barely feel your pulse, and your mom was staring daggers at me like, *you did this to him.* And I sort of...started to cry.'

'Sorry,' I say. 'She has that effect on people.'

'What made it weird was how much she looks like you. It's uncanny. Like a little old Tommy, *J'accuse!* It crushed me, like I really had done this to you somehow, you know?'

'But you didn't.'

'But it felt like I had. Then I couldn't stop, bawling like a baby in front of everybody. I was so afraid if I let go of your hand...'

'But you didn't.' She shakes her head, no.

'You should've been there. Apparently we're all a lot fonder of you than you think. We were all crying a little. Even Fluke.'

'All right, now you're just pulling my leg.'

Shakes her head. 'You didn't even blink. Mysto walked in and hollered at us to cut the downer vibe, what you needed was a song. So we wiped our eyes and started arguing over what to sing.'

'Oh, don't tell me. Fluke wanted doo-wop—'

'No, Johnny Mathis. Your mom wanted a lullaby, and Ricky pointed out that what we wanted to do was wake you up, and U-Boy was going to sing Beach Boys to piss you off, and all I could think was Billie Holiday. Ray got fed up and started to sing, so we just joined in.'

'What'd he sing? Do it.' Can't believe I missed all this. Boy, turn your back for two days.

'No, I'm terrible, and we petered out after one verse. I think Fluke knew one more, but Ray and your mom sang the whole thing.'

'So do it, already!'

'Sounded better with all of us, but...okay.' She sits up and begins to sing in a sweet, wavering voice. 'As I went walking that ribbon of highway...'

Punch to the gut; the pain is back, with all the buddies it could muster. The last of the Demerol clocks out, fleeing my bloodstream. Avoiding it is not easy, the only song every American agrees on—but I've managed it for years. I can handle his others: the tunes we used to sing at rallies, even 'Pastures of Plenty.' But not that one.

The checklist of Huntington's Chorea: depression, dementia, delusions, not to mention the muscle spasms and atrophy that take their sweet time in killing you off, relishing your suffering. God only knows how much longer Death is going to toy with him, and he really did not have this shit coming. Guthrie was—no, he *is*, he still is, that old Okie's still with us, tough as nails—one of our best, and he's paid a lot more dues than most. And when all the Pinkertons and bulls in the world couldn't beat him, his own body stepped up to the job. He'll never hop another freight, never again walk through a green field telling the workers to rise up against their oppressors. At this point he can barely move out of his wheelchair. What's worse, it's a damned lie.

This is not our land anymore, if it ever was. They've driven us all into cities or reservations or straight to the edges; we're hanging by our nails and I can see the boot coming down and just...not that one.

'Stop,' I say. My voice sounds cold and choked-off.

'I warned you. I can't carry a tune with a suitcase.'

'No, you're great. Keep singing, okay? Anything else.'

Shoots me a look, but starts crooning 'Mack the Knife,' just like Billie. She's pretty good for a still-breathing white girl, untouched by years of heroin; that strange Venusian style unlike anyone else in the world.

I stare up at the ceiling, and try not to let the sharks in.

You do see them coming sometimes, although there isn't always much you can do. Fluke and I were sitting out on the point late one morning when I was sixteen, sleepy with sun, when something brushed by my foot and a fin broke the water right in front of me. The bad kind. The kind that's Indisputably Not a Dolphin. My mouth went dry, I tried to cry out a warning, and nothing emerged but a very minor squeak.

'I see it,' Fluke says quietly, and then another one appears.

'Should we run for it?'

'Do...not...move. Pull your feet up, nice and easy.' He's whispering, as if they could hear us and get even more pissed off. 'Lie down flat.'

I do so, quickly. Another one appears, circling. And another.

And then there were four. Boss shark party, with us as the main dish. Round and round they go, trying to hypnotize us into falling off the boards. All I can think about is Sambo and the tigers, and maybe they'll turn into shark butter we can put on our pancakes, we should be so lucky. They do not. Round and round and round, at a cool even pace.

My heart's drumming so fast I'm about to black out. Breathe, I think, in and out, breathe. One way or another, this will all be over soon. Don't imagine rows of teeth tearing off your face. Just breathe, as moments ooze by like cold molasses and centuries pass, and why won't they stop fucking with our heads and leave? Fluke peers over the side at our new chums, playing ring-around-the-rosy only inches away. All I have to do is reach out and—no.

'Hammerheads,' he murmurs. 'Not so bad, really. They only nibble.'

I don't want to be nibbled. Not one teeny-weeny little bit. I want to be home in bed reading a book, with all my limbs and face intact.

'Be cool,' he says, casting me a worried look. 'Don't pass out. They'll get bored eventually.'

We'd been out for about an hour by then. The sun is directly overhead and I'm starting to feel thirsty. I can see Ricky on the beach, shading his eyes and staring out in our direction. I don't know the wigwag for 'motherfucking sharks help,' so just wave as frantically as I can without rocking the board. He waves back, then heads into his shack, as my heart sinks into my heels.

We're going to be slaughtered right here in front of half of LA, and they'll just gawk and point and do nothing, and maybe tomorrow we'll be famous, our bloody remains in the 'Times' for everyone to weep and cluck and do more nothing. Glance at Fluke, suddenly overwhelmed by tenderness for those snapping black eyes, that sharp elfin nose and stubborn cleft chin, the mole on his jaw. It's a nice face, serviceable and friendly. I don't believe it should end up in some shark's belly.

'Listen,' I tell Fluke. 'I just want you to know—'

'Sssh,' he says. 'I know. It's okay.'

'No,' I say. My teeth are chattering, although it's eighty degrees. 'It's not okay. If a shark tries to eat you, I will punch it so hard it'll be shitting teeth forever. There is so much out there waiting for us, and you're my best friend, and I'm not gonna let some jerkwad megalodon make you miss even a second of it.'

He laughs shakily. 'Listen, if they're not gone in ten minutes, I say we go for it. I don't think my heart's gonna hold up much longer.'

And like that, they take off, plummeting under, gone—and this may be a trick, but we don't wait around to find out, breaking all previous records for fastest time anyone has ever paddled that distance, catching a wave halfway there and beaching so fast we leave skid marks halfway up the shore. That's all we have in us for a while but hysterical laughter, down on the sand pounding each other on the back, unable to believe we're still alive, not even a scratch.

Me being me, of course, after we've had a rest and a few beers, I want to go back in. My Irish is up, and I'm pretty sure otherwise I'll never surf again. Fluke whaps me upside the head.

'Get your board and get in the car, Tommy. We're going home.'

'But—'

'No 'buts', buddy. God doesn't make more than one miracle a day, not for shmoes like us.'

'God is dead,' I sulk, secretly very relieved.

'You're gonna be dead, you don't get in the car. Jesus, this is what I get for taking you out when you're on the rag. Sharks and backtalk.'

I get in the car. And I'm fine the next day, although we both stay pretty close to shore for a few weeks. But we survived, and it makes for a great story around the fire. We've all got them; it's kind of a rite of passage, and some even have the scars and chomped boards to prove it. Just a few months ago Ricky was cornered by a Great White in Santa Cruz, and a gang of dolphins swooped in out of nowhere and chased it off. Can you believe it? Dolphins. It's like they think he's one of them.

I sit up now, grab her by the arm. She helps, and I swing my legs out, look at my bare feet for a moment. Gotta pee like a racehorse, but I'm not sure how I'm going to make it. Come up, groaning, and stagger down the hall, leaning on her. As soon as I pee it feels a little better, enough that I can walk. Open the door to find her anxiously waiting on the other side.

'Look,' I say. 'Whee! Time machine! This is me at ninety. Still in?'

'You big spaz. How can I help?'

'I dunno. Maybe just baby me a little? And a dumptruck of drugs would be nice; Stein said the first two days are going to be the hardest. I'll be fine on my own after that.'

'Jeez, didn't they give you anything for the pain? I think I have some Brofen in my purse.'

'Just some aspirin, Tic-Tacs basically. What's Brofen?'

'For my period. Oh, don't give me that look. It's an anti-inflammatory, it's not going to turn you into Liberace.'

'Well, ain't you the walking pharmacy? Sure, lay it on me.'

I dry-swallow the pills as she goes to get some water. Just breathe, man. In and out. It's not helping. I can feel myself turning into this uptight shark-ridden guy, poised to slam the shit out of the nearest head.

'I need to tell you something, Georgia.'

'Me, too.'

'Ladies first.'

Bites her lip, looks away. 'Um, all right. Don't get mad, but I thought you might not want to see me after we slept together. I know, I know it's dumb, and not who you...but you disappeared, and...well.'

'Huh,' I say. I know this is a thing some guys do, but I never got it. If anything, the option of sex on top of hanging out makes it much more likely I'll stick around. 'You don't still think that, right? So then...why sleep with me in the first place?'

Shakes her head, silent, but the tight way she's holding herself makes me tense up, too, knowing only that I got there too late, after all; that some trusted, twisted dimwit hurt her like this. That she rushed into it with me, just wanting to get on with the acid test. Girls, man. Girls, and their pearls before swine.

'Look,' I say. 'That was one of the best days I ever had. Followed by my waking up and finding out that not only had you not ditched my comatose ass in the hospital, you'd kept me company even though I was probably about as entertaining as a cardboard box. You'll have to try a little harder than that to make me go away.'

'So you weren't pulling some kind of...subconscious appendicitis?'

'Yes, that's my passive-aggressive superpower. Rather than tell you how crazy I am about you, I try to off myself.'

'Oh—just that I'm not going to be a barrel of monkeys this week. I plan to bitch and moan and in general be a real asshole, and you don't have to hang around for that. You can play Florence Nightingale if you want, but be prepared for a serious ingrate of a patient.'

She grins.

'It's not funny, babe. You're the last person I want to snap at, and I'm probably going to snap.'

'It's a little funny, grumpfish—you really are ninety today. But you're going to be nineteen again.'

'Yeah, well, there's the rub. I get like this when I'm nineteen, too.'

'Everybody has bad days.'

'Not like this. Ever read *Hamlet*?'

'Okay, now you're just being melodramatic.'

'No, some days really are like, 'stale, flat, unprofitable, check.' I'd be running people through with swords if I could get off the floor. I'm not doing it on purpose, I swear; I'd give anything not to feel this way—and I know I should snap out of it, but my brain won't listen.'

'Hon, you're so...I don't know what to call it. It's like you float through life with no idea other people have stuff going on, too. My mom was at Dachau, Tommy. You think I don't know what depression looks like?'

I say nothing. Spade's a spade, and this was a paltry hand to begin with.

She pulls me to her. 'You're just lucky you look cute in pajamas.'

'Seriously, get out now.' I kiss her. 'I'm a big myopic mess, and I haven't even worked up a good head of steam yet. Is your mom like this too?'

'Myopic, that's the word. Mom's worse—but she calls them 'migraines.' I was ten before I realized that wasn't the medical term for lying in a dark room for hours every afternoon, even though there was nothing wrong. She'd bite your head off if you knocked. Not crying or sleeping. Just lying there, like...'

'So she can switch it off, then? Just get up, when she has to?'

'In a way. I think my dad keeps her going. As soon as he comes home, she's right as rain.'

'But not for you?' Touch the soft warmth of her.

She shrugs. 'I'm blood. Not allowed to leave.'

'But he wouldn't, would he? Doesn't seem like the leaving type.'

'Never in a million years. He doesn't even cheat—and trust me, he has ample opportunity—but she can't believe that. She doesn't hound him. But you can tell she feels like it's all going to collapse one day.'

'Don't take this the wrong way, but how do you know? That he doesn't cheat, I mean?'

'He'd smell different if he cheated. And he'd tell me. We don't keep secrets from each other.'

'What about me?' I ask, intrigued. 'Do I smell like a cheater?'

'You smell like you need a bath.'

'Yeah, sorry about that. Can't get the stitches wet—but you can give me a sponge bath while I have sexy nurse fantasies, if you like.'

'Oh, you're on. I'll be Helen Hayes, and you be Gary Coop—what?'

'Ah-ha-ha, fuck. Nothing. Just, ouch, maybe not just yet.'

Scopes me out. 'Oh, shit, shit! Make it stop, it's pulling on your stitches! What do we do?' She's chortling, one hand over her mouth.

'Goddammit, Georgia.' But I'm laughing too.

'Sorry,' she snorts. 'I'm sorry, it's really, it's not funny, I don't mean to— it's just so weird. I suppose the usual is out?'

'Mmm, probably. Ow.' I can't imagine how much coming would hurt, though part of me really wouldn't mind finding out. The bell rings, and Georgia goes off to answer the door, while I fan myself ineffectually and think hard about cold showers.

'Hey, there, bud,' Fluke pops his head in. 'Hear we got guy problems.'

'That's all I said, Tommy, hand to God, didn't say 'woody.' Whoops.'

Throw a pillow at them. 'Will someone get me a fucking icepack? The two of you! I'm dying here!'

He glances at Georgia. 'Should we set him up in a gallery? Like the lost Rodin: 'Sad Jew with Boner."

I fracture, my dick subsides, and the relief is surreal. 'Say, bud, you're looking pretty duded up for a sick visit.'

He grins and cocks his eyebrow as he shrugs off his blazer, hangs it up. Ahh. Guess he didn't take my advice after all. I shake my head.

'Okay, Studly Do-Right. You, I'll pump later. What I need now is grub, and pronto. I'm about to eat my pillow.'

'Your mom left the Vitamix on the counter,' says Georgia. 'Here.'

They watch as I take a resigned slug of the beige sludge. Grimace.

'How bad is it?' Fluke asks. I hand it over; words really wouldn't do it justice. He sniffs, then gives it a shot, chokes, looks desperately around for somewhere to spit, and swallows.

'Lightweights,' Georgia scoffs. 'Watch and learn.' Takes a gulp, then gags it back in the glass. 'Ho, hah, gah, get it off me! It'th on my tongue! Why does this *exist*? It can't possibly be good for you!'

'How about I make some soup?' Fluke offers. 'A nice minestrone?'

'Really? You'd do that for me?'

'Sure. Boner kills, pills, soup—I'm a regular candyman, baby.'

'You guys cook; I'm going shopping,' says Georgia. 'Those morons. I don't know what our medical establishment is coming to, sending you home with baby aspirin and this Black Lagoon bilgewater, but we'll fix you up. Fluke, you're on sponge bath. Enjoy.'

She whisks out, as Fluke rubs his hands together. 'Oh, boy. Scartime.'

'You're not,' I tell him. 'Behave, and I'll let you change the dressing.'

I give myself a thorough whore's bath in the sink, as he perches on the john to dole out the lowdown on last night. After their date they went back to her place—and talked. Made out a little, but mostly just hung out, drank coffee and listened to music, getting up to dance from time to time. Before they knew it the sun was rising and Sheila had to get ready for work, so they made breakfast....he trails off. I finish brushing my teeth and spit.

'And then what?' I say, considering my jeans. I'm ready to get dressed, but I'm going to need to sit down, and may have to forgo shoes entirely. 'Did she make you eat haggis?'

'No, coffee and scrambled eggs,' he says absently. 'But it felt...right. Sort of familiar, you know?'

'So when do you see her again? Scoot over.'

'I don't know. We were both pretty zonked, and it didn't come up. Gotcha something, though.' He stands and pulls a vial from his pocket, half-full of little white pills.

'Oh, honey,' I say. 'You remembered.' I shake one out for each of us, and we click, *Salud*.

'All right,' I say. 'Moment we've all been waiting for. Pass me that bag behind you, and the scissors. No, the other—yeah. And check the chest, pretty sure we've got alcohol in there.' Tentatively start peeling the tape off my lower right torso.

'Got it,' he says, and eases the bandage off. 'Whoa. She's a beaut.'

We contemplate the wound. How odd, that you could just open up my body, reach inside and ferret around in there. Looks a little sad still, but better than it did with the tube.

'Yeah, Stein said it was some of his best work. Fourteen stitches, but they're tiny. Won't be invisible, but hardly a hack job. Did you wash your hands? Wash your hands first, cholera boy.'

He does, and we redress. He sighs happily. 'I feel like Doubting Thomas now, all faith restored.'

'What? Help me with the jeans there, just from the bottom. Who?'

'You know, the disciple that thrust his hands into Jesus' wounds?'

I stand, jeans sagging around my hips. 'Is that who I'm named after? What a dick! Why would he do such a thing?'

Fluke shrugs. 'Why'd they do any of the shit they did to that guy? Let's go feed you up.'

He puts me to work chopping carrots and zucchini at the table as he putters around in the pantry, boils water and adds tomatoes, celery and garlic, then shakes in oregano and basil.

'Can you have salt?' he asks, scraping onions into the pot.

'Course, it's not heart disease. So what now?' The smell is getting to me; I'm on the verge of eating Fluke, St. Jude's medallion and all.

'I dunno. Poker? It's gotta simmer a while.'

He grabs the cards as I flick on the radio, and we play four rounds of Spit in the Ocean and two of Acey-Deucey, then he blends it—by now my tongue is lolling out like a dog's—and it's the best damn thing I've ever scarfed down in my life, I kid you not.

'So what about the shop?' I ask, as he hands me bowl two.

'We put a deposit on the site. The rest is on hiatus, till you get better.'

'You didn't tell Georgia, right? Still can't believe you fucking narked us out to Ricky.'

'Oh, come on, you know you were never going to get it together, and it was turning into this whole big thing.'

'Well, you should've told me then.'

'What, and miss the fun of watching you squirm? Not on your life.'

'You're a cruel fuck, Fallootch.'

'*Mangia*, you invalid. You look like shit.'

The pills kick in by the time Georgia gets home, our world melting into a slow pleasant drift. We greet her with happy slurred drawls, then collapse in giggles. 'Stop,' I gasp. 'Oh, God, oh please *please* don't make me laugh. Ow, ow, fuck.' The pain makes me laugh even harder; I belch like a foghorn, unable to hold it back. Fluke falls off his chair, upending what's left of my third bowl of soup, as she sets a few paper bags down on the counter, shaking her head in dismay.

'Can't I leave you knuckleheads alone for a minute? What're you on?'

'Whoa, Millie,' groans Fluke from the floor, grabbing at her ankle. '*Toujours gai,* baby, *toujours gai.* Come on down, the view's to die for. No, wait—you *are* the view. Stay where you are.'

'Help yourself,' I tell her, handing over the bottle. 'Look at this one. Happy as a clam.'

'Ugh, fine. But I want some soup, too; I could smell it from the street.' She pops one, examines the label. 'Say, this is pretty high-dose stuff. Who's Sheila Mackenzie?'

Takes a sec. 'Fluke, the fuck? Tell me you didn't!'

He sits up, unabashed. 'Oh, the scrip's from a year ago, she won't even notice it's gone.'

'For the love of—' I dab furiously at the spill with a napkin. 'Sheila's his girl. Was, most likely. Now he'll be lucky to get arrested.'

'Damn, Tommo, don't flip. I'll put it back, okay? We'd been up all night, and I wasn't thinking straight.'

I bite my lip, high fleeing, dumb with guilt.

'It'll be okay,' Georgia reassures us. 'Really. And I think you can swing this so it's more than okay. Bring it by her place with the truth: that you were desperate for a sick friend who was in a bad funk, and are terribly sorry, and never again. Just be super calm and adult about it. Do you have a tweed jacket?'

'Tweed?' He gets up and shakes off. 'It's August. No need for tweed.'

'Something classy, then. You know what I mean. Skip the tie, leave the top button open; serious, but sexy—and shut up after the apology. Not a word. Just sit there: manly, silent, a little vulnerable. She'll think it over, and if she takes your hand, you're golden. A girl will never offer to hold your hand unless she actually digs you. And then it's this crisis you two have fielded together, and you're the decent guy who'll go to any lengths for someone he cares about. New level.' She pauses, frowning. 'Unless she kicks you out, in which case I can always set you up with a nice Jewish girl. And none of that Aqua Velva mustard gas crap. It's a testimony to your charm that any woman comes within a mile.'

'Oh, she's good. You're good,' he tells her. 'Should I bring Tom along? One look at those Bambi eyes, and she'll melt.'

They size me up as I glower. 'No, you can't exploit me for your evil plot!' Clutch my belly and growl, 'Just put her pills back and run for it!'

'See what I mean?' Fluke says. 'Crabby, but oh, that thin earnest face.'

'He's irresistible. But you're under a deadline, and he's in no shape.'

'If no one's gonna listen to me, I'm just going back to bed.'

'You can't,' says Georgia reasonably. 'I'm dosing you with all this stuff I got from the *yerberia*, and then we're watching 'Guiding Light."

'Get outta town,' says Fluke. 'You watch that too?'

'Only religiously. I've scheduled my entire life around it. You?'

'Me? Oh, no, no. I just, my sisters, it's kinda...Jesus, how could Mike just *leave* her like that?'

'How *could* he? Venezuela, asshole? Stay and fight for your woman!'

'Well, she moved on in a hurry. Alex, that evil bastard? Shit, I was glad when she lost the baby, glad, even if it means I go to hell. What a snake-in-the grass he is—twice as bad as Karl!'

'But maybe today Mike'll put him in a coma too.'

'And they can get back together! No, staying strong. That hussy didn't even wait till the ink was dry on the annulment.'

'You're both out of your minds, and I'm not watching soaps,' I grumble. What if Mama came home to check on me? I think I'd rather have her walk in on me jerking off.

Fluke clucks, 'Oh, it's fifteen minutes of your oh-so-busy day, ya big wet blanket. And madly romantic, so right up your alley.'

'My alley's not romantic,' I protest. 'It's hard as nails.'

They bust up, and she hands me a creamy drink, tastier than Vitamix. I relax a little as she strokes my hair.

'Face it, darling, daytime tube is the pillhead trade-off. In a week you'll be knee-deep in 'Dialing for Dollars,' playing Mah-Jongg in your robe. I'll teach you to curse in Yiddish and buy you a carton of Tareytons, and then you'll be all set for your new life.'

'I just went cold turkey.' Turn Bambi eyes on Fluke, who only bares his teeth at me in a feral grin. 'Too late, buddy, we're not playing Scrabble or reading Wordsworth or whatever tedious pansy crap you've got in mind. You're outnumbered. Now go sit your ass down, or you'll make me miss my story.'

'You guys hate me,' I say sadly.

'Very astute,' says Georgia. 'That's why we're holed up here, instead of down at the beach.'

'All for one, and one for all,' says Fluke. 'Solidarity forever.'

"Oh, you can't scare me, I'm sticking to the union," sings Georgia.

'Jeez, you're a terrible singer,' Fluke tells her. 'I mean, really, really—'

'Don't care,' she shoots back. "Sticking to the union, till the day I die!"

They bundle me onto the couch, and we watch 'Search for Tomorrow' and 'As the World Turns' as well, as they bring me cups of fragrant herbal tea and bowls of soup and pudding, too busy shouting at the screen to answer my questions. I have to confess it's a lot more fun than I figured, this roller-coaster ride of human drama. So strange, the shit you let yourself miss out on, just because you feel like it's going to compromise you somehow.

'Hey, Georgia, did you hear Tommy got religion in the hospital? So freakin' cheap, Tom. One little old near-death experience—'

'Shut up, Fluke,' I say, and mean it. My cheeks are burning.

'Oh, come on, man, it's cool.'

Georgia pats my hand. 'It is cool, Tommy. But you don't have to talk about it if you don't want.'

'Bible's righteous.' Fluke says, and scuzzles my head. 'Jesus surfed.'

'You know, I always suspected that. One of us, too, nice Jewish boy who couldn't keep his mouth shut to save his life.'

'Moses surfed,' says Georgia. 'That's how he rescued us from Egypt.'

'Isaiah surfed, too,' I allow. "I am the Lord thy God, that divided the sea whose waves roared."

'See, Georgia, ain't he da kine? He's gonna pull a Little Richard on us now, turn preacher. I say, Amen! Can I get a hallelujah?'

'Rabbi, you mean?'

'Oh, yeah, yeah! He'll be a surf rabbi, like Doc Paskowitz! Righteous! 'Rabbi Beck will now lead us in the prayer for boss sets, followed by two Ventures hymns and a luau. Shaloha. All rise."

She hoots. 'Doc Paskowitz, I'll have you know, is the Jewish boogeyman. We've all heard the story: 'Once upon a time there was a nice boy who had it all: money, brains, a first-rate Stanford education. A successful doctor for years, and he threw it all away to become...a *surfer*! A *bum*! Ach, such a *shandeh*. Broke his poor mother's heart."

'Do they mention how much fun he's having?' I ask, curious. 'He has a wife and kids, and they surf, too. Just live in a trailer and travel all over, helping the poor and spreading the aloha. And he prays every morning, with the shawl and everything.'

'You guys should do that, Tommy,' Fluke yawns. 'No lie, I think you'd be really happy.'

'I can't,' I say without thinking. 'We've got the shaaahhh...'

'What?' says Georgia.

'Shah of Iran,' I say quickly, unwilling to tell her and jinx our little plan. 'I hear he surfs too. Right, Fluke?'

No answer; he's conked out on the arm of the couch. Georgia and I get up, turn off the TV, and put a pillow under his head. As we make our way upstairs, I say, 'That union song...that's Woody, too. Where'd you pick it up?'

'I don't remember. Hebrew school, probably.'

'Really,' I say. 'That's, well, that's...huh.'

'You can come by *shul*, if you're curious. I think you'd like our rabbi.'

'Oh, I don't know.'

'Just think of it like going to Disneyland. You don't have to stay there forever. No, you know what, it's more like a library.'

'How so?'

'We're there to read a book. It's like, oh boy, gonna read the book, and here we are reading the book, what a great chapter, let's talk about it. We sing a little, and then we eat. It's pretty low-key.'

'I don't know. I'm still kinda nervous.'

'Of what?'

'That they'll...stone me?'

'You do know we don't do that anymore, right?'

'Metaphorically, I mean. For being a bad Jew.'

'The prodigal son fixer-upper? They'll be all over you.'

'They'll hate me for being a gold-digging Commie, out to nab their girl.'

She rolls her eyes. 'Please, half our members are still in the Party. Jews invented Communism long before Marx came along. And Conservatives don't care about money—that's a Reform thing.'

'But they won't think I'm good enough for you.'

'Well, that's up to me, isn't it?'

We've paused for a breather. This is killing me, and I'm running out of excuses. Pretty sure God will be as angry at me as I am at him—or won't exist at all, and we'll just be standing in a room for no reason, swaying and talking to the wall like shmucks.

'I'm not a real Jew, Georgia,' I confess. 'Not really. I don't observe; I was never bar-mitzvahed. I don't even have a Jewish name.'

Her hand slips around my waist, squeezes me softly. 'Yes, you do.'

'What do you mean?'

'Tom. It's Hebrew.'

'What's it mean?' She smiles to herself. 'No, c'mon, tell me!'

'Come to *shul*, look it up.'

My eyes snag on the picture of Grandpa Joe over her shoulder. *Oh, go ahead*, his eyes tell me. *I grew up around this nonsense, and so did she. We came out fine.*

'Maybe I will,' I say, then dare it. 'No, not maybe. I will.'

'I love you, Tommy.' And she does. She *does*. Isn't that nuts? I could be ninety and she'd love me anyway, if I never set foot in her humdrum opium den, even if I'm poor and in pain and not good for much, just as shabby and dark as our house and everything in it. Hard to believe, but she does, and maybe it wouldn't be the worst thing to take a stab at being who I am once in a while.

'I love you, too, babe. Thanks for, you know—for hanging out today.'

'Nowhere else I'd rather be, babe. I mean that.'

And she does. Something shifts in that moment; she's no longer a girl I have a hard case of the hots for, but a human who needs me as much as I do her. This is for good. She's not gonna run off with no explanation, breaking my heart. I can trust her.

194

Funny how all you have to do is let go, even of stuff you thought was set in stone. We're in this for the long haul, I know we are, because in that moment every shark is gone, vanished without a ripple; all gloom and doom skedaddled, leaving nothing here but this warm easy joy I know I'll carry with me to the end of my days. Might be a trick, sure—but I'm going to take a deep breath and swim like hell for shore.

Two weeks after my eighteenth birthday, I went on a date with Fluke. For the record, I asked him out, and when he wanted to know if we could bring girls, I said no. Why not? Well, I explained, it was 'Exodus,' so there was a distinct possibility I was gonna...you know.

'Gotcha,' he nods. When we get there, I realize he's come equipped.

'What's in the bag?' I whisper suspiciously, as we take our seats.

'Dinner,' he says, and starts hauling it out—two bottles of Chianti, some sausage, garlic bread, gnocchi, and God knows what else.

'You're nuts, you know that? Please tell me you don't have candles and Mario Lanza's Greatest Fucking Hits in there. Why can't we just do popcorn, like normal people?'

'Tommy, calm yourself. It's a highly emotional four-hour movie, and I'm gonna need the sustenance.'

People are already looking amused askance at the spread. I slide down in my seat, groaning.

'Didn't ask you to partake, bud. Feel free to go get your nasty popcorn.'

'Why do I take you *anywhere*?'

'Cause I'm fun. Hold this.' Passes me the bottle, lays a napkin over his knees, and digs in as they roll it.

I'll be honest: this flick was like having the flu. Moments of feverish excitement followed by long stretches of disembodied exposition, and dialogue so pointless it seemed like some sort of code. Just as you were about to die of boredom, something would blow up, or someone would get killed, or Sal Mineo would confess to having been raped by the Gestapo, which for reasons unclear qualified him to join the Irgun, wage guerilla warfare on the brutal British Mandate and orchestrate a massive prison break to free his comrades.

By the second reel, I'm drinking heavily, Fluke is talking to the screen—all Falluccis do this, firmly believing the world is their living room—and no one's even shushing him. By reel three he's made friends with half the theater, and they're all joking around and taking bets on who's gonna die first.

I know what he's doing. He knew what this shit meant to me, and how Hollywood could break your heart unless you laughed in its face. But I never toughened up. Like falling in love. Every time, I'd think, this is it, this is gonna be the one. I'd hope, and hope, and pick my shattered self up off the floor to hope some more.

True story, too: summer of '47, the rustbucket SS Exodus sailed from France, bearing 4500 Holocaust survivors headed for the Promised Land. Brits tailed her the whole way, and when the Jews attempted to dock in Haifa, surrounded and boarded her, waging a battle with the unarmed passengers, many of them pregnant women refusing to turn back. Several were killed or injured. They were forced at gunpoint onto more seaworthy vessels and returned to France—to be herded into camps identical to the ones they'd escaped. Britain's main concern, of course, was not the insane cruelty, but how to rationalize it so they didn't look like the monsters they were. They needn't have bothered. The world huffed and puffed for a few days, then moved on.

But the wheels started turning. Leon Uris wrote a fictionalized version of the event, in which the refugees wound up in internment camps on Cyprus and were rescued by a crew of Israeli freedom fighters headed by Ari Ben Canaan—only to have to fight Arabs, Nazis and Brits alike for the right to a homeland, just some small place to not be dead, to raise crops and kids. I read the whole thing in one night, stoked despite all my years of carefully cultivated diffidence. Yeah, that's right, you motherfuckers. That's right. We're *back*.

So I confess I was kind of looking forward to them not dropping the ball with the adaptation. It's not unheard of. 'Grapes of Wrath' was pretty good, and...well, okay, maybe just that. But I honestly didn't see how you could take a story this righteous and fuck it up.

Surprise: they fucked it up.

This exciting tale of love and death, triumph and despair, with some of the best—Otto Preminger, Dalton Trumbo, Paul Newman—and it was like watching a group of heavily sedated strangers sitting in a sandbox. By the final reel even they knew they'd lost us, so we got not one but two tear-jerker deaths, that Disney last resort of resuscitation.

A grief-stricken Sal Mineo, who played Dov Landau with such fury I couldn't look away, swears vengeance on the killers, but Paul Newman pops up to wax rhapsodic with all the emotion of someone reciting the phone book to insist his Arab childhood friend and the young Jewish girl be buried in one grave, because some day there'll be peace, blah, blah, blah. At this point Fluke boos, and is heartily seconded by several others. Like the never-ending massacre of my people is some kind of act of a god who could be mollified with human sacrifice and cutesy symbolism. Feel free to just stop *killing* us any time, assholes.

I don't even wait for the credits to roll. Just walk out.

Fluke finds me on the sidewalk a couple minutes later, staring at the traffic. Doesn't say a word about how they blew this one shot. Doesn't mention the politics of Hollywood or the Middle East, how Newman and Preminger could've buried the hatchet and made a solid story here, or how there'll be other movies. Doesn't point out that the only actor who wasn't an embarrassment was Italian, or that every flick ever made about his people is all gangsters or mindless wine, women and song—never how they nearly starved after unification, then hauled their asses over to America, only to be treated like whores, savages and criminals. Just hands me a Tupperware. I open it up: tiramisu.

'How'd she know?' I ask him.

'Well, Ma figured one way or another you were gonna need it.'

'Looks great, but I'm not that hungry.'

'No surprise, asshole. You ate all my fucking food.'

Oh. No wonder I feel sick. 'You know, we *built* this fucking town. So much for us controlling it. One flick, just one, that says something *real* about us. That's all I ask.'

He laughs, lights a cigarette. 'It is a little weird.'

198

'God, that *bullshit* ending!'

'Ah, you know how it is. We should all play nice. But if you and some guy are holding guns to each other's heads—don't be the first to lower yours, okay?'

I promise, still grumbling. We split the cake, fingering the creamy rum-soaked crumbs into our mouths, and then we go home.

'Exodus' won Best Soundtrack, the Oscar booby prize; the theme was playing everywhere for months. Mineo was nominated for Supporting, but lost to Ustinov in 'Spartacus.' His career went downhill after that, plagued by drugs, fights and his flagrant bisexuality. Eventually he was stabbed to death in a dark alley behind a bar in West Hollywood.

With two blockbusters under Trumbo's belt in one year, the ten-year blacklist was officially broken, and Hollywood went back to business as usual—but I couldn't help noticing that they shut up about Israel and Judaism alike for a very long time.

It's a beautiful day: the September sun is shining like a benign miracle, we're outside the Bank of Italy, dressed to the nines, and Fluke is kicking the living shit out of a tree. I want to stop him—it's hardly the tree's fault—but am kinda more tempted to join in.

We do clean up nice, if I may say so. Mama made me try on one of Grandpa's old suits, which I thought at first was a joke, cause the guy was a giant, no way was I not going to swim in it. But the blue serge goes on perfect, just a little tight around the shoulders. Waist's baggy, and we look at each other for a sec, trying to keep it together with how much I look like him, I nod, and she spends the afternoon tailoring it up. Fluke has on his funerals-and-weddings best, and we shaved close, put on deodorant, combed our hair, the whole shebang. We look sharp, and talked a good game like we actually knew what we were doing, and anyone in their right mind would've handed over the money and let us unleash the dogs of commerce.

It's harder than you'd think to hide who you are, though, and surfers have that look to them, like a gorilla married a ballerina and their kid walks funny and got left out in the sun till his nose had burned and peeled a thousand times. The man eyes us skeptically as we go on about respectable sporting goods, baseball gloves and footballs and hully-gee, and I can see the wheels turning in his head: Venice, surfers, bad risk, clunk. He's all but got the red stamp ready when Mr. Fallucci asks us to wait for him outside, so we politely shake hands and leave—and that's when Fluke totally loses his mind.

I'm surprised, to be honest, because nothing ever fazes him. I mean, nada. Neither wind nor rain nor wipeouts nor pregnancy scares; he's the easy-goingest cat you ever met, a real antidote for my freakout over the least little thing, so it's kinda weird that I'm the one whistling 'Officer Krupke' with my hands in my pockets, grinning pacifically at the passersby while he's pummeling the hell out of the massive oak buckling up the sidewalk.

'All right,' I say, and grab him. 'Cut it out, you're gonna hurt yourself.'

Too late. His knuckles are bleeding, and his little tantrum has left him with deranged eyes. He curses for a time, and I let him, even learn some new words: *brutto stronze, maledett, schifoss*. The ones about the guy's mother, I already knew. After a minute, he stops struggling.

'This is *bullshit*, Tommy,' he says. 'I'm so sick of this shit. I'm *somebody*, for Chrissake. Not a loser, not a bum. All through high school, when everybody was rooting for the football team and I could kick every one of their punk asses, I was polite and shut up, and fuck that. People think what we do is worthless, and it's not. It's hard as fuck, and we're the best at it and get no respect, just condescending looks from kooks who could never do what we do in a thousand years, and I'm polite and say nothing, and fuck that from now on, and fuck them too. We know this scene inside-out, we're two smart guys sitting on a goddamned gold mine, and that bastard has his head so far up his own ass he can't even see it.' He shakes himself irritably. 'Let me go.'

I let him go. "I coulda had class," I mourn. "I coulda been somebody, instead of a bum. It was *you*, Eddie. You sent me, straight to—"

'You're not funny.'

'I'm a little bit funny.' He heaves a sigh, shoulders going slack in a way that's worse than all his kicking and screaming. 'Listen,' I go on, 'Forget that douche. There are other ways of getting money, you know that. We'll pull this together on a shoestring. Might be rough at first, but then we'll be raking in the dough, and we'll come back in six months to spit in his face. Or not, and then we're no worse off than we are now— and we won't have to worry about you guys losing your fucking house. And hey, we can always get a job selling insurance, right?'

It's an old joke. Some poor misguided fool actually gave us a job selling insurance once; after weeks of us abruptly disappearing, then skulking back hours later to drip all over the forms, we both got canned. I've got Tony's, and Fluke has his delivery job, but we're probably never going to be able to hack it in the real world. He doesn't laugh, though.

'Look,' I say. 'One way or another, it's gotta happen. That site is a steal, it's a sign. That prick sits on his ass all day, robbing people with a pen instead of a pistol, and he doesn't get to dictate. We can do this on our own, *capisce*?'

'You think?' There's a flicker of hope in his eyes.

'Shit, yeah. Look, we need first and last for the shop, that's $500. Some lumber, paint and drywall to fix it up, maybe another hundred. Blanks we can get on credit, and we'll screen the shirts ourselves. My mom can throw some wetsuits together, easy. I did that show last year at KCRW, and got to know a few of the company guys. They'll basically give us records if it'll boost sales figures.'

'Sophia could help on the register. And paint the mural.'

'We'll do it together. I've got the whole thing blocked out, it'll be fun. Remember our deal?'

'Yeah,' he admits ruefully. 'This was supposed to be fun.'

'So we can do this for under a grand, easy. I've got $200 in my new car fund I don't need, cause let's face it, I'm never getting rid of Mayhem.'

He laughs. 'It worries me, how much you love that useless jalopy.'

'That car is deep. You never did understand her.'

'I understand her, all right; I understand that she's a gurgly piece of shit who strands you every other day.'

'Well, that's between me and her.'

'Not if I'm the one picking up the pieces! Man, if I had a nickel for every hour of my life I've wasted putting that car back together, I could fund this goddamned place myself.'

'Okay, you know what—let's make a million dollars, I'll get a Porsche. Brand new, breaks down just as often, and a C-note says after a week you're bitching about how much you miss the old girl.'

'You're on, sucker. What about the business license?'

'There's, uh...a little more to it than I thought.' I'd spent the day down at City Hall, as turns out there were a dozen state, municipality and tax requirements, unexpected bullshit that required prolonged interaction with humorless grumps in cat's-eye glasses. I'd gotten the wheels turning, but that was a lot of forms, and it could be weeks. 'Let's face it, some folks'll try to take us down just for yuks. I'm on it, though.'

'Hey, you know who could help? Ray! Man, I bet if you pulled him off the rockets, he'd shape like a son-of-a-bitch.'

'Ahhh,' I hesitate. 'He...I don't think so. He never got this at all.' That's putting it mildly. All Ray's ever cared to know about surfing is that it's the reason I'm never home, so he gets saddled with the chores.

'Do me a solid and ask, okay? There'll be money in it eventually.'

'Okay. But he'll say no, and give me a hard time. You know who should get in on this, though? Pip! He could be our silent partner!'

He looks doubtful. 'Well, he'd work, all right, but--I dunno. You know how he is around people.'

'Oh, c'mon, man, he needs this. No one else is gonna give him a shot.'

And they won't. I don't know if that kid ever got a shot in his life.

We'd just come out of the water a couple years ago, when Fluke wiped his face off and squinted down the shore. The sun was coming up, and there was something under the pier, like a pile of old clothes. Fluke took a few steps, then dropped his board and started to run. Just a kid, I thought during those first few seconds when we were sure he was dead. Just this little kid someone had beaten half to death, then dumped in the water to drown. But he wasn't dead yet, and after we work him over he pukes up half the Pacific and slaps our hands away, snapping like a Chihuahua.

'Whoa,' Fluke says. 'Cool your jets, man, we come in peace. Y'okay? Where's your folks?'

Silence. Sea-green eyes, flicking from one strange face to the other.

'Who did this?' If you didn't know Fluke, you'd think he sounded calm.

Silence. The purpling bruises, the split lip.

'Got a name?' I ask.

'Maybe he's a little slow?' Fluke is holding his face, fingers searching the skull for damage. The kid growls low in his throat, like this is a theory he could stand never to hear again. I don't think slow is the problem.

'Should we take him to the hospital?' He tenses up. Guess not.

'All right, listen,' I say. 'We're gonna take you up the beach a ways, get you fixed up, just till we figure out what to do. Is that okay?'

He nods, and we carry him up to Ricky, who shocks us all by not only taking him in and chasing us out, but playing nursemaid for the next few days until the kid can walk around again. Still hasn't said a word, though, and shies from our touch until we quit touching him. Out of earshot, we fret over what we're going to do, and Ricky finally gets one of the more sympathetic lifeguards to put in some casual inquiries with the cops.

No one is looking for him; no one's even heard of him. We let it go, not wanting to get charged with kidnapping—and not wanting, as Ricky points out, for him to get packed off to some godawful home where they'd probably kill him off altogether. But he's ours now, and we don't have the faintest idea what to do with him.

He needs a name, we do know that much, but no amount of coaxing produces it. Mysto's on a Dickens kick, plugging for Pip, and the kid, who I guess was listening in on our christening plans, comes out of the shack to announce, 'Pip is okay.' We jump up to bombard him with questions—and that's the last thing he says for two months. You get used to it. Everyone pitches in, bringing him home for meals, baths and surreptitious nights on the couch when the weather is bad, just hoping that Pip will, in fact, be okay.

The cops don't give a shit, but we know from bitter experience that the truancy boys are another matter, up our asses like *la migra* until the day we turn sixteen. We ask Pip his age, and he holds up ten and four fingers. He's not even five feet tall, skinny as hell, and just...childlike, you know? Never does acquire any of those obnoxious teenaged habits we're all guilty of; doesn't fart or belch or tell long dumb jokes.

Seems both younger and infinitely older than the rest of us, wandering the pit like a Trappist monk until the day he puts a hand on Ricky's arm and nods with his chin out to sea. We'd never seen Ricky smile like that. He gives him a few lessons and turns him loose, and after that it's Katy bar the door, can't drag him out of the water for anything.

He gets his own stick, one of Ricky's treasured 9'6" Velzy's, and a couple pairs of hand-me-down trunks, and that's what he lives in, sleeping in the hammock under the palm awning to the shack. We make sure he brushes his teeth and eats now and then, and take him to Sears, where Fluke charms the cashier while we walk out with $60 worth of school clothes and a new jacket. Register him as a freshman with some story about a cousin from Oklahoma and records lost in a fire, and Fluke has a quiet word with his English teacher, a kind old lady who always went to bat for him. We tell her the whole story after swearing her to zipped lips, and she promises to keep tabs on him and call the payphone on the pier if anything goes awry.

Something, of course, instantly goes awry, and we spend a lot of time that year hauling him back to school, explaining yet again *they're gonna take your ass away, Pip, you have to try harder*, as he's nodding like a madman, *yes, yes, absolutely*, and half the time he's back at the beach before we are. And how can we stay angry at those sweet apologetic eyes? We were no better, and when the cry goes up, *T-Bird!* we don't have to teach him to rush into the dunes along with half the kids here, to hide in the long grass until the LA County Truancy Department has gotten tired of querying a bunch of somnolent surf hoods and departed for more fruitful pastures.

But something must've sunk in along the way. He does a quicker sum than any of us, follows our conversations intently—and he reads the 'New Yorker' every week, though no one can ever figure out where he's getting it from. Laughs at the cartoons and everything. And on the day he turns sixteen, he fills out his high school withdrawal forms in an enviable copperplate, signing with a flourish: Philip Pirrip. Done, a free man. We have a big party and attempt to get him laid, but he's not interested, just another teenaged thing he isn't into, and we feel dumb and somewhat douchey for trying.

His hair is halfway down his back by now, with no one badgering him to cut it, and he never really hangs out with anyone but us, who are so attuned to his every gesture or twitch of brow he doesn't have to speak at all. So he's kind of...limited in what he can do, and doesn't always do the right thing. Or maybe it is, on some other planet.

Some muscled lugnut walked by a few weeks ago, sneering, 'Can't tell if it's a boy or a girl.' We closed ranks, *back off, hode,* and Mysto snapped, 'Why'ncha suck his dick and find out?' and the guy shoved him, hard enough that he fell on his ass. Before we could move, *whammo,* Pip jumped in like a pit viper and punched the guy right in the throat.

He went down all purple, and we thought, well, that's that, he smashed his windpipe and now we're going to have to smuggle him out of the country and why oh why Pip do you have to make our lives this fucking complicated? Guy turned out to be okay, though he didn't have a great deal to say after that, just skulked off with his tail between his legs. We went wild, hollering at Pip, applauding his *cojones,* but he just smiled, waved us off, and out he went. Our little Harpo.

So you see what I mean. We can't shelter him forever. He's got to have some kind of income—we can at least do that, keep him that safe from this shitty world. Maybe help him find a place of his own, wouldn't that be something? And, oh, if we could find him a girl, someone to really look after him. That'd take a weight off. Girls are crazy for him, and he lets them crowd around and play with his hair, but he's...no, he's not like Ricky. Ricky has the occasional girlfriend. Pip, it's like that part of his brain doesn't exist at all. But we can give him a job, and Fluke knows we have to, whatever ensues. If we don't take care of each other, well, what's the point to any of this?

Mr. Fallucci emerges from the bank then, dejected and embarrassed, and we pounce on him to explain the new plan. He brightens a little.

'Ahh, I knew they wouldn't be able to keep you two numbskulls down for long. This is going to be cutting it pretty close to the bone, though. What about the lease?'

'Five-year,' I say brightly. 'I'll sign it. I wasn't doing anything with my credit rating anyway.'

He sighs, shaking his head. But then he looks at Fluke. You should never do that; it impairs your judgment, and this is his firstborn son and more than anything he wants something solid for him in this life. 'All right. We don't need that *cambiavalud*; I'll lend you the rest of the money. Do *not* screw this up. And don't tell your mother.'

Then all is cheers and hosannas, and we go off to sign the lease.

Something we tend to overlook, when talking about the great glorious myth of the Gold Rush, is that hardly any of those guys made much money off the actual gold. James Marshall, who found that first tiny nugget in a lumber mill on the American River, sure didn't, and his boss John Sutter tried to shut him up and secure the land, but you really can't outrun this sort of madness.

As luck would've had it, the Mexican-American War had just ended the week before, with the agreement that Mexico would give us western America, and we'd give them a few million bucks and stop kicking their asses. So it was all ours now—and we didn't have to beg for settlers to join our sparse ranks anymore, simply step aside. Pretty soon the whole place was infested with hopeful miners, and even Sutter never did get much more out of the bargain than a lot of streets named after him. Both he and Marshall died penniless.

The first comers did okay, but they had exhausted the vein by the time half the world came barging over in 1849, many with wives and kids in tow. They'd missed their wave. There wasn't much left, but they refused to believe it. Carried on, losing their shirts, abandoning their families, chasing this crazy destitute dream. Worse, they turned on each other: taxing the foreigners, lynching the Chinese, massacring the Indians. Nearly half a million people showed up to get in the game, and believe me, California was not an easy place to reach back then. People died, trying to get here. They ate each other. San Francisco exploded, going from a tiny mission of 200 to a lunatic boomtown of 150,000 people in only a few years. A forest of masts sprang up in the Embarcadero, ships abandoned by their gold-fevered crews.

But a few folks stepped back and thought, you know, I bet I can do something else here that isn't backbreaking and pointless, maybe make a little dough on the side. They turned those ships into hotels, taverns, brothels—even a jail, for when customers had overindulged. They set up shops, selling mining equipment and groceries at grossly inflated prices. Women opened boarding houses; Chinese people would cook your food and do your laundry. Samuel Colt perfected his Navy revolver in 1850, the better to defend your stake, *mine mine mine,* and died a millionaire. California wasn't destined to be a dreamy El Dorado utopia after all, just one more joint governed by the same needs that have always driven humanity: greed, sex, violence, and well-made trousers.

In 1870, a woman brought her husband's torn pants to a Latvian Jewish tailor, begging for a tougher make. He reinforced the pockets and fly with copper rivets, then took his idea to a German tentmaker with money to invest. They brought in a shipment of canvas, dyed it blue, and started turning out pants named after the source of the fabric: Nimes and Genoa. Denim jeans, not only for the desperate miners stranded on our shore, but for lumberjacks, cowboys, railroad workers. Jeans so goddamned good, they still sell like hotcakes a century later, to everyone from socialites to Socialists. Marilyn, Brando, and Einstein look cool in them—and the rest of us do, too.

We can learn from history, you see. A hundred shapers are already vying for custom in this town, and maybe Ricky is right; maybe this scene is dead, the vein tapped out. But no one else knows that yet—and we're not gonna be the miners here, down on our knees in a cold creek 18 hours a day, busting ass for barely enough dust to buy one more day's sourdough.

We're going to be Jacob Davis and Levi Strauss.

And yeah, I know: even though Davis was the one who came up with the whole idea in the first place, the jeans aren't called 'Jacob's.' But that's not going to happen with us. Fifty-fifty on the fortune and fame, straight down the line till the wheels come off.

Two days later, early evening, we're at the hardware store. The last 48 hours have been a blur of phone calls and forms and driving all over Santa Monica and Venice, picking things up and dropping them off; we've gotten very little sleep and no surf at all, but we do get into a big argument on Aisle Three over shelves and liability. Earthquakes are considered, and surfers with a tendency to climb on things, and in the end we just went for some steel babies we'd bolt to the walls.

'What's eating you, crabapple?'

'Nothing. Big day.' Slides his eyes over at me. It *was* a big day, and far from over yet. I'm falling-down tired, the scar's taking turns itching and aching, and I can't handle much more of this.

'Turquoise or cerulean?' I say, holding up paint samples.

'I don't fucking care, I'm color-blind.'

'You're brown-green, and quit being a dick. Just for the sky.'

'Cerulean, then. Gonna make the ocean a different color on each wall?'

'Kinda. I'm thinking turquoise for Hawaii, but not sure about Australia.'

'Brownish-green? One of these days I want to go check out Torquay, sharks be damned. You think kangaroos surf?'

'Why not? They balance on their tails and box.' I brace myself on a shelf and kick up at Fluke with both feet; he deflects me with a swat.

'Think they have birthdays in Australia?'

'Course. They're not Jehovah's Witnesses, just upside-down with crazy animals. Is that all of it?'

'I guess so.' He sighs heavily.

We're loading the camper, when I slap my hand to my forehead, aghast. 'Goddammit! Your birthday!'

'How could you fucking *forget*? You never forget! I've been dropping anvils all day!'

'Oh, man, I just got so caught up in...look, I'll make it up to you, swear. We'll drop all this stuff off and go out for a beer.'

'Well, I don't know that I want to, as you so obviously don't give a shit.'

'Oh, boo-fucking-hoo. C'mon, boy's night out, but this is really it, okay? Last of the petty cash.'

Hump the stuff up to the shop, where I unlock the door and flick on the lights. We're hauling the shelves in, when the back room bursts open and a mob streams out, screaming, 'Surprise!!' We both leap about a mile, Fluke drops the shelf on my toe, and I'm hopping around holding my foot as we both curse mightily.

'Get over here, you clown,' hollers Mr. Fallucci. 'You kiss your mother with that mouth?'

'Son of a goddamned *gun*!' Fluke gasps, clutching his chest. 'You nearly gave me a friggin' heart attack!'

Then we're engulfed in a sea of humanity—his whole family's here, even Angela and her boys, down from the Bay Area for the first time since Easter. Ray and Mama, and all the guys including Ricky, though there's nothing to boost and I'd warned him I'd break his fingers if he tried. Couple of old school buddies, and Sheila, who has forgiven the Miltown Disaster, though it may be a while before he sees any action there—all swarming around with well-wishes, hugs, and so much love this tiny space is hardly enough to contain it.

Flips me the bird over the crowd, grinning, and he's right. I set him up. Shaking him for long enough to pull this off was no cinch, but I wanted it to be a night to remember. Mysto and U help me bring the rest of the stuff inside, by which time he's been dragged back into the workshop, where a table is covered with potluck dishes, beer and wine, and a large cake with blue frosting and a little plastic surfer cavorting amidst the twenty-three candles.

Later that night, after we've eaten our fill and are dancing—you haven't lived till you've seen Mrs. Fallucci do the Tarantella with Ricky as Leo shows Sheila the finer points of the Watusi—I wander outside, full of warm boozy camaraderie. Watch the adagio crowd toss each other in the air under the palms, then hunt down a pay phone.

'Howdy, stranger.' Her voice is deep with sleep.

'Did I wake you? Sorry to call so late.'

'Three days, so I assumed you were gone.' She yawns. 'Daddy fixed me up with Tab Hunter. Dull, but there may be hidden potential there.'

'Very well-hidden,' I say wryly. 'I miss you.'

'I miss *you*. Call, okay? My mind goes 'dead in a ditch' very easily.'

'I'm kinda...busy with something. It's a surprise. I'll show you in a few weeks, but it's got to be just right.'

'Don't do anything for me, okay? I like you fine the way you are.'

'It isn't for you. Not entirely. You were kind of the inspiration, though.'

'Well, glad I serve some purpose. Still want to come for dinner Friday?'

'Try and stop me. But then I'm gonna vanish again for a while, so don't ditch me for Tab just yet.'

'This better be the surprise of the century.'

'Oh, it will,' I say. 'It will. Can't wait to see your face.'

'I've got more than that to show you.' She sounds giddy. 'U-Boy's been teaching me a few moves.'

'Aces. No one's got moves like U. How's it going?'

'Ah, you know—he's a little antsy, but he comes across. It's just...'

'What?'

'The girls have kinda been giving me a hard time.'

'Like how?' I ask, heart sinking. I know how.

'I dunno, neither fish nor flesh. Not one of your gang, and I never was into the girly scene—but girls'll turn on you no matter what you do.'

'*You* don't.'

'You haven't seen me. I put up with stuff for ages, then go full volcano.'

'Let me at 'em. Ricky's not the only Machiavellian on the beach. I can make life pretty difficult for snotty bitches, if I'm in the right mood.'

She sighs. 'Just forget it, Tommy, really. They can't make up their minds if I'm a dyke or a slut. It's too dumb to even bother with.'

'They're jealous as hell, what'd you expect? You had the gall to be better than them. Believe it or not, guys can be just as bad. We'll figure it out, okay?' She says nothing. 'Listen, I gotta go, but—'

'Are you gonna do that thing where you make me hang up first?'

'No-oo,' I say, doing it. But eventually we wrest ourselves away from our proxy transceivers, and I lean against the booth.

I've never been good at keeping secrets, not even happy ones. That poker-faced betrayal. I'd rather get everything out in the open—and as God is my witness, I'm never going to keep anything from her again. But I wanted just once to present someone with a masterpiece, finished and perfect. For them to be suitably impressed. Watching it go through the awkward first stages isn't the same. I know she loves me, but I want her to respect me, too. To think I'm somebody. Because Fluke's right. We're aces, and it's time the world knew that.

Walk back to the shop, pause outside the window. They've turned off the lights and lit a bunch of candles, all those faces softly mysterious in the gold-rose glow like a Renaissance painting. Ray's deep in discussion with Mysto and Elena, gesturing with a slice of pizza. U-Boy's playing peek-a-boo with Angela's baby, Mama and Mrs. Fallucci are cleaning up, and a few couples are swaying to the Platters, tired and at peace.

I knew in that moment: we weren't going to fail. This mission wouldn't be aborted. This was *exactly* what we were supposed to do with our lives. It was going to soar, and we were going to be rich as Croesus and show them all, the bankers and surfers and hard-hearted towel girls, that you can be a surf bum and still know how to work the system; that you can be a dork and a righteous rocker too. Not looking cool, maybe. But being cool.

Fluke and Pip are off in the corner, and Pip is saying something to him, I can see his lips moving, and Fluke's expression...it's hard to tell what's going on there, but after a moment I turn away, unable to bear how it's twisting up my heart. I won't ask, but I hope it was good. I hope it was really, really good. They both deserve it.

GLORIOUS FOOD

The defining mark of any surfer, maybe even more than the need to be out on the water, is hunger. It's comical, really, how much we eat. Fluke and I sat down with the Adele Davis once and figured we burn off about thirty donuts a day. Five loaves of bread, six sticks of butter, a hundred pieces of bacon. Leftovers never make it to the fridge. At parties, we're always the ones in the corner, upending the entire buffet table into our mouths. We're rarely welcome anywhere in groups larger than two, as we have an effect on houses similar to that of termites.

Like Esau, we even sold our birthright for grub. He got pottage, which I'll assume involves weed in some way, while we got some of Gidget's peanut butter-and-radish sandwiches, which tasted just as nasty as they sound—but boy, didn't we gobble them down and beg for more. Taught her how to surf in trade, and she went home and told her dad, and he told the world, and it was all downhill after that. My advice? If you find a gold nugget in a creek, shut up about it—even if someone does offer you a grub stake.

So food is a very big deal for us, to the extent that we pass around the 'Women's Wear Daily' recipe sections as often as we do the 'Playboy' centerfold, and spend more time around the fire discussing who's going to make the burger run or that time U-Boy ate twenty slices of pizza, than we do gabbing about who got laid the night before. Easy to laugh about all this on a full stomach, but things look entirely different when that desperate vacuum is sucking up everything you hold dear. I don't know how people did it in the camps. No part of me could've survived that; after a month I'd have sold out everyone I'd ever met for a peanut-butter-and-radish sandwich.

My first week on solids was, no lie, like being born again. Chewing was a miracle, this thing I vaguely remembered doing once, and the textures on my tongue, it was all so *good*. That feeling of fullness, like a drug; you just want more of it. I got strong—I'd been half-assedly doing the physical therapy exercises they gave me, and Georgia had been coaxing me out of the house for longer walks each day—but that first morning my stomach could handle some eggs and toast, I went out and started running down the street, laughing and waving my arms like a little kid.

I was so stoked not to be dead, to be doing this again. It hurt like hell, and I was winded before I even got around the block, but it made me so happy I went home and scarfed down a mixing bowl of Rice Krispies and bananas, snap-crackle-pop.

Let me tell you something about bananas: they figure very heavily into any weight-gain program, and one can tire of them really goddamned fast. But I'd lost almost twenty pounds, and there hadn't been much fat on me to begin with, so bananas it was, bananas and peanut butter and tuna fish and ice cream, and many, many jokes about King-Kong and Chiquita and Harry Belafonte, and U thought it particularly clever one day to pretend to be sucking off a banana like a queer, and by that time I was in no mood and pinned him down in the sand, force-feeding him bananas till he apologized, hard to do when you're laughing hysterically through a mouthful of gloop.

But I'm doing push-ups now, and agonizing sit-ups; working in the shop and running on the beach with Fluke, griping the whole way. And venturing back out on the water, at last. Something's missing, though, something I'll have to ease back into.

Surfing isn't like riding a bike, you see—there's a certain mojo required, being attuned to eighteen things at once while shutting it all down so nothing reacts but your body. The size and direction of the swell, the strength and speed of the waves and the forecast and time of the tides; if you're on a rhino chaser or a chip, what the rocker and fin are up for. What you are. Our pecking order, lineup density, who's liable to drop in on whom, how to reciprocate. The chain reaction of manic feuding with fellow surfers, lifeguards and bust-hungry cops liable to be set off by one careless gesture.

People think we're bone-lazy morons—and we're not, honest. But your subconscious gets so consumed with complexities of wave physics and etiquette, they push aside jobs and school and remembering not to put your socks in the oven. And yeah, sometimes you want to say, fuck it, hang back on the sand with a beer, digging on the Shirelles and the tan oiled flesh all around. But the sea is calling, calling, luring you in with the promise of that one perfect wave. My God, what if you missed it? How would you *live*?

214

Surfing is like riding a bike—but blindfolded, through an ever-changing obstacle course, in the rain, and I've lost my handle on it, am wiping out even in the kiddie bowl; everyone and their asshole cousin seems determined to drop in on me today, the scar's pulling on my abs so that every turn is a bitch, and after a while I'm so frustrated I'm ready to throttle every kook on the beach, not a state of mind particularly conducive to blissful union with the sea.

Paddle out to the break and just sit, disconsolate. Mysto pulls up beside me and pats me on the back. We all have our off days. I give it one last shot, only to wipe like a clown. The board lands hard on my shoulder as I scream in frustration, silenced by a mouthful of saltwater. My ass feels strongly that it's been kicked enough for one day, so I head home, ice up, shower and get ready to go over to Georgia's for Shabbat dinner. At least she wasn't there to witness my humiliation; she had some kind of horse thing going on.

Pulls me up to her room, all excited, to show me a first-place trophy, a bronze horse rearing up with a jodphured girl astride.

'Why didn't you tell me this was some big equestria-palooza? I'd have come out to cheer you on, brought my pom-poms and everything.'

'Oh, it wasn't a big deal.' Her eyes say otherwise.

'Did everyone lose their minds? Or do you just say, 'Raw-ther, old chap,' and like that?'

'Well, there's applause, but I wasn't listening. Buckley barely made the last jump, and I was sure we were going down. Happens sometimes, and it's pretty grim.' She sits beside me. 'You ever compete?'

'Nah. I've entered a few things just for laughs, but most contests have the top five or six guys, and no one else stands a chance. All Hawaiians, pretty much, or guys that've been there for awhile. Ricky's solid, if he can get his head right, and Mickey Muñoz. Dewey, Corky, Phil, a few others. The rest of us have been dodging bodies in this piddly *wahine* surf for so long, they're the only ones who can really stand up to those guys. I used to be okay, but I might've sized out, like a jockey.'

She looks skeptical. 'Do you *want* to compete?'

'You know...not really. There's some money, which would be nice, but mostly it's just bragging rights and magazine covers, that sort of thing. Competition is kind of the opposite of why I surf.'

'How'd it go today?'

I shake my head. 'Too much on my mind, I guess.'

'Oh, oh, that reminds me! Close your eyes and listen—it's like he wrote this just for you.'

I hear her futzing with the hi-fi, the scritch of record, then a rollicking folk guitar and a voice that sounds like a carhorn aping Guthrie. Oh. Dylan. Gave the first record a shot when it came out, and passed. Just another chubby-cheeked folk gremmie doing the same tired old covers, with that annoying whine that makes you want to break his nose by the second verse. But this is *him*. Too many people, all too hard to please.

'C'mere.' She perches on my lap, and we touch foreheads, kiss. 'You did good, centauressa. Let me know next time. I'll come out and watch, and be so genteel you won't even know I'm there.' Run my hands down her thighs. 'I dig this, by the way—he may actually grow on me.'

'He's Jewish, you know.'

'Who, Dylan? Well, he's from New York. Everyone's Jewish there.'

'He's not, though. He's from Hibbing, Minnesota.'

'That's where Tom Blake is from! Wait, there's Jews in Minnesota?'

'Jews are everywhere, we're like dandelions.' She blows on an imaginary flower. 'Who's Tom Blake?'

'Oh, no one. The world's only perfect surfer, is all. But that reminds *me*. Do I need to do anything special tonight? Like, wear a yarmulke? Your parents know I'm not really...up to speed, right?'

'Just be yourself, you'll do fine. You ready to go down?'

'Always.' I pretend to dive under her dress, and she pushes me away, giggling. 'Get off me, you big oaf. Later. I'm starving.'

216

'Me, too. Ever since I started eating again, I'm in this permanent state of Oliver Twistiness.'

'Mmmm,' she says, and her hands move down my back, feeling my ribs. 'I know the feeling. Please, sir, may I have some—'

'Behave yourself, fornicator. It's Shabbat.'

'But that's exactly when we're supposed to misbehave.'

'Really? Nah, you're screwing with me. Don't mock the rookie.'

'No, cross my heart. It's in the Talmud, a mitzvah to fuck on Friday. Be fruitful and multiply, make lots of lucky little Jewish babies. Shabbat's wide open, so what better time?'

I laugh out loud, never having heard of a religion that encouraged its adherents to get in each other's pants. Her mother calls 'Dinner!' so we head for the stairs, and I'm not entirely sure what 'Talmud' or 'mitzvah' mean, but I think I'm going to like it here.

'It's Tommy's first Shabbat,' Georgia explains as we pull up around the table. 'So go easy on him, please.'

'What?' says her dad. 'But I thought you were—'

'His grandpa was a Red, Daddy. Opiate of the masses and all.'

'He was,' I confess. This is usually the point where I get thrown out on my ear, but Hollywood Jews tend to have a more sympathetic take. 'He was pretty adamant, and my folks didn't care either way, so we just grew up with...books, I guess. Science. Thanksgiving and Halloween. We went to a lot of marches. May Day was big.'

'Nothing? No Shabbat, Passover? Rosh HaShana?' Ira looks confounded, as if I'd told him I'd never been to the movies.

'Rosh HaShana—that's where you blow the shofar, right?'

'That's the one,' says Georgia. ''Cause we're so good to the help.'

Takes a sec. I have to bite my lip not to bust out laughing.

'Georgia!' says her dad, scandalized.

217

He shakes his head ruefully. 'You do know you can have all those things and Judaism too, right? Hell, we encourage it. It's not a cult.'

I sigh. Atheism is like being a vegetarian; hard for some to digest. But this is LA—we're all mad here, and my friends never gave me a hard time about it. Not like anybody's dying to be a Jew in the first place, and there was no danger I'd be anything else. Catholicism seems nice, with the incense and Latin, but I'm not real big on forgiveness. Do the crime, do the time.

'His father was observant, but they had a parting of ways when he was a teen. And after the war...well, he didn't want to know from God. Sorta felt like religion was a cop-out, you know? That we should try harder to make a perfect world for its own sake.' I gaze around at the tablecloth, the braids of bread under their embroidered cover. It all seems oddly familiar, like a half-forgotten dream.

'And how do you feel?' asks her mom. She really is so beautiful it hurts to look at her for long. I keep calling Ira 'Sira,' recalling only mid-word his desire for informality, but she's just Ma'am, and no one corrects me. She's kind of scary. Cheekbones you could cut yourself on, and those eyes...I focus on the bread.

'I keep an open mind,' I say. 'Been reading some. Seems cool, if a little heavy on the animal sacrifice. So fill me in; I'm ready.'

'Welcome to our table, stranger,' grins Ira. 'We'll fill you in, all right—if nothing else, the brisket should convert you.' He looks just like Georgia when he smiles: that sudden warmth, just for you.

Beth covers her hair with a lace kerchief, says the blessing, and strikes a match. Sounds cheesy, but watching her light the candles, their flames reflected in her eyes, thinking about all she survived to be able to keep doing this—this innocuous act a bigger 'fuck you' than all their guns and barbed wire—it burns. There's a tug in my heart that's been there for a while. These ceremonies and strange guttural words I can almost understand, they're something I've been pushing away for years, to satisfy a stubborn ghost. All I have to do is relax and let it in.

And do I. Ira says the blessing over the Manischewitz, the worst wine I've ever tasted, grape Nehi gone to the dogs, but then Georgia blesses the challah, and it's delicious, like strudel and French toast had a baby. I look around to find no one else having seconds—but then they start slinging food at me like it's going out of style. Mrs. Fallucci was always my standard for cramming, but she's got nothing on these guys.

There's chicken soup with carrots and egg noodles; I have two bowls of that, and crackers with smoked salmon and celery, and Mrs. Lustgarten notices me eying the challah, slides it over, and I eat three pieces before sitting on my hands to stop myself. A salad with iceberg lettuce and mini-tomatoes, another with fruit in Jello, and half a dozen side dishes, all of which I have to at least taste. And the piece of resistance, as Fluke would say: the brisket. Let me tell you, I've had meat in my life, but this baby is *profound*. You barely have to chew it; my mouth is dissolving with ecstasy. This isn't food—it's like I'm about to catch the spirit and start dancing around, flailing and speaking in tongues.

'I'm sorry,' I laugh, coming out of my reverie to find them all looking at me. 'I'm being a complete...' *Don't say anything in German.* 'It's just hard to stop, this is so good.'

'Ahh, *fress, boychik*,' says Ira. 'You're growing. Makes us happy, and you could obviously use it.'

Consider explaining my whacked metabolism, but don't want to protest too much. Neither do I want them to think I'm some sad surf urchin, though, desperate for a handout, so I finish my third helping of brisket and roast potatoes and sit back, wiping my mouth. Even the napkins are stunning, satin striped scarlet and blue, with fancy brass rings, their Hebrew letters rising like flames.

'My compliments,' I tell Mrs. Lustgarten. 'That was incredible.'

She laughs softly. 'I'm limited to the occasional hard-boiled egg, I'm afraid. This is all Carmela, and the brisket recipe is from Ira's mother. Georgia got all the cooking talent in our family.'

'No kidding,' I say. 'She taught me to bake a cake, and I'd never made anything more complicated than grilled cheese. Did you taste it?'

There is an odd awkward silence, in which no one looks at me.

Georgia frowns down at her plate, and Ira says hastily, 'But I hear you're giving her surfing lessons. How's she doing?'

I'm happy to enthuse about her progress, though you learn to foresee the glazed eyes when you go on and on about your obsession. I've never seen a learning curve like this on anyone but Pip; it's like she's been doing it her whole entire life.

'If I'm that good, maybe I could compete, Tommy.' She's gazing at me, cheek on her fist. 'Head out to Hawaii for boot camp, then come back and kick everyone's butt.'

I hesitate. 'Much as I'd pay to see that...'

'What?'

'The real comps aren't for girls. Huntington Women's got some ace surfers, the Calhoun mafia, Marge and her daughters, and there's some serious new talent—but they don't get any support. More people show up for the T-shirt contest than to watch the girls surf. And no credit for style, they just want you to follow the rules. Plus the men's contests are all invitationals, so it's kind of a popular kids' party, and they'll never go co-ed in a million years. Shame, cause some of those girls can charge. They could take me easy, and maybe even Ricky, too.'

'Any prize money?' I shake my head. "Surfer' covers?'

'Oh, you kid. According to 'Surfer,' chicks stay on the beach where they belong. There's this one goofyfooter though, your age, from Encinitas. Real scrapper—she took Huntington and Makaha when she was only fifteen, won three times now. First girl to crack Waimea, too—charged it like a little Greg Noll: half the size, twice the...ah, guts. Linda Benson. You guys should get together, she could teach you a lot.'

'Benson, you say?' says Ira. 'I think her dad used to drum for Dorsey.'

'Get outta town. Buddy Rich is Linda's dad?'

'No, different drummer. But he had a kid he couldn't ever drag out of the water. And Georgia could get that good?' He sighs happily, gazing at her with pride. 'You'll be on every cover, darling, I guarantee it. My daughter, the Susan B. Anthony of surfing. But it's not too late?'

220

'Never too late to start having fun,' I say noncommittally, and stand. 'Can I help clear the dishes?'

'Tchah, Tom, sit down,' Ira says. 'You're our guest. Carm can get them.'

And that's when my sinuses let loose. Hazard of the profession; you get a lot of seawater up your nose, and it won't come out, just sits up there biding its time until your eyeballs feel like they're being pushed out of their sockets—and it invariably happens without warning, just when you're trying hardest to look cool. To clarify: it's not a drip, it's buckets. Real sight to behold, especially if you've never seen it before.

The Lustgartens cry out as I'm bent over, hands over my nose, pouring the Pacific onto their parquet floor, stammering, *it's water, just water, haha, sorry, dishtowel?* Cause no way am I sullying those napkins with my dishonorable discharge. Ira starts busting up, Georgia joins in, and Mrs. Lustgarten grabs a dishtowel and holds it to my nose as we argue over who's going to get the floor. I know I see victory in her eyes. She's won here without a shot fired, and I'm now the clown who doesn't stand a chance with her daughter. Takes the towel and disappears.

Georgia asks if I'm okay. I grumble that I'm fine, though I may need an ambulance for my dignity. Ira tells us about the Seder when he drank an entire bottle of Manishewitz and threw up on his Aunt Milka, and by the time Beth gets back, I feel very slightly better.

Carmela comes in, bearing coffee and a pineapple upside-down cake on a silver platter. A sturdy Mexican in her early twenties, she deposits it on the table and collects the dishes, then disappears without a word, as I stare down at my lap. My kind of people don't hire help, not even in LA, where labor is cheap. Maybe you pay some kid to mow the lawn or babysit, but that's it. Cleanup has always been me and Ray's job, so my hands get antsy when it's done for me, like a voice is whispering, *get off your ass, parasite.*

Fluke and his dad used to hold me down while the girls cleared the table, and finally just allowed my weird habit of helping the people who had fed me. But I'd felt safe with them, secure in their love. I dunno. Whatever. I managed not to flee the dinner, despite my little *faux pas*, and get my just dessert now. Achieve the Herculean feat of restraining myself to two slices of cake, and Georgia is reaching for another when her mom shoots her a look.

'Oh, Mom, please? It's so good!' I agree. It's all good. This whole house is like some kind of surfer's wet dream, with the food and the pool and forty-inch color TV. Were it on the beach like the Adamson house, you couldn't get me out of here with a crowbar. But her mom lays a hand on hers, eyes narrowed.

'Just one slice,' Georgia protests. 'I've been riding all day, on salad!'

'We'll discuss this later.' Jeez, now that's a mad-dog. Rowdy Yates never knew what hit him.

Georgia narrows her eyes right back, and cuts herself a slice; her mom bangs her hand down on the table so hard her wineglass falls over, then stalks out of the room. We watch the purple spread across the white linen—*you can get that out with salt*, is all my stunned brain can come up with. Then Georgia excuses herself, lips tight, to storm up the stairs.

Slam.

Slam.

What the hell just happened? We were fine. We were *fine*.

Is she actually telling her daughter not to eat, after what she went through? I'd eat all the time, feed strangers in the street, no one could stop me. Hell, I'd probably wander around supermarkets, jerking off. This makes no sense—and is this how Jewish families fight? I'd always assumed they were like Italians, threatening each other with violent death before hugging and pledging eternal fealty—but maybe they're more like WASP's, with the martinis and the silent treatment? I want to run upstairs and shake Beth till her teeth rattle, but I guess that wouldn't go over too well.

Don't recall any prohibitions in Leviticus about cake; it was mostly pigs, shrimp and grasshoppers you wanted to avoid. Kind of a boring book, though, all lepers and liability, and I might've dozed off, so it's probably something to do with torts. But who fights over cake? Isn't the whole point to eat it, if you're lucky enough to have some?

'I, um,' I say helpfully. 'Is this...should I leave? Or go check up on her?'

'No, no,' Ira says. He looks like a man who's walked a long way along a highway after his car ran out of gas. 'It's between them, it'll pass. Don't get involved, or they'll both turn on you.'

'Well, maybe. Hmm.' I blow some air out, struggle for something to say. 'So...are you still into jazz?' Hi-ho, a bomb just went off at the dinner table, let's talk Bird and Trane.

Drains his wineglass and lights a smoke. 'Not as much as I used to be. Got busy, I guess. Doesn't seem quite as life-or-death as it did back in the Mocambo days.'

'Nah, you're right. It's no good anymore. Not sure what happened there, but even Satch sold out with all the Vegas crap. It was gone stuff, you know? The best. And then it was just...gone.'

Tries on a smile. 'Like Picasso? Again with the passion?'

'Well, come on, it matters. Bebop's okay, but the new stuff is so cold. Detached. I'll probably be struck by lightning for saying this, but Miles Davis doesn't do zip for me.'

'Yeah, I don't dig him either. And poor Chet, rotting away in Italy...'

'Oh, he's out now. Just doesn't want to come back home.'

He barks a laugh. 'Who could blame him?'

'Yeah. Hum.' Fidget a little with my napkin. 'Look, I'm sorry, but I have to go make sure she's okay. Even if she bites my head off. Just doesn't feel right. Do you mind?'

'Nah, go ahead. I have to make a call.' He hesitates. 'You do make her happy, Tom. Happier than I've seen in a while—and don't mind Beth. She means well, just wants things...to go right for her. She can lose sight of the forest for the trees.'

'I don't know how anybody raises a kid, to be honest. Hat's off. But isn't she cool? One of the smartest people I ever met, so you must be doing something right.' Don't let anyone hurt her, I want to add. Not even *your precious martyr wife. Fuck the cars and clothes. Let her eat some goddamned cake*

He shoots me a look of such gratitude it knocks me out. Like no one's ever told him this, and he genuinely didn't know. There's more I want to tell him: how he can trust me, I'll build a fortress around her if I have to. That surfing isn't a waste of time, but like jazz, guys getting together to riff, though in the long run kind of a lonely pursuit. That I want it to make her happy, even as I want to tell her to run away fast, before it pulls her under. There's something he wants to say, too, I can tell, it's pushing at his mouth. He's silent, but I hear it anyway.

You make her happy. For now.

I smile back quickly, uncertainly, and head for the stairs.

No response to my knock. Then a quiet, 'I'm in here.'

The room is empty, bathroom door closed and locked.

'Can I come in?'

'No.'

'Is this about some stupid diet? You're not fat. That's insane.'

'It's more than that, Tommy.' The voice is coming from the floor, quiet; I kneel down to hear. 'She has to control every single part of my life, and I'm this dumb broken Barbie doll that never satisfies her. I don't think she even understands that I'm human.'

'Oh, she does. Come on. Moms just get pissy sometimes.'

'No, Tommy. She hates me, and I don't know why. Everybody thinks I'm making drama, and I can't stand being this cliché of the poor little Jewish princess whose mother walks all over her, but God, if I told you some of the things—no, no, I can't. I'm a good person, but I just can't anymore. I can't, I'm sorry, but I can't.' Her voice trails off into a sob.

'Can I come in, please? You're freaking me out.'

'No.'

224

I feel her on the other side of the door, nothing but wood between us.

'Want me to go hang her out the window till she apologizes?'

She sniffles, gulps a laugh. 'I love you, nutcase.'

'I'd do it. You don't get to use the Holocaust to be a jerk to your kid.'

'Oh, she would've been this way anyway. People are who they are. The shit they go through just makes them more so.'

My arms ache to hug her. I'm going to take her away from all this if it kills me, go someplace real and clear. Make her feel like the treasure she is every day for the rest of her life. I'm sure her parents mean well, and they can both go straight to hell.

'Just hang in there, okay? You'll be off to college before you know it, and your real life will begin. I'll show you Rincon, we'll go to Hawaii for Christmas break, and you'll be surfing circles around everyone.'

'Even Ricky?'

'Especially Ricky. And you'll get a trophy, if I have to forge it myself.'

The door opens so abruptly I fall in. She's taken off her pink sheath dress and is standing in her bra and panties. I gaze up at her tan body, her tearstained face. The bloody scratches across her thighs. Sit up, and touch them gently. 'Fuckin' A, Georgia! Why would you do this?'

She brushes my hand away brusquely, as if shooing a fly. 'I'm just so mad right now, Tommy. Something's not right, it's not, I can't figure out what. I barely eat, but I'm still packing it on, my skin's breaking out, and—God, she's right. I'm gross. Not voluptuous or zaftig or baby fat; I'm just fucking *fat*. It's disgusting.'

I'm on my feet, holding her face. 'I swear I'd tell you the truth about this, babe, cause I can see it matters to you. You're not fat, you're...no, fuck perfect. Perfect's left in the dust. Don't ever hurt yourself like this again, okay? Come scratch me instead.'

'You're not listening to me, Tommy. Something's *wrong*.' Slaps the wall, frantic. 'It's like I'm right before my period all the time, hormonal and weepy, and it's been months and months and...'

225

The light goes on for us both. Fuck. I can see it dawn in her eyes, but neither wants to be the first to say it out loud, lose our lucky charm

Hormones.

Those fucking pills. You can ignore the reality right in front of you, that you allowed inside you like the sad rube you are, because you needed to trust these doctors, with their *first do no harm*, and *try a cigarette instead of a sweet*, and *have some thalidomide, little lady, what could possibly go wrong?* It's like they're not even trying. I want to ram their goddamned pills up their asses.

'So much for our free lunch,' I manage.

'Maybe I'll get used to it,' she whispers. 'Maybe it'll stop.'

'How long has it been?'

Her fingers move in a quick minuet. 'Four months...no, five.'

'You're not gonna get used to it. And you don't have to.'

'Really?'

'What're you, kidding me? That's why God invented rubbers, right? That shit is gone. Hand it over.'

Pry open the medicine chest. Wow. A treasure trove of the usual stuff, plus a tidy selection of Seconal, Miltown, Dexedrine, five different kinds of diet pills, stuff I've never even heard of. Ricky would bust a nut. 'Well, howdy do. Which ones are they?'

She pulls out a round foil pack, letters and numbers on it like a kiddy decoder ring. I crumple it up, toss it in the toilet. We watch solemnly as it circles down in a rush and is gone.

'She made me take them,' she says.

I don't know what to say to that. 'I'm sorry.'

'Caught me with a guy, and marched the little whore-child straight down to the clinic. That was a fun day. And I should've figured this out by now on my own. That's how dumb she makes me.'

226

I put my arms around her, head to hers. Soon, I think. Soon.

She hands me the Seconal. I hesitate for a brief nasty second—I could get twenty bucks for it, easy—then unscrew the lid. *Sure?* She's sure. Tosses them in herself, a red rain of tinkling splashes, flush.

She's laughing now, at least, so we go wild, throw them all in, kissing each other, every pill gone for good, a hundred bucks flushed down the drain. Let the fish get high as shit tonight. We don't need this anymore, any of it. Better living through chemistry, my ass. We can make our own lives clear, like stepping out of a plane into nothing, like walking on water, forever and ever, amen.

'Better?' I ask as the last one swirls away.

She sighs. 'Yeah. A little shaky, maybe, but better. Now what?'

I touch her cheek. 'Can I ask you something stupid?'

'Still not slumming.'

'No, not that. It's just—do you really not know how beautiful you are? Like, are you kidding me? Fishing for compliments or something?'

'I'm okay, I guess. I don't think about it, I swear, it's so superficial, and everyone's so obsessed with it. But then someone like Marie Johnson shows up on the beach, and I feel like this dowdy shrimp bumpkin. She has this way of looking down her nose at you...'

'She does that to everyone. Even me, and I'm a foot taller than she is.'

Marie's a piece of work, all right. As far as I can tell, her only goal in life is to be noticed, with her big blonde bouffant and her slam-dunk body. She has these two fifteen-year old bodyguards, twin lunks who follow her everywhere, like freaky human accessories. We all fell about in raptures when she first started coming down, but it got old pretty fast once we saw we had no chance of getting in those size-six short shorts. It's not her morals; she just couldn't stand to muss her hair. Never goes into the water, or says a single interesting thing. Blahsville.

'Do you think she's pretty?'

'Who, Marie? Sure. Pretty as an Oscar, and probably as much fun in bed. But you'd have to ask Ricky about that.'

'Whoa, stop the press! Ricky banged Marie, and you're just telling me?'

'Oh, Marie doesn't put out for anyone. I mean he sleeps with an Oscar.'

She chuckles. 'He won an Oscar? For what, his outstanding work on 'Beach Baby Blowjob?''

'Let's just say he didn't so much 'win' it, as ripped it off from a party. Cops pulled us over, but they didn't look under the passenger seat.'

Laughs harder. 'How does he get away with this shit? The *chutzpah!*'

'Balls?'

'Yeah.' Cups mine, like she owns them. 'What about my mother?'

'What about your mother?'

'She's pretty hot stuff. I bet you'd sleep with her, wouldn't you?'

Hoo boy. Consider this, running fingers through her hair. There's no right answer here, so I might as well be honest and lay it out. 'She's the most gorgeous woman I've ever seen, but she's not good to you, and she scares the shit out of me. I can't get a read on her at all. But even if I could, and was into her, and she didn't look at me like I was something she'd scraped off her shoe, why the hell would I do that to you?'

Smiles to herself, a tight little smile. 'Tell me how pretty I am.'

'Please, you're not even slightly pretty,' I scoff. 'Pretty goes away.'

Her face relaxes; she runs one finger under her bra strap so it falls off her shoulder, and I feel a strange current running all through me: down my elbows, up my legs, seizing at my heart and lungs, coursing into my spine to swirl round my mind. Humans have this crazy notion that babies don't remember. We really do believe some weird shit: a savage can't feel pain, an animal can't think, neither goes to heaven. It makes life easier, believing the baby brain will be wiped clean. But breasts, we remember. That warm nourishing comfort.

I don't know a single guy who isn't into them, even the ass and leg men, even the precious gems who claim only to love a woman for her mind. I'm not a gem, mind you. I'd never date an ugly girl. But then, I've never seen an ugly girl. I guess we don't have that many here, but I've never seen any in pictures—even the plain Janes in glasses, you see that ironic intelligence glinting from their eyes. Bearded ladies of the circus, you think how comforting it would be to stroke that strange silky fur every night as you drift off. But breasts are really where it's at, and Georgia's are top notch.

Not that huge, I'd say maybe a 38C, but so right, how they feel under my hands. Pale and proud with those tiny rose nipples, and when she guides me to them I have a fierce memory of sucking, lips and tongue happily waiting for that surge of sweet warmth down my throat. It's not the milk I expect, exactly, more the promise that grace will roll down like a mighty stream, filling me with the spirit till I am hungry no more. I get this crazy vision sometimes when we're together, of me eating her whole, like Saturn with Venus. Keeping her in my belly for years, till it was safe to come out again. It's weird, I know. Don't freak, I wouldn't really do it. I just sort of...want to.

Weaning's the worst thing ever to happen to us, I think; seems like we spend the rest of our lives in an oral daze, brooding, trying to fill that hole. Fluke is definitely a breast man, and a real charmer so access is plentiful—yet he still smokes like a fucking fiend. But we're all fixated, chicks too. I mean, they *have* them, can't get away from them, and must feel themselves up all the time. I know I would. But they check out the knocker situation even more than we do, comparing. Like dicks, except that we get to put ours away. Women are just—they're right out there, you know? Vulnerable, nowhere to hide.

And yet, lovely as Georgia's breasts are, they're way down on the list of my favorite things. She's just so *human*. Honest and smart, awkward in all these ways that make me want to hug her till her bones crack. We kiss for a long time as I unhook her bra, run my lips over her nipples, slide my fingers between her legs as she moans: *please sir, may I have— ohh, please sir, please.*

the wall and God, I am so ready, with weeks of waiting, with the hard-on I've had for her since the moment we met.

She's touching the scar, the exquisite agony of it, and we're staggering a little, kicking off the last of our clothes, watching the images of these wide eyes and freckles and fingers on lips in the mirror and I whisper, *say it, say it now, tell me how fucking beautiful you are,* she shakes her head. I fuck her anyway, our last get-out-of-jail-freebie, and we're trying in vain to be quiet, knocking shit over, laughing, banging on the wall till she explodes like Pele, moaning into my neck. If you were standing just outside, you probably would've thought she was in pain.

She wasn't, though. I'm pretty sure she wasn't.

Then we skip *shul*, throw her board in the car, and head out without saying goodbye.

Round midnight, we're lying on my board, me cradled between her legs, head on her belly, gazing up at the moon, the occasional sudsy froth of cloud floating by. She forgot to bring her suit, so has my red trunks on and one of Fluke's T's that hides absolutely nothing, and the degree to which she doesn't care is like this drug for us both, the guys' gazes sliding off her like she's waxed. Her bottom turn is still a wreck, though, and I'm not doing much better.

After awhile we get tired of wiping out, so dry off and crouch down by the fire for a beer and a few laughs. Pip touches the scratches on her thighs, looking worried, but she shakes her head, *it's nothing, forget it.* His fingers linger for a second before he meets my eyes and withdraws, and we head out again, tandem this time, just to float for a while, rising and falling with the waves.

'You really read it all?' She's asked me this twice already.

'Just the Old Testament. Wasn't like much else was going on.'

'Remember the very first chapter? In the beginning?'

'Who could forget? Nothing but water and darkness and chaos.'

'He didn't make the water, though. He just named it: *mayim*. And on the second day he put some up in the sky: *sham-mayim*. There-water. That's all there was, for all eternity: water, and wind over the face of it. The first wave was here even before God. He just sort of...sorted it out.'

'Will there be any surfboards in heaven,' I sing softly. 'Will they tell us that we cannot ride?'

We're quiet, counting the stars, half-asleep, rocked by the swells.

'Tell me,' I say, and swirl my toes gently through the water.

'Hmmm?' She sounds drowsy.

'What happened with the cake? The one we made?'

'Oh, hell, I don't want to talk about that.'

'Come on. This is going to kill me. I loved that cake.'

'Will you tell me about your dad?'

I stop stroking her calf. 'Nothing to tell.'

'Then it won't take long. Come on, Tommy. We've been together two months, and you haven't said word one about him. Not a word.'

Sit up then, it's like my jaw is wired shut. I can't joke about it, or change the subject, or even breathe for a moment. Let it go, is what I've been telling everyone from Mama to Fluke to my guidance counselor, for eight long years. Let it the fuck go. Blow out a few quick puffs, then take it all in, a deep shuddering gasp; slip over the side without a word, stroke down. Exploring the depths, feeling my way, all moonlight gone, nothing here but the safety of darkness. Down and down and down. *Nimm mich tiefer, tiefer.* Deeper still.

Aho Loa, they called it, the breath-holding contests in old Hawaii, and they didn't screw around: diving for pearls at first, then just for the glory of it. Most people can do a minute, maybe two if they're good. Those guys would go ten, fifteen—even twenty. I've never made it past eight; even then your brain starts to cannibalize you for oxygen, your muscles seize up, and you slip into this sleepy euphoria until you don't want to come up, maybe ever.

The deeper you go, the easier it is to stay, all that water holding you down where you belong. That's why it's not a good idea to do this on your own. Fluke quit after the first time I passed out, but Mysto doesn't seem to mind, just sits up top with a stopwatch and dives in to check things out at the six mark. He gets that sometimes you want to be really good at just one thing, even if it's something everyone else thinks is dangerous and pointless. It's different when you're not drowning, when you're down there by choice. You give yourself up, to life or death. Either way, the surrender is wholly yours.

I hit bottom, feel the sand rise up around me, relax into it, holding onto kelp, ears popping, heartbeat slowing to lag mode. Not too deep—the reason Malibu has such mellow waves is because we don't have serious dropoff; there's nowhere for the swells to spend their fury, so they just ease on in. Took a while to keep my eyes open, but you get used to it. It doesn't burn as bad when everything you know is made of tears.

I packed him away long ago, into a Pandora's box of bitter wrongs and useless regrets, one I'd rather not look into, ever again. Does she really need to know about...shit, about any of this? It doesn't affect us. I will never, ever do the things he's done. Even letting him in for a moment leaves me naked with rage, so I'll just live down here alone in the dark till I'm human again, inner time growing as the world above shrinks to nil. Stay focused, now. My lung capacity isn't that tremendous, but I've always needed to show myself I can live without air, or love, or money, or any these things we've deemed so essential.

Minute four is when it gets interesting. Your body grows suspicious, no longer falling for tricks—the slowed metabolism, the alphabet game—and begins to punch at you to rise, rebelling against your will.

There is a splash overhead, and she is briefly silhouetted against the surface, swimming down to me, unable to see. I let the air out, follow the bubbles up, move into her arms, and her mouth is on mine, feeding me oxygen from those kind lips. This girl's trying to save my sorry ass; the least I can do is be straight with her.

We surface next to the board, gasping, and I blurt it out before I push it back down: 'He was a bad guy. He did some really fucked-up shit to my mom, Ray and I were too little to stop him, it would've made it worse if we tried—and we left and had nothing, thought we were going to starve and no one would care. Mama pulled us out of that, but it took a lot out of her, so I'm sorry if...she's a good person, you have to know that. And I'm a good person, too, at least I think I am—but if I saw him today, I'd kill him where he fucking stood. That's inside me now forever, that shittiness. I don't get to flush it and be done. It's never going away, and all talking about does is make me furious, because you know what? He was hurting her, and I should have done something. So let's never talk about him again. Ever.'

The board is rocking, and she dives under, puts her arms around me, hands over my heart. Says nothing until the shaking subsides. Then, so quiet I can barely hear, she says, 'He doesn't get to live here anymore.' Shake my head, but I'm not agreeing. He does get to live here. He serves a purpose: that I will never hurt her, and I will never leave.

She never did tell me what happened with the cake, that cake we'd put our hearts into, but I can imagine, I guess. Those dumb horrible scenes we have with the ones we love, who are supposed to love us back. You think you'll get over them, but instead they build up like residue on a painting, until every color is dull and dirty, and you can barely see the pure image that once thrilled you so. These people do get to live here—all of them, forever—just as you do with them. So don't fuck it up.

At last she says, 'I'm starving, Tommy. Wanna go get some tacos?'

I laugh into the board, weary to the bone, and against all odds hungry again myself. 'Yeah. Yeah, baby, I do.'

It's pitch dark in here, but I know it's a tunnel. Shout, *hello*, and hear the sound echo down its length: *low, low, low*. Full of abandoned cars. Not sure what happened, but figure I should get out before the whole thing collapses. No light from either end, so I just pick a direction and fumble along, barking shins, stubbing toes, nearly falling a few times. Spot a flashlight bobbing up ahead: Georgia, here to guide me out.

Malibu never looked so sweet as when we emerge, the moonlight laying gentle fingers on the unscathed empty cars. No catastrophe I can see, everyone's just...gone. She points up at the cliff, to an enormous mural of a mermaid. Once we gain some distance, though, I look back and see it's simply a woman, greenery grown over her running legs.

What is she running from? Or toward? There's a bunch of flowers in her hand, so maybe she's on her way to meet a lover. Close my eyes to imagine the shock of the encounter. Her throwing her giant self upon him, the sudden reality of all that warm flesh in his arms.

The smell of earth after the rain. Open my eyes, and my arms are thick with it up to the elbow, furrow upon furrow, waiting to receive us. Georgia's wandering down a row, hair tied back with a blue bandanna, overalls loose around her like Johnny Appleseed.

Calls over, 'You want to go straight? Or mix it all up?'

'I don't know,' I say. 'I'm planting potatoes.'

'Potatoes are a winter crop, silly. It's spring.'

'Potatoes can grow anytime. Just cut 'em up and toss 'em out.'

'I want to plant an Indian garden. Corn, beans, and squash. What's that word again...synchronicity? Symbiosis, that's it. And herbs under your bedroom window.'

'What kind of herbs?'

'Sage, oregano, and cilantro. All of the locals, and every kind of thyme. 'Rosemary, that's for remembrance.'

'Pansies are nice,' I allow.

'Oh, I love pansies. A whole garden of thoughtful fairies.'

'"You must wear your rue with a difference.' What *is* rue, anyway?'

'Another herb. I think it's poison.'

'That's yew.'

'No, rue too. There's loads of poisonous plants. All the lilies.'

'"Consider the lilies of the field. They toil not, neither do they spin.' Now we know why; they're quietly plotting our demise.'

'And foxglove—all those 'accidental' deaths in Agatha Christie. Put the Brits right off salad forever.'

'Did you know she surfed? Agatha Christie was the first English surfer. Isabel Letham in Australia, Heather Price in South Africa, Kelea and the queens out in Maui. You were there from the start.'

'Christie, huh? Last of the hard-boiled Dames.' She sounds wistful. 'And there's oleander—but you can't cook with that.'

'I never trusted oleander anyway; all those spiky dagger leaves, and that sticky milk-sap. Morning Glories are cool.'

'We'll plant some by the fence. Pretty blue flowers to greet us at dawn.'

'It's a hallucinogen,' I tell her. 'Like jimson weed. You chew the seeds, or make tea. Too many'll kill you, though.'

'Did you know you can kill someone with a pack of cigarettes?'

'Be sure and tell Fluke.'

'No, really, you soak them in a glass of water. Drink it and—'she draws a finger across her throat. 'Kaput. Acute nicotine poisoning.'

'Well, the trick would be getting them to drink it.'

'Oh, no, that'd be the easy part. I can get anybody to do anything.'

'And the hard part?'

'Deciding who to kill, of course.'

'Not me, right?'

'Duh.' She rolls her eyes. 'But they don't mean to be that way; it's just a defense mechanism so they don't get eaten. It's how you fight without teeth and claws. And they're all useful in moderation, like for medicine and anesthesia and stuff. The only trick is not to overdo it.'

'This is fun.' I finish digging and look around for a faucet, trying to get some of the dirt off my hands. 'We should do this every day.'

'We can if you want. You kinda have to, with gardens. All that weeding.'

'Not potatoes. Forget about them, and six months later: hey, dinner.'

'This is really nice, Tommy. I always wanted my own garden.'

'Our own little Eden.'

'Nah, not like that.'

'Why not?'

'Because not. Not everything is like something else. It's not Candide's garden, or Lear's, or anybody else's. Just ours, okay?'

'Which Lear? King or Edward?'

'Edward, natch. 'There was an old man in a garden, who always begged everyone's pardon..."'

Wipe my hands on my jeans. 'I do that, don't I? Not even sure why.'

She comes over and takes my hand, presses it to her cheek, and all around us the garden begins to grow. Little shoots poke out of the earth to become stalwart bushes; every kind of flower appears, from humble violets to elegant Calla lilies. Long vines of ivy, wisteria and Morning Glory twine over the fence, as a wave of poppies washes through, licks at our legs. Bees buzz around, and a hummingbird zips out of the sky as

236

an orange tree bursts into bloom. *Lustgarten*, the garden-joy. Dizzied with color and fragrance, with the ease of all this perilous beauty, I close my eyes.

And then I'm alone on a boat, out on the ocean. Ship the oars for a sec to try to figure out where I am, then row east, trying to get back west. The water is dead calm. Pacific.

I'm not worried, in the dream. I know eventually I'll get wherever I'm going; the boat seems sound, and there's the water and food Georgia packed, and a little jar of honey. Oh wonderful Pussy, oh Pussy my love. No five-pound note, but nowhere to spend it anyway. I'll be okay.

I row and row for a long time, as night creeps over the sky. It's entirely possible I may never get anywhere, just spend my whole life in this boat in the middle of the ocean, dip and pull, only the seagulls to keep me company. I don't feel discouraged, though. It's weird, but I don't even feel that lonely. Just like, well, here's what we're doing now, so let's get a move on. Row some more.

Eventually I wake up, zombie-zonked. My arms ache all day. I do tell Fluke about this one, and he says, almost enviously, 'You have the weirdest fucking dreams of anyone I know, Tommy.' Ask him what he dreams about, and he says cars and Jayne Mansfield.

'Nothing else? Not even surfing?'

Shakes his head. 'Not even once. I think surfing *is* the dream, y'know? How about you?'

'Yeah,' I say. 'All the time.'

'Good dreams?'

'Well, they're all good dreams,' I say. 'At first.'

Michelangelo never wanted to paint the Sistine Chapel in the first place; he was more of a sculptor, really, and was happily puttering away with a big marble piece when the Pope's goons showed up to frogmarch him down to the Vatican. No one says no to the Pope, so bam, three years of his life up on a ladder, and his back was never the same. Pretty bitchen result, though. Mine is nowhere near, of course, but it's coming along a lot better than expected.

I'd thought getting back into this was would be some big artist's-block nightmare, so was surprised at how easily my hands remembered how to do it. Got home from the hospital, pulled a sketchbook out of the closet, and after a few awkward doodles, a dam burst. Sat in bed for a week surrounded by books, snapshots and magazines, sketching out our world of waves: Malibu, Makaha, Torquay, Biarritz. A flaming sun in a cloudless sky, smiling down over us. Walk into the shop and you're on an island in the middle of it all, can almost hear the crash of surf and gulls screeching, feel the spray on your face.

'Hey, Sophia, check it out!' High on paint fumes, I just added shades and a shaka to the surfing kangaroo, unable to think of any significant Aussie surfers. Plane fare's impossible—but reports say they're killing it Down Under, upside-down or not. The waves are slabs of dark-green; a shark fin lurks off in the distance.

No answer. She's over in the corner by Hawaii, passed out on the floor, still holding a paintbrush. Poor kid, we've had her up since five, surfer hours, and now it's almost...ten? Jesus. And working our asses off the whole time, only a few breaks for soda and snacks. I hop off the ladder, cap the paint, toss our brushes in the cleanup jar. Check out the racks in back: three figures hard at work in a buzzing snowstorm.

'Hey!' I shout over the noise. 'Hey, Ray, let's go! Bedtime, Bonzo!'

The planer goes quiet, goggles and dust masks pulled off faces.

'You guys all done out there?'

Fluke's hair is white—all of him is but for the circles round his eyes. Pip and Ray look just as bad, plucking bits of foam off their tongues. We need to set up some kind of ventilation system in here before we start glassing, something more serious than propping open the back door, or we're all going to suffocate.

'Almost, just a few more touches—but we should get Sophia home, or your ma'll have our heads.'

Ray slouches into the head to clean up; I can hear him exclaiming at the sight in the mirror. Fluke brushes himself off, and we wake Sophia up. 'Hey kiddo.' He shakes her shoulder.

'Lava,' she murmurs. There's a smear of blue on her lip, like a mustache.

'No lava. Home-a.'

She opens her eyes, then. 'Oh, Eddie...you have ashes in your hair.'

'Nah, just foam. See?' He combs some out, lets it drop to the floor.

'I...huh. I had the craziest dream.' Sits up, rubs her eyes. 'A volcano blew up the whole world, and we were flying through space, and...'

'And you were there, Tin Man?'

'No, it was *real*. We were fine, just shooting off in different directions, but we couldn't talk to each other. Wasn't even that scary, just lonely. Lonely and dark, and really empty.'

No one can hear you scream, I think.

'Well, you're back, safe and sound.' Holds out a hand. 'On your feet, cosmonaut—you're too big for me to carry anymore.'

I drop Pip off at the beach, Ray climbs into the front seat, and we head home. At the light I dust some white off the nape of his neck. He hasn't shaved today, not that either of us really needs to, and is starting to bear an unfortunate resemblance to our father. He always had that fall of hair over his dark eyes, but now his nose and jaw are taking on that sharp, cruel look, too. Handsome—I can see why Mama fell for the fucker in the first place—but this is Ray, and my hands long to rub it out. It's not who he is.

'Not too bad, so far.' Cracks his back. 'I'm into it. Got a few ideas.'

'Oh, yeah? Well, shit. Lay 'em on me, Tesla.'

'Nah, probably stuff that's been done before. Never mind.'

'Ah, come on, spill.'

'Buncha stuff. Mostly speed. Speed is good, right?'

'Depends on what you're shooting for. Helps catch, but then your trim's out of control. It's harder to steer.'

'Right, okay. So we'd make up for it in other ways. Go shorter, by a lot—and then if we did a hydrodynamic combination on the rocker, convex at the front, ease into concave, you'd still have the speed, but with just enough drag to...and channel the deck—and something with the rails. The fins, though. The fins are what's bugging me. There's gotta be some way to steer, like a rudder.'

'Too complicated. On a paddleboard, maybe.'

'Like a lever you could press with your heel.'

'But that's sailing, Ray. *You're* supposed to be the rudder. And you feel the water, you don't dominate it. Get too technical out there, and it's no fun anymore.'

'Ahh, you're not ready for my brilliant innovations, old man.'

'Well, someday we'll all be flying around in jetpacks and getting meals in pill form. Till then, let's just turn out some boards.'

He's quiet for a while, lost in thought.

'So you gonna tell me about her?' Hang a left, trying for casual.

'Who?'

'Um, the girl I found you in bed with, you nasty little bastard.'

'Oh. Hmmm. Just a girl.'

'Yeah, I gathered as much. Kinda caught me by surprise there.'

'Well, that'd explain why you screamed and ran out of the house.'

'Gee, I'm sorry, *nerdus pervium*. You wanted me to stay and watch?'

Laughs a little, squeezing his temples. 'Can we not talk about this?'

'First time?'

Silence. His head turned away, watching the cars.

'Hmm?'

'You know, you miss a lot when you're never home, Tommy.' He shrugs. 'Let's just say your legacy wasn't all teachers getting revenge on your delinquent ass. There were perks. No one messed with me, and a lot of girls were very eager to find out if lightning had struck twice with Da Rod's dorky kid brother.'

There's a rushing in my ears. Pussy can be a torturous row to hoe on your own, and I was supposed to keep him safe. That was my job, and I was always out with my friends or off in a dream. All those times I could've sworn I smelled that funk in our room...but no way, he was right there, reading a book or diagramming a circuit, and why on earth would anyone sully this pure soul? Pretty brazen, though—even I never dared bring them home. Headlights blaze in my eyes, a car swinging wide round the bend, and I nearly swerve into a pine tree. The narrow road that runs over the twining ridge may not be the best place to discuss this, but now I'm piqued.

'You could've dropped a hint, man. You were always so quiet, I didn't think...I mean, shit, did anybody even give you the talk? You know, birds, bees, social disease—'

'Mama did. She was changing the sheets and some panties fell out.'

'Mama did.' I hum an anxious little tune. 'Our Mama.'

He nods stoically.

'Ho dogs...how bad was it?'

'Not really the high point of my life, to be honest. She was pretty, um, comprehensive. Cucumbers were involved.'

I groan. 'You coulda come to me. Either of you. I'm right here.'

'But you're not, Tom. You took off when I was nine, and we've barely seen you since. You ditched us. Like you'd joined the Merchant Marine, but without the postcards from Shanghai.'

I pull up by the house. She left the porch light on for us, but he makes no move to get out. Waiting.

'I had a life, Ray,' I say uncomfortably. 'Not a federal offense.'

'You know what I mean. It's not just sex talks and mowing the lawn.'

'Oh, c'mon, don't give me that. You never cared about surfing.'

'*Du hast mich nie gefragt*, Tommy.'

'What would you have said?'

'No, probably. But you could've asked.'

'Ray?'

'What?'

'You wanna go surfing?'

'No.' He sighs. 'I mean, not right this minute. But I guess I'm going to have to at some point, right? Do me one favor, though—don't let your fucking friends laugh at me, okay?'

'They're not like that, man. They wouldn't. But I know a break where there's no one around, great waves, it'd be perfect. Next week?'

'Sure.' He wrestles open the door; it's been squinchy ever since I got sideswiped by some jerk on La Cienega. 'Just so you know, Tommy— you're a space-case most of the time, but as brothers go, you're all right. I mean, I wouldn't trade you in or anything.

242

'Yeah, good to know. Now get your ass in the shower, you've got gunk in your ears. And your nuts, too, trust me. Don't leave it too long, or it'll itch like a mother. *Hasta.*'

'Where to now?'

'Gotta go see a girl about a girl.'

'Tell her I said hi.'

'Yeah, back off, Romeo. You got yours.'

He chuckles, and I drive off. My fucking baby brother.

On the nod at a light until a horn blares me awake and I drive on. Just wanted to see her before I went to bed, if only for a kiss. Surprise her. I brought her a bouquet of roses from the yard last night; she was on her way out to the movies with a girlfriend and tried to drag me along, but I had to get back. I wanted to keep my promise, the Saturday night thing, but she looked like she was in good hands. *Is this the fabled boyfriend?* the girl had asked, and Georgia gazed at me, her eyes radiant. *Oh, no, better. This is Tommy.*

Maybe she's not home. No, it's nearly midnight on a Sunday, where else would she be? I jump the gate, shinny up the old jacaranda outside her window, and am poised to throw a pebble at the glass, when I stop.

The curtains are open, and she's feeding the fish—she has this big aquarium full of zebras and angels and mollies, little snails and suckers, a peacock eel, even a benign miniature shark. Watches them as they race for the crumbs at the top, a smile playing around her lips, then starts to undress for bed by the dim light of a reading lamp. Stops. Goes over to the mirror, examines herself, puts one hand to the glass as if encountering a friend she hasn't seen in a while. Turns, traces the chiaroscuro curve of breasts and hips, sucks in her stomach, then turns back. Tries for a bicep, and frowns. Tries harder. We can do it.

All thoughts of attracting attention are gone; she can't know I've seen her like this. But neither can I stop watching, like an unexpectedly good Late Show, and the creepy feeling in my belly just makes it better. Then

She drops to the floor, out of sight, and I have to stand to see. Push-ups. Go, kiddo. Makes it to twelve before dropping, exhausted, and I think it's okay, all the time in the world, go to sleep. I love you. But she starts again, hair in her face, body ramrod-straight in girdle and bra, barely making it. Up and down and up again.

I'm there for a long time, half-dreaming as she struggles. She passed the 200 mark, her arms are shuddering, she's still at it—but why? I know why, as I slide silently down the tree and drive home. I know why, and it breaks me that she does this alone, like something to be ashamed of. Strong arms mean speed; they help you catch. But then the trim's out of control. It's harder to steer.

I never bought the Pygmalion myth, you know? You can't turn a person into someone else, no matter how badly you want to. Even Aphrodite couldn't. People will wrestle their own selves out of who they are, to become who they're meant to be. That woman yearned to be more than just a pretty marble statue, and it wasn't some pervy sculptor's kiss that made her flesh.

Drifting off to sleep, though, I can't help but think: I want this for her. Whatever she's aiming for, whoever she wants to be. There's something strange happening in there, a chrysalis stirring right in front of me, and I can't wait to see what emerges.

I'm a lucky man, I think: she's nuts, this girl, there's this ferocity to her, she can do anything in the world she sets her sights on, and I get to be along for the ride, maybe...and then the alarm is going off and it's time to get back to the shop. Put my shirt on inside-out, and may just leave it that way. Ray tumbles out of bed, too, hair all bent up and wild, and starts pulling on his pants.

'Where you going?'

'Coming down with you.'

'School. Monday. You've got school. Go back to bed.'

'You need the help—and there's no school today, Dopey.'

Shit. I don't even know what—oh, right. Labor Day.

244

'Listen, just sleep in, okay? Enjoy your last day of freedom. You can come over tomorrow after...y'know, classes.' My bed is singing a warm sweet song, hard to tune out. 'Once you've finished your homework. Because college and...stuff. Future. Fuck.'

'Uh-huh. I'll start the coffee.'

I shouldn't be working today, either. Labor Day was sacred when we were growing up, a government guilt-grant from 1894 after a massacre of striking Pullman porters. Americans work so hard, and are so easily mollified by the occasional holiday, falling for the dangled leisure carrot every time. But the shirts are ready to be silkscreened, and I'm the only one who can do it. One day, I tell myself. Hell, even Hank Greenberg played on Yom Kippur—oh. No, he didn't. Middle of the '34 pennant, he flipped them off and sat it out. Hell, it's just one day. Next year I'll be back out there marching with SAG and the garment workers.

The unions took a while to make it out west, and the rag trade was one of the last to fall. 'Open Shop,' they called it, meaning you could exploit the hell out of desperate seamstresses, hire the lowest bidders, saddle them with inhumane hours, then send them home with piecework to boot. The East Coast garment unions just hummed and looked the other way, because what're you gonna do—everyone knows you can't organize Mexicans, right?

Well, yeah, turns out you can. Rose Perotta, a Jewish anarchist and ILGWU activist, came out in '33—this was after the New Deal began half-assedly enforcing bargaining rights, but Los Angeles was still like, *haha, Fed fuckers can't tell us what to do*—got some Spanish speakers on board, and they went around and knocked on every door, preaching the gospel of solidarity and resistance. And one day all these quiet little seamstresses stood up from their machines, chanting, '*Huelga! Huelga!*' Walked out for a month, picketing the factories, singing and speaking in the streets, pelting the scabs with tomatoes, and getting arrested none too gently by the LAPD's Red Squad.

And they did it. Strikers shut her down, and Angelenos will go without food before we'll forgo new clothes, so they got their Local 96, along with a 35-hour work week, decent conditions and no more piecework. Started a Spanish community radio station—and organized themselves from then on, men and women together.

Isn't that the greatest? Because in truth, it is kinda hard to organize Mexicans—or was. They're nice people, and nice people are doormats in this town. The whole state took note, and backed off to pick on the Okies for a while, but that's another story.

The following year, over one and a half million Americans struck for better wages. Most of the strikes failed, and the strikers were arrested, beaten, murdered—but they changed our country for good, made our brilliant quasi-Socialist economy possible. The Wagner Act was passed, legalizing unions, collective bargaining and strikes. In 1938 Roosevelt passed the Fair Labor Standards Act, guaranteeing a minimum wage and 40-hour work week. The owners raised merry hell, but they had to go with it—for the time being. This shit matters, and we all know what happens to liberty when you relax your vigilance.

This is a bone of contention between me and Fluke. He had a contact who could get the shirts on the cheap, but when I asked if they were union, he wiffled and waffled and finally acknowledged that they were some kind of Taiwanese sweatshop bullshit.

'It's half the price,' he growls. 'Could you for once not break my balls?'

'You know how I feel about this, man. Union or bust.'

'We're *already* bust, goddammit, and they'll cost a buck apiece!'

'So we'll just get a couple dozen, then, and charge three.'

'The hell you on? No one in their right mind is gonna pay three bucks for a T-shirt.'

'Guess we'll see. But that and the Beach Boys are my only conditions.'

'What's this about the Beach Boys? You're not still on that shit!'

'You don't get to sing about something you don't do. Period.'

'Uh-huh. So what'd your good friend down at Capitol say when you explained this to him?'

'Nothing. I didn't tell him. He sent them along with the others.'

He riffles quickly through the boxes of LP's and 45's, as I busy myself with a pile of forms. We're going to have to wait a couple of months till we have money for the premiums, but I want to get this out of the way now, otherwise I know it'll get buried.

'Tommy?'

'Hmm?' I am all innocence, preoccupied with insurance clauses.

'Where are they?'

Jerk a thumb at the door. 'Out in the trash, where they belong.'

He takes a breath. 'Tommy, I am this close to beating your dumb ass to doomsday. You can't have a store that sells nothing but surf shit, then refuse to stock the top-selling surf band. You can't, that's all there is to it. It's like a pizzeria that won't do pepperoni.'

Goes out to the alley, comes back a minute later with an armload of records. 'You don't have to approve, man. You don't even have to listen. All you have to do is fucking sell them.'

'And all they have to do is get on a fucking board. Just once. *Once!*'

'They're not axe murderers, for Chrissake, just dorks. You go to bat for dorks all the time!'

'We don't support scabs, or candy-ass *poseurs*. I'll burn this place to the ground first, and I'm through talking about this. Can we go shape now?'

He takes the records home, and Sophia, who agrees with me, won't touch them either, and eventually Leo takes them to Scouts, where they get turned into ashtrays.

I doze a little, waiting for the emulsion to harden on the silkscreens. Weirdest thing happened when I went down to order the stuff, check out the available merch and figure out prices. Eventually we're going to branch out to towels and bikinis, but right now we have just about enough for some T's and a dozen trunks, and that's it. The voice on the line sounded oddly familiar, and when I walk into the brick building off 10th and Maple, the girl at the desk waves me off for a sec as she finishes her phone call. I'm leafing through a catalog, when she says, 'Tommy?'

My head snaps up. Oh...no way. It can't be. Holy shit. Just like that, I'm tongue-tied and twelve again.

She stands, one hand to her cheek. 'Jeez, it *is* you! Damn, you got *tall*. What happened?'

'Uh...hey, Tina.' Scintillating, dorkus. *Plus ça change.* No wonder she dumped you. She skips out to throw herself in for a hug, and I recover. 'I can't believe...how *are* you? Where you been hiding yourself?'

'You know me, here and there, this and that. Secretarial school, then my uncle swung me this job. You?'

'Ah, surfing, mostly.' It's true. That's all I've done with my life for seven years, paddled out on a board and got pushed back to shore. Even Sisyphus would raise an eyebrow.

She clicks her tongue. 'You and the *chingado* surf. I never got it.'

'Well, good thing you didn't have to.' The hurt is still there, you can hear it. Thought I was over her after all this time, but I thought wrong. She's grown herself—not taller, but fleshed out, no longer the skinny sardonic child I was so obsessed with, that wild hair tamed into a tidy professional bun now. The way she deflated all my drama, made me laugh again; I never found another girl who kissed me like that, with such clean, unfettered affection.

Flash on our first time, her legs around my back in the garden shed: the terror of hurting her, of being found out. The thrill of discovery, that precarious sense of no longer being alone. Possessed by her soft heat, so grateful to lose myself in the delicious jungle of her body. And then one day she pushed me off a cliff, and I never saw her again.

She pulls back, eyes me. 'Tommy, why do you think we broke up?'

''Cause I wasn't cool enough.' Aim for flip, but it's more of a mumble.

'No, baby, you were plenty cool. But every date turned into 'oh, let's go down to the beach, I just want to show you this one boss thing!'—then you'd ditch me for hours while you were out with your friends.'

Hang my head; she's right. I did that constantly, desperate to impress. Twice I came out and she wasn't even there, had caught a ride home with one of the older guys. I'd stand there like a dope, dripping on the sand, abandoned and abashed. And I never learned.

'Don't know what to say, Teen. You were great, and I was just a dumb kid who didn't appreciate.'

'Ahh,' and she waves it off. 'Water under the board, right? But how can I help you today?'

The way she says it makes me instantly think of a dozen things, none of which have much to do with surfwear, but I shake them off and explain our predicament. She nods.

'And you'll have the money for a larger order by the 20th?'

'Pretty sure. End of the month at the latest.'

'All right, I'll see what I can do. But *andale*, let's go get you squared.'

It's my first time walking the floor of one of these places. Sewing at home is a quiet affair, Mama humming through the pins in her mouth, cussing from time to time. But there are a million different machines here, all roaring away: sergers, cutters and mangles; rows of solid old Singers. The fabric dust floats thick in the shafts of sunlight filtering down from the overhead windows, tickling your nose and throat. The women don't seem to mind, shaking back their heads to stare me down, curious as cats. One asks Tina a quiet question; she laughs low, says, *pasado*, and they all start with the wolf-whistles and the *cariñosos* as I ham it up for them, bowing and blowing kisses until Tina shouts, *¡calmense, sinverguenzas!* and pulls me through a door in back.

We go through the piles of shirts, and I pick out a few colors, and she throws in a wide-necked nautical style with blue and white stripes she says is very big right now in France. And then we talk shorts. Just the usual trunks, I tell her, but I've got ideas about a new style, when we have a little more cash to play with.

'There's too much fabric,' I explain. 'It gets heavy, and bunches up.'

'So you need tighter.'

'Just a little. Mostly shorter.' Boards used to rip the shit out of us; you could tell a true surfer by his hairless inner thighs. For a long time we

249

surfed in sailor pants or jeans, cut off at the knee. Then along came Nancy Katin, the tiny chainsmoking seamstress saint of Huntington and her indestructible Kanvas Katins have been hanging off our hips ever since. They're heavy as shit, though, and the wax and boards are smoother. We're ready for a change.

'Why not just go with Speedos?'

'No, trust me, we'd be falling out all over, and no one needs to see that. Something a little more reliable, you know?'

She grins. 'You want a sort of trunk-bikini, then?'

'Kinda. We need the support, but the less we feel, the better. Thin and flexible, but sturdy. Is that too much? Use strong nylon, maybe even a dual-layer—but not so short that you can see, you know...'

'So you want to surf naked, but not get arrested. Yeah, I think we can do that. How much you looking to spend?'

'I can give you thirty today. We'll try it out, then get a few more and— depends how they sell. We can do a percentage, or just a straight buy.'

'All right, deal. Take your pants off.'

'What? Uh, take—what?' I stammer.

Pulls a tape measure from around her neck, laughing. 'Can't help you if you don't take your pants off, Tommy. Try to design this on the fly, it'll be a mess. Don't go shy on me, it's nothing I ain't seen before.'

I unzip and drop trou, then stare up at the ceiling, trying to hold still as she runs the tape around my waist, from hip to thigh, hip to hip, under my groin, as I'm thinking *don't get wood don't get wood* and of course instantly get insane wood, and she's jotting figures down in a notebook, and then her thumb is at the base of my cock through my boxers, and she's measuring that too, and I pull back.

'Hey there now, hey-hey, I know you don't need that. Didn't fall off the turnip truck just yesterday.'

'For support, extra protection. Shorts this flimsy, a cute girl walks by—'

'Whoa, really? You can do that?' Boner camouflage is the holy grail of men's swimsuits. We're gonna be millionaires. Surreptitiously rearrange myself and zip up.

'Nah, just messing with you. But it's something to put on your resume.'

'Why, you little...' I laugh. 'You got some gall, Vasquez. I oughtta turn you over my knee.'

'Oh, yeah? Whatcha doing tonight?'

Shit. 'There's...I'm sorry. There's someone else.' So help me, it feels like a betrayal of them both. For a terrible instant, I can't recall her name.

'Ahh. Lucky girl. Well, if that changes, you know where to find me. See you in a week.'

And that wasn't even the weird part. Nor was meeting her again after all those years. It's that ever since, I haven't been able to get her out of my head—and knowing her, she probably knows it, too.

Fluke and Pip shamble in at ten with a thermos of coffee and a bag of tacos, as the shirts are drying all over the shop. It's a nice array; we've got 'Duke University,' Kahanamoku standing proudly at Makaha with a fourteen-foot *olo*; 'Shaka Zulu,' the African warrior king sailing through a barrel, spear in one hand, surfer's salute in the other; 'Jesus Surfed,' and half a dozen more with just our logo.

'Oh, plus they put some extra stuff into the box by mistake,' I tell them. 'I was gonna send them back, but then I had a better idea.'

Two dozen white cotton panties are spread over the boards, dry now. 'X,' they state in black Roman font, and in smaller letters underneath: 'Mark Your Spot.'

'See? 'Don't Get Your Panties in a Bunch, Incorporated," I gloat. 'Came through after all.'

'Damn, Tommy,' says Fluke. 'You're gonna get us shut down. 'Jesus' is bad enough.'

'What're you talking about? I ran 'Jesus' by your ma, and she loved it! Even your dad thought it was funny!'

'Yeah, well, Catholics have a sense of humor. It's those Pentecostals we need to worry about, the snake handlers. Pip, take those off your head, you're gonna stretch them out.'

Pip pulls the elastic over his nose, eyes us through the leg holes.

'It's not a bad look,' I muse. 'We could send him out to rob banks.'

'I dunno,' Fluke says. 'Maybe something a little more...pedestrian.'

'But we're not pedestrians,' I point out. 'We're rogue Aquarians.'

'Oh, good one. Do that. You gonna help us glass?'

'Sure, give me a couple minutes to finish up the mural.'

An hour later, he pokes my calf. 'Hey, asshole. You promised to help.'

'Look,' I exclaim. 'Look, I made a compass rose! And the latitude and longitude for each beach!'

'It's amazing, dorkus. Now help.'

'Can you tell who that is?'

He glances at it; you could spot that stance from space. 'Ricky.'

'And Biarritz?'

'I dunno, some old guy? Oh, it's John. From that picture he sent you.'

Duke, of course, owns Hawaii. He owns the whole shebang, really. The rest of us will be trailing in his wake for all eternity, picking up the sets he generously leaves behind. I come down off the ladder, slug some coffee, and start producing something that isn't useless—or maybe is, depending on how you look at it.

It was Oscar Wilde who acknowledged that all art is completely useless, and he was smirking when he said it, in that irresistible way he had, but it's true. Surfing is as useless as art; that's what makes it beautiful. The flower blossoms for its own joy, Wilde went on, and man may sell the flower for gain—but that is accidental. It is a misuse.

And that's our life for the next two weeks. Sophia and Ray come in after school; we shape and glass forty boards, setting up two fans, opening both doors and nearly passing out anyway, the foul toxins of fiberglass resin creeping into our noses, raising dizzy hell in our bloodstreams, altering our brains. Move them out into the sun to dry. Tuesday afternoon I'm putting the shelves together, when I hear Fluke holler, 'Hey! Hey!! Get back here, you junkie fucks!' and then a slam and crash as he and Pip tear off down the alley.

Race out in time to see a pick-up screech down the street with one of our nicest boards, the Mahalo model. Son of a bitch. They're not going to be able to sell it—still a coat shy of waterproof and the skegs aren't on. That's how those cocksuckers operate, though, bumbling around stealing everything that isn't nailed down. Like Ricky, but without any sort of planning or finesse. Thirty-nine boards, then, okay. Hard knocks tax. You learn.

After that, we keep a close guard, and the next day Fluke shows up with a Luger his dad brought home from the war, with its curved butt and narrow barrel. Safety's on: *gesichert*. Secured. We do feel safer knowing it's in there, though the magazine is long gone and we wouldn't know where to find bullets. All you have to do with a gun is wave it around anyway, right? We keep it locked up in a drawer under the register— and we used to be such nice people, too.

Get a phone in, finish filing the forms, receive our business license in the mail. Fluke and Pip take a break on Sunday, and I'm on Saturday, just to get in a little surf and sleep, but Lord am I gonna be happy when all this shit is over, and we can just relax and let the money roll in.

And every day I notice some minor detail that could be improved on the mural that'll just take a sec, and Fluke has to pull me off the ladder an hour later, to come deal with the real work.

Late Thursday afternoon his dad comes over, and they put the sign up. Fluke won't let me come out until it's done, and when I catch sight of it

I actually stagger back a little, it's that breathtaking. Dark wrought iron, a huge 'X' surrounded by kelp and fish. Serious masterpiece. People are starting to notice and bug us about the opening, but we didn't think that far ahead. Should there be a party?

We're fresh out of money, down to pennies, and the bills are starting to pile up. Saturday night, we figure. Shit's practically covered by now, and we can take the day off, put the word out, maybe have some kind of minor gala. When surfers get together, necessities tend to materialize, usually in the form of beer.

'Still, though,' Fluke frets. 'No need for wine and cheese and fralala; it's not the Ferus Gallery. But we're the hosts, so we should probably put out a keg or two, get 'em all drunk and spendy.'

We've exhausted all avenues for extra revenue at this point, however. Mr. Fallucci gave us everything he could, and all his tools besides. Can't ask John—he's not a handout guy, and I'll cut my heart out before I go to my dad. None of the guys have any spare dough, and we cashed our last paychecks a week ago, closed out our accounts. Sophia used her babysitting money to get business cards, and Pip showed up last week with a bandage on his arm, selling blood downtown with the winos for extra resin. Well, in for a penny, in for a pound.

Fluke comes back in later, the bell tinkling. 'Tommy? Where you at?'

I emerge from the john, pulling at my pants. 'What's up?'

'Don't lose it, but...some prick stole your board outta Mayhem.'

I laugh a little, unconvincingly. Hold up the ticket. He groans.

'Oh, come *on!* Not your lucky board, Tommy!'

It was all I had left worth anything. The week after we finished it, I took it to bed every night, I swear, murmuring and fondling the rails in my sleep. I think that's when Ray really started to worry about me.

'I'll get it back, Fluke. That's the point of pawnshops. And hey, I got seventeen bucks, and we can have a pretty decent do with that, right?'

We look at each other for a long moment, and there is something like fear in our faces. You go out in rough surf, seize a wave, paddle straight up on the lip and look down into the fury several feet below into which you're about to launch yourself—and there is this split-second of time that seems so much longer, where you can just say, *hell no, this shit will kill me.* You can still back down then. Closed out, not worth the risk.

I think we just passed that. Here goes nothing.

Friday afternoon, we've got the place tidied up; boards racked by the wall, wetsuits hung, shirts and shorts stacked on shelves, records in cases on either side. A little display of magazines, postcards and wax, and a scrapbook up on the counter we started a while ago, full of pics, surf quotes and anecdotes, clippings about contests, and Rick Griffin cartoons from 'Surfer.' U-Boy and Mysto are on security and music, keg and snacks are procured. No chairs, we agreed—keep them circulating. Restless people buy more.

At least a hundred are going to show up for sure, and we've blanketed the city with a mysterioso little flyer: our name, time and date and address, 'Mark Your Spot' at the bottom. I guess we're ready, but I'm so nervous I've gone out the other side, can't feel anything but this dazed calm. Few more things to do. People have been peering in for weeks, so I'm kind of used to it, but as I finish screwing the padlock onto the small wooden chest under the shirt display I can feel a prickling on the back of my neck. Turn to see a girl in a cheerleader outfit, hands to her forehead to cut the glare. Oh. Ohhh.

'Hey,' I say, unlocking the door and holding it open. 'Surprise! I had something a little cooler in mind for this moment, like with me not all covered in paint, but—well. How'd you find me?'

Georgia nods back to the café across the way. 'I was hanging out with a friend. Saw the sign.'

'Well, come on in. You look adorable, by the way. Go Normans. Didn't realize you were a—'

She holds a finger to her lips, shushing me. Prowls around the place, checking out the mural for a time, as I belatedly realize there aren't any women in it. Dozens of boss surfer chicks, and I included a kangaroo. 'Did you paint this?'

musing over the Gothic letters on the little wooden box: 'Bluebeard's Chest: Key at Register.'

'What's in here? Do I want to know?'

I take the key off my neck, hand it over. She slips it into the padlock, opens the chest, pauses for a moment. Holds up a pair of panties.

'Yeah, definitely want to keep these locked up. No blood, though? No dead bodies? Bluebeard can't have all the fun.'

'That's up to you, my friend. Mark your spot.'

She smiles to herself. 'How much?'

'Buck-ninety-nine.' My mouth tries to say something obnoxious about working it off in trade, but my brain subdues it. 'For you, a dollar.'

Shakes her head, passes me two bucks. 'Lesson one: no freebies. All you get from that is hurt feelings and bankruptcy. Treat your friends like your customers, your customers like your friends, you'll be fine.'

I tilt my head, tape one of the dollars to the register. 'Mazal tov.'

'First sale?'

'Yup. But what do you think? Don't leave me hanging!'

She holds her arms out, and I move into her, that solid warmth against my chest, golden wisps falling from her ponytail. It's like retrieving the best part of my self. Don't know how I could even look at another girl. After awhile: 'Are you...crying? Don't cry. Not a good sign.'

'I'm not,' she says. 'This is just...I thought it might be something along these lines, but I didn't...it's so brave, Tommy, and frankly, I'm scared.' Wipes her eyes. 'Cause it is really, really hard to run your own business. I don't know if you know that yet.'

'Starting to figure it out, yeah.'

'You think there's going to be a stopping point, and there just never, ever is. You take everything so to heart—I'm afraid it's going to fail, and you'll be crushed. Or worse, that it'll succeed, and...'

'And what?'

She pulls away, walks over to the boards to run a finger down the smooth pinstriped gloss of the Malibu Champion. 'We weren't always rich, you know. My dad came out from Philly when he was sixteen, flat broke, during the Depression. He drove a beer truck, and was working these connections he'd made at the clubs, you know, just doing favors for friends, putting people together, cause he's good like that—and then he realized he could make money from it.' She turns back, looks me in the eye.

'But he had to learn things that weren't in his nature. How to be mean, and put his foot down, lay a dollar sign on stuff that had been about love before. When he got back from the war, it was a different town. Almost everyone he'd known was gone, and my mom was with him— they got married in Hamburg, and she was already pregnant with me— so he had to start all over, under pretty serious pressure.'

'I can be mean,' I say. 'And I can start from scratch just dandy.'

'I believe you,' she says, and comes back, takes my hand. Looks like she lost some weight over the past two weeks. A lot of weight, mostly in her face. Her cheekbones—that softness is gone. 'But the hardest thing he had to learn was how not to have a life. A regular job, you come home, your time is yours. You get to be with the people you love. But with your own business, you don't have that anymore. My whole life, he was busting ass morning till night so people would take him seriously. I ran away once when I was eight, just to make him take a vacation.'

'Really?'

'Yup. I was gone for four days. Slept in a vacant house, lived on peanut butter and oranges while he had the whole town out looking for me. He takes vacations now.' She fingers a postcard, a palm tree on a white empty shore. 'But it's not just that. You have to be twelve different guys a day, sometimes all in one hour. You lose yourself.'

'I know who I am,' I tell her. 'I'll be okay.'

'But wait, there's more.' She laughs bitterly. 'What makes you happy, Tommy? You told me. Surfing, and hanging out with your friends. Truth now—how much of that have you done in the past few weeks?'

I say nothing.

'Do you even remember the last time you saw me?'

Saturday. Came over to the house, kissed her, and promptly passed out on the couch. We talked on the phone...Tuesday, I think. No, Monday.

'Surfing?'

Shake my head. I don't even have anything to surf on, at this point.

'And the people—?'

'Okay, I get it. It's hard work, sacrifice, all that. But this is gonna mean something, Georgia. If it takes off—Mama can catch a break from time to time. I might be able to send Ray to MIT, like he deserves. I can get my own place, help my friends out. Me and you—maybe the 'M' word, or just live somewhere that isn't a hovel. I'll have choices, for a change.'

'Yeah, you're right. You're absolutely right. But will you be happy?'

'You know, I will. Different kind of happy, maybe, but it counts.'

She bites her lip. 'Tommy, will you promise me something?'

'Sure.'

'In a year, we're gonna go away, just you and me. No matter what else is going on, I'll come get you, September 14, 1963, and we'll head out to...I don't even care where, as long as it's far from here. I want you to think hard about this then, figure out if it's really what you want to do with your life. I told you I don't care about the money, and I meant it. Vets make decent pay—give me a few years, and I can support us both.'

My jaw stiffens and I look away. 'I can't let you do that, Georgia. Come on. There are limits.'

'But you do all this stuff for other people, and the surfing was the one thing...the one thing...when I saw you on the beach that day, I thought,

258

that guy's doing *exactly* what he needs to with his life. Please don't let that go, not yet. Please?'

'But I won't, I swear. Look, Venice Beach is right here. All I have to do is roll out the door.'

'Oh, God, this is my fault. I never should've told you to make money off this. You were *fine*.'

I take her shoulders. 'I'm fine *now*, really—and this started long before I even met you. You want to blame anybody, blame...' Oh, forget it. She'd never believe me anyway.

'Okay,' she sighs. 'I have to get. Crazy homework, and two reports due Monday. But can I come to the opening?' She flicks one of the flyers.

'Of course! I was going to pick you up at seven, after I'd showed you the place tonight.'

'All right, see you then. You don't have to pick me up, I'm sure you'll be busy. And I don't mean to be a drag. World's worst cheerleader, right? You guys should be proud of what you did here. And that mural—it ain't just Super Cali. It's supercalifragilisticexpialidocious.'

'What?' I bust up laughing. 'What'd you just say? Is this one of your dad's words?'

'Yeah, some jazz thing, I think. Gloria Turner came up with it. 'Atoning for education through delicate beauty."

'Write it down, would you? I wanna put it on a shirt.'

'Later. I better split. I love you, Tommy, and this is so cool. It is, and as for the rest...we'll figure it out, I promise.'

She kisses me for a long time, and I can feel this new person thrusting through her, rising under those soft lips—but by the time I open my eyes for a closer look, she's gone.

September 14, 1963. No idea who we'll be by then, what the world'll look like. Everything's so up in the air right now. We didn't wind up going, in the end. Just didn't work out. Life seldom does.

One more thing to do, before I head home to sleep like the dead. Fight rush hour traffic across town to the Getty Building, take the elevator up and smile at the secretary, getting ready to go home herself.

'Can you please tell Mr. Getty that, um, Tom Beck is here to see him? Won't be but a minute.' Jesus, just let him remember me, and not think I'm a complete lunatic. 'Tell him, uh...just say the surfer.'

John appears at the door in his shirtsleeves. 'Tom! Come on in, boy! Honey, bring us some coffee before you go.'

'Just water for me, thanks.' I've been mainlining doughnuts, adrenalin and bennies all week; there's so much crap in my system at this point my eyeballs are skittery. Ushers me in, and I sink into the butter-soft leather chair by his desk.

'Now, what can I do for you?'

'Just wanted to return a courtesy, sir.' Hand over one of our business cards, swallowing my smile.

He gazes at it for a moment. 'Surf shop, eh? You need money?'

'No!' I say, too loudly. 'No, nothing like that, we're set. I just—you were our first customer, kinda got the ball rolling with this. So, you know, you can come on by sometime, or call if you need anything. We deliver. And I wanted to show you this.' I pass him a Polaroid: me and Fluke, triumphant shakas by the Biarritz mural.

The secretary comes in with our drinks; I sip the water, watching his face. He must play a hell of a hand of poker, as his expression doesn't change a bit. But he's doing this thing with his thumb, rubbing circles on his forefinger, as if trying to comfort himself somehow, I'm not sure why. He waves the picture.

'That's me.'

I nod. He pushes his chair back, stands and walks over to the window overlooking downtown LA. Goes quiet for a while as I wait, unsure why I'm even here. This man represents a system I spent my life fighting, he shits where he surfs with his oil—and yet, I like him. I do. He's weirdly cool, and it would mean something if he respected me.

'You seem like a bright boy, Tom, and I'll assume you put a fair amount of thought into this, so I won't insult you by giving you unsolicited business advice. But mark my words: trust no one, from now on.' I can hear a trace of Okie over the Minnesota in his voice: *fur amahnt*. It's oddly reassuring, like listening to Woody Guthrie, though you couldn't imagine two more different guys. 'Your best friend will turn on you over money. No one ever thinks it'll happen to them, but it always does.'

'Not to contradict you, sir, but I'm pretty sure that's not in the cards. Neither of us is really in it for the money—and Fluke's my...' I hesitate. 'Best friend' doesn't describe it, not even 'brother.' I can't imagine life without Fluke; he's like my heart or my liver. 'We're pretty close.'

Nods to himself, hands clasped behind his back. 'You hang on to that. That's hen's teeth, right there. Always thought I'd find it with a woman, but turns out none of them were copacetic with the...well, the hours I kept. Happy enough to spend the money, though.'

'Yeah, my girl's already up in arms, and she's not a nag, either, she's wonderful. You'd like her. But I want to have something to offer her, and this is all I really know how to do.'

'How is she with the surfing?' He turns back, watching me.

'That, she gets. Probably what drew her in the first place.'

'Well, that's all right, then. But I want you to do one thing for me.'

'What's that?' Let me guess: he wants us to take a road-trip together. Next September, say.

'If she's a good girl, and I'll wager she is, and the business starts to send you two to pieces, just walk away from it. I had five wives and quite a few lady friends, and I screwed it up every goddamned time. Too late now, but if there were one thing I could change about my life, it would be that. A woman who really understands you—she'll love you anyway, money or not. Don't throw that away.'

I'm staring at him, still holding the water glass, speechless. Christ, isn't *anybody* gonna be happy for me? Rich people always think they have it all figured out, don't they? They love to lean out of their castle windows yelling down at us about how we're doing it wrong. But I'm touched by the concern in his eyes, in Georgia's — and I get where they're coming from. For a moment I can see myself across the desk fifty years from now, busting some poor kid's balls about this, some kid who's going to smile and nod and then go out and fuck it all up anyway. John probably thinks I'm an idiot who isn't listening to an old man go on, but I'm not, and I am. I am, I swear it. I hear every fucking word.

Later that night, waking up on the couch, I feel Mama's hand stroking my hair. She leans over, unlaces my sneakers, gently pulls them off, and for once, I let her.

'*Ich bin so müde,*' I murmur, relaxing into her warmth.

'*Es ist alles gut, mein Sohn. Schläfst jetzt.*'

'*Es tut mir leid,*' I say, '*Dass ich nicht für dich da war. Für Ray.* I should have been here more, helped you guys out.'

'Ach, silly bear. Better to see you a little bit, but see you happy, no?'

'*Ich liebe dich, Mama. Für immer.*'

Drift off to her singing a lullaby about the fish in the clear high tide, the little kids that wake up early; God knows and loves them all, and they are happy and without sorrow. It was my favorite, and Grandpa's too. Even if he were in one of his moods, he'd wind up humming along.

Wake again at dawn. She's covered me with an old chenille spread, and I sink back down with the comforting thought that not only can I sleep till noon today, but that if I want to, I can every day. I'm lucky to have people who love me enough to make that my life, and I'm choosing to give it back to them. This is what will make me truly happy.

The Rondanini Pietà was the last thing Michelangelo ever created, and frankly, it's the poser of the bunch. At first glance it kinda seems like a piece of shit: goofy long legs on Jesus, and not even finished, a third of it still unhewn marble, dull and roughly crystalline. I still remember my disappointment: *twelve years on this*? It made no sense, cause the guy was a charger, could knock out masterpieces eighteen to the dozen, just

262

bam, bam, bam, a year or two at most on each, every fleshy cheek and sensuous curve of drapery begging to be touched, marble more real than most people can ever hope to be. Seemed an odd choice for his last statement, like he was rejecting everything he'd ever done: either this useless statue goes or I do.

Look closer, though, and you realize: he's not trying to make an artifact we can all marvel over, he's explaining sculpture to us. You don't bang away at it, imposing your will on a passive piece of stone, but approach it slowly, feeling the intricacies of the crystal connections. Listening to the figure trying to wrestle its way out.

If it's a warrior, any attempt to turn it into a pretty girl will guarantee a mess. And if it's a helpless, anguished woman holding the body of her dead son, not giving a shit that he's the messiah, knowing only that her own sweet baby was in this awful pain, crying out with it for days, lost to her forever now, for no reason at all—then that's what it's got to be. Something like that isn't going to be pretty; it's horrifying, that's the point. You help where you can, with whatever tools you have, but don't think you're some special genius. You're only letting it emerge.

No one ever considers the sculptor, though, taking his free will for granted. Unlike the nameless stone girl who later on became Galatea, Pinocchio and Eliza Doolittle, Pygmalion had an identity: the creator. It didn't matter, though, cause he's not the story here, just some creepy shlub defined by his creation. But I can't help but wonder: did he get to do anything else with his life? Who was he supposed to become?

I may be reading too much into all this, of course. Maybe Michelangelo was just a lonely old man whose only children were stone and clay. Maybe he was sick of hacking away at rocks for ingrates, and his back and neck hurt, and he was almost ninety, tired of all this shit, and ready to go home. Either way.

Rearview mirror, it's hard to see why we worried. About 300 people had congregated outside the doors by the time we opened, and when Fluke walked out with his spiel of 'Welcome all, but fire marshal says no more than fifty at a time,' it was like one of those Don Martin cartoons where the guy's flattened with footprints all over his face. I struggle through the tide to rescue him, and Sophia rushes to pull Ray to safety behind the counter, but I'll be honest, the scene was completely out of hand for a minute or two.

Many more show up over the next hour, including a reporter from the 'Times,' several members of Ricky's Hollywood crowd, and two quiet guys in shades that, if I didn't know any better, could have sworn were Paul Newman and Steve McQueen. By the time I head over for a closer look they're gone, but plenty more are swarming in to take their place.

Mostly girls, which none of us were expecting, and they are super loud, all bopping around the shop in halter-tops screaming hysterically—but they've got money to spend, and for some reason they're spending it here. Large chick groups scare me, to be honest. They have this insane energy, feeding on each other, quiet all this time but then get together and get all brazen and crazy, wasted Maenads dying to tear you limb from limb. The air is thick with smoke and perfumed sweat, tanned limbs and blond hair, hundreds all crammed in here together, ravenous for something I'm not sure I can give them.

This wasn't really how I saw this going.

Someone gets the chest open, and they're shrieking blue murder over the panties, passing them from hand to hand as I burn with second thoughts and belated shame, a dirty old man of nineteen—and then the panties are gone and I pull a chameleon up against the wall, Cadillacs blasting over the crowd, *they often call me Speedoo cause I don't believe in wasting time,* and I should probably be doing something right about now, but I have no idea what. I get pretty antsy at parties, and the ones where you don't know anybody and your entire life depends on making a good impression are the absolute worst.

Fluke directs a girl with a shiny black bob to the sign: 'Yes, we have no Beach Boys,' under which he's written, 'Tommy's idea—he's an idiot. Feel free to tell him so,' and I've written 'Screw you,' and he's written, 'Screw you too,' and so on. She argues, but winds up buying Dick Dale instead, so ha-ha, screw *you*, Brian Fucking Wilson.

Everyone's scooping up wetsuits and T's, struggling out of the store with boards—and we sell out in forty minutes flat, not so much as a postcard or Ventures 45 left. The guys had followed the girls inside, and were slouching around being cool, thinking things over, and they got left in the dust, so are looking a mite aggrieved.

Fluke grabs my arm. 'Now what?' His hat is battered, rosebud limp in his lapel. At least his trunks are still intact.

'If they look even remotely legal, give them beer,' I say. 'And tell them to come back in a week.'

Mysto and U-Boy, bless them, are passing out suds as fast as they can and gently maneuvering folks towards the exit. Sophia has the genius idea of taking orders before they go, and by nine we've got fifty orders for boards and at least twice that for shirts—and everyone wants in on the panties. I'm glad we convinced our parents to stay home tonight, and I feel weird watching Sophia ring up sexy underwear, but oh well, right? Because *money*.

Jesus, so much money. By eleven we're out of beer, too, so we throw out last of the stragglers, send Mysto and U home, lock up and go back to the shaping room. Nothing left but the mural, the register, and us. Sophia dumps the drawer out on the worktable, and we all fondle the big pile of green in silence for a while, in shock.

'God-diggity-*damn*,' says Ray at last, pulling off his shades.

'Count it,' says Sophia. There are dark circles under her eyes, but I've never seen her this stoked. 'Count it, count it already!'

So we do, and it's over three grand.

I flip through a wad of fives. 'Pawn shop's still open, right?'

'Where the fuck is Pip?' Fluke's face is stuck somewhere between pissed and worried, our default expression when we don't know where the fuck Pip is. I'd been searching the crowd all night for his curly mop, desperate for riot control, but he never showed up. Sorta thought he might not be up for it, but I can't believe Georgia didn't come either. She knew what this meant to me. They both did.

'No idea, and...where are your shirts?' We were all sporting X shirts tonight, store pride. They grin sheepishly at each other, then pull tens from their pockets and toss them on the pile.

For a moment or two I don't get it. 'Hold up. You guys got *ten bucks* for your T-shirts?'

'A biker offered me twenty after we were out,' admits Ray. 'You need to make more, pronto. I can't tell him no again; he actually thought I was trying to drive him up.'

'Well, thanks for cutting me in on that action!'

'Oh, please. Those girls were bad enough tonight without you parading around out there half-naked.'

'Hmmph. Well, welcome to the first meeting of the board.'

'Heh,' says Ray. 'Board.'

'As Chairman, I move to get started.'

'Why do you get to be Chairman?' asks Sophia. 'Why not Eddie?'

'Because I'm the only one here who's appropriately garbed, dorklet— and I didn't recognize you, so you're out of order.'

'Boo. Boo, usurper. Fascist. I'm bored already. Booo.'

I hold my hand up for silence, totting up the figures. '3,182 dollars and 85 cents. Sweet Tapdancing Christ.'

'Is this a dream? Am I fucking dreaming?' says Fluke. 'How the fuck did anyone even know who we were?'

'Told you so.' I toss the pile of fives in the air. 'I fucking *told* you so!'

Sophia plucks one up and mimes lighting a cigar. '*Madon*', we're gonna be rich, we're gonna be so fucking *rich!*'

'Language, missy.' But Fluke's laughing too, kind of breathless.

'All right, brass tacks,' I say. 'We're gonna need two grand to reinvest on blanks and shirts and rent and stuff. Pay back your dad. The rest we can divvy up, pay you guys for all your time.'

'Oh, no, you don't,' says Ray. 'We're investing, too.'

'No, keep it. You worked your asses off.' Sophia stubbornly shakes her head, and I sigh. 'Mr. Fallucci, our Chief Enforcement Officer of Hard Truths, will explain how this works.'

'Just take the money and run,' he says. 'You earned it. Pretty sure what you saw tonight was, for lack of a better word, a fluke. Fata Morgana or something. No idea if it'll happen again, and we're the owners, so they can come after us for everything if we go under, and I mean everything: our stock, our cars, even our boards. Later we can maybe bring you in, but for this first year, let's just play it as it lays. Pip gets $300, you each get $150, and we'll make do with the rest. Tommy gets his board out of hock, we save the change for petty cash, and that's it.'

'You guys get paid first,' I add. 'And you don't need to take the risk.'

'Our capitalist overlords,' teases Sophia. 'Boy, that didn't take too long. Come, Mr. Tallyman, hand it ovah. I'm spending every last dime on liquor and Beach Boys records.'

'You're fired, sassafrass,' I tell her, and she comes round and hugs me, kisses Fluke on the cheek.

'You guys are the nuts. Best brothers ever,' she says, 'C'mon, Ray, let's go tackle the wreckage. I wanna go home and tell Ma.'

Pleased, I glance at Fluke to see if he noticed the slip, but he seems kind of preoccupied. We're both zonked out of our gourds, yet so wired I'm pretty sure neither's going to sleep tonight.

'Wait,' I say. 'No, they can't. Worst they can do is evict.'

'Not selling stock, Tommy. Not tonight, not ever. This is our thing.'

'Well, okay,' I say. 'But you coulda just said that. They'd get it.'

'Fata Morgana,' he mutters. 'I told you what that is, right?'

'Sure. The Sicilian mirage, with mermaids luring sailors to their death or something. Or was it Morgana le Fay? Okay, I don't remember, but like that thing we saw—'

'We opened a surf shop, Tommy. And sure, we talked about how we were gonna sell overpriced stuff to grems, but I thought real surfers would be in here, too. There was free beer, and not one came. Not one. I know you noticed. I've been watching you notice all night.'

'Ricky came.'

'Ricky.' He snorts. 'Ricky showed up cause the rest of us were here, so we could play surf clowns for his rich friends. What'd he get us for?'

'Just wax. But I may have bested his ass. You'll see.'

Ricky'd met my eyes, leaning against the wall all scruffy and sunburned, sneering at his surroundings, and I'd waded through the crowd to his side. A skinny young thing with a blond beehive pops up and pokes me in the chest: 'Hey, I know you! I do! You're that guy!'

'You got me,' I say, and she asks Ricky, 'Isn't he ginchy?'

'The ginchiest,' Ricky assures her solemnly, and then she's gone again.

'Kook City, Rods. Happy now?'

'Very. Is that a stick of Parowax in your pocket, buddy, or are you just excited to see me?'

Signal to the *Times* photographer, and put an arm around him tight as the flash pops in our faces. Whisper through the side of my grin, 'Smile, fuckhead, cause it's this or a mugshot. Tonight's on the house. I love your klepto ass, but don't ever steal from us again.'

It comes out the next morning in the Sunday Sports section, and it's not a flattering shot. He looks like a jowly muskrat, and if you'd never seen the poise and grace of this man in his element, his sheer outlandish elegance, you might wonder why we worshipped him so. The few polite paragraphs do little to clarify what happened, but I buy two copies—one for the scrapbook, one to be framed and hung over the register: 'Ricky Morrow Boosts Here—All Others Pay Cash.'

Fluke runs a hand through his hair, nudges the hat into the pile of bills. 'You know how shit works in this town. You have thirty seconds to be hot before poof, the lady vanishes. And if we don't get that core of steady buyers, if we're stuck out here in January with no one coming in, not even chicks and kooks, we're gonna be fucked.'

'This is all uncharted waters, Fluke. You knew that going in.'

'Yeah, I know. I just see this shit at the track sometimes. One big win drives you wild, you wind up throwing good money after bad.'

'But that's not—look, we tripled our investment, and we're not going wild. Might as well roll again. Give your dad his money back, and keep the rest safe till we can open an account. I've got a few tricks up my sleeve that may get the real guys in here.'

'Oh yeah?' He starts stacking the twenties. 'Such as?'

'New trunks, for one. Me and...uh, one of the garment girls, we've been playing around with the design, and it seems pretty solid. I'll bring in a couple pairs on Monday, we can try them out.'

'One of the garment girls?'

'What?'

'Nothing. You had a look.'

He's bound to find out sooner or later. 'It's Tina. Tina Vasquez.'

Looks blank. Then: 'Get the fuck outta town. Not...?'

'The very one. Happy reunion, but not too happy, if you read me, so try to keep it under your hat. She really knows her shit, though, so I think we're in good hands.'

I can see the dozen ways Flake *wants to run with this, but he just raises* his eyebrows, draws a zipper across his lips. I sweep the coins off the table into a coffee can.

'And Ray's got an idea for a board that, the more I think about it, the more I realize it could change...well, everything. It's that different. It'll be short, for one. And fast. Like, super fast.'

'How fast?'

'Don't know, we haven't made it yet. Maybe too fast. Wanna go for it?'

'Sure, why not. No real reason to stick to rhino chasers, right? You told Mysto and U? Speed's their catnip, they're gonna be amped.'

'No. And don't you tell anyone either, especially not Ricky. Loose lips. He'll just piss all over it, then steal the idea out from under us and give it to Noll—and we're gonna have to mess with it a little, get it just right before we go to market.'

'"Go to market." I love you, you crazy cocksucker.'

'You ready to make some money?'

'I was fucking born ready to make some money. Let's call our folks.'

'Don't tell them either.'

'Not telling anybody, for Chrissake. Just us and Pip. Where *is* Pip?'

'I'll find him. Can you drop Ray home? I have to get my board.'

'Sure.' He counts off $300 for Pip, a twenty for me, and tucks the rest in his pocket. We stand.

'Listen,' I tell him. 'No idea what's gonna go down, in January or points north—but we did good here. We did. Whatever Ricky or anybody may say, this counts for something.'

He socks me in the shoulder. 'Wouldn't have done it with anyone else in the world, either, you little prick. You know it.'

'Yeah.' I swallow. 'Let's go call, though. Our moms are probably on the ceiling by now. Meeting adjourned.'

270

I'm standing across the street from the place, clutching the ticket. Neon lights are flickering at me, searing the night: Tiburón P-A-W-N. I know the guy said thirty days, but who the hell knows with these people? They might've sold her anyway, and I can't bear to think of anybody else's dirty paws all over my baby. Just go on in, asshole. They're about to close. Move it, come on.

The college kid behind the register is deep in a history textbook, and I spot her right away, relief flooding in so hard I feel dazed. Plunk the twenty and the ticket down on the counter, and he glances at them, then checks the ledger.

'Still gonna have to charge you a buck, man.'

I nod, unable to take my eyes off her, up against the wall helpless and alone, surrounded by guitars and shotguns. I'm relieved to see I'm not the only asshole who had to give up his most cherished possession. Not even the only surfer; there's four other boards up there. Nice ones, too: couple of Velzy's, a Weber, even a Quigg. He nods back, and I go over and lay my head against the gull on the nose for second. I'm so sorry, baby. Never again. Not for any reason.

Then I shoulder her and am outta there, the bell tinkling behind me and the guy—who seems awfully nice to be working in a pawnshop, you'd think they'd screen them for sleazability—shouts after me, 'Hey, man, hey, you forgot your change!' Wave him off, which I've never done before in my life. Like throwing a little something back into the jaws of the hurricane that hit us tonight.

Over the grass, the courts and boardwalk, down to the sand. Safe again, breathing deep, hushed by the waves. Tide's going out, mellow lefts, just what I need right now. Kick off my huaraches, peel off the shirt that has in a few hours somehow become more valuable than my board. Crazy old world, huh?

And then I see them.

My eyes aren't quite used to the dark yet, so at first they look like any other couple that comes down here on Saturday night to mess around: arms resting around each other, the girl in a red party dress, the guy ghostly in white jeans and T-shirt, pale blond hair. Pale *long* blond hair.

For an instant this does not add up, and then I'm hit by a wrecking ball of rage and betrayal, *wham*, right in the belly. I've seen the way he looks at her. It's pretty much how we all look at her, but this is Pip, and whoever coined the term 'puppy love' never met a puppy. Once they decide you're the one, you can ignore and kick and starve them all you want, and they'll still follow you around forever, that sad infatuation radiating from their eyes. If you have half a heart, it's hard to resist. And she does, she can't help it. But neither can I. Someday this will all start to shimmer before it disappears altogether—and if I only knew when, I think I'd be okay.

Fluke and I were at Rincon a few years back, lazily paddling out, when he stopped short and pointed to the horizon, startled.

'Hey, you see that?'

There's a ship out there in the haze, what looks to be an old galleon. It's no trick—you can see every detail: rigging straggling from the masts, cannons poking out from the side, a carved mermaid on the prow. I rub my eyes. Still there.

'Anyone on it?' You hear about this stuff sometimes, read about it in books, never thinking it'll happen to you.

'I can't tell,' he says. 'Should we go check it out?'

'Nah, bad idea.'

'Oh, c'mon, where's your sense of adventure? It's a pirate ship, Tommy!'

'It's two miles out—and even if it is real, they probably all died of the plague or something, and I'm in no mood for buboes. Gotta be at least two hundred years old.'

'But that's impossible! How come nobody ever came across it?'

I squint; our Flying Dutchman looks more real than ever. Oars from the galley, ragged sails hanging limp. 'It's a pretty big ocean.'

He shrugs. 'All right, but if it's still there in an hour, to hell with it, I'm going out.' Starts to sing, his righteous voice like molasses rolling down: 'It's that ohh-llld...ship of Zion...'

I nudge him. 'Don't jinx it, man.'

We catch a few waves and rest on the sand for a while, and by that time the ship is floating above the water, wavering and changing, and okay, not really real, but what the hell? One of the local fishermen walks by, so we tackle him and he tells us about the galleon that comes around, trick of the light. Looks like a castle sometimes, he says, and then Fluke cries out in recognition. His nonna had told him about the fairy castles that would appear over the Straits of Messina: sailors would go crazy and jump overboard, unable to swim or to resist this vision of paradise. It rarely ended well.

We check one more time before heading out—and it's gone. Vanished. Nothing out there but the waves.

I never asked her about the guys who came before me. What's the point, right? Pick a number between one and a hundred, either way, you're going to drive yourself nuts. She had hers, I had mine, and all that matters is that now we have each other. And yet my mind is always thinking: was it two, four, a dozen? Does she still think of them? Were they smarter, smoother, did they have money and fast cars and nice homes and bright futures and pasts they could stand to talk about? Would they do things to her, touch her in places I never dreamed of? Did they never say a single boring thing—or maybe never say anything at all? How long have I *got*?

But that's not what's going on here, it's not. They're a cute couple, but this is Georgia. This is Pip. They're real, and they're your friends. Just calm down, asshole. Steady as she goes.

'Hey, guys,' I say, and no cucumber was ever this cool. Plant my board.

Her head jerks up. 'Tommy,' she murmurs, sleepy and glad, and that's all she has to say. Nothing happened. 'You found us.'

Pip's conked out on her shoulder. She pats the sand beside her, smiling up at me, and I sit.

'Where were you?' I whisper, still kind of afraid to touch her.

'Hmm, funny story.' She stretches her legs. 'I got there late, no parking anywhere, so I doubled back on 23rd and was gonna come in through the back door. Which you really oughtta keep locked—'

'Fire exit.'

'Oh, right. But then I tripped over Pip sitting out there. And he really did not want to come in.'

'Figured as much. I told him he didn't have to.'

'He didn't want to disappoint you.' Her breath, soft against my ear.

'He tell you that?'

'Not in so many words.' She sighs. 'So we hung out, waiting for things to calm down, but it was sounding like a total madhouse, and I couldn't just ditch him, so we went for a walk and wound up here. I knew you'd find us, though. And you did.'

Pip doesn't stir, but I can feel him listening. I reach over, tug softly at one salt-rough curl. 'Guy's best worker runs off with guy's best gal, with ensuing shenanigans. Screenplay writes itself. But who'll play Pip?'

'I don't know. No guy is cute enough, and no girl is this sad.'

'Tuesday Weld?'

She ponders this, taking Pip's hand, one thumb tracing the webbing between his fingers. 'Maybe. And me?'

'She could play you both, like in 'Parent Trap."

'And you?' Pip is peering at me over her shoulder.

'Don't laugh, but Paul Newman. I've had an unwholesome crush on that guy since I was a kid. Nice half-Jewish boy, too.'

'No halfsies with us. Only Jew or not-Jew. He's pretty easy on the eyes, though, so I'll let him in the tribe.'

'Could swear I saw him tonight, but I'd believe anything at this point.'

She clears her throat, looks away.

'What?' I say. 'Wait, did you—you did, didn't you?'

'Don't know what you're talking about.'

'And the reporter!'

She grins. 'Okay, the reporter was me. But the rest was you, Tommy. You guys know a lot of people, and they all have pretty big mouths.'

'Are you kidding? I knew exactly one person there tonight who wasn't working—Ricky.'

'Well, they all know you. Natasha came, right?'

'Who?'

'My friend, the one I went to the movies with? She promised to give you a hard time about the Beach Boys.'

'Black bob, like Louise Brooks?' She nods. 'Yeah, she bugged Fluke for a while. I was just in hiding by then.'

Her laugh is gleeful. 'So did they all buy stuff?'

'They bought *all* the stuff. Wiped us out.'

'That's fantastic, Tommy. Isn't it?'

'We'll see. Oh, but that reminds me—' I pull the wad of cash from my pocket, hold it out to Pip, and I swear this is one of the high points of my entire life. 'Your pay, sir.'

He looks at it, confused, then shakes his head.

'No, this is moolah, it's good. You can get a place now. Eat whenever you want. You won't have to depend on anyone for handouts.'

He pushes my hand away.

'Jesus, Pip, just take it.' Georgia elbows me in the ribs, gets to her feet and pulls me after her under the lifeguard tower.

'He didn't do it for the money, you dope.'

I wince. 'Okay, he did it for me—and I'm doing this for him. That's how work works. He's not my slave.'

'What's he gonna do with it, Tommy? Where's he going to keep it, with Ricky? How's he going to rent a place, pay the bills? He's just a kid, and he doesn't even talk.'

When you're broke, it feels like all you need to do is lay your hands on some money, and shit will magically uncomplicate itself. Not so. Just different complications. I lean back against the tower, rub my forehead, and try to think as she waits.

'Okay. Okay. Pip?' He sidles over, head low.

'Quit it, man. I'm not mad, just wasn't thinking. What if—look, what if I take the money, and rent a place for us both? We'd be roommates. Would you be cool with that?'

He considers this. Nods.

'All right. Monday we'll go look at some places, right here in Venice. You know you're a royal pain in my ass, right?'

He grins, ducks his head. Whispers something.

'What's that?'

'I can make spaghetti.'

'Right on, then. Spaghetti's my favorite.'

He socks me happily in the arm, and Georgia's eyes meet mine over his head. I think, *I'm not doing this to impress you, you know,* and her eyes say, *I know.* She offers to take him back to Malibu so I can finally get out on the water before my head explodes, but makes me promise not to leave just yet, cause she has a surprise for me.

276

I explain that I can't take any more surprises, tonight and possibly ever, and she races back, sandals in hand, slips something into my pocket, kisses my cheek and runs off again.

I wait till they're out of sight before having a look: a room key to the motel across the way. The Tropicana's a cheap joint—the phones are chained to the wall and the carpets come with sandfleas pre-installed—but they rent to minors and don't ask questions, and I get to wake up tomorrow in the arms of the woman I love, who loves me too. Who isn't going to disappear, no matter what.

Drop the key on my shirt, grab my board and head out into the water, my baby to my belly, nose to the west, pulling me out, back into myself. No noise, no neon, no insanity. Just this calm and this dark and this air and this water, and my board solid under me, rolling with the waves— and if I can trust this, I can trust it all.

The night after Fluke and I had seen our pirate ship at Rincon, I was drifting off to sleep, when suddenly I sat straight up in bed.

'Ray! Ray, you awake?'

No answer. I creep over and shake his arm. 'Wake up, man.'

'Hrrgnnh? Whaddaya want?'

'I need to know how a Fata Morgana works.'

Blinks at me. 'Muh?'

'When you see shit on the water that's not there. A mirage.'

Most people would not be overly generous at this point, but Ray's used to it, so he drowsily explains about the hot air meeting the cold water, and how the atmosphere bends to refract the light and trick the eye. Doesn't answer my question.

'But we saw the exact same thing! I mean, *exactly*!'

He moans a little. 'Go to sleep, Tommy.'

I relent and go back to bed, brain buzzing. The point of a hallucination is that it's an individual experience; no one else can see what you're seeing, and either you've got some direct link to the beyond, or you need to be locked up. But Fluke and I agreed on every detail: the Jolly Roger, the mermaid, everything. This seemed even more miraculous to me than the vision itself.

Was it a visit from some other dimension? A time traveler? How many people would've seen the same thing we did? Hundreds, thousands? The whole country? How many, exactly, can collaborate on the same mass delusion? I have no idea, and no way of replicating this, so wind up just sticking it in the box in my brain labeled Very Mysterioso and going back to sleep.

Later that night, I awake to an empty space beside me. She's over by the window, hand on the pane like a cat waiting to be let out. Her smell is on my fingers, all over me, making even these crummy sheets a place I want to dwell forever. Roll over to watch her, quiet.

'You were right.' She doesn't turn. 'It never ends. The waves just keep on coming. I don't know why that should surprise me.'

'When I was a kid, I thought it'd disappear if I looked away.' I'm beyond exhausted, vision blurry, but if she's here, I want to be here too. 'All the water would recede into a hold, fish and all, boats stranded on the sand, a deserted desert. But as long as even one pair of eyes was watching, the ocean would stay. We could will it into being: sending it away, then watching it roll back to us.'

She's smiling to herself. 'That's a lot of pressure.'

'Well, there's a lot of people. Someone's always watching.'

'Tommy?'

'Yeah?'

'Can I tell you something that's scaring me?'

Wiser man would hesitate. But I'm Tom Beck—I can fix this. 'Sure.'

'I think I'm going to screw this up. You and me, I mean.'

Funny, I feel the same. Can't shake it. Don't know how, but I know I'm going to find a way to blow it. It hurts, fumbling in the dark, helpless on the ropes as fate socks the living hell out of you. I never really got the concept of rolling with the punches; they all hurt, you know. And you recall every one, forever.

Sit up and rub the sleep from my eyes, the better to see her: breasts and thighs silvered blue by moonlight, shreds of pink and yellow neon from the hotel sign flitting soft across her face. Wait for her to turn and look at me, but she doesn't, just stares out to sea.

'Ever since I was little, marriage felt like this...doom, just looming over me. I didn't want it, I knew that like you know what color your eyes are. Staying with one person, even a nice one, till death did us part, seemed like more of a prison sentence than love. But part of me wanted to believe what everyone said: that I was going to meet the right guy one day and change my mind.' Glances at me, maybe waiting for argument. I'm a little hurt, but say nothing.

'I'm not much of a mind-changer, though. I come by that honestly. And let's face it: we can delude ourselves all we want about how marriage doesn't matter if you have your heart set on something, but in truth, if you want to be anything but a housewife, slip that ring on, and that's all she wrote. You'll always be second-rate, at one or the other.'

Clear my throat. 'I don't buy that, Georgia. I'll do whatever it takes to give you your time, your space, all that Virginia Woolf stuff. Doesn't mean you have to marry me, but you should know that.'

'Well, that's what makes this hard, Tommy. Because I did meet the right guy. Except that—' her voice breaks, and I feel the floor give way, knowing I'm about to hear something harsh and irrevocable.

Comes over, kneels and runs her hands over me, her touch so cool it's like I'm running a fever. 'There, um. There's something else, and you won't understand, even though you're the smartest person I know, and already you get me better than anyone but my dad. It's going to hurt, and I hate that, but I'm not going to be a sneak about it.'

'You're killing me here,' I say, and mean it. 'Out with it.'

'I kissed him, Tommy.' She doesn't need to say who. 'I could see how badly he needed it, and I thought, oh, why the hell not. I love him—anyone who doesn't is a damned idiot—and Tommy's just going to have to deal with it. And that's all it was, a kiss. We stopped before it went any further. But it was good. It felt right.'

Lays her head on my knees. My heart is pounding, but I can't help but stroke her hair. As if I'm forgiving her, as if I get to. It's just Pip, I tell myself. Just a kid, just a kiss. I can live with that.

She laughs a little; it's not a happy sound. 'This is gonna sound nuts, but you know how God and Israel always had this fucked-up, fractious relationship, Israel chasing after other gods, and God losing his mind and shipping them off to Babylon or whatever?'

'Sure,' I say. 'Made for some interesting diatribes from the prophets, but after a while you sorta want everyone to shit or get off the pot.'

She's raised her head, watching me.

'So...you're saying you have a thing for Philistines?'

'I'm saying I'll want to be with other people, Tommy. Not right now, or because you don't satisfy me. There's nothing wrong or lacking about you. You're like no one else I've ever met—but you're just one person. There are going to be others I'll want to know in that way.'

'Well, everyone feels like that. It comes up, you sit on it. It's a sacrifice you make, if you love someone.'

'I can't, though.' She sits beside me, her hand on mine. 'And I don't see why I should. I mean, we've created this mean-spirited idea of love that boxes us up, and I don't get the point of it. I've *tried*, I swear. I'd like nothing more than to be nice and normal and never hurt anyone, and you know what? I'll never know how to do that. Connecting with people like that, that intensity—it's pure, efficient. It means something, Tommy, and it wouldn't take anything away from how I feel about you. I'm not sure why we've all convinced ourselves this is some big sinful affront, but it's pointless. Do you see what I'm saying?'

Oh, I see, all right. 'It's a slippery slope, though. You lose yourself.'

'I won't, though. And you and I, we're different. We can approach this carefully, together. I know we can.'

'But I don't *want* to approach it.'

She swallows. 'Do you want to break up, then?'

'No,' I say quickly. 'I want you to control yourself.'

'I control myself just fine,' she says. She sounds angry. 'I'm not a whore. And I'm not going behind your back, or lying to you. I never will.'

'I didn't say that, come on. But I don't want to share you with anyone else; I want to be enough.'

'But you are, don't you see that? You're exactly enough Tommy for me, more than enough. I love you in ways I'll never love another human being. But it's like having the world's greatest steak, and then nothing but steak for the rest of your life. It doesn't make sense to me. I don't know why it makes sense to anyone.'

'Oh, so I'm steak now? Or still a Philistine? Not following.'

'No, and I'm making a mess of this, because I'm so tired. But we have to be truthful, okay? I can deal with anything as long as there's that. This is important, so try to hear me. You're, uh...' She rubs her hands over her face, hard. 'You're my home, Tommy. That's the only way I can put it. If you want me to go away and never see you again, I'll understand. But it would be—it would *hurt*.'

'So don't!' I say desperately. 'Stay with me. I'll try harder.'

'But you don't have to, that's the point! Neither of us has to. We can both stop trying so hard to be who my mother or yours or Ricky or anyone thinks we're supposed to be, and just be who we *are*. You be Tommy, and I'll be Georgia, and I'll stay with you forever, if you'll have me—and there's no one else, I swear, no one. Not yet. But you need to know...there will be.'

I roll over on the bed, back to her. A swarm of bees is all around me, in my brain. This isn't how this works. None of this is how this works. I wanted to marry her, just the two of us against the world. I'd die in her arms, and it would be a life well-lived, because she'd loved me.

Try to picture her kissing me, smelling of another man, his sweat. His goddamned come. It's a terrifying image, nearly as bad as the thought of her absence. *Don't, please—you're really pretty, but please don't.* The look in Mama's eyes when I mention her name. *There are worse things than lonely.* Ice fracturing under a child's feet. Nine weeks, I've known this girl. How the fuck did we get here so fast?

I'd wanted perfection, was how. My whole life had been one long dues-paying mess, and I didn't even know what union was collecting them, or for what. But I'd needed a fairytale to drop into my palm like the last pill in a bottle: this. This will be the one that'll turn the trick, the peak experience, the perfect wave. The cure for all that's ever ailed you. You will never have to struggle for this again.

Put up all the cynical bulwarks you want, but when a princess shows up out of nowhere to carry you off on a horse, it's going to take a lot to drag you out of that cocksure belief in a happy ending. But what if said princess were someone beyond perfection, outside that realm entirely? What if the word, the rules, didn't apply here at all? What if everything we thought we knew about love and happiness, was just some dumb delusion we'd talked ourselves into?

Anything that comes out of my mouth right now will sound like some freaked-out little kid, though, and she's probably feeling the same. Here we are, laying ourselves bare, trying so hard to be both honest and kind, managing only to drive knives into one another's hearts. No wonder people lie to each other all the goddamned time.

'I don't know what to say, Georgia. Really, I don't. For once in my life, I've got absolutely nothing.'

'We don't have to say anything, okay? Just let it be for now.' She pauses. 'Can I lie down? Or do you not want me touching you?'

'Course you can.' I always want her touching me.

'Are you okay?'

'Not really.'

'I love you, Tommy, and I'm sorry. I know this makes me seem selfish and flighty and kind of a shitty person, but this is who I am. It wouldn't be fair, to pretend I'm not.'

Reach around, hold her hand over my heart, and we just lie like that for a while, warm and silent against each other.

How did we get here?

Was it fate? God? Was there a God up there after all, with delusional agenda of his own, tossing us about like a kid with tin soldiers? Did that motherfucker turn his back on the six million simply so the two of us could get together, torture ourselves into some new mode of existence?

All right, don't do that. You always fucking do that, dive right into the self-centered histrionics. Random osmosis, is all. She could be any one of a billion Brownian passersby. But she isn't. There are things you can sit on, too. Sacrifices you can make, even if they tear you apart.

'Do you want to fuck?' she says at last. 'Would that help? Or would you rather just hug?'

'Not if it's some kind of pity deal.'

She shakes with half-suppressed laughter, squeezes my arm. 'Dork.'

'Can we maybe do both?'

'Oh, Tommy,' she says. 'Of course we can. We can do both, or neither, or anything at all, really. Don't you see that? *Anything.*'

She's got a point, I guess. We are strong, we two. We've learned to roll with the punches after all, after a fashion. We're smart, good-looking, resilient. Blessed by the gods of this strange fickle city. She and I will never be this young again, this stoked with lust and hubris, flush with dreams, cash and passion. Almost seems a pity not to practice these while we may. And we're Americans, by God, our gorgeous cornucopia overflowing with options. We can do whatever we want, however nuts it may seem to the rest of the world, or even to our unmoored selves. Look beyond, beyond. Anything at all.

So we do. Not like we had a choice, right?

It was a good year, that year. In hindsight it may seem strange to call it that, but it was, overall, one of the better ones. Adventurous. And we were pretty brave about it all, you know? Braver than we ever thought we could be. We changed in ways none of us saw coming, and found happiness we never knew existed, barely knew *could* exist. We created a home for ourselves that was honest and kind, good and full of love, in a little clapboard house in Venice with butter-yellow walls, an orange tree out back, and a haphazard garden we worked with our own hands. And we ate a lot of fucking spaghetti.

I am three years old and drowning. A wave has knocked me ass over teakettle, and although I can't swim, I'm quite calm, sure I'll be fine if I can only get my footing. I can't. Held under, rolled over and over, breathless and dizzy; sand, seaweed and shells flashing by, the dark murky brine all around...and then another wave sweeps me up and deposits me on the shore. This was on San Francisco's Ocean Beach, maybe Kelly's Cove, though it could have been Mendocino or Santa Cruz or Malibu or Tijuana. My peripatetic biodad would take me to all these beaches up and down the coast of California, because he could drink beer up on the sand all day without anyone giving him a hard time. And the ocean never let me drown, not once.

The seagulls and surfers both seemed an integral part of it all, as if they'd been there forever. Nameless surf music seeped into my blood, so that years later, riding the bus to school in Israel, I'd find myself comforted by the funky theme of the morning show on the radio, these sounds from my distant California past that had somehow made it all the way over the sea. 'Walk Don't Run,' by the Ventures. These tunes never failed to assure me of the stalwart rightness of life, even if I couldn't always find my footing.

Last July, Sheila Weller reposted her 2006 'Vanity Fair' article, 'The Lost Boys of Malibu.' Oh, surfers, yay! My brain growled, 'No articles, you. Get back to work.' I clicked on it anyway, in dire need of a little mindless fun.

Then read it again. And again.

Sheila is both a knockout writer and a truly generous human being, feeding you all this great stuff which makes you hunger for so much more, even about people you knew, or thought you did. I was fascinated by these boys and girls who were nothing like the carefree invulnerable types I'd always assumed all surfers to be. They seemed both brazen and broken; surfing their salvation, and often not even that. And I kind of...well, I wanted to write about them.

'Don't be absurd,' said my buzzkill brain. 'You know zip about the early 60's. You're a NorCal girl who goes to LA every five years, more familiar with Scientology than surfing. 'Pump-House' and 'Point Break' don't count for anything, and you know it.'

But this urge didn't quit; it just kept getting stronger. Finally I thought, 'Well, Ray Bradbury never went to Mars. I could do some research, and write a short piece. A haiku, say.' Came home from the library with an armload of books, and halfway through David Rensin's Miki Dora bio *All for a Few Perfect Waves* thought, 'Oh, boy, I may be in trouble here.' Read all the books I could lay my hands on, watched every movie from 'Riding Giants' and 'Step Into Liquid' to the Frankie-and-Annettes—and then it came flooding out.

Okay, that's not true. This was not an easy book to write. I learned German for it, the geography and history of the LA area, the strange synchronicity of its inhabitants' lives. I'm in a wheelchair, so had never been on a surfboard before—yes, we do surf, but I needed someone to show me how. All the programs were far away, so I felt like a shameful poser trying to approximate this sensation, though I'd skated and swam and sailed once upon a time, body- and windsurfed and paddleboarded and even lived on various beaches.

Despite the research, I was still dumb as paint about this deceptively simple process of surfing and its culture, how waves worked and were they measured in heads or feet or increments of fear; if lefts or rights were better for goofyfooters and the functional difference between a stringer and a rocker, and how utterly, insanely addictive this sport could be, even if you weren't actually doing it.

Everything in the world was suddenly very dark after November, and all I wanted to do was hide in this 55-year old story that was building and building in my head till I was crying in the shower with how utterly inadequate I was to tell it, and how all these awful things were going to happen to all these nice people who didn't actually exist.

And then I found Matt Warshaw.

Matt Warshaw is the Godfather of Surf, an above-average tube-rider and extremely smart cat. What he doesn't know about surfing may as well not exist, and all through that winter my son Max would yell, 'It's

two o'clock in the morning, get off 'Encyclopedia of Surfing,'" and I'd
say, 'I'm not! Ha ha!' then hide under the covers with my phone cause I
needed to find out just one more thing about George Freeth or the
shortboard revolution. Matt forked over all this stuff that lent structure
and integrity to the story, and was extremely nice about answering my
frantic emails. But he was also an exacting fucker, and in my mind
became this ghostly Maxwell Perkins I had work my ass off to appease.
I'm truly grateful, Matt. If this book is any good at all, that's mostly
down to you—and I tried not to anthropomorphize the sea.

Max would come home from school and wonder why I was still in my
robe; I'd read him my pages, and he'd tell me I was an awesome writer,
and I'd wail that no, I was shitty, and he'd laugh. As soon as I finished
each chapter, I'd fire it off to my mom in Israel, who would fact-check,
reminding me that McCarthy was dead by '57 (true) and no one had sex
before '66 (umm)—and to my friend Yael up in Portland, who has
patiently read all my stuff since she sat down next to me at SF State
twenty years ago and said, 'Hey, are you from Israel too?' and always
gives the best feedback, useful and kind. Even my friend Teo, who'd
often fall asleep while I read, claimed it gave him great dreams.

They really were great dreams, weren't they? We were the kings of the
universe back then, cowering under our desks, our passion and music
and hopes stomped almost into oblivion, worried about Bolshies and
black oppression and becoming hopeless squares, slaves to a terrible
system—but always, always getting back up again with ideas about how
we were going to change it all for the better.

This is mainly a work of fiction. Some events actually happened, and
John Paul Getty really was a Malibu surfer, although he'd left America
by then, never to return. The Nazi stuff is all true. I wish it weren't.
Everything else was made up or synthesized from surfer lore. Ricky
Morrow shares much with Miki Dora, who never lived on the beach nor
did anything nice for anyone if he could help it, though I believe there
is more to him than the asshole/genius argument would evidence. The
Beach Boys were never booed out of the Rendezvous, that sort of thing.
Take all this apocrypha with a grain of salt, and don't sue me. It's tacky,
and I don't have any money anyway.

288

Many thanks to Barbara Tuchman, James Michener, Larry Gonick, Derek Waters and Lin-Manuel Miranda, who taught me that there are many ways of learning history, some more fun than you might expect.

To Raymond Chandler, Joan Didion and James Ellroy, who wrote the savage lovely truth of Los Angeles, and whose work is very entertaining when it isn't about to kill you. I snuck two 'Farewell My Lovely' refs in, just for the Chandler acolytes.

To my father, who grew up during this tumultuous time, for all the tales, beautiful and horrible. For my brother Judah and his skater crew: Nolan, Jamie, M'sou, Bakari, Aron and the badass Courtney Cole. Even the nefarious Chick Sheriff had her place in your saga, and Judah's karmic getback on Security Guards with Delusions of Grandeur remains one of the all-time greats.

To all the surfers who befriended me and were good enough to share their wisdom about waves and shaping and slang and pranks and sharks and 'dude, don't say 'dude,' no one ever said 'dude' before 1972' and 'we really didn't say 'fuck' that much either.' Tommy Beck has a lot to say 'fuck' about, though. I went through like Twain's wife and took out as many as I could, but there's still quite a few in there.

For the remarkable Allan Gibbons, who can do anything well, and who designed the book even as flames were licking at his house, tactfully correcting me on many details so I didn't sound like a kook.

For Vinz Klefer, photographer extraordinaire, who let me use a version of 'Big Wave' for the cover. This was the only image in the world I wanted, and I'd looked at thousands.

At some point a reader said, 'Look, this is kind of a dark book. I don't know that people are going to want to read something this dark.' To which I laughed, 'You kidding me? This is the *Sunlight* Zone! Just wait till we get to the Abyss!' Because there are going to be more books. Course there are. And they get a lot bleaker, but there are bright spots all along, and there's a happy ending, because this is America. Turns out there's a *lot* to say about friendship and love; surfing and addiction; Nazism, communism, and Judaism; music, movies, and what it means to be an American. So much for haikus.

For the music makers and the dreamers of the dream: the revolutionary Dick Dale, the original dork-rocker Buddy Holly, The Ventures, The Coasters, The Shirelles, Chuck Berry, Little Richard, Jerry Lee. For Woody Guthrie and Bob Dylan and the incomparable Billie Holiday. God bless you all. You made it bearable.

And for every girl who got on a board and said, 'Yeah, screw you guys, I'm doing this. Stop checking out my ass.' You are my *wahine* queens, all of you: Kathy Kohner, Keala Kennelly, Bethany Hamilton, Isabel Letham, Dottie Hawkins Ault, Marge Calhoun, Linda Benson, Coco Ho, Mozelle Gooch, Rell Sun, Lisa Anderson, Navah Paskowitz Asner, Anat Lelior, and so many more whose names should flame forever in the pantheon. The waves are yours; they always have been. *Mahalo.*

But mostly for Kathy Kessler, whose fearlessly kind life and early death plunged an icicle into my soul nothing will ever melt. This book is for you—and for the guy who spoke of you so tenderly, half a century later. No way could I have abandoned that story; it's not like I had a choice.

Right?

Made in the USA
Las Vegas, NV
12 October 2022

57140902R00166